THE COPPER
ROAD

Also by Richard Buxton
Whirligig (Book 1 of Shire's Union)

BOOK 2 OF SHIRE'S UNION

THE COPPER ROAD

BEYOND THE PROMISE

RICHARD BUXTON

OCOEE PUBLISHING

First published 2020 by Ocoee Publishing
www.richardbuxton.net

ISBN Paperback 978-0-9957693-3-5
eBook 978-0-9957693-4-2

This is a work of fiction. Names, characters, places and incidents are
either a product of the author's imagination or are used fictitiously.
Any resemblance to actual people living or dead, events or locales is
entirely coincidental.

British Library Cataloguing in Publication Data
A CIP catalogue record for this book is available from
the British Library.

Cover design by JD Smith Design
Typesetting by Aimee Dewar

For Sally

Richard lives with his family in the South Downs, Sussex, England. He completed an MA in Creative Writing at Chichester University in 2014. He has an abiding relationship with America, having studied at Syracuse University, New York State, in the late eighties. His short stories have won the Exeter Story Prize, the Bedford International Writing Competition and the Nivalis Short Story Award.

Richard's first novel, *Whirligig*, was published in 2017 and shortlisted for the Rubery International Book Award. To learn more about Richard's writing visit www.richardbuxton.net.

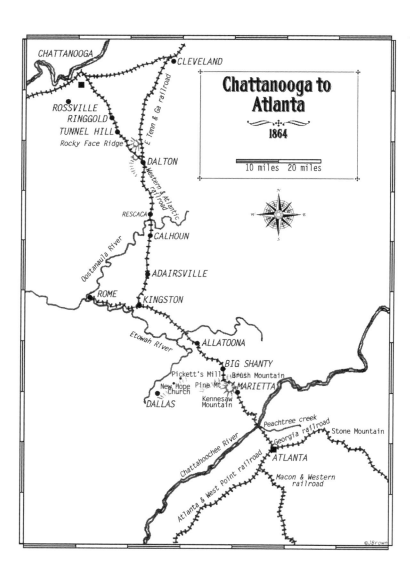

Chattanooga to Atlanta

1864

10 miles 20 miles

CHATTANOOGA

CLEVELAND

ROSSVILLE
RINGGOLD
TUNNEL HILL
Rocky Face Ridge

E Tenn & Ga railroad

DALTON

Western & Atlantic railroad

RESCACA

CALHOUN

Oostanaula River

ADAIRSVILLE

ROME

KINGSTON

Etowah River

ALLATOONA

BIG SHANTY

Pickett's Mill · Brush Mountain
New Hope · Pine Mt. · MARIETTA
Church · Kennesaw Mountain

DALLAS

Peachtree creek

Chattahoochee River

Georgia railroad

Stone Mountain

ATLANTA

Macon & Western railroad

Atlanta & West Point railroad

©JBrown

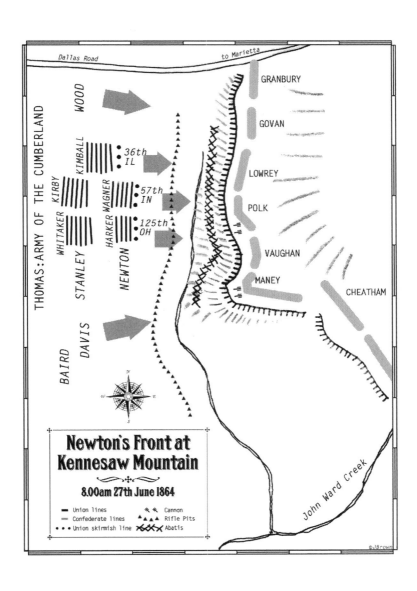

Newton's Front at
Kennesaw Mountain

8.00am 27th June 1864

PART I

Dandridge, Tennessee – January 17th 1864

It was impossible to sustain an even supply of fear day after day. A year ago, Shire would have twitched at every far-off rifle snap. He might have moved quickly into column and an inner file where a bullet would have to work hard to find him. When the sergeant selected guards or pickets, Shire used to avoid his eyes. These days, fear was suppressed by many things: the numbing cold of a Tennessee winter; the hunger of an army on half-rations; the simple boredom of marching from wet, barren county to wet, barren county. Fear had been reduced to a tightly wrapped knot resident in his gut and nourished by the memory of battles fought, of friends bleeding out, of death as random as a tumbling flock of crows.

It hadn't rained today, though this low gray sky held the threat. It wasn't easy to read the signs, this not being his part of the world. Recent days, similar to this, had stayed dry; others had seemed set fair until, with little warning, wet weather rolled in from the mountains to the north or the east.

A bugle sounded somewhere out in front. There was a crackle of gunfire. What cavalry they had cantered back to the safety of the pickets: the spaced line of men stationed out in the open ground to briefly check any approach from the enemy.

'Someone's gotten our horsey friends all riled,' said Tuck. 'Takes a big stick to knock *them* backward.'

A trooper came on ahead of the others. They parted to let him through the main regimental line. Shire looked over his shoulder but wasn't able to hear the man's report to Colonel Moore. It couldn't have been good news as the order came for a second company to re-enforce the picket. Not his company though, not Company B. They stayed facing forward in battle formation. That wasn't so unusual: they'd been bumping into Rebels all week. Whenever they were threatened, Colonel Moore – commanding this month in Colonel Opdycke's absence – found good ground, stopped the column and had them face the most likely direction of attack. It never came to anything. It wasn't worth getting anxious about.

In a sense his whole regiment, the 125th Ohio, were on picket duty. So was the 93rd. They were two regiments and a detachment of cavalry, miles forward of their brigade, out foraging in the cold valleys and hills while being mindful that Longstreet's Rebel army was out here somewhere. Shire knew their job as did all the veterans of the 125th: if Longstreet showed up, give him a bloody nose and fall back toward Knoxville.

'Looky there,' said Mason, his new corporal stripes accentuating the direction he pointed. 'That'll be the stick.'

To their left was a small valley and on the far slope, higher than the 125th, was a mass of Rebel cavalry descending the hill. Shire spotted two pieces of field artillery. His knot of fear began to unravel, sending tendrils of nervous energy into his arms and hands, a dryness into his throat. 'So many.'

'They're gonna have to dismount to come at us through those woods,' said Mason. 'Won't look so many then.'

Colonel Moore advanced them twenty paces to the top edge of a gentle slope. There was no cover, only clear ground before them running down to the woods. Tuck and Cleves were in the front rank and took a step down the slope so that Shire and the second rank could fire over their shoulders.

Tuck slipped, cursed, and grabbed Cleves' arm, almost pulling him down. 'I prefer honest wet mud,' Tuck said, 'not this half-breed variety. You can trust deep mud. You know where you are with deep mud.'

They were ordered to load. Shire reached under the flap of the cartridge box that hung on his right hip. He pulled out a new charge without once taking his eyes from the enemy. He bit the paper open, tipped powder and ball into the barrel, then drew out his ramrod – right hand, thumb down – and tapped the ball home. This might yet come to nothing. He might later find himself firing the round into the sky just to clear the barrel.

A dozen or more rabbits broke from the woods in panic. Behind them, men in gray emerged on foot. They still looked a good number: many more than the two Ohio regiments. This wasn't a feint.

'Looks like a busy afternoon for us,' said Mason.

'Someone put a rope on Shire.' It was Cleves. 'So we can find him after.'

'Button up, Cleves,' said Mason. 'This ain't the time. Face front.'

'Alright, Corporal, but it ain't your shoulder he's shooting over.'

Shire inched his cap box along his belt, nearer the buckle where he preferred it. He said nothing. He'd proved himself more times than that weasel Cleves ever had. What counted against him was his brief capture at Chickamauga, and then, by hard necessity, his temporary desertion after the Union Army had fought its way out of Chattanooga. He was still on a charge for that, though the Colonel had done nothing about it for six weeks. At reveille bugle call, some bright spark – often Cleves – would call out, 'Where's Shire? Where's the

Englishman?' And at rollcall there'd always be a sarcastic cheer when he answered his name.

The two cannon boomed from across the valley, overshooting into the trees behind the 125th. Too much powder, but it was enough to set Shire's fear entirely free. He'd have to live within it now, have to use it.

The Rebels came up the valley side quicker than expected. Evidently it had caught Colonel Moore by surprise as he was only just in time giving the order for the left flank to angle back and face the charge. Company B was on the right next to the 93rd and stayed put. The Rebels were coming at the left. They rushed the picket which fell back in panic and prevented the regiment from opening fire until everyone was back inside the line. By then the Rebels were no more than thirty yards away, so when the left fired the first volley, billowing white smoke out over the slope, it hit them hard. The Rebels got off a ragged volley of their own, but one more from the Union and the attackers were already edging away. Company B hadn't fired a shot.

Ahead of Shire, more Rebels – many more – stepped out of the woods and came on in tight formation looking to fix the center while others flanked around the 93rd. At the command, Shire lifted his rifle over Cleves' shoulder, ensuring the hammer was away from Cleve's ear. He aimed at the Rebels' legs, knowing his barrel would kick up when he pulled the trigger. Captain Elmer bellowed, 'Fire!' There was the comforting rip of rifles from either side. White smoke lifted away into the winter air. Down the slope men twisted and collapsed onto wet grass. Whether any of them fell to Shire's bullet, he couldn't know; the company fired rather than the man. They reloaded and the enemy stole ten paces. The Rebel captain's saber fell and summoned a row of yellow flashes. In the same instant, minie balls thudded into the mud in front of the first rank, others whistled above Shire's head. He heard a familiar sickening slap and looked to his left in time to see Lieutenant Seabury Smith tip sideways from his horse, no more life in him than a wet bag of sand.

'Fire by rank! Front rank... fire!'

Shire lined up on the advancing Rebels, waited his turn. Cleves began cavorting in front of him, clutching at his eyes. 'Tarnation!'

'Second rank... fire!'

Shire couldn't shoot with Cleves dancing around.

Tuck reached over and pulled Cleves' hands away. There was no blood. 'Ain't nothin' but powder smoke.'

'I can't see nothin'!'

Shire had no time for this. 'Get the hell out of my way.' He grabbed the back of Cleves' coat and yanked him up the hill, dropped him in the mud then stepped forward and took his place in the front line beside Tuck. Shire was the only one loaded. The Rebel officer waved his men forward with his saber, urged them to charge home. Shire drew a bead on him, breathed out and fired. The saber dropped into the grass and the officer knelt, clutching at his arm, but then struggled to his feet and ordered his men on. Shire loaded quickly as the Rebels raced at them, bayonets lowered. He was late getting his rifle to his shoulder, but the captain took an extra beat and Shire was able to aim with the whole company. This was how to fight, despite the fear. You were never going to run so to hell with it. Stand tall, hold your gun steady. Let them see you close an eye while you wait for the order.

'Fire!'

The rifle stock punched his shoulder. There was the momentary flash of the guns. He held his breath for half a second to let the smoke clear. They were all as one; one strength, one weapon, one intent. They were the Tigers of the 125th Ohio and it would take more than this chancer's charge to reach them.

The Rebels stopped. More fell. Many cried out. Some stood and looked for their officers; others started to back away. Company B loaded again. Fear melted away with the gun smoke. Shire wanted to step out, to charge and sweep them down the slope, but there was no need. The Union held the high ground. One or two Rebels got off a parting shot as they sullenly backed down the hill, not prepared to face away. He reached for a percussion cap and felt a kick. His first thought was it must be Cleves somewhere behind him. He turned in anger but fell, his left leg careless of his weight. And then the hot sting, as if a cooked nail was being pulled through his calf. Tuck was there and Sergeant Ocks who tore open Shire's trouser leg. 'Right in the meat,' he said. 'Best place.'

There was a good deal of blood on the big sergeant's hands.

'Get him behind the line.'

Tuck helped him away, tied a tourniquet above the wound with quick hands, patted Shire's back. 'Rest up. We got this fight.'

There were other charges to defend, but Shire played no part. He was left on the cold grass close to the colors and dead Lieutenant Smith. The Union and the regimental flags – his flags – were planted side by side, untended. The firing and shouting went on just ahead, but it was as if he'd moved to a different world, outside of the company machine, discarded. The fight was still in him. He wanted his rifle. The minutes passed and he journeyed into a new sort of fear. Despite the tourniquet, the pain in his leg grew sore and hotter still. He wanted to reach down and soothe it, but sitting up made it worse. He thought of the singing bone saws, of the careless log-pile of wet limbs stacked outside the army hospital in Chattanooga. What good was he sitting here? He needed to fight; that was the only way through. The regimental flag hung lifeless in the winter air, the eagle and stars lost in the limp folds. The last time he caught a bullet he was carrying that very staff over the crest on Missionary Ridge. The bullet had been spent, but the bruise was only recently faded on his left breast, and there was a circle of darker skin the size of an Indian head cent that he'd forever keep as a reminder. Which flag was he collecting wounds for? For the Union? Or for a regiment that seemed apt to spit him out, an Englishman that didn't taste right in the first place?

The Rebel artillery never found its range and continued to overshoot. Later in the afternoon, after the final Rebel charge, Shire was lifted onto the Lieutenant's horse. Colonel Moore led them back up the hill and into the woods along with the 93rd. After dusk they lit fires, many more fires than they needed and, while they were burning down, the two regiments slunk away. It was time to find the safety of the brigade. They'd given Longstreet his bloody nose.

Pennsylvania – February 1864

Pennsylvania was just the other side of the window, sliding by the train. Tod knew it was there, but it might have been any state in the rump Union for all he could see. The winter darkness had come on quickly after they'd rattled and bumped their way east out of Pittsburgh. He would have made his move back then, but he needed the dark. The rivulets that washed across the cold glass were a blessing: it would be harder to track a man in the rain.

It was mostly dark in the carriage too, only the Yankee guard's lantern ghosting up and down the aisle. Through the hard, wooden seat, and through the bare panel against his back, he tried to translate the creaks and groans of the train into an estimate of speed. The train tended to complain a deal more on the corners as the car bent its coupling against the one behind. Just now the squeaks were dying away as they straightened and the engine picked up the pace. The carriage established a gentle sway and there was an accelerating rhythmic 'clack-clack' from below.

'You sure you wanna do this?' whispered Wrigley. 'It's a hell of a long way back to the army in Georgia and, likely as not, your legs will break as soon as they hit Pennsylvania.'

'I'm sure,' said Tod. 'I've had enough of Union prisons.'

'Baltimore might be better than Johnson's Island. It sure as hell can't be as cold.'

Tod felt his decision had been made well back down the track. 'You're gonna have to help me get out that window. The sash'll only come down a third, I reckon. If I get stuck, don't go trying to haul me back in. Push all you have to.'

'Alright, alright, I got it, Captain, but you forgive me ahead of time. I could push you off a hillside or into a river. No way of tellin'.'

'I forgive you. Just don't pitch me into a telegraph pole.'

The lantern swayed toward them. The guard, his free hand moving from seat to seat, looked half-asleep. He reached their end of the carriage and stood for a few slow seconds riding the sway, his lids heavy. For a moment Tod thought that he was going to say something, that he suspected what Tod was about and would throw him back in the boxcar.

'Sir?' said Tod, as he might do to wake a sleeping child. 'Sir?'

The guard started. 'What?'

'Looked like you'd gone there, sir. I didn't want you to drop the lantern.'

The guard gave him no thanks, turned and started back up the carriage.

They'd only been moved into the passenger car when Tod had demanded to see the officer in charge. It hadn't been a ruse on his part, there was genuine need. When he was forced into the boxcar with Wrigley and the other officers at Willard station, it was beyond full: men packed in tighter than bristles on a brush. The prisoners already loaded were from an Alabama unit, all lower ranks, and it had been hard to keep a lid on their tempers; they weren't about to take orders from a Tennessee captain who, by his arrival, had made the problem worse. There was no room for the sick to lie down and mercy, the smell... When, torturous hours later, the boxcar door slid open in Pittsburgh, a Yankee colonel was standing there like he was on parade, a waxed moustache above any number of polished silver buttons; the sort of Yankee Tod had no time for. He'd told the man that if they couldn't get more air into the car, then he would only be delivering a collection of corpses to Maryland. He'd challenged him to climb up, come and see if he could squeeze his way from one end of the car to the other without stepping in puke, invited him to empty the one bucket they had for their needs.

The colonel had declined his offer but ordered the glass to be smashed out from the two tiny, barred windows. He'd said he'd take ten men out – no privates – to ride in the passenger car. The right thing to do would have been to let someone else go in his stead, but Tod had seen it for the gilt-edged chance it was. This fool was the sort to think that as he'd shown some charity, Tod would be honor-bound not to try and escape. To hell with that.

He'd taken Wrigley and his other lieutenants along as well as some first sergeants and corporals who'd pushed themselves forward. When they'd been led into the passenger car and taken their seats, the few civilians had scurried up the other end as if a bunch of dead men had just come aboard. He supposed they were a sight in their tired and dirty gray uniforms, stains overlapping from the war and the prison, bringing with them the odor of the boxcar. As they left Pittsburgh the guard had taken up his patrol, a slow walk to the middle of the car, the temporary border between the Union and the captured Confederacy.

Tod figured that they could easily rush the man; he was walking right by them, only the Yankee colonel had taken a seat up near to the civilians. He had a pistol and a second officer with him. Tod had the rank to order the men with him to attempt the escape too, but he was no longer sure he had the right. Most of them were just happy to have left Johnson's Island and didn't want any further part in the war. Some said they wouldn't take parole if it was offered, convinced they'd be forced to break it as soon as they were turned out into the Confederacy. They'd help him though. The word had been passed along. He hadn't been able to persuade Wrigley to come with him. He supposed you had to be a little crazy to jump from a train that was moving along purposefully in the dark and the wet. It was still going much too fast and he was getting further and further from Pittsburgh. That's where he figured to head. It would be easier to lose yourself in a big city.

A second guard opened the thin door and stepped into the car from the plate outside. A rush of wet air blew over Tod's hands. The guard shook his head as if he could cast off the cold.

A year ago, Tod would have thought the word 'cold' good enough to use for any eventuality where he didn't feel warm, but after the last few months, he could grade cold like you might different shades of blue in a dying Tennessee sky. This passing draught was no inconvenience at all, it merely served to tell you how pleasantly warm you were once the guard closed the door. He could remember the cold high up on Missionary Ridge, camped there with next to no cover for the best part of two months last fall, looking down on the Union Army in Chattanooga. There the freezing rain would whip down off Lookout Mountain and steal the slightest comfort from their pitiful campfires. He'd thought that was as cold as a man could get until after the battle, after his beloved Confederate Army was defeated, he was shipped north with thousands of other men.

To begin with they were taken to Louisville, only to be sent on to Sandusky, Ohio, and from there out to the officers' prison on Johnson's Island in Lake Erie. It was December, but the Yankees were stupid enough to keep a gunboat out on the water as if someone might think to take a brisk swim for the mainland. It was the running joke in the prison huts that had no more than a small box-stove and where, sometimes, if you could bear to stay outside for more than a minute, you could brush the frozen lice from your hair like they were fine winter hail. There were never enough blankets. Mid-January they'd lost a man. Tod helped carry the body to a dilapidated shed that was half-smothered by snow where the corpse would wait until the ground thawed in the spring. Whether the new prison in Baltimore would be any warmer he didn't know. Maybe it would, but he had no intention of finding out.

The guards traded places, the sleepy one heading out for his turn on the plate. That was an option: to step through the door and overpower the man, jump from there, but he didn't know for certain there wasn't a second man. And besides, he was realistic enough to know he'd lose in a straight fight. He had no real strength left in him; only enough to fuel his determination.

'Wrigley, you awake?'

'It ain't conducive to sleep, waiting to throw a man from a train.'

'We should get ready.'

'We're going too fast. Wait a while. Pennsylvania must have some hills. We'll hit one soon enough. And then *you'll* hit one.'

The boredom would be the same in Baltimore. Tod knew that much. He picked up his small pack and lay it in his lap. It held all his writing. When under arms he used to write dispatches for the *Chattanooga Daily Rebel*, patriotic prose for the fighting Confederacy under the pseudonym of Mint Julep. Lately, it had been only for his private consumption, no more than the day-to-day life on a frozen prison island, but it kept him sane. He was lucky the Yankees had let him keep the pack. On Missionary Ridge it had been taken from him by a Yankee soldier while the cannon were yet to cool. After searching it and finding Tod's letter to his home in Franklin, the man had given it back.

It was a curious matter. He'd thought on it often. For a start the boy had a peculiar way of talking. It might have been an English accent, he wasn't sure. The soldier, much his own age, said he'd met Tod's brother, Moscow, and his father when billeted in Franklin last spring. He claimed that he'd helped them gin some cotton, as if they'd come over as good neighbors to help. Though it was more than two and a half years since he was home, Tod knew for certain that wasn't the way it was. He'd heard too much. He imagined the farms and, in all likelihood, his own home to be desolated; the slaves all gone away and the cattle taken for the Union Army. There were tales of starving families, of horses stolen and women violated. No doubt a tale grew as it passed from campfire to campfire. In his letters for the *Chattanooga Daily Rebel*, he was no stranger to a little embellishment. It was to be expected in a partisan paper, to provide elevated rhetoric, to concentrate the minds of the people toward the evils done upon their countrymen. He'd heard the rumors too often to not credit them. The Yankee Englishman must have been a simpleton or some such.

'I can't face it,' said Tod.

'What?'

'I can't face another Yankee prison while my family is suffering. Not when there's this chance.'

'Some chance. Chance to break your neck falling or have it broken by a Yankee noose. The war's in Georgia now. It's passed by Franklin. It might not be so bad at home.'

'You know the stories same as me. We heard them while we were fighting and we heard them in prison. Credible stories, from people who'd been to Williamson County, or at least to Nashville.'

'Maybe that's all they are. Stories. People don't invest time passing on tales of how things is mostly alright and nothing much is happening. Where's the story in that? You take the gossip too much to heart. You always have. Best thing you can do for your family is to last out the war, be there to help when it's over.'

'It's not in my nature, Wrigley.'

'I guess not. Needed sayin' all the same.'

They were quiet for a time and he began to doze; the car was so warm, or at least *so not cold*. Through his fogged mind he became aware that the 'clack-clack' of the train was slowing along with his heartbeat. He started awake. There was the sense that the other end of the car was tilting gently upward in the dark. The couplings beyond the door began to complain as the carriage was led around a bend.

Wrigley spoke with his eyes closed. 'You wanna get some air, Captain?'

Tod clutched his pack. 'Yeah. Too comfortable for me in here anyway.'

They waited until the guard was at his most distant. Wrigley whispered into the next set of seats and it was passed on in turn. Tod saw Carlton down the car rise up in the dim lantern light. 'You sonofabitch!' He hauled up the man next to him, struck his hat from his head and received a convincing punch in return.

The guard hurried at them. 'Cut it out.'

Tod didn't have much time; the Union colonel would take an interest. He stood and forced the window down into its housing as far as it would go. There was barely enough room to throw out a small boy. Standing on his seat, he got his head outside into the cold rain where the engine effort and the clack-clack were much louder. The free air turned thick with soot and he closed his eyes, tried to spit out the taste of warm ashes. He'd never get out. He should pull back inside and try to kick out the window, but before he could make the attempt, Wrigley grabbed both his legs and tried to stuff him through. His ribs were caught on the metal strip that ran along the top of the glass and he believed the window would break anyway. He wrestled his pack outside. Wrigley let go only to slam back into him. His ribs scraped over the window strip one at a time, like a roughly played washboard. Left hanging from his waist, he cried out, his body flat to the wet window. His pack dangled toward vaguely seen crossties that were passing by much faster than seemed healthy. He lifted his head and looked through the window. Inside was an inverted, tangled scene of men fighting, but he could hear nothing above the metal roll of the wheels. Out of the upside-down world and the dim lantern light Wrigley charged again. There was no way to brace himself. Wrigley hit hard and Tod fell free of the train, wide enough to miss the crossties. He balled up for the impact that might end it all here and now. It knocked the wind from him but he was still falling, tumbling and flailing down, until he hit hard and wrapped around a tree trunk. There were long moments while he struggled to breathe, to find the courage to gingerly move and discover which parts of him weren't broken. He moved his neck first and by the tail light of the train found he was looking up a tall branchless tree. That bastard Wrigley had thrown him into a telegraph pole after all.

Comrie, Tennessee – February 1864

Shire stood behind the horse and brushed out the very last tangles until George's tail hung long and straight. The grand stables at Comrie, Clara's home in the hills, were bone cold, but at least offered protection from the chill Tennessee wind. He picked up the shears he'd found hanging in the tack-room, carefully pulled the tail straight and cut the thick hair a hand-span's up from the raggedy end. George shifted his weight. Whether it was down to the sudden butcher-like scrape of the shears, or the unasked-for depletion of his tail, Shire couldn't tell. 'Easy, old fella.'

Shire moved over to the trough. There was no need to disguise his limp; Clara wasn't here. He soaked a cloth to wipe through the tail. It would make it easier to separate into three even parts. It was as if he'd last done this only a few days ago rather than a year and a half back, and then on the other side of the Atlantic. He had always found grooming a soothing pastime, a break from the heavier work on the Ridgmont farm, a chance to talk to the horses. Most seemed to find it restful. George was no exception.

He wondered at his own state of mind, this mild undercurrent of anxiety that had crept up on him the last week or two. By rights he should be more than content given the recent removal of some of the harsher realities of army life. First and foremost, the constant worry over when he might next eat. Clara might describe Comrie as shorthanded, despite upward of two dozen blacks about the place. It was certainly self-sufficient. He'd yet to discover where the root-cellar was, but every meal had a plentiful supply of potatoes or yams; even corn, tight on a cob that might have been picked yesterday though here they were into the thin end of winter. In the army, by necessity, he was preoccupied by food. A good four-fifths of their time was spent foraging for supplies rather than concerning themselves with Rebels. Until he'd been settled into the small hospital tent at Loudon, where the brigade initially set up winter quarters, he'd not been fed a full ration in two months. At Comrie, he'd gotten into the happy late afternoon habit of walking by the handsome, standalone brick-kitchen to sniff the air and guess what might be destined for the small dining table he nightly shared with Clara. It made him wonder how effective a fully-fed army might be: if it would be slovenly, slow to get underway and its men, free from the mind-worms of numbing hunger, would be disinclined to line up against their former countrymen to trade shot and shell.

He recalled a farm south of Knoxville that his company had ransacked. The farmer might well have been a Union man, and his wife and three little ones the same by association, but the squad hadn't bothered to ask. Instead they'd levered up a couple of loose floorboards to steal the family's winter supplies, leaving them with nothing more than an army docket in poor exchange. Shire had an itchy conscience at the time and a worse one now, but it hadn't stopped him scooping out his share of pickled-peppers and blackberry preserve.

In the hospital tent you didn't have the distraction of searching for food. You lay in bed dwelling on its absence for long hours, only to find the day's main event was yet another variation on a thin and meatless broth.

That had been a long count of days. It was a good clean wound the surgeon had said: 'That ball hit nothing but muscle on the way through, nothing but muscle. Should heal up just fine.'

Shire had known men lose their limbs or their lives over smaller scratches. The first morning in the hospital, he'd passed pleasantries with a soldier wounded in the shoulder whose bed had thoughtfully been placed next to the tent entrance. When the cold breeze wafted inside, Shire would receive the flavor of meat left overlong in a pantry, rotted meat that needed to be thrown out, or better yet, buried. That had been the way of it a few days later.

Shire's own wound had started to itch. When he turned over, he began to believe he could feel something moving in his flesh. He spoke on it once too often and the surgeon brought over his junior and armed him with a thin metal prod tipped with porcelain. After unwinding the bandage from Shire's calf, the surgeon encouraged his novice to have a good dig around and see if he could get any trace of a lead ball to mark the porcelain. The boy had set to it with a will as if it was a challenge for him personally, rather than for Shire, who writhed every other part of himself across the bed in an attempt to keep his leg still. It might as well have been the glowing end of a fired stick that he went digging with. The surgeon pronounced the wound clean. No matter that it bled as freshly as it had when Shire lay on the grass at Dandridge. After that, he kept quiet, tended to his soup and didn't complain when his wound prickled.

George took a step forward and Shire realized he was working the plait too tight. He tried to backtrack and let it loosen a little.

The soup was better at Comrie, closer to a ham and vegetable stew. It occurred to him that not only did he no longer have to worry over food, neither did he have to do that as part of a crowd. In fact, while away from the army he didn't have to do anything in enforced company. Of course he missed Tuck and Mason, but he didn't miss dipping his head into a pungent tent and negotiating for a space to sit. It had been more common on the winter slog around Knoxville to have no tents and to simply sleep where the day's march ended. But a regiment of men could still crowd a wood or conspire to pack an open field. To be here alone, in these oversized, high-beamed stables was both luxurious and slightly unnerving.

And then there was the complete lack of orders; his return to a long-lost state of being where he could do what he wanted, go *where* he wanted.

The summed removal of all these constraints: the semi-starvation, the enforced company and the constant orders, had almost overwhelmed him when he returned to Comrie. Like the first surfacing breath of a man underwater too long. All he could do was convulsively take the first desperate lungful of this temporary freedom. It had taken several more days for his state of mind to acclimatize, for him to try and judge how far he might be from the safety of shore.

He'd hoped perhaps for a rebirth of the younger Shire, the one he recalled from before a mix of happenstance, friendship and love – love had the majority share – had pulled him away from his English home and into an America at war with itself. Instead, at times, he felt he was becoming reacquainted with some distant cousin who'd traveled abroad for a number of years and returned worn and slightly saddened by the experience. It shouldn't be such a surprise, he thought. The healing wound in his leg was only the latest added to his collection. There was the dent above his heart from the spent minie ball that he'd stopped on Missionary Ridge. More on show was the tear-shaped scar on his right cheek. He'd gained that well over a year ago after arriving in New York: It was the product of fat dripped from a burning, hanging soul who the gangs had lynched for having the effrontery not to be white. The scar was stubbornly and redly on show whenever he came to shave; if only it would hint at fading then perhaps the memory might too.

This new Shire, this partial stranger, had to be negotiated with, taken on horse rides in the hills, quieted before he could get to sleep. It left him suspicious that he might not be so unhappy to get back to the army where his disparate selves could just get on with the more directed, albeit crowded, business of being a soldier.

He'd interrupted a crowd in the stables just two days ago when he'd come looking for Moses. Finding the cold yard and the kitchen wholly empty, he'd slipped in between the oversized carriage doors and into the rear of a stand-up meeting. All the blacks were there in the dusty half-light, field-hands and former house-slaves, babies and old-timers like Moses, who stood in the open carriage as if it were a pulpit. Shire went unnoticed long enough to hear him say, 'This ain't the time. Freedom don't mean you have to head out into a cold winter and a war that's yet to settle.'

A broad-shouldered boy, directly in front of Shire, pushed an angry arm into the air. 'There's no pay here,' he said. 'Ain't nobody seen a Union cent.'

There was a mumbled affirmation from the crowd. Moses, his gaze drawn this way by the claim, spotted Shire. 'You ain't gone hungry yet, neither,' he said. 'Something we can help you with, Mr Shire?'

Everyone had turned to stare.

Alone in the stables today, he was halfway down George's tail but the higher section of the braid looked ragged. It wouldn't do. He shouldn't let his mind wander. Working it all free, he brushed the tail out again. George twisted his head in mild enquiry.

'What's the rush?' said Shire. 'We've got all afternoon. Perhaps if I stay long enough, we'll get a visitor.'

A week ago, he surely would have. It had been Clara's idea for him to recuperate as her guest at Comrie. For the first few days she couldn't do enough for him. He'd been practically grateful for this light wound that had bought him the boon of spending so much time with her, but even then there was an anxious, almost frantic edge to Clara. She looked after him, but her mind was somewhere else.

When the brigade, and the hospital with it, had moved down to Cleveland, Tennessee, he was back within a few miles of Clara. His wound was healing, but the best he could do was lever around the hospital tent on crutches. He'd written to her of the injury from Loudon and, now closer, had been planning to get another letter up to Comrie, but one afternoon he woke from a nap to find her beside him, her fingers woven into his.

It was Tuck's doing. He'd gotten a message up into the hills somehow. Tuck always found a way. Clara – beautiful, dark-eyed Clara – had appeared happy, more than happy. After an hour, she'd excused herself and when she came back said, 'I've spoken to your major. It's all arranged. You can convalesce at Comrie.'

For once Shire didn't mind the jibes from Company B as Clara helped him to the buggy. He would have her all to himself soon. Tuck had collected the things he'd need. 'If that leg starts healing too quickly, kick it with the other one.'

It was a fine buggy, but not matched by the uneven pair in harness. There was George, somewhat on the old side, but he was the dandy compared to the curved-back gray mule that kept him company. There could have been pigs in the traces for all Shire cared.

That was the high point. It had been fine for a while at Comrie too: Hany, Clara's maid, and Mitilde fussed over him nearly as much as Clara, but things had been on the slide ever since.

It was still too cold to sit out on the porch, and Comrie's rooms were empty of furniture, all of it hidden away somewhere deeper in the hills which were judged too lawless to venture into for its recovery. Instead there was a makeshift room, a study devoid of books with blankets at the windows to keep out the winter. The fire was always tended, here and in the smaller and still-furnished hunting den, but if you left those rooms you might as well step into an ice-house. Clara and Shire took their meals there, spent the first few days swapping tales of their time in America, summoning from their English childhood happier memories of the Ridgmont estate. It was as if those memories acted as a palliative for Clara; a balm to ease her more recent trauma. Day by day, they stopped working.

As the weeks passed, she began to leave Shire more and more to himself. She'd busy about Comrie with the blacks. If once he found her, it never seemed long before she had to be somewhere else. Promises to meet later in the day were missed. Time together was whittled down to no more than meal-times and short evenings. It remained an abundance, a precious windfall, but Clara appeared restless, whether with his company or her own he couldn't quite tell. Perhaps it was both.

'Why does she stay?' he asked George. 'What's to keep her? She's not signed up for three years like me. She could be away back home to England.' The business with Taylor, her late husband, was an embarrassment, of course it was. But if she told her father, the Duke, he could hush it up if anyone could.

Last night, at dinner, he'd asked her straight out. Why not find her way to New York and sail home? She'd looked at him in a way that suggested that the answer ought to be obvious, then cleared away the plates herself rather than wait for Mitilde. She'd not returned to share the fire.

He'd let go of George's tail and it had come undone again. 'Never mind, George,' he said quietly. 'Perhaps tails are just meant to be tails. Maybe we shouldn't worry overmuch if they pick up a tangle or two.'

Comrie, Tennessee – February 1864

There was barely anything that Clara cared to take. Mrs Thackery had left behind little in the way of usable furniture. Her former tenant had carted up back in December to get closer to her soldier husband in Georgia. 'To reside on the more Godly side of the line,' as she'd put it.

Abandoned to the Union and the Devil was a heavy looking oak table, roughly hewn, by Mr Thackery perhaps. Clara hoped he was a finer soldier than he was a carpenter, that his eye lined up better with a musket than a lathe. There were no chairs but instead two plain wooden benches pulled close under the table. So alike in crudeness were all three items that they might have been wrestled from the same tree. Maybe she could use the table in her bedroom. It would be something at least, given that her walnut writing desk was waiting out the war deep in a copper ore seam along with the rest of Comrie's adornments.

Clara had tried to persuade Mrs Thackery to stay, for the sake of those two little ones if nothing else. It had wrenched her heart to see them led out and lifted up onto the wagon, bound for who knew where. 'There's nothing to fear,' Clara had said. What depredations there had been, after the Union Army arrived, were over. And they were never aimed at the likes of Mrs Thackery. 'There are old slave cabins at the house if it would make you feel safer?'

Mrs Thackery had straightened and said that if it was all the same to Clara she 'didn't much care to. Fine homecoming that would be fer my Sherborne, his two boys housed no better than slaves. I 'magine he'd think that cut hard against the grain of what he's been fightin' fer.'

Clara's Confederate husband was not long dead after wearing the same colors. In point of fact, he'd been Mr Thackary's colonel. So Clara felt it wasn't the time to contend with the sentiment. Even if she felt more inclined to make a case for Mr Lincoln's view of the world, her own past was too compromised.

The forest would start to take the place back if she failed to find another tenant. She had the sudden thought of herself climbing into a wagon, *bound for who knew where.* Would that be so bad? So many people were on the move. Julius Raht, the manager of the mines at Ducktown and one of the few people she could call a friend, had ridden up to Comrie yesterday to say goodbye. She'd insisted he stay for dinner, not that much insistence was needed where Julius and food was concerned. It had made a change from only Shire's company, kept at bay any temptation toward deeper conversation. Julius said his mines were as good as useless while the war lasted. 'No men to work them and no market for the copper.' He was taking his family to Cincinnati to wait out the war. He invited her to come and visit, to escape Comrie, if only for a while. Shire had sided with Julius and said it would be good for her, as if he knew better than she did. That had set her squarely against the idea.

When Julius rode away, she'd had the familiar melancholy of being left behind while the rest of the world moved on. She'd endured the most trying months of the winter in her cold and empty house. She despaired of recovering Comrie's furniture from its hiding place deep in the hills, and still deeper in the Ducktown mines, but it seemed important to do that to set Comrie right – a necessary step.

There was no doubt that Mrs Thackery's leavings belonged to Clara. She'd passed up to the wagon all the Confederate money she had. It was worthless in the Union. But to Clara's mind, if what she was doing wasn't theft, it bore a close resemblance. Coming into this home uninvited, disdainful of what little there was, pained she had to take anything at all.

The ever-fresh memory played out once more. She was chained and manacled, alone in the bare hut with Taylor high on the hill, the wind howling outside. The heavy slave-collar was about her neck. He knelt over her. She felt again the cold certainty that she was about to suffer and die. He placed his dirty hand tightly over her scream.

The rumble and ache of a wagon jolted her back to the present. She stepped outside from the musty parlor, patted her horse and took a head-clearing draft of cold air. Mist swirled through the trees, not substantial enough to dampen her bonnet or gloves. From the gloom spoke a round sing-song voice, Mitilde's voice, that Clara heard every waking day. 'I ain't sayin' he's perfect, but you show me another man who'll take her and her child on. I ain't ever seen a girl as needs a father as much. Needs a father and a firm hand.'

'He's ain't for stayin'.' It was Moses. 'All day and every day he's talkin' someone into headin' out. He's a dis-con-tent. She needs someone settled.'

'Whole world's discontent, you ole fool. Armies marchin' this way an' that on account of it. The young ones need to find their own ground now they's allowed.'

An old mule, as yet unnamed, one Clara had recently acquired from a copper hauler whose trade had ceased to exist, eased out of the mirk, head down. Behind her, seated on the wagon, emerged familiar black faces. Mitilde claimed two thirds of the sprung driving-bench on account of circumference and gesticulation. Next to her sat Moses, his wooly hair the same shade as the mist. He held the reins as easily as he might do a fishing pole after several hours of waiting.

'She needs a husband,' Mitilde said. 'Things is changed.'

Moses nudged Mitilde with his knee and she altered tack. 'Here we is, Miss Clara. Here we is.' The mule drew up at the Thackery house.

It was clear to Clara they had been talking about her maid, Hany, but it was news to her that Hany might have a match. Why had Mitilde buttoned up as if Clara would have a care? Maybe it was only tittle-tattle, but there was little else to talk about. She lifted an arm toward Mrs Thackery's abandoned home. 'There's nothing I truly want, but I need the table and benches in my bedroom.'

Moses climbed down slowly and came around to help Mitilde as she lowered herself. 'I don't need no help,' she said, swatting at him behind her back, but he stayed in close quarters to bravely support her weight and she let him be. Clara smothered a half-smile. If he could support Mitilde, he'd have little enough trouble with the oak table. She led them inside.

'If there's anything the staff need, take that too.'

She'd started to call them staff. She knew Mitilde found it amusing. It suggested butlers in livery, maids in pinafores with white caps, footmen. In fact, it was this couple, this old man and his latter-life paramour, who headed up the collection of former slaves who had chosen to stay at Comrie. Stay for now, at least, while they all worked out the true parameters of freedom.

When Mitilde moved the benches, a robin flew up from beneath the table and close by Clara's head. 'Out you go, Mister Robin,' laughed Mitilde. 'No business in here. Best to make use of what you can, Miss Clara. Ain't nobody about to haul the Comrie furniture from the hills any time soon.'

'No, Miss,' Moses said. 'No army goin' into those hills. Atlanta's where they all thinkin' of. The Copper Road and Ducktown can go to hell for all they care.'

Mitilde smacked his arm. 'You mind your mouth in front of a lady and get the other end of this here table.'

Moses was right. The Union Army was garrisoned down in Cleveland but never came into the hills. The Copper Road to Ducktown was hardly used at all. Every week some new story whispered out of the hills: a robbery or a murder. Old scores, most from long before the war, were being settled while there was no one to watch. Her furniture might come to live in the hills for as long as the copper had.

Comrie was not unlike her life, she thought: devoid of components, cleared out of all that mattered. It was hateful to have to wait. Wait until the war ended and the law edged its way back into the hills so she could recover what belonged to Comrie – all of it hers now, not Taylor's. After that, anything she'd taken from departed tenants could fuel Comrie's fires for all she cared.

She tried to lend a hand but Mitilde wouldn't have it so she mounted her horse. For an old couple they made light work of wrestling the furniture onto the wagon. Moses pushed Mitilde up and then led the mule in a wide turn before he climbed aboard himself. Clara could have trotted on ahead, but preferred to let her horse amble behind.

Shire would be waiting at the house. It was easier to get irritated with him than dwell on the wider inertia of her life. He'd offered to come and help, over-keen as ever. He'd been that way for as long as she'd known him, which was to say always. You'd think keenness would be an attractive quality and to her advantage. Yet attraction was nonsensical and didn't work that way, rather it was some subtle concoction of attention, indifference and scarcity. Shire was getting the proportions all wrong. She'd come to Mrs Thackery's without him in order to help with the scarcity.

After a short while, the wagon slowed as the mule started to struggle with the gradient. The road broke from the trees and switched back and forth in several short lengths across a steep meadow. At the top was Comrie, its red tiled roof muted by the mist, the tall columns fronting the entire mansion were a dirty gray rather than Grecian white. It was like looking up at a prison window. Shire stood in front of the columns at the top of the wide steps and waved as if he'd not seen her in a month of Sundays.

She was aware of being utterly unfair. Shire had left everything, spent a year of his young life fighting and suffering to get to her and save her from a bigamous marriage. Perhaps only his particularly extreme variety of devotion might serve to make someone do that. And where had it got him? Stuck in the army and in a war that wasn't his quarrel, his father dead in England, his future so fragile that it wasn't worth a single thought beyond the summer.

And he *had* saved her. Her husband, Taylor, was dead and rotting in a shallow grave way up the hill behind the house. She detested that: Taylor being *above* her even now. While his body slowly leeched into Tennessee's red soil, his shade was no doubt laughing at the quandary he'd left her, as if he still reigned here, godlike, watching and waiting on high. She felt his dead weight in the heavy air as she followed the wagon and climbed toward the house.

The matter of her marriage was unresolved, and she might never learn the exact date of Taylor's secret wife's death back in England. On that single fact rested so much: whether she'd ever legally been married, whether she owned Comrie and its wider wealth, whether she could mark time as the supposed heartbroken widow of a Confederate colonel and then re-emerge into a new life, with that no more than a badge of suffering. Or, instead, would she be revealed as his sullied victim, worthless to herself and her 'noble' line, Comrie never hers to begin with? Such was her true inheritance from Taylor Spencer-Ridgmont. Such was Shire's rescue.

And how could she resolve her predicament? She could hardly write home to a father who was ignorant of the secret store of shame that lived precariously on the other side of the Atlantic.

Dear Father, could you please be so good as to look into the matter of the death of one Grace Harland, daughter of your former estate vicar and once on your staff as a second seamstress. I require to know the date of this wretched woman's death. On that fact, balances my very existence.

There was no confidant she could employ. And if once the enquiry became known and subjected to wider scrutiny, what then? If she was proved to be legally married, she would still have been publicly disgraced, a scandal to the distant great and good in England and to the leavings of the war here in Polk County. Too ashamed to leave these hills she'd be known as the widow who was tricked from her ducal home back in the mother country. She envisaged herself living out beyond the horizon of her current life and into old age, nothing more than a local curiosity. Her future seemed locked away, trapped, as inaccessible as the Comrie treasures in the mine. How did Shire plan to rescue her from that?

Pennsylvania – February 1864

Tod half climbed, half crawled, back up onto the tracks. His ribs screamed like they had been prized from their home and set to cook on a hot brick. He'd have cried out but it wasn't the thing for a runaway to do, and besides, it hurt just drawing what air he needed. He placed both feet on a crosstie, tried to straighten up but could only manage half-way and stood there like he'd been gut shot.

The train's yellow tail-light was fading into the rain, the dog pant of the engine working hard on the incline, but then came a short squeal of brakes, metal on metal. The engine sent out a single long hiss that blurred into the wind. Tod hurried as best he could to the north side of the track and started to climb up the slope and into the trees. He figured they'd look on the side he'd jumped and would assume he'd head downhill. They had no dogs, at least none that he'd seen.

He tried to tell himself that pain didn't matter, *couldn't* matter. He was blowing already. The tail-light was his only point of reference and disappeared as soon as he was in the woods. There was no moon, no stars. His feet slid on wet leaves and he cast his hands blindly out in front. All he'd done was come up fifty feet from the track and he was spent. He slumped against a tree and struggled to manage the choice between pain and air. The trees shook their gathered rain onto his head in big, cold February drops. The rich must of the forest was almost heady. He heard voices over the whisper of the branches and saw a lone lantern down on the track. He could make out a pair of boots but that was all. If he could see the light then the light must be on him, but he had no strength left; it had all been bled away at Johnson's Island. All he could do was furtively dig his hands under the leaves and rub the wet, loamy soil onto his face. He had an insane urge to call out, to yell, 'Here I am,' as if he was a boy again, hiding from his younger brother, Francis. It had somehow always been better to jump out if he knew he was about to be discovered.

As far as he could tell, the lantern was hung out over the other side of the track. Only two men. There weren't so many guards on the train; they could hardly abandon all the prisoners to come look for him. It would go badly for Wrigley and the others. They would probably all be shoved back into the boxcar. The train whistle sent out a short scream and Tod jumped as if it had called his name. The lantern hurried away back up the track. Was that all they were going to do? It appeared so. The engine started forward again with a stutter of steam and a yank on the couplings. Tod sat and listened until he could hear nothing above the wind and rain. He felt elated and bereft at the same time.

The rail line was the only orientation he had unless the clouds cleared. He figured the Yankee colonel couldn't get a wire off until the next station, so slid back down to the track. His eyes had become more accustomed to the dark. There was a wet sheen on the two rails that invited him back to the west, toward Pittsburgh. He felt a long way from anywhere and anyone, alone in an enemy winter with only these two stretched-out strips of metal to help him begin a long journey. He put aside the memory of his warm seat on the train.

He picked a pace that he might be able to sustain. The crossties were too far apart for the stride of a tired man so he would step on, off and over – on, off and over. The rhythm of it allowed for no other thought. Time blurred, measured only by each on, off and over. He used what little strength he had to keep his balance in the wind and rain. He lost count of how many times he tripped before he fell down hard between the rails, setting his ribs aflame again. He turned his head sideways and rested it on a crosstie like it was the softest pillow in Pennsylvania.

He might have slept had the rails not began to murmur. At first Tod thought it must be his imagination, but when he stretched a hand to the metal he could feel it. The sound rose, like a sword endlessly pulled from its sheath. He got to his knees and ahead of him silver light raced toward him along each rail, tracing out a corner. He stood and hauled himself and his pack toward the dim shapes of the trees. The engine arrived, paying him no heed. It granted him only one warm breath of steam before abandoning him to the dark and the cold.

He had no idea how long it was until dawn but knew he couldn't go on. He used his last strength to move further into the woods and lay down on the leeward side of a wide trunk. The leaves were sodden, but no more than he was.

When he woke, it was still dark. He sat up and something heavy raced away through the leaves and twigs. His heart came quickly up to speed. A bear, maybe? More likely a deer. Whatever it was, it was gone. The wind had stopped and the rain too, though the trees passed on the memory of it. He stood and rubbed his stubbled face. His hands felt like they belonged to someone else; someone cold and dead the morning after a battle. A hint of light crept into the world under the patched canopy of winter. He should get moving, generate some warmth. He was hungry, but used to that. As a soldier and a prisoner, he'd learned to hold hunger in its place. Now, with miles beyond measure ahead of him, there wasn't even the prospect of food.

He crossed to the south of the rails; it felt nearer home. The light came on reluctantly with gray clouds low above the trees, but that wasn't such a bad thing if he didn't want to be seen. The land was flatter and the maples and elms began to thin out. He chanced on a one-man path that led to a two-rut track, considered which way might be west and trudged on. He was blowing again, worn out. After a muddy half-mile the trees either side stopped at a worm-rail fence with a handsome five-bar gate. Beyond was a pasture and then a fine farm that, despite his weariness, Tod could admire. He would have tipped back his hat if he'd had one. There was a large wooden barn, big enough for a church, painted cherry red as was the house close beside it. He edged along the fence and found a tree that split at head height so that he could rest against the trunk and watch through the V. To look at, the farm was nothing like his brick home in Franklin, but there was an honest self-sufficiency, a simple orderliness, that caught him in the chest and had him weeping. He wished it was home that he was trying to escape to. It was a low moment to endure.

By now, most sheriffs along the rail line would know there was a soldier on the loose. He'd need clothes and food if he was to get further. He caught himself looking for slave huts before he remembered where he was. A rooster started up. There was no sign of a dog. The barn door was open and a pale light inside withered as the clouds broke. A man pushed a barrow loaded with manure out and around the back. As he returned, a woman came from the house with a young boy who walked on ahead, swinging an empty bucket that was too big for him. They all entered the barn. This might be his best chance. Was today Sunday? He thought it might be but couldn't waste the day waiting on them leaving for church. Best be quick.

He followed the fence until he could come across the field from the opposite side to the barn. He climbed up to the porch as quietly as his heavy, wet boots would allow but tripped on the top step, his stumble covered by lowing from the barn. The door to the house was wide open and he stepped inside. There was a steep staircase to the right. Upstairs would be the best place to find clothes. Down the hall was an open kitchen door. His stomach howled at the sight. He'd need to visit both anyway. Why not start with the kitchen?

He was at once a fox in a henhouse, wanting to find and eat everything. There was a crock hiding the rump of a loaf, cheese under a cloth. He took a bite of both and crammed the rest into his pack. He lifted a full jug and gulped at it, forcing down the food, almost choking, the milk dribbling down through his stubble. He wiped it with his sleeve, but stopped short when he found himself looking into the stern eyes of a young child, a boy of no more than two or three.

He knew how to converse with children: he had younger siblings, nephews and nieces aplenty, not to mention the slave children, but it had been a long time and this one had him at a disadvantage. He could tell that the frown the child wore wasn't down to there being a stranger in his house, but rather that this stranger was making liberal with the food. Tod retrieved the cheese and bent down. He held out a hand but couldn't stop it from shaking, and offered the child a good size piece. A smaller but steadier hand took it and the boy turned to leave the room, no doubt to enjoy it in a place of his choosing, only to run straight into the folds of his mother's dress.

Women had been a rarity in Tod's recent life too, and this one, maybe for that reason, looked shockingly pretty. With her dark hair loosely tied for her morning chores she could have been Venus herself. She still meant capture and a hanging tree. She may as well have been the sheriff. She turned the child by the shoulders. The boy did his best to hide the cheese.

'*Was hat dir dieser Herr geschenkt*, Joshua?'

Joshua plainly wasn't up to answering, preferring to let the scene play out.

The woman reached for a hand-bell on the dresser that was big enough to start a school day. 'Sir, I'm going to ring this bell and that'll bring my husband.' Her accent was heavy. 'It would be as well when he gets here that you aren't holding that knife like you mean us harm.'

Tod looked to his trembling hand like it had deserted him. Sure enough, he was gripping a knife low to his side, the blade angled up. He slowly placed it on the table and edged backward. Chickens clucked outside the kitchen window. Milk dripped from his chin to the floor. How must he look? He wanted to apologize but could do no more than dumbly open his mouth.

She rang the bell. Joshua stuffed the cheese into his mouth and put his hands over his ears. Tod sank to his knees. So much for escape. He'd not lasted a full day before being captured by a Yankee mother and child.

Comrie, Tennessee – February 1864

Shire was alone again. Every day now, after the midday meal, Clara abandoned him, no longer troubling to provide a reason. It was as if he caused offence simply by being there. Since his well-beaten trail of tangled thought had once more ended in a thicket, he sought out old Moses and found him in his cabin. Shire had no plain clothes so was in his Union blue minus his kepi hat. Moses looked surprised to have a soldier knocking at his door but invited Shire into a room of simple comforts: a low bed, a high-backed rocker and a small black stove with a skinny chimney pipe. There was a bridle on the floor, a rag and the smell of vinegar.

'Can I help?' Shire asked.

'I's about done.' Moses pulled a drying shirt from the rocker's back and threw it on the bed. 'I don't get visitors so much.' He waved Shire to the chair. 'This is a visit, ain't it? Or did you need me for somethin'?'

'It's a visit.'

'Uh huh. Thought so. I ain't got no coffee.' He held up a finger then knelt down stiffly and reached under the bed to stretch and recover a plain glass bottle half full of clear liquid. He made to pull the cork with his teeth but then thought better of it and passed the bottle to Shire. 'You can take care of that.' From the bedside he collected and wiped-out a chipped porcelain tea-cup, an outcast from the big house. 'I can drink from the bottle.'

'We can share.' Shire bit out the cork, swapped the bottle for the cup and let Moses pour. There was no pattern on the inside of the cup – it was clean white. Feeling the whiskey burn his throat, Shire wondered if this was by design or the result of regular use.

Moses chuckled. 'Plenty in these hills if you know how to get it. I had to hide it better than under the mattress when Master Taylor was alive. These days I only need to keep it out of Mitilde's sight, in case she puts her head in.'

Shire was still blinking away the sting of it. 'She wouldn't begrudge you a drink, would she?'

'Maybe not, but it ain't worth the finding out.'

'You don't plan to marry her then?'

'Well, you sure ain't one for warming your hands before you start the milking. Ain't we supposed to talk on the weather or the war before pickin' over my weddin' prospects?'

'The whiskey must have loosened my tongue.' It wasn't like they hadn't talked before. Perhaps he had been on the direct side. He liked Moses; liked an older man's company. He could hardly compare Moses' life experience to Father's, God rest him, yet somehow the world seemed to have hammered a similar shape of wisdom into both of them.

Moses took his turn at the cup, gave it another charge from the bottle then sat on the bed. 'I don't see that there's much need to change things.'

'But it's your choice now, right? No need to get permission from anyone.'

Moses passed back the cup. 'Only Mitilde, but that's my point. You start asking permission for that and end up asking for everything else. I like having my own cabin.'

'Hers is bigger.' Shire bravely took another swig.

'You been visiting there too?'

'Clara was saying.'

'Is that what you talk about over the chicken and gravy?

Which cabin Mitilde and I ought to settle on?'

'She's fond of you both, wants to see you happy.'

There was a quiet moment or two while they let the whiskey ease into their blood.

'I guess,' said Shire, 'I don't understand that if two people care for each other, love each other, why they wouldn't choose to be together.'

Moses nodded slowly, sipped more whiskey and let out a low chuckle.

'Something funny?' said Shire.

'Just thinkin'.'

'Just thinking what?'

'How kind it is of this young Englishman to take the time to pay me a visit and give me the benefit of his long experience of love. Maybe old love ain't the same as young love.' Moses made himself comfortable on the bed with his back to the wooden wall. He took a swig straight from the bottle. 'There was a copper-hauler, a muleteer, long before the war but after the Cherokee had been cleared out. He set up with a wagon hauling supplies up the newly finished road to the mines at Ducktown, then copper ore or smelted copper back to the railway at Cleveland. It's a two-day trip each way so he only spent one night in four with his wife. She got into the habit of cramming four days' news into a single evenin'. He was always away early the morning after. He loved to listen to the fast river beside the road and to know the names of all the birds and animals.'

Outside in the yard, Hany yelled and summoned Shire out of the story. 'Cele, get yourself down offa there. Come help me peg out this washin'. Miss Clara gonna send you away again f' sure if you don't make yourself useful 'round here. Get down I said. Cele!'

Moses waited out the interruption. 'The couple had but one child and she was married off young, so one fine day his wife said she'd like to ride beside him into the hills. He didn't think it a bad idea but, by mid-morning, he discovered she was intent on filling the time between the here and now and the second coming with any sort of mindless news or town gossip, never once commenting on what beauty was ahead of them on the road. After the trip back, she said she had nothing much to do on the home front and would come again and cook for him. That way he wouldn't have to frequent the Halfway House tavern that was the stop-off point for all the hauliers. Summer passed to fall and still she rode with him, all the colors on God's earth passing left or right, never mentioned. What he couldn't fathom was how she was keeping up on the news from town when they were never a moment parted. Late fall, they were on the ferry crossing Greasy Creek when a bird, twenty different shades of blue, 'lighted on a branch ahead of them and started to sing.'

'"What bird is that?"' his wife asked.

'He was just thinkin' how dumb do you have to be to not know the name of such a common bird, when he realized he couldn't bring it to mind hisself. His wife remarked how she'd thought he would a known that, what with all the years he'd been riding the road, and then asked him had he heard the price of sugar lately. Once they got home, and as soon as his wife was asleep, the word 'bluejay' popped right into his head.

'Next day a heavy storm came in and all the hauliers in town kept to their homes. He felt strongly that the folks in Ducktown shouldn't go without supplies, but lovingly insisted his wife stay home on account of the weather. By the time he got to Ducktown there was a foot of snow and no way back for a long and silent month.'

Shire realized he was lightly rocking the chair but felt no inclination to stop. 'Some might say that he didn't truly love her.'

'Some might say you can have too much of a good thing. On a cold night I can be over to Mitilde's cabin and into her warm bed so quick as to barely feel the draft. And it's a wider bed than mine, by necessity.'

The old man laughed so richly that Shire couldn't help laughing with him.

'Now your predicament… well, that's another matter and I don't pretend to understand the ins and outs, but you have love to work with. That's plain. Maybe it's not the right time.'

'It's complicated,' Shire said. How could he explain to Moses the gulf between a schoolmaster and a Duke's daughter? As far as Shire was aware, Moses knew nothing of Taylor's secret marriage. 'She has no time for me.'

'We came and got you from the hospital, didn't we? No one's idea but hers.'

'But she's free to choose now. Like you and Mitilde are free.'

'You think? A few blue soldiers wander this way and everything changes for the better? For the young ones, maybe. They's all full of it. Head north, head west, but what they gonna find when they get there? Freedom don't come with a home, don't find you work. There are different grades of freedom. Some of us have been here so long it's hard to get caught up in the notion of it. Master Taylor is dead. That's all the freedom I need. And in a few days, you can come back up that hill with me and we can burn those slave prisons up there.'

'Clara wants to move his body, bring him down off the hill and put him with his mother and brother.'

'You should talk her out of that. He's best left where I buried him.'

'She doesn't listen to me. She's not done with him.'

'Are you surprised? Him only a few months dead. You didn't know him, did you?'

'Some,' said Shire. He thought of a boy he'd known, Tom Muncie; a young man really, but with a boy's mind, a boy's face. Taylor had shot him, executed him while Shire was in touching distance. 'I wish I'd known him less.'

Moses swung his legs off the bed and stood up, impressively steady for an old man oiled with whiskey. He pulled his shirt over his head and took up the clean one. He could have stayed facing Shire, there was no reason to turn, but as he pushed in his head and arms he twisted away. Shire had a moment to see his back. Scars, paler than Moses' old brown skin, some tending to pink, angled every which way: from shoulder across to rib, looped high around the waist like a cheap belt, cut straight down beside the spine. When Shire dwelt on it later, he considered that there was less unmarked skin on that back than he possessed on the ball of his thumb.

'His father was a violent man,' said Moses, 'and he raised a violent son. The day that freedom arrived, we didn't all suddenly break even. You think Cele is the only leavings of Taylor running around out there? There's plenty Miss Clara don't know, and she shouldn't know. How d'you imagine it was in their bed?'

It wasn't a place to which Shire had let his mind wander.

'You think after a marriage vow he turned into a southern gentleman? He never gave out anything but pain and spite.

And here's you wanting to hold hands and find a new life before he's had time to rot. Maybe you should wait until a warm summer's been an' gone, until he's had a chance to mulch down a mite more.'

Comrie, Tennessee – February 1864

After lunch, Clara had sought out the sanctuary of the kitchen, her nerves worn thin by Shire. Their conversation had again become depressingly anchored in the past. Depressing because Clara realized it was for want of a clear future. It was less chafing to be with the women and work in the present. The standalone kitchen was warm and complete, not cold and empty like the house. Different rules applied; she wasn't obliged to be in charge. Mitilde let her roll out some pastry and appeared sensitive enough to Clara's mood not to criticize the angry weight she was bearing down with. 'You sure like your pastry thin,' was all she said.

Shire, Clara realized, sat at the nexus of all her frets about the past and the future. He was only here again at her instigation. It had seemed an obvious and wonderful idea at the time. Her friend of longstanding, her childhood and *best* friend, who knew her better than anyone alive or dead. Perhaps that was the nub: that she could hide none of herself from him. While doing or saying nothing provocative at all, Shire acted as an agitator, a worry magnet that drew out, taut and stark, the very worst of her fears.

Mitilde was right, this pastry was too thin. She balled it up, pushed her knuckles in deep and got it ready to roll again.

Hany and her little girl, Cele, clattered in through the door, all noise and bustle.

Mitilde fired a warning shot. 'This here's a kitchen, go play somewhere else.'

Neither Hany nor Cele paid any heed, Hany's happy eyes following her child's every action. Hany still wore her hair short and parted in the middle but not as neatly as she used to. Grooming time was spent on Cele.

The child was as pretty as her mother: skin as shiny as molasses and wide, bright eyes always looking for the next new thing. She was here due to another of Clara's invitations, for Cele to come and live with her mother at Comrie. It was only Christian to suggest such a thing. Throughout Polk and the neighboring counties people needed to sort out new living arrangements after the Union and freedom arrived, sifting lives through a mesh of old, moot transactions. It was a slow process. There were never so many slaves in Bradley or Polk County to start with – Comrie was an exception – and, it appeared to Clara, no one had quite known what to do; least of all former slaves. Freedom had only ever been a fanciful notion. Things were only slowly settling out. Husbands and wives, sold apart in the years and decades before the war, found the means to come together. It was beautiful if you stopped to think about it: all that invisible healing out in the low country below Comrie. Hany and Cele were part of the same story. How could she resent that? Maybe because she was held outside. An onlooker. No settling out for *her* life. Taylor's ghost would never allow it.

So far, Comrie had seen more comings than goings. It seemed to Clara that her home was considered a temporary refuge, benignly run despite its past, but she was aware that not everyone viewed her kindly, especially newcomers, particularly the young. She caught the odd sour look, mumbled comments that wouldn't have been risked the year before. It was understandable: only she was left to represent the old regime. She hadn't turned anyone away. The huts behind the great house lived under the steep slope that rose up to Taylor's grave high in the hills. Over the turn of the year, they had become crowded with men, women and children. Yet it all lacked an air of permanence. It had more the feel, she imagined, of a frontier wagon stop with people excited to be together, but anxious to head out toward a new future. It left her feeling wistful and excluded, as if she might find herself the last person here, waving the final wagon goodbye. She envied them their excitement, uncertain though their futures were.

Cele, small for her nearly six years, her big eyes level with the table edge, looked on while Clara finished rolling out the pastry. She moved a hand to Clara's dress to gain purchase. 'Can I make pastry? Can I cut out the pie?' Giggling, she blew the loose flour so it dusted over the table.

'Cele!' said Hany. 'Miss Clara don't need your type o' help.'

Cele got in another rushed blow before her mother swept her up and away.

'She's no bother,' lied Clara.

Lovely as she was, Cele stood out among all the other children as a running, jumping insult to Clara. She was Taylor's daughter, conceived in violence well before Clara came from England to marry him. It had been several years before Hany told Clara the truth: that the little girl Hany used to visit down in town was her daughter and not her sister as everyone had conspired to pretend. Clara considered the sister relationship a better fit: Hany had always been full of childish ways. She was Cele's partner in crime, if not an instigator then at least a willing participant. Hany smiled like a mother though; that much had changed. But on a daily basis, just by leaving small muddy footprints on the stone hall floor, or singing from the top of the sweeping stairs, the child pointed up Clara's stupidity, and how utterly she'd failed to see Taylor for what he was until it was too late.

Beyond that, Cele presented herself as daily evidence that Clara was likely barren. Lovemaking with Taylor – though she'd never found an ounce of love in it – had been months apart with him away in the war. That had been a blessing, but he'd taken his fill when home. At the time she'd been glad not to conceive. Where might that have left her? But one thing that seemed painted over in her future was the comfort of a child. She could feel that future now, hollow and cavernous in her womb. If Mitilde and Moses were right and Hany had a beau, Clara mused, someone who wanted to leave, maybe Taylor's little reminder would become part of a future exodus.

She stopped for a moment and looked through the window. Shire emerged smiling from Moses' hut, wandered through the herb garden and on toward the house, no doubt to look for her. He was more attractive when he didn't know he was watched and wasn't trying to hide his limp. She loved him. Of course she loved him. There had never been any question of that. Shire was *there* to be loved. It was one of his uses, but there was no way forward with him. She'd known him too long. That particular love was set in its mold. Besides, he was no more than a young schoolmaster who'd become a rank and file soldier.

She'd heard tales of him in battle: from Tuck when he was here after Taylor's death and from the surgeon when she'd visited the hospital. 'Wonderful, Miss. Just wonderful if you can take him away to rest. We'll be needing him back though. The regiment can't do without its Englishman. Carried our flag over Mission Ridge he did.'

She found it hard to reconcile the hero stories with *her* Shire; the Shire she'd had to talk down from trees when they were children. Recent signs of wear and tear were there to see: the scar, the limp, his brown eyes looked older, but she could see through to the boy who'd always belonged to her. Almost like a favorite and deeply loved dog. That was an unkind thought and unworthy of her, but there was some truth in it. She only had to clap her hands and he'd come running. Maybe it would be easier to love him again when he'd gone.

This pastry was better. Never mind that it wasn't perfectly round. She laid it over the filling, glad to be doing something where she could affect the outcome, even if it was only to badly cap an apple and blackberry pie. She rotated the dish and pressed her thumbs to crinkle the edges. Cele caught sight of it from across the kitchen and ran over, bouncing off Mitilde on the way. 'I wanna help. I wanna push the pie.'

Clara wasn't quick enough to lift the dish away and two tiny black digits reached up over the table and blindly poked holes through the newly laid crust.

Hany stifled a giggle.

'Get her out!' shouted Clara.

'It's only a pie, Miss.'

'Don't you answer back to me!' She swept the pie off the table with such force it smashed and broke against the oven. 'There was a time, not so long ago, when the only children allowed in this kitchen were those old enough to help.'

Hany, close to tears, picked up her daughter. Cele, her fruity fingers in her mouth, appeared more interested in the commotion than upset by it. Clara imagined it, she must have, but there seemed a moment where the indifferent stare of the little girl, the slight angled set of her mouth, might have belonged to her father.

Hany carried Cele outside, leaving the door swinging.

'Miss Clara,' said Mitilde, her voice soft and low, 'there was a time, not so long ago, when many things were different.'

Clara didn't need the lesson or the soothing. While she felt wretched that all her worries had spilled over onto the child, part of her felt elated, relieved... better. She began to clear up the mess.

'I'll do that,' said Mitilde. 'Go be with your soldier.'

Her soldier. She'd only find frustration there. Instead she half-ran around to the front of the mansion and climbed the long steps to the porch. It was really too cold to sit out. Regardless, she took a rocker and pulled it back into a shadowy corner out of the wind where no one would see her or hear the slow sway of the chair. If Taylor was intent on speaking to her from his grave, then he didn't deserve to be left in peace.

Westmoreland County, Pennsylvania – February 1864

Tod sat well back inside the covered buggy to avoid being seen by the Amish. Beside him, Luther leaned forward in the sunlight to make best use of the reins, encouraging the horse into a trot where the track allowed. Despite his hiding place, Tod felt conspicuous. He had not left the farm since he'd arrived five days ago.

It was a wrench to drive away from his refuge, leaving the simple Christian kindness of Luther and his young family. It felt like stepping onto an open stage. He was wearing the fresh Amish garb that Rachel had left outside his bedroom before first light. The jacket was so oversized that, when he'd stood before her to say goodbye, his hands were hidden in the cuffs and the suspenders were wholly in use for the trousers. He didn't like to complain, but worried that the suit might draw attention to him once they reached the station down in Latrobe.

There were so many farms, each one as neat as the next, and so close to where he'd been hiding. The fields were empty of crops but as tidy as a swept kitchen floor. It was a dry day and the Amish were out making best use of it: tending their cattle, mending roofs, sweeping wet leaves from porches. Every man and boy was dressed as Luther was, with the same flat-brimmed hat, the same black suit and waistcoat over a white shirt. The women and girls wore plain navy-blue dresses, a white apron and a white prayer cap tied under the chin.

Luther tipped his hat to anyone who looked their way, which was to say everyone. As they edged past a buggy on the track he drew the rein and conversed in German to a man of similar middle years. Tod turned his face, developing a sudden and earnest interest in the hedgerow. It was a good while before Luther nodded his goodbyes and they set off again.

'Perhaps we should have picked a quieter time of day to make this trip,' said Tod.

'There *is* no quieter time of day, not when the sun is up.'

'Well, given you're carrying a runaway, you think we oughta press on rather than stop to chew the cud?'

'Later, once we are closer to Latrobe. Among my people, *not* stopping would attract attention. Besides, everyone knows who you are.'

'What?'

Luther turned his head, smiled with his whole face. 'Do not worry. No one will say anything.'

Tod shrunk back further into the shadow of the cab. The looks and waves from the Amish took on a different light.

'I didn't tell you before as I didn't want you to worry.'

'If everyone knows about me then why have I been hiding in the house all this time?'

'Outsiders can arrive unannounced, like you did.'

When Tod had stumbled into Luther's farm, only for Rachel and young Joshua to take him captive, he'd thought himself lucky that they led a remote life, a goodly way from the nearest sheriff. But on Saturday, when he was beginning to believe himself safe, Rachel let in several other women to help in the kitchen. It had been tortuous listening from his bedroom: not only the women's sweet voices and laughter, but the aromas... Dear Lord.

Then on Sunday, he'd watched through lace curtains as an oversized wagon pulled into the yard and unloaded a dozen or more benches. Luther and the driver carried them into the house along with open crates of crockery and a box of hymnals. Later in the morning, the whole community pitched up. The buggies were backed up out of the yard, their horses led off one at a time into Luther's barn. Family after family, in the same suits and dresses, funneled toward the door below Tod's window. The house bubbled with chatter. He cracked open the door so he could listen, but it was all in German. Had it been Greek or Latin, as he'd studied at the Harpeth Academy in faraway Franklin, he might have had a better chance. The prayer started up, nearly all of it intoned rather than spoken. It had lasted for hours. Mercifully, after that, Rachel had slipped upstairs and given Tod a plate of food.

Luther's buggy reached the end of the track and climbed up onto a raised and wider turnpike. 'You have to understand,' he said, 'I could make no decision on my own when it might affect everyone.'

Tod recalled that many of the older men had stayed after the Sunday service. 'When church was over? You told them about me then?'

'It was a prayer meeting. We don't have a church. And no, I told them the day you arrived, while you slept.'

All that time spent hiding, while any number of strangers discussed his fate, but then they could hardly invite him along. It would have been worse still to sit among them not understanding a word. 'I guess I'm just grateful I wasn't turned in. Wasn't that the obvious thing to do? I'm your enemy. You would be harshly treated if I was found.'

'Do you truly think of yourself as our enemy?' Luther sounded genuinely perplexed.

Tod considered what to say. 'I guess I've come not to. How could I, after all the kindness you've shown, after coming to know your family?' He recalled the first time he was allowed back into the kitchen; Joshua had taught him to churn butter and Tod had feigned incompetence. 'But I'm a soldier of the South. If you had an older son in a blue uniform, I'd take issue with him.'

'Our sons have been spared from this war.'

'That's a luxury we don't have in the South, whatever our beliefs.'

'Yet there remained a choice.'

'When your state's will is ignored? When your home is invaded?'

'You have a choice again now.'

'I have a regiment. I belong to that regiment. There might be years left in this fight.'

'If you live each short hour with God, then the years will take care of themselves. We understand you intend to get back into the war. That troubles us. If you fight again, and if you take only one life, we will have merely saved you that you might kill someone else.'

Tod took on board the philosophical problem. His mind wandered to lessons on Bentham. You could never square that sort of thinking. At least, he couldn't. He was more concerned with the consequences if he didn't fight. 'What I do after I leave isn't your responsibility. You didn't will the war any more than I did. If it helps, I'm a quartermaster. My job is to see that the men are fed and supplied.' It didn't seem the time to mention he'd done his share of shooting as well.

'That magnifies the problem. A good quartermaster supplies the bullets for many men to kill many other men. It would help if you were a poor quartermaster.'

'I'm sorry,' said Tod. 'I can't help you there. I know my business.' A ragged queue of gray soldiers appeared in his mind's eye, waiting in line for him to hand over their ration of cartridges.

'It was suggested I should invite you to stay with us, to wait out the war, but I already knew your answer, and sending you to hang is simply violence by proxy. So putting you in Saul's clothes and driving you to the station was the only thing for us to do.'

'I'm grateful,' said Tod, 'to all of you. And thank Saul for me.' He tried to square his shoulders inside the ill-fitting jacket. 'Although he could stand to lose a few pounds.'

'Saul died last week.'

They rode in silence for a while, Tod feeling uncomfortable in a whole new way.

They crossed a tidy plank bridge over a thin creek. Luther gently reined in the horse and the squeak of the wheels died. There was no traffic ahead or behind, nothing more than the light Pennsylvania breeze and the blowing of the horse. They stepped out and Luther collected the animal some water. Tod stretched and tilted back his hat. From the banked-up turnpike he drank in the rounded richness of the country. Luther and Rachel had their own little paradise if they were prepared to put aside the rest of the world. 'It's a beautiful country I'm at war with, and it's a crime that it wasn't avoided, but contented people never run for office.'

Luther smiled and put a hand on Tod's shoulder. 'We don't begrudge you your freedom, but we... I... would ask something of you.'

'I'm in your debt.'

'Your only debt is to God. He led you to us.' Luther held Tod's eye with the earnest stare of a preacher. 'If you make it back to your army, no doubt the time will come to kill again. You will have a choice. Remember us, remember our home, how it is possible to live without violence. It's just a different kind of bravery.'

If only it was that simple. 'I'll remember you, Luther, and I'll pray for your family, but in my army, that would be called desertion.'

'In God's kingdom, it would be called peace.'

Comrie, Tennessee – February 1864

It was a poor day for grave digging. The ground was frozen after two clear nights. Shire could feel the topology of the smallest ridge or runnel through his boots. He stamped his feet on the hard ground but failed to generate any warmth, just a fizzy numbness that slowly dissolved to leave them achingly cold.

Clara stood beside him, made all the paler by the low gray sky that had eased over the hills as they'd climbed up here at first light. Why was she doing this? What purpose could it possibly serve? She made no entreaty to warmth other than to work each ungloved hand tightly over the other. She'd been doing that more and more as the week had gone on, inside or out. She wore only a gray shawl over a black dress while she watched the gravediggers at work. He thought to take off his army coat and wrap her, play the chivalrous soldier, but any approach he'd made this morning had been ignored or curtly dealt with. Best to leave her be.

She'd ridden off yesterday late in the afternoon. No one knew where she was going. She'd refused to wait for Shire to get a horse tacked up to go with her. It was after dark when she'd returned and Mitilde had ragged on her like she was a truant child and steered her to the fire in the den. After she'd made Clara eat, Mitilde had laid into Shire. 'You so lame that you can't stop this girl from ridin' off? What you here for if not to mind her?'

It was useless to tell Mitilde that it had never been that way.

Clara had picked at her food and calmly told them that men would arrive early in the morning. A father and son she'd found in Ocoee would come up and move Taylor since everyone here refused to do it. Mitilde had looked horrified and clutched at the doorframe. When she'd steadied herself, she said, 'I'll tell Moses to be ready.' Then she left.

'We won't need Moses,' Clara had called after.

Now, before Shire in the cold morning, the father and son chipped away at the frozen ground, the wiry older man doing most of the work. He talked all the while. 'Miss, I'd be obliged if you would leave us to it. Or at least let this boy walk you away while we get the leavings out. It ain't a sight a lady should see, and there's no casket you say.'

Clara gave no sign of having heard a word.

Shire assumed he was the boy referred to, as Moses – usually an 'old boy' – was back in the trees gathering dead branches. There were a few other graves up here on account of this boy, he thought. Well, himself and Tuck. He wasn't boastful of it. It wasn't a happy thought, but also not one without a certain kick of pride, almost comfort. It was a strange emotion to get a grip on.

The son was a paroled Confederate, done with the war. Shire wondered what he made of digging up his own colonel. He had heard enough to know that Taylor wasn't loved among his men; he'd been too reckless for that. All the same, Clara was taking a big risk. Even if rumors had leaked out from Comrie that Taylor had met his end here, and not, as circulated, in the November rout from Chattanooga, these men were going to put that speculation beyond doubt. The point of interest would then settle firmly on what had happened here.

The crosspiece had fallen from the crude grave-marker sometime during the winter, so all that identified Taylor's grave was a broken chair leg taken from one of the two long huts nearby. Lined up next to him were five unmarked low mounds waiting on their first spring to gain so much as a blade of grass.

The gravediggers decided to take a different tack. They asked where they could find water to soften the ground. It was a long way back down to the house, too far to make it practicable, but Clara and Shire didn't know where the water was up here. They all walked over to Moses who'd emerged from the woods and was busy dragging what dry wood he'd found up to the walls of the huts. He pointed the men to a trickle-creek that hatched somewhere in the pass above and they went to find it.

Moses had been ready and waiting first thing in the yard at Comrie. He hadn't asked if they needed help but just slotted in behind Clara as they started up the long steep path to the grave. It was slow going as the gravediggers had to manhandle the pine casket along the narrow path. Moses had been agitated. He chivvied along close behind Clara and tried to persuade her no good would come of this, and that Taylor should be left where he died. He had no right to a better place. Clara had ignored him until he got so worked up he jumped in front and stood in her path. Shire bunched up behind.

Clara took a moment to catch her breath. 'You think I'm doing this for Taylor?' she said. 'Go home, Moses, you don't have to watch this.'

'Then let me move him, not these folks.'

'I wouldn't ask that. You don't owe him any loyalty.'

'I ain't sayin' I do.'

'Go then.'

Moses stood his ground. 'Guess I'll come witness.'

'Alright. Maybe it's time to burn the huts too. You could do that.'

Shire knew all about the huts, shackled as he briefly had been in one of them. Before the war, they were used for trade, housing illegal slaves newly stolen from Africa and marched up from the coast, kept here while their futures were sold all across the South. Moses had been forced to feed and water them in secret. Along with everything else, Clara had discovered this: that her husband – if he ever was that – was a slave driver and trader too. Not in American-bred slaves, that would have been legal in Tennessee although shameful enough, but in Africans, shunning a law that Tuck told Shire had been variously ignored in the South for decades.

Moses sullenly prepared for the fire while the gravediggers poured pail after pail over the grave until the three-inch frost was softened enough for them to take up their shovels again. The minutes played out. Thinking of words that might offer comfort or distraction was beyond Shire. It wasn't a deep grave. The diggers were surprised to hit metal. By degree they unearthed a thick link of chain and the father decided it was easier to pull on it than to dig it out. Shire turned to Clara. 'There's nothing to be gained by watching this.'

She struck away his hand and stepped past him; spoke through clenched teeth while staring toward the grave. 'Nothing for you perhaps, but I will look on him and see he is rotted and gone.'

Several feet of chain came away easily but then it pulled taut and would only give up a stubborn link at a time. The boy stepped over and gripped the chain like his father and leaned his weight away from the grave. The ground stirred and finally gave way. Both arms, half-rotted but with enough sinew to hold the yellow bones in place, lifted from the ground like a sinner's first earnest prayer to God. They were manacled at the wrist.

Clara wavered then spun and put her face onto Shire's chest. He feared for a moment he might retch himself, but then he'd seen a lot of dead men this last year.

The gravediggers gave some slack and Taylor's arms dropped back. 'You sure this is the right grave?' asked the father. 'Don't make much sense having these bracelets on a white man. Don't make much sense burying the metal at all.'

Clara stirred from Shire's chest and he followed her gaze over to Moses who'd stopped work and was watching on from a distance. Expressionless, he turned his back and set fire to the huts.

Comrie, Tennessee – February 1864

The darkness was absolute. Shire was tempted to reach out a hand from under the covers to test it. To see if this black air was some substance he could grasp, that might then ooze between his fingers like a thin honey. Ten men could be standing in the room and he wouldn't know, but he was certain there was no one in this mansion but himself and Clara. Not even Hany was on hand; that would have meant having that busy child Cele in the house and Clara wouldn't have that. What would it be like for Clara when he was gone? She'd be utterly alone in this place. Maybe that was what she wanted. He beat at the pillow, lay on his side and pulled the blankets over his head so only his face was exposed to the cold. Occasionally a twist of wind swept the rain against his window. It was a comfort; something to interrupt the night.

The day had ended unfinished, incomplete, in as much as Taylor was not yet back in the ground. The huts had burned merrily, as if glad to hurry from the world. The smoke from each had conjoined and lifted into a single column, angling up until a wind off the highest ridge knocked it sideways to dissolve way over Comrie, over its fields and people.

The gravediggers had been spooked by the chains and the hellish feel of the fire. They insisted that Clara go away before they set hands on her husband. Shire had kept hold of her as they walked to the graveside, but there was nothing to see in the cold earth but the decayed and manacled arms. She'd broken away and left. He'd stayed a while longer, but once the diggers got to their knees and began to reach in with their bare hands, he'd left too. Back at the house he hadn't bothered to seek Clara out; it was clear she had no use for him.

It was time to think about leaving. For the first time the company of Tuck and Mason, the idea of being back with the 125th, felt a better prospect than staying at Comrie. His leg was almost healed; they'd likely put him on light duties for a while. What had he truly expected to happen with Clara anyway? He'd kept his childhood promise to her last year, to come if she ever needed help. It was done, used up in the effort, bet like a last lucky coin and lost.

He'd not seen her again until well into the afternoon when Moses and the gravediggers came off the hill with the casket and set it down in the yard. Shire had joined Clara outside. The blacks looked out from behind half-opened doors and twitched curtains.

'It took us a while longer than expected,' the father had said, 'what with the hard ground. Your nigger has the chains. We'll have time to do a better job on the new grave if we come back tomorrow.'

Clara had argued with them, strident, said that wasn't what was agreed and that she wanted him buried again today.

'Ma'am, I'm thinking you expect it done right this time, to the right depth. There's no time to do that before the dark comes on. We'll be back soon after first light and get to it, but you need to tell us where you want him to spend tonight. You have a cellar?'

'In the house?' Clara turned ashen.

'Anywhere on the cool side.'

That included pretty much everywhere, Shire thought.

'We haven't nailed the lid. If you wanted to make up a posy for us to put in tomorrow, or maybe a Bible. His men weren't fond of him, my boy will attest to that, but he was a hard fighter.'

Clara said nothing.

The father called after her as she walked away. 'We just need somewhere to lay him tonight. Ma'am?'

Shire moved to intercede but Moses took care of it and told them to follow him.

For the rest of the day, all of Comrie was subdued. The blacks kept to their huts, the wind got up and a few squally showers swept through. Clara was silent at dinner and pushed at her food. Shire felt guilty for having an appetite.

The rain rattled against his bedroom window once more. That was decided then: he would see Taylor reburied tomorrow, but then would talk to Clara and ask if Moses could take him back down to Cleveland in a day or two.

He realized his eyes were open. An unsteady line of yellow light grew beneath the door and slowly spread around the frame. The handle turned and an angel stepped inside.

*

Clara halted on the path through the herb garden. She wore a gown over her nightdress, nothing on her feet. It had taken an act of will to come this far. She held herself and the dim lantern against the swirling wind and occasional pepper of rain. The wet and the cold had sobered her state of mind enough for her to ask what in God's name she was doing. What would happen if someone should see her, wandering the night like a wraith? They'd think her mad. Perhaps she *was* mad. Mad people must have moments like this, moments of lucidity when they discover they have stepped outside the parameters of a normal life. But she couldn't turn back; couldn't deny the raw imperative to see this through, to break free of him.

It hadn't been enough to see Taylor tugged from the ground, decayed and shackled as he was. He had won again. Instead of being below her as intended, down the hill in the place of her choosing, he was back at Comrie and lodging for the night. She was forced to wonder on him; wonder on a casket not nailed closed, but loose, so his spirit hands might come and push it to the floor and lift his cadaver out and free. The wind rose and she took a backward step.

These ghoulish thoughts, if she allowed them, were just another form of domination. She'd lain in bed and imagined him walking into the hunting room. His dead hands reached for the decanter. He seated himself in the armchair, talked up at her yet down to her, as he always had. No. She would not permit it. She would have the last word.

Lifting the lantern, she stepped forward, walked across the cold, hard dirt of the yard and behind the stables to a small shed with its roof pitched low at the back. She stood rooted two paces back from the shed door. They called it the birthing shed. It was only big enough for a single sty inside. If there was a sick animal or one that was due to drop, they'd bring it here. On occasion, she had looked on while Moses or another slipped a hand inside a struggling mother to rope a calf and haul it into the world. It was a magical place, a portal. Now Taylor was in there, putrid and stinking.

The wind swirled more forcefully, as if urging her in. She stepped forward, drew back the bolt and followed the lantern inside. The casket lay in the middle of the floor, the lid on, the chains and manacles loaded untidily on top as if to keep it so. She closed the door on the night. The sudden quiet was shocking and she backed to the side of the shed. The smell was of sweet manure.

She looked at the chains and thought of Moses, of all

the suffering he'd seen and endured at Taylor's hands, of the long-fermented anger that drove him to manacle his dead master before burying him. She moved slowly toward the coffin, each shaking step a triumph. She wanted to scream and run, but would do this.

She knelt.

The chains were vastly heavier than expected and it was easier to just pull the whole bundle toward her and onto the floor. From her pocket she took a long blue ribbon of pins, her engagement token from Taylor. The prettier ones with jeweled heads sparkled in the low lamplight.

The gravedigger's thought had stayed with her all evening, the idea to put something inside. She would return this to Taylor, spurn him as she should have when he'd proposed. It had been a false gift, his first lie; given when asking for her hand though Taylor had already wed.

She considered the best way to raise the lid without looking inside and moved to the foot of the casket. She held her breath and kept her eyes up, gripped the edge of the coarse pine lid and scraped it open a few inches. Grasping for the ribbon, she pricked herself and dropped it to the floor. She had to look down to find it, cried and fumbled like an old woman. More carefully this time she picked it up and dropped it into the casket. She had to breathe, couldn't help but suck in the musk and decay. It settled in the back of her throat. In death Taylor was no different to the stink of a rotting fox in a ditch. She made to close the lid, to let no more of him out, but found herself staring at the chains. Moses was right: they were a better gift. Yes. She moved around to the side and eased the lid over a little more. For an irresistible moment she looked down to find in the shadow the taut and wasted face. Taylor's hair was as thick and long as ever.

'From both of us. From Moses and me.' She dropped in the manacles. 'From all of us.' She picked up a loop of chain and fed it into the coffin like slippery viscera until the last link slid inside, then pulled the lid over and wriggled backward in her nightgown across the dirty floor.

She was quickly back to the house, gulping fresh air all the way. There. It was behind her. She'd get up early and find Moses, tell him what she'd done and get him to nail the coffin closed before the diggers came and wondered at its added weight. Back in her room she had a cold wash, found fresh nightclothes, climbed into bed and tried to let her breathing settle. She closed her eyes but instantly found herself back in the shed looking into an empty coffin. She could smell something. At first it was only slight, lingering on the edge of her senses, some partial aroma which, all at once, she recognized. It might have been no more than his last sweat dried into his faded Confederate cloth, but it was there, in her mouth, the taste of Taylor. And *he* was here, in their marriage bed and above her, inside her, rutting away. His stink filled the room. She stood and brushed wildly at her nightdress, lit a candle and hurried out to the hallway. The night-drafts of the house toyed with the flame. Shadows of Taylor twitched across the walls. She needed to smother him, put something, *someone*, between them. She turned and hurried toward the other end of the house.

*

Shire's angel blew out her candle. The darkness was all the more profound given the recent dose of light. It was quiet outside. He could hear nothing and began to imagine he'd been dreaming or it had been some waking vision, but then heard something soft fall to the floor. There was weight on the bed. The blankets were lifted from him. He could sense Clara, her scent of early autumn – sweet, earthy, rich. There was a pace to her warm breath that brushed his face. She was so close in the dark. He wore nothing. Conscious of his arousal, he angled his loins away.

She kissed his neck, her hair cold and fresh on his cheek. He felt her touch on his waist, encouraging him closer. His hand found the round of her hip, smooth and warm as a pebble in the sun. She edged closer still so he could feel her softness against his chest. So many times, in the weeks ahead, he would wish he'd said nothing at all. 'Are you frightened?'

'Yes,' she said.

'You've been so distant, so hard to read.'

'Am I hard to read now?' She pressed a kiss to his lips.

He kissed her back, put his hand underneath her hair, tried to lock up his doubts, but felt anxiety in her touch, her kiss, some driving need not aligned to passion. Her hand stroked low across his stomach. He moved to stop her and as their hands met under the covers they entwined instantly, like they always had as children. Clara pulled back from the kiss. 'Isn't this what you want?'

'Of course. You know that.'

'Then give in to it.'

'What is it I'm giving in to?'

'Maybe it would be better if we didn't talk.'

'Maybe it would be best if we did.'

'I need you, Shire. Please.' She tried to untangle their hands but he held her.

'Why are you here?'

'Can't you do this for me?' She was angry. 'Most men would do this for me.'

'Most men might not love you.'

Clara spoke more loudly, 'I'm not asking you to love me.'

'Then what are you asking of me?'

She pulled her hand free and slid away from him so they were no longer touching. He wanted her back; wanted the softness again.

'Too much it seems.'

'He's gone, Clara. Wherever you choose to bury him, he's dead and gone.'

She was quiet for a while. He slowly reached out for her face in the dark.

'Gone for you, perhaps,' she said. 'Your home wasn't his home. He doesn't laugh at you through the eyes of a child. You don't feel his hands or smell his breath.'

Shire felt his anger win out over sympathy. How could she be this ungrateful? It was all he could do to not to say, *I left my own home for you, lost father and friends, have a war to return to that I signed up for just to reach you.* Instead he said, 'I love you. You know that… But I'll be damned if the first time we lie together is on his account.'

He got out and found his clothes in the dark. 'You can stay. Taylor's not in here.' He left and went to her room, climbed into her empty marriage bed. He couldn't sleep. It wasn't the anger that kept him awake, nor the unspent passion. It was the aching part of him that wished he'd shown her that gentle and real love was there for the taking, and the anguish that his chance might never come again.

Pittsburgh, Pennsylvania – March 1864

What difference could one man make? Tod kept circling back to that thought. It was his first day off from the arsenal, nearly two weeks since he had left the other world of Luther's farm. This morning he'd walked the couple of miles from Lawrenceville to Pittsburgh, taken the last bridge over the Monongahela River and climbed to the top of Coal Hill. The 'hill' part of the name struck him as a misnomer: rather it was a high – very high – bluff that started from the south side of the river and extended away both west and east. The 'coal' part of the name was certainly accurate. On his climb he passed several places where coal was being quarried from open seams and lowered on steep rails to river barges below. It was as easy as raking in a crop of dollar coins. Why had providence provided such easy bounty to the Yankees?

The spot he'd chosen to eat his lunch wasn't random. After climbing the bluff, he'd worked west until he could look directly down at the very tip of the dying point of land on which Pittsburgh was built. That spot marked the death of the Monongahela and Allegheny Rivers and the birth of the great Ohio. He'd wanted to see their unification from up here, from a creator's viewpoint. Perhaps feeling godlike might help him make sense of things. Instead it had turned him wistful; views like this could do that to a man.

It wasn't so much the scale of the Ohio, already maybe four hundred yards wide and stretching the best part of a thousand miles to the Mississippi. It was more the use the Yankees put it to. As a quartermaster, he couldn't stop himself from taking inventory. He could see twenty-seven boats afloat: fine, high, two-wheel paddle-steamers, sternwheelers, open barges or great rafts of logs tied to smaller steamers, every boat with single or twin smoke-stacks that pumped every shade of gray into a blue March sky. And that was a fraction compared to the moored boats. From his viewpoint the docks on the Allegheny were out of sight, but just on the north bank of the Monongahela he could count three dozen before the bridges and the slow turn of the river obscured more. In between sat Pittsburgh, its foundries and factories with higher chimneys of their own, as if it were a great city battlefield with every last cannon pointed directly at the heavens.

What could one man do? The South could set nothing against this. New Orleans maybe, but New Orleans had been lost. The Mississippi was lost too and the great Gulf and Atlantic ports were blockaded. Once their coal was mined and the cannon were built, all the damned Yankees had to do was load them aboard a boat and float them off to war. What depressed him still more was that from his time walking the wharves, he knew that the greater share of those boats had nothing to do with the war. It was simple trade in goods with the growing cities in the west. It was steel for the railroads that reached further and further into the younger states and new territories. There were passenger steamers for people to go and visit their kin. There was a pleasure boat down there; he could see ladies twirling parasols even in March. The South had no time for such frivolities. No time and no means; the war was all consuming. The Yankees fought with one hand. It made what he planned to do seem all the more insignificant. He chewed on tough city bread and took some water to get it down.

He considered how episodic his life had become. From this distance, his nine weeks living in the ice-box prison on Johnson's Island felt shortened, concatenated. There was his escape from the train and his night in the wet Pennsylvania woods, a man lost to the world. His time with the Amish, with Rachel and Luther, seemed far in the past, yet it was no time back at all.

It was tempting to shrug off their kindness and the risk that they had taken: the Amish weren't real Yankees, absented as they were from the war and the wider world. The couple had made light of the danger to themselves. Yankees or not, they had shown there was a different approach to life, that there was a choice – at least from within their community – a choice to stay out of the war.

He rubbed his cheek, pinched at its returned health. He remembered the shock of doing the same in prison and finding it concave and thin. Was his week with Luther's family truly a blessing? That was a rather one-sided argument: he'd washed the prison from his skin and the lice from his hair and, once he came to believe Luther wasn't going to turn him in, he'd rested and made the best of every meal. What was to set against those blessings? Nothing tangible, just an ill-defined feeling that he had left their home with an obligation, something wrapped and waiting in his Christian heart.

Whenever he thought back to the farm, Rachel was ever-present. He'd come to terms with that. Longing was different to lust. And anyway, who could hold him to account if he *did* feel lustful. He hadn't let it show. Longing was the greater part, longing for a wife who lightly wore the beauty of a young mother, envious of the certainty of love stored up for Luther's future.

There were girls aplenty at the Allegheny Arsenal: countless city girls who made up cartridges and packed ordnance. Some were too young to flirt with, but Tod had picked out favorites in each hut and had banked a fortune in smiles, blushes and coy looks. Would it be so wrong to take some comfort there?

Down below, on the spear-tip of land between the rivers, he could make out stony lines and angles from old Fort Pitt, lost to Pittsburgh's past. He wondered what defenses there were in the hills around the city today. He'd not seen any from the train. Perhaps this far north they felt there was no need to worry? Gettysburg wasn't so far, two hundred miles perhaps. Rumor had it that last year's battle might have taken a different turn. What then? General Lee might have thought Washington too well defended. Perhaps Lee's mind and his army might have come west instead to this great arsenal of the North. This bluff was so close to the city. He imagined Lee laying out a hundred cannon, letting the guns' silhouettes show on the skyline while the populace raced for the bridges over the Allegheny, and when the city was emptied, Tod himself spirited onto Lee's staff, directing his attention to the armories and the cannon foundries, watching the shells arc and fall until the city was nothing but flame and the last chimney fallen into rubble.

The shrill whistle of a departing steamer brought him back to himself. There was no General Lee, no cannon. The wind that rose up the bluff from the rivers had freshened and the sweat he'd built on his climb had turned cold on his back. He brushed the crumbs from his lap, stood and started his way back along the heights until he reached the path that angled down to the bridge. He felt guilty for his fantasy of destruction. Luther wouldn't approve.

He crossed over the Monongahela and into Pittsburgh. The sidewalks were busy. The smell of the foundries, tanneries and machine shops won out over the muddy manure of the riverfront. He took a tin mug of coffee from a corner cart and stood there, burying himself in its aroma.

It had been easy to lose himself in the city when he stepped off the train. Luther had gifted him a spare set of regular clothes and a hat, saying he used them himself when traveling. 'Sometimes it's just easier,' he'd said. It was certainly easier for Tod; the clothes were more his size, and he couldn't realistically have rolled up at the arsenal in Amish garb and expected them to take him seriously.

Instead of a city job he could have worked his passage on a steamer down to Louisville or Memphis, but he figured that sooner or later he'd need some money in his pocket beyond the dollar Luther had pressed into his hand. Why not make it here? Once the idea of working at the arsenal occurred, it won out over wharf or mill work. He'd sell himself for what he was, a quartermaster. The pay would be better and the work lighter. And he'd see what he could learn about Yankee munitions. It might prove useful.

As to a name, he'd given this some thought on the train. Steering close to the truth, he recalled a Tennessee regiment on the Union side, the 2nd Tennessee Volunteers. Turncoats to a man, but he'd make use of them. He'd claimed to be a quartermaster's assistant, discharged after a year's service, with the imagined name of Luke Edwards.

'Can you start today?' was all they said.

Ten days in, he was already considered an old hand. The turnover in employees was so fast. Men found better paid jobs, went west or just plain disappeared.

When he'd finished his coffee, he walked north until

he hit Liberty Avenue which would take him back toward Lawrenceville, then alternated north and east to get closer to Fort Pitt Foundry on the way. The place was mentioned so often at the arsenal. He crossed railway spurs and sidings that served the great gun works. It was as busy as a beehive on a workday. His direction of travel was across the grain and he gave way to tired, soot-stained men with their heads down who were walking away from the works. Another host, only marginally cleaner, were headed the other way toward the varied collection of high red-brick sheds that were between Tod and the Allegheny waterfront. From this distance he could barely see into the windows but formed the impression that many of the buildings were hollow. He could hear chains and hammers. The smell reminded him of a smithy, scaled up a hundred times in steam, metal and sweat.

There were a few guards on the gates. Maybe he could have scammed his way past, but instead he walked beyond the last building and found a way down to the river so he could look back at the works from the riverfront. There were any number of derricks and one lifted a cannon barrel in a wooden cradle, swung it slowly across and down into the hold of a waiting steamer. It was hard to judge from where he stood, but it looked perhaps like an eight-inch barrel; field artillery most probably. Edging closer he could see a dozen canon cradled up, waiting their turn. Were they headed for Sherman perhaps, via Louisville, Nashville and Chattanooga, guns to push the Yankee army on to Atlanta? He felt his blood rise. He recalled the celebrations when his regiment captured a cannon at Chickamauga, not only a trophy, but a prize to be turned against the enemy. New Confederate cannon had been a rare sight in the months before his capture. There were so few foundries and the raw materials were in short supply. They'd had to steal whiskey stills and beg the church bells from Tennessee early in the war. Here the bells had been in full cry on Sunday, a jibe to a Southern heart.

The two-story high doors to the tallest shed swayed open and accompanying shouts drew Tod's attention. There was the sound of metal rolling on metal and then a horse team emerged, hauling along the rails a gun bigger than any Tod had ever seen. The full diameter across the muzzle must have been three-feet; at the breech it was twice that. Heaven only knew how much it weighed and how it didn't crush the wooden trolley that bore it. Under the careful guidance of many men the great gun slowly took the bend in the rails and turned toward Tod, as if it had singled him out. He could see directly into its great, dark maw. A fort gun, no doubt, or a harbor gun, not remotely capable of being moved in the field. What weight of shot it could throw he couldn't imagine. Slowly it squealed along the track, a Yankee weight of evil and oppression. A minute later it swung again to be heaved into the nearest shed and the men pulled closed the doors. Tod was left alone, listening to the lap of the river on the shore.

What Luther had said might have made sense in his world, but not in this one. *What could one man do?* It was a matter of circumstance, of opportunity. A quartermaster at an arsenal, with access to the inventory and the stores: that one man could blow the arsenal to hell and back.

Atlanta, Georgia – March 1864

George Trenholm looked out on the city as he and his son progressed in fits and starts through the clogged streets. Not for the first time, a resentful face turned his way. Perhaps, he thought, the weary citizens of Atlanta were noting the fine open carriage, its polished sheen not yet completely obscured by dirt. Officers, unsticking their boots from the mud, may have been wondering why so fine a black horse wasn't in the cavalry, or more pointedly, why a wealthy gentleman and his son wore the high-hatted uniform of business rather than that of a blooded soldier. He could hardly blame them for being suspicious of wealth in a city where prices were sky high. Perhaps he'd have done better to hire a simple hackney carriage rather than loan the hotel's finest.

The weight of pedestrians stopped them once more. Atlanta had changed again. Trenholm found that if he was absent for more than a season then it was like visiting a new city. Even before the war, it used to grow at a startling rate, like his youngest, Frank, who sat across from him. Recently, if he turned away from Frank, say to pick up his hat, on turning back he would be surprised anew at the boy's height. It was the same with Atlanta, a youthful city, sprouting in the fertile soil of war.

He liked to think of himself as one of the city's midwives. Through his commercial and political allies, he had encouraged the growth of Atlanta as a rail hub, fostered its banks. There were any number of places across the South – and the North for that matter – where his money had been planted, but he felt a special affection for Atlanta. He wanted to protect it. He wanted it to live a long and prosperous life. He was here to find a way to help.

It might have been better to have walked to the rolling-mill; it was no more than a mile. The Negro driver, supplied along with the carriage by the Trout House Hotel, was taking a roundabout route to avoid the very worst of the mud. At least while Trenholm was marooned in the carriage no one could impose with a telegram from Richmond to ask his advice, or from Charleston with news of another ship taken or sunk. In business, he'd always known which plates to keep spinning: the ones that made the best return. In war there were other measures to set against self-interest. More and more he had to sacrifice his time to his young country, to the wider good. But then there were greater sacrifices than time.

Outside a bakery a stump of a man lay, asleep and wide-mouthed, next to a begging hat – all he had left of a uniform. The proprietor emerged and lightly kicked him, testing the vagrant for life. There was no evidence on show and he pushed the legless body along the boardwalk, away from his shop-front. Vagrants were hardly invented by the war, Trenholm thought, it simply multiplied them.

They began to move again.

The Trout House was his favorite haunt, presently back in business as a hotel. In recent years, like most of Atlanta's central hotels, it had on occasion been pressed into service as a hospital. He had stayed there back in December, again with Frank, after the Federals had broken free from Chattanooga and stormed Missionary Ridge. At that time, the area around the hotel and the Car Shed, the great passenger terminus for the railways, was glutted with a carpet of wounded inside and out, all waiting to be cleared to the surgeons or to the

Almighty. By then, the new hospitals out at the fairgrounds had been built, so from the hotel he was able to watch the ambulances roll back and forth.

He liked to stand on the balcony and look out over State Square and the Car Shed, like a doctor testing a patient's fever. He liked the Car Shed too, the huge red-bricked, arch-roofed passenger terminus surrounded by engine houses and depots that belonged to the four railroads that met at Atlanta. It appealed to the empire builder in him, a nexus of endeavor and expansion. Nowadays, it was a terminus for hope and grief; he'd like to think in equal measure, but he knew better than that. With less fighting during the winter, the city gave the appearance of healing, but it was only a pause. The Union would come on in the spring with the earnest intention to claim Atlanta for itself. State Square would be carpeted once more. In a few months, it might be too late to help.

Trenholm wished they'd pass a smithy or a tannery, so the smell of a burning hoof or a half-cured hide could drown out the human stink from the side-alleys and from beneath the boardwalks.

Frank was quiet, not unusually. They spent so much time together that he shouldn't worry at the silence. His son's gaze was ever toward the soldiers, scruffy home guard as most of them were. If the war lasted another year then he couldn't reasonably keep his youngest out of uniform. The boy chafed to get to the front as it was. Ironically, the need was to extend the war. It was beyond winning outright, last year had seen to that. Instead it had to be stretched, its price in blood and money so high that the Union would be made sick of it.

How would he feel if Frank became part of the price? Would he put that in the cost column? 'What do you notice? What's different from December?'

Frank cast his gaze wider. 'Fewer ambulances. The injured are on crutches rather than stretchers. More army than before, I think.'

He was right. 'Since Chattanooga was taken last year, I guess this has become the furlough town for Johnston's Army. What else?'

'The street signs, were they here before?'

The driver interjected over his shoulder. 'They's new. Owin' to so many outsiders. Soldiers, business folk, the sick on the mend, the runaways from Nashville or Chattanooga. They all come to Atlanta but they don't know the place like we does. The signs is to keep ev'body from gettin' in each other's way.'

'Has it worked?'

'Not so I's noticed, but then there's more people week on week.'

An old timer with a battered top hat every bit as tall as Trenholm's acknowledged them with his unsteady bottle. Trenholm wished again that they were less conspicuous. He'd always found the armor of wealth, it's clear and overt display, more helpful than dressing down: it set almost everyone, especially the trading classes, back on their heels. Maybe it was time to think differently.

He was wealthy before the war. That wealth had since been sustained by blockade running, bringing in goods both needed and desired then charging the earth. It was simple supply and demand, no sin in that. Though in wartime the demand outstripped the supply to such an extent that he baulked when he heard what prices his goods were fetching. But that was America as he understood it to be: a place where you sucked up as much money as you could with no mind to the donor. It was all a great game and the bank kept the score.

Ahead on their left was a wood mill where Decatur Street angled toward the Georgia Railroad. Across the several tracks rose the smoking Atlanta Machine Works, an armory for the western war and the destination for much of the output from Trenholm's rolling-mill. A train, steam spent and squeaking, crawled across his view and toward the freight depot. Blocked from crossing the rails, the carriage driver kept east along the road.

Like the hot metal in the works, the youthful Atlanta was malleable, he thought. It hadn't resisted being turned toward the purpose of war. Not like his home town of Charleston, its colonial stiffness borne in old stone. Atlanta had a younger mind, new money. There were more people on the make per acre than anywhere else in the South.

It was time to get out of blockade running. He didn't need his conscience to provoke him on that score. The Yankee Navy was getting better. These days, from any seaward vantage point in Charleston you could watch the blockade squadrons beyond Sullivan's Island. It was a standing insult that the people of South Carolina could do nothing about. His captains used to make it through eight times out of nine using the night and the shallows. Now it was more like two times out of three.

The government was taking over the risk and he was encouraging them to do so. He ordered them faster boats from Liverpool and Glasgow, sold them his own, recommended captains; anything to help him divest. The trend was the same in Atlanta: wherever production was failing to meet the needs of the army, the government stepped in. Private owners could accept government bonds, Confederate currency or, if they didn't like that, take nothing at all. The South was at war; that's how it had to be.

There was any number of worn-out freight cars off the rails alongside the Georgia railroad. All were occupied as far as he could see. A barefoot young woman, her dark hair tied back, brushed her family dirt out of the sliding doors as if that were her front porch. A couple of urchins played behind her. He wondered where their true home had been.

As chair of a committee of bankers he had recently written to Secretary Memminger at the Confederate Treasury, warning that inflation was becoming rampant, setting out measures that might help. It was the collective economy he'd had in mind as he wrote: the conditions for business, the survival of the state. Farmers near Charleston had refused to take Confederate money, preferring to be paid in cloth produced from government mills. If that sort of sentiment spread, what would happen to commerce? But what about this young family living in a boxcar? He should be considering them. How could they afford anything at all?

His mind skipped to Clara and cast north across the rising hills of Georgia and into Tennessee. He'd not seen her since Chattanooga fell last summer. She'd sent a final letter to his home in Charleston via Ducktown early in the New Year, before that high road became dangerous and less traveled. It had told him everything, of Taylor's betrayal and death, of his secret marriage. She didn't suspect that he'd known of the marriage, had fought to keep it secret to protect his own and the Confederacy's interests. Not much credit due him there. He felt a debt of care to her, but what could he do with Comrie back in the Union? In letters passed through the lines he'd asked his friend and business associate Julius Raht, who managed the mines at Ducktown, to look out for her, but Raht had left for Cincinnati. She was beyond his protection. It didn't help to worry.

Out from the city-center they moved on more quickly. They stopped only to take their turn at the rail crossing. Soon, the belching line of chimneys from the rolling-mill loomed above them. When they arrived, they stepped down from the carriage to the sound of the engines driving the rollers. Did he imagine it or could he feel the heat from the furnaces from here, outside the mill? A hundred yards or so down the line were pile after pile of worn or broken rails waiting to be reworked and sent to where they were needed.

'That's a deal more rails than we saw last time,' said Frank.

'The Yankees don't let up.' It was impossible to keep pace. On the plus side, he thought grimly, with Tennessee lost and the Confederacy shrinking, there was less track left to fix. 'You want to be in on this meeting or would you rather go see the furnaces?'

'I've seen them before. I want to hear what Colonel Wright has to say.'

'Alright.' He could hardly expect Frank to pass up a chance to meet the soldier responsible for building Atlanta's defenses.

The offices were a heavy stone's throw from the rolling-mill. The clash of metal on metal muffled as they stepped inside and climbed the stairs. He pressed as many hands and recalled as many names as he could – encouragement cost nothing. Colonel Wright was waiting at the table as they entered the room. He stood to greet them.

'My apologies, Colonel,' said Trenholm. 'You obviously negotiated the Atlanta mud better than we did.'

'No apology needed, sir. It's a pleasure to visit your mill.'

Trenholm called for some fresh coffee. He could see Frank admiring how smartly turned out the Colonel was, his buttons given an extra polish for this meeting perhaps. To Trenholm's eye, beneath his careful side-parting, Wright looked worn down for a man not far into his thirties. Little wonder, with Atlanta the next western city on the Yankees' list.

He knew Wright to be a capable man who'd headed the arsenal in Nashville and arranged for its evacuation to Atlanta two years ago. Now Wright ran the arsenal here as well as granting army contracts to the city's various ordinance manufacturers. Given he was in charge of the city defenses as well, there would be many generals in the field less vital to the cause than this young colonel.

Trenholm poured the coffee. 'Bostwick, my general manager, can see us afterwards if you have time. He met me at the hotel last night.' Trenholm thought that Wright might be more candid in private. Frank didn't count. 'In short, Colonel, I need your advice. The demands on the mill are more than it can meet. I make money on everything: army contracts, government contracts, on a deal from Georgia or any other state. Profit isn't the issue. Atlanta's survival is the issue. I have formed a picture of the need from a distance, but you are better placed to advise where to focus production to best help defend the city.'

Wright's fingers toyed with his cup. 'What's your current split?'

'Around seventy-five percent on rail production or reuse, twenty percent armor-plating. The remainder are metals rolled to order, mostly iron and mostly wheeled directly to the machine works for armament production. All the furnaces are running around the clock. We can't give more; we can only change the mix.'

Wright pressed a hand over his hair. 'Well, sir, let's start with your armor-plate. Is all that twenty percent for the navy?'

'Yes, what *passes* for our navy.'

'I'm not Secretary of War, sir, and if some armor-plate helps break the blockade, I'm all for it, but if your metal is headed for some tortoise shell monster being constructed in a backwater bayou, then I think it's a crying waste. We've lost the war for the rivers. The Mississippi, the Tennessee and the Cumberland. All gone. If we're to triumph or even compete, it must be done with our armies.'

'Alright then.'

'As to the rails,' said Wright, 'you are never going to meet the demand. As well as the Yankees ripping up track, the traffic on the rails is constant, the loads heavy. Most of the pile outside is from wear and tear rather than Union vandalism, but I'd sooner see the work go on the rails than on the plate.

'But, sir,' continued Wright, 'changing the mix here isn't going to change the outlook over much. I have contracts out for all the ordnance and weaponry General Johnston wants, some fulfilled in Atlanta, some out in the towns hereabouts. And we've built laboratories and factories at the racecourse.' Wright sat forward. 'We turn out rounds for small arms by the million, thousands of rounds of field artillery, friction primers, gun carriages, caissons, wagons—'

Trenholm held up a hand, 'Colonel—'

Wright's hands balled into fists on the table. 'I work with Major Cunningham at the Quartermaster Department. We're in each other's pockets every day of the week. He has over three-thousand women working for him on woolen jackets, pants, shirts. Three-thousand! He needs saddles, harnesses, buckles, buttons, spurs, sabers, scabbards, canteens, haversacks. Should I list the food as well? Do you know how many crackers an army eats a day? We ship them by the train load.'

As if in support, a train whistle sounded outside and had better luck stopping Wright's rant than Trenholm had. Frank looked anxious. Trenholm waited. Was this all his trip to Atlanta would turn up, a colonel on the edge of despair?

Wright, as if suddenly aware of himself, sat up straight, became more soldier like. 'Sir, we can't produce enough of one single product. Not one. We're short everywhere. Even with what we do produce, we don't have enough boxcars to carry it... Major Cunningham and I shared a drink last week. He got out his notebook and we did some sums. What we need, Mr Trenholm, conservatively speaking, is at least three more Atlantas.'

Trenholm sat up to speak but Frank got in first. 'Are you short of soldiers?'

'Not now, Frank.'

'Well it's true, isn't it?'

Wright put a warm smile on his tired face. 'Son, the Confederacy's always been short of soldiers, their manufacturing process being necessarily drawn out. Chances are, we'll still need soldiers next year.'

'Colonel Wright,' said Trenholm, grateful for how he'd handled Frank, 'I understand. I truly do. I have the same overwhelming demands made of me each day. All we can do is make the best choices and trust to fortune. It's election year, Colonel, back in the old Union. We don't have to win the war; we just have to make it so painful for the Yankees that they vote Lincoln out and sue for peace. November. We must hold onto Atlanta until then.'

He couldn't achieve much more here; Wright wasn't in a settled state of mind. 'How about we talk again tomorrow? Come to the hotel and we'll have dinner. I'm not a soldier, Colonel, but I flatter myself that I have influence, in

Richmond, and with President Davis. He knows of this meeting. We want to support you, Colonel. *I* want to support you. Is there any one thing, anything that is hurting us, anything I can try to help with?'

'I'm sorry, sir. I shouldn't have run on as I did.'

'It's alright.'

'Copper, sir.'

'Copper?'

'Yes. We need more. The percussion caps that fire our rifles are made out of pure copper, or brass if we have the zinc, but we're running low on the copper and there's no natural supply. We've reused all we can. If I can't supply the army with percussion caps, we might as well surrender Atlanta today. That or throw rocks at the Yankees. We have stocks, but it'll be a fighting summer. Unless I get a new supply, I'll have to cut production. With respect, sir, I'm sure your influence can move mountains, but can you talk up a copper mine?'

Trenholm shared a sideways look with Frank. They both knew a copper mine, barely over the Tennessee line at Ducktown, a mine that had been stockpiling smelted copper for a year or more. The trouble was it was deep in the hills, behind Union lines, and there was no road worthy of the name in from the south. Hell, he had shares in that mine, though he never expected to see a return again. Maybe he should take out his investment in kind. 'Let me think on it, Colonel. Let me think.'

Pittsburgh, Pennsylvania – March 1864

The girl inclined her bare neck and held Tod's stare longer than he thought called for in polite company. Her hair was hidden beneath a white cotton cap. 'When I heard the first blast,' she said, 'I knew straight away it was the arsenal. We were at home. That's a good mile away, but I could feel it through the ground.'

Tod imagined Ellen was sixteen or seventeen. She had high cheekbones below wide hazel eyes. He tried to ignore her coy looks. He'd do better to concentrate on her story. Besides, flirting was at odds with the subject.

'There was a boiler blew on a steamer startin' out on the Allegheny once, but it weren't nothing like this. I looked at Ma and we were both thinking the same thing. Who's on shift? We always looked to get the same day off if we could. We still do.

'We stepped outside, everybody did, and there was a great tower of smoke climbing into the sky. Then more explosions, a whining and a whizzing. The cartridges started cracklin' and went on and on. People with daughters and wives started runnin' up here though new buildings were catching and exploding all the time. Crazy what people will do. I guess we'd all run straight into hell for a loved one. Don't you think so, Mr Edwards?'

Tod tore his eyes up from that neck, recalled he was supposed to be Mr Edwards. 'I guess,' he said. Ellen briefly returned her attention to the machine, feeding it steadily with a rod of soft lead while another girl worked the wheel. A blade rhythmically sliced off two-inch slugs and they dropped into the inner workings of the press. It wasn't Tod's job to oversee its mechanics but he ran his hand over the casing, glanced into the inner workings as if he was some sort of expert. 'Did you go with them?'

'I followed on. I had so many friends here.' She looked away. 'But I wish I hadn't come. First thing I saw was a girl walkin' home naked and burned. I didn't recognize her. A man tried to wrap a cloak on her but she screamed and beat him away. I saw a smokin' shoe that had blown a full block from the gates and for some reason went to collect it, only it weren't empty. There was any number of crazy sights. Half a hoop-skirt came down out of the sky with the ashes and settled in a tree. I didn't go any closer. They said most of the bodies weren't fit to look on and that they burned like pine logs. Seventy or more dead. I could name twenty of them for you right here and now.'

Under his shirt, Tod's makeshift fuse was wrapped twice around his waist. It had been itching all day. He shifted his weight in an effort not to scratch.

The machine spat bullets into a bucket with the same two-second interval that it chomped the lead. Tod imagined most would ultimately come to rest plugged in the trunk of a Virginian tree or in the brown loam of a Mississippi cotton field. It took no effort at all to bring to mind the variant sounds of a bullet smacking into a muscle, a jaw, a forehead. Some Union soldier would aim the rifle, but each bullet's journey started here with pretty Ellen and her friend who took the bucket and, using a tin mug, doled out shares to the rows of girls sat at the tables. He mustn't let these bullets head out into the world in search of a Confederate heart. 'It must have been hard for you to manage, without any work I mean.'

'Oh they had new huts up in days,' said Ellen. 'They didn't wait on the enquiry.'

Tod had hoped he would be able to dent production for several weeks.

'They got the idea that some of the powder barrels had leaked onto the road and a horseshoe had sparked it. Imagine that; a single horse step, but they don't know any better than I do. All the same, these days we only use the barrels once. The company that supplies the powder ain't allowed to take them back for fear they'll wear and come to leak.'

The quartermaster, Tod's boss, had drilled this into him. It was part of his job to check the barrels were sound. He nodded all the same.

'That was a year and a half ago,' said Ellen, 'and we're still pressing bullets and rolling cartridges. Every day Ma and I say a prayer for the girls that were lost, but we say a louder one hopin' it won't come to pass again.'

Tod touched his hat brim and backed away from Ellen's overworked eyelashes. He walked slowly behind a line of girls and checked their work. There was rarely an issue with quality. If there was, he didn't like to correct them. They knew better than he did how to roll a paper tube, fill it with gunpowder and tie off the end. It was only toward the end of the ten-hour shift when they started to tire. Despite having to play the part while he waited for his main chance, he baulked at improving the quality of Yankee munitions, not least because he expected to be on the receiving end of them again one day.

Ten cartridges were wrapped into a pack and the packs were collected and stacked in boxes; around 40,000 cartridges a day. Tod made the entries himself. In other parts of the arsenal they made percussion caps, put case shot and canister into artillery shells. They made saddles and spurs, sword-belts and stirrups. If the Union Army wanted it, it was either made here or brought here from the city's tanneries and smithies before being shipped down the Ohio or back east by rail. What wouldn't his Confederate army give for a day's output from Pittsburgh.

The cartridge boxes were removed from the work-hut as soon as they were full. Tod took the latest outside and across to one of the magazines. There were five work-huts dedicated to the production of cartridges. Tod tallied the output from each. He moved into the dim light of the magazine, stacked the box, collected the ledger and moved back into the light of the door to make the entry. Out of sight at last, he was able to lift his shirt and scratch to his heart's content.

Blowing up the arsenal was easy; as easy as being careless. The problem came in trying not to blow up all the girls who worked here, not to mention himself. Ellen wasn't the first person to tell him about the disaster in '62. Mr Riordan, Tod's boss, had spent half of Tod's first day going over the measures the army had introduced to avoid a repeat. Like Tod, Riordan was a civilian employed by the military.

Tod's puzzle was how to delay a fire or an explosion until well into the night, when there were only military guards on site. He'd spent his last few nights working on a solution. There were fuses for the artillery but they lasted no longer than a shell in flight, and running a line of powder was hazardous and would give him merely seconds to get away. Also, he couldn't be in the compound out of hours, so that wouldn't help the girls.

In the end he'd stolen a length of thin rope from the stores and soaked a few inches into melted wax to make a kind of thick wick. He'd taken it down to the riverside and found a quiet spot where he could set a match to it and count off the rate as best he could without a timepiece. He reckoned it would burn around six inches in an hour if it stayed alight which it might well not, so that argued against a lengthy fuse. Similarly, the smell of wax might alert the guards. He'd cut a short fuse when the time came.

His target wasn't the cartridge store. His last job of the day was to return unused gunpowder to the powder magazine. If that went up, then most of the buildings nearby would go too. He usually had a minute or so alone inside. He'd made a point of getting on good terms with the bearded old guard, Jasper.

There was, of course, the disagreeable matter of striking a match inside the powder store to light the fuse. If he dallied on his way to the magazine, chewed the cud with Jasper, then most of the girls would be through and out the armory gate. If the powder decided to go up there and then, so be it; war wasn't a risk-free venture and he doubted he would ever know what had happened. He tucked his shirt back in and went to check the next hut.

Today was payday and early afternoon the girls filed out of the huts and over to the pay clerk to draw their wages. Tod was mindful that it might be their last for a while but there was nothing he could do about that. He took his turn at the end. It was good to have a few dollars to his name, even if he was in the pay of the U.S. Ordnance Department. After the rent, last week's money had largely gone on candles.

He'd spent first light yesterday at the docks on the Allegheny. It took him barely any time to satisfy himself that he'd have no problem getting hired as an extra hand. All the other men who'd turned up looking for work were taken on by one boat or another. If, after the explosion, he didn't show up at the arsenal to try and help put out the fire then Mr Riordan might get suspicious, but Tod would be steaming down the Ohio before anyone started to ask questions.

After he collected his pay there was nothing to distract his mind from what lay ahead. His skin was raw under the fuse where he'd clawed at it. He had to step to the privy so he could tie it tighter. Waxed as it was, it kept sliding down. The sky was gray. He would have to delay his plan if any heavy rain came on; he wanted a fire to take hold after the explosion.

The light began to fade. The girls finished the set of ten they were on and then poured outside. Tod collected a few final smiles. He made himself wait in one hut and count to a hundred before he started to tend to the powder. It had been managed well between the huts during the day, so there was only one half-full barrel that Tod needed to take to the powder magazine. He stoppered it, muscled it out of the hut and into a barrow.

Now the moment had come, he felt oddly detached and his mind took a semi-philosophical bent like it used to before a battle. If he blew himself up or if he didn't, who would know? If his life ended today, his family and regiment would in time assume he had either died in the Pennsylvanian woods or headed out west. At least after a fight there was a reckoning, a story to tell, a letter for his colonel to write. If he succeeded and survived, he doubted he would ever tell a soul. As he slowly wheeled the barrow to the powder magazine, Luther's voice came back to him: '*The time will come when you have a choice.*' He supposed this was that moment, though he could reason that by destroying the munitions he might conceivably save more lives in the long run. He'd privately won this inner argument with Luther so many times. This was war. Luther barely knew what that meant. Let him have *his* home invaded. Let someone else's army steal his animals, take his crops, push their way of life down his throat.

'Is something wrong, sir?'

'What?' It was a new guard, a young guard.

'Only you were wearing a pretty mean look walking over.'

'Where's Jasper?'

'Took sick. The sergeant detailed me to look after the powder magazine.' The boy squared his shoulders and put out his chin. He didn't look a deal older than Ellen. 'But I knew you was coming, Mr Edwards. I can let you in.' The boy leaned his rifle against the wall and, the magazine being partially buried, stepped down to the door. He fumbled with a bunch of keys but got it open. The light was low and it was dark inside.

Tod stood there, angry at Luther, like he'd had some part in this and putting this boy here was his last play. Well there were plenty of Southern boys younger than this one who might be spared from a bullet or a shell if Tod held his nerve.

'You want some help with the barrel?'

'No. No thank you. I can manage.' The boy wore a Union uniform; that was the end of the matter. He took a step down into the dark.

'Stop that man!'

Tod turned and the guard reached for his rifle.

Mr Riordan hurried toward them as best he could; he was far from the thinnest of men. He waved a piece of folded paper in the air like it was an arrest warrant. Tod's mind raced. He was so close. He could still step inside and strike the match.

'There you are, Edwards,' said Riordan, arriving breathless. 'I thought I might have to come and find your lodgings.'

Riordan's manner didn't seem threatening.

'Why?' asked Tod. 'What can't wait until tomorrow?'

'*The Spirit of Kentucky.*'

'Pardon me, sir?'

Riordan caught his breath. 'She can't wait. She's loaded. She sails tonight and I need you on board. I can't turn up that no good shirker Wiggins for love nor money. He's either drunk in a bar or dead in a ditch and I don't care which. He was due to sail with her. I need someone I can trust to get everything properly signed for in Memphis. There have been too many irregularities before now.'

Tod's waxy belt started to itch again at the mention of trust. 'What about the huts?'

'I can find a man for tomorrow. And I can put this powder away. The boat sails in an hour. Here's the inventory. It's all loaded, but I want you to double check it against the manifest when you're on board. And see it's all stowed safely. It's mixed munitions, mostly.' He handed over the paperwork and with an arm at Tod's back started him on his way. 'There's a pass too, it allows you to get the train back as if you were military. And ten dollars toward expenses that you'll need to account for. I know your folks are somewhere in Tennessee but I need you back here quick as a jackrabbit, so no home visits.'

Within the hour, Tod found himself climbing a gangplank. He showed the inventory by way of identification. They pointed him aft and told him where to find his berth. He sweated despite the month, having raced to his lodgings to collect his backpack with all his writing material. He'd left the Amish clothes.

The whistle sounded close and loud and he went to the rail. *The Spirit of Kentucky* had two covered side-wheels and, in no time, they were well out into the Allegheny and racing with the current. They passed Fort Pitt Foundry, all bricks and smoke. Tod could see more cannon lined up for loading. Five minutes later, the land between the rivers faded to a point and he knew he was on the Ohio. He hadn't come to Pittsburgh to do it harm, but he had left a failure. As things had turned out, he'd not only helped produce the damned bullets for the Union but he was delivering them as well.

He found his cabin; one thin bunk above another but not a lot else. He stepped inside and closed the door on the world. How could he ever justify this? Pulling himself onto the top bunk, he rolled over painfully, only then realizing he still had several feet of self-made fuse wound around his waist.

Cincinnati, Ohio – March 1864

Clara woke abruptly to shouts and curses below her window. There was a moment's pleasurable disorientation before she remembered she was in Cincinnati, at Julius Raht's new home. The cursing softened to laughter. It mixed with the roll and creak of wagons and the tread of heavy steps on a boardwalk. Her room was small and cold, the mattress over-soft, but she enjoyed the heady pleasure of being somewhere new, somewhere different. It mingled with her more permanent, unresolved disquiet. Together they hinted at the possibility of change. She was hungry. She swung herself out of bed onto the cold floor and put on her mourning clothes. It was hateful to start every day by honoring Taylor. The black dress seemed to preserve him as part of her physical world.

They'd arrived yesterday in the late afternoon. The evening with Julius and his wife had been pleasant enough. Mrs Raht's German cooking was heavier than Clara was used to and no doubt accounted for Julius' girth. They'd exchanged news, but she had little to contribute. Julius was far more connected to the wider world. The Union appeared confident, he said, that this year would bring an end to the war. Grant would push for Richmond and his friend Sherman would march on Atlanta. If they were successful, what would be left for the South to fight for? Julius had put off talk of Clara's finances until this morning. 'I find I make better business in daylight,' he'd said. She hoped so.

She stood aside on the narrow stairs as three children raced up and past her. Julius was in the kitchen with Mrs Raht and yet more children – none of whom looked underfed.

She'd reconsidered the invitation from Julius after Shire left Comrie. She was still angry with him: angry at being left alone in his bed, angry at being left to wear Taylor's stink. Where had Shire acquired the sureness of mind to reject her?

His colonel, Opdycke, had arrived at Comrie unannounced to check the veracity of Shire's defense for his desertion after Missionary Ridge: that it was the only way to save her. She couldn't deny the truth of it and she hadn't wanted to. She'd spoken for him but then insisted the Colonel take Shire back to the regiment. It was a spite born out of hurt, she knew that, but there was no easy path back to their childhood; too much had happened. What settled into her most in the days after he rode away, was that she'd been left alone again, even if she had instigated it this time. It was always someone else moving away and into the world while she stayed where she was, wedded to Comrie if to nothing else. But the North was open now and there was the standing invitation from Julius. Nothing would change if she stayed at Comrie. She was glad to be in Cincinnati. Everywhere outside this house was new territory, new possibilities.

Mitilde arrived in the kitchen, Moses behind her. Mitilde wore a hurt look, no doubt unhappy that Clara had gotten ready without her help. Much as Clara would have liked to have come away alone, it wouldn't be proper, and she couldn't abide the idea of bringing Hany. She'd thought to ask Moses if he'd come. He was good company and content to spend plenty of time alone with his thoughts. The mistake she'd made was to ask him in front of Mitilde.

'Why you wanna take that old man? More likely you'll be 'tending to him. He ain't never been further than Bradley County.'

Moses had puffed himself up. 'And you have, I s'pose?'

'I's been to Chattanooga. You know I has. Besides, that's not the tellin' fact. I know how to look after a lady and see off unwelcome types. They ain't gonna mess with me, no sir.'

'Well, you got that right.'

To forestall a longer argument, Clara had suggested they both come.

'I'll look out your mourning clothes,' said Mitilde.

Her mistake was already evident on the wagon-ride to the station. Stopping those two from arguing was, she imagined, like beating out a forest fire when the wind was up. For two long days on crowded trains they kept at it. They took to listing all the people and families at Comrie: who would leave, who might stay. Clara learned more by staying quiet. She realized they were losing something in exchange for freedom: the harsh certainty of the past, a domain they had long worked within and even helped to run. Every departure was a lessening of their authority, a rejection. Now they were looking out on a new world, one that, despite the arrival of liberty, they viewed with old and suspicious eyes; busy Yankee cities that weren't to be trusted.

Only the view from the window occasionally calmed them. They had to change trains at Nashville and as they came into the city, Clara watched them both marvel at the endless houses and churches, at the city smoke and at all the people. Mitilde's hand searched for Moses'. He patted it gently and Clara found she was jealous. It made her think of Shire again, that she might have broken something that mattered, and that, undeniably, he had done the right thing.

Julius Raht's house wasn't big enough for someone with so many children. And now they needed space for Mitilde and Moses as well. Julius tried to put them in the one room, but

Mitilde flat refused. Clara knew – she suspected even Julius knew – that Moses rarely slept in his own hut at Comrie. If there had been time enough left in the day, she'd have suggested they get married before bed time, but then there'd been nothing stopping them doing that since Taylor died. In the end, Mrs Raht had shuffled the children to make space.

Mitilde and Moses irritated her far more than they should; not just their bickering but their stubbornness when it came to marrying. Perhaps her own false marriage was at the root: they had a way forward and wouldn't take it while she had none at all. Even their arguments were more intimate than anything she could look forward to.

Julius rescued her from the busy kitchen and carried their coffee into the parlor. He set it down on a low table and turned to shut out the clamor. Clara took a seat. Julius was the closest thing she had to a guardian these days. She was beginning to correspond with her parents again, but they didn't understand her state of affairs. They knew nothing of Taylor's secret marriage. Apart from Shire, Trenholm was the only person who knew the truth, and he was the other side of the lines. She wished he was here, but Julius had her interests at heart. As a long-term friend to Taylor's family, he knew Comrie's past business better than she did. She could afford to be honest with him about most things. 'I need money, Julius, or at least the prospect of some. Comrie can't go on as things are.'

Julius squeezed into the chair opposite. 'A large amount of money?'

'I don't know how much, not precisely. There's no income for Comrie while the war continues. The mines are closed; the railways aren't paying dividends. Taylor spent practically all we had in the bank on his regiment.'

'You have shares in that bank.'

'I do, but there'll be nothing from there this year. People have barely begun to recover. Julius, I need to pay my workers. For a few weeks after the Union came, we all sat tight, everybody was content to work to get fed, but they know their rights. I *want* to pay them. Some have already left. Moses and Mitilde are saying many more of will leave soon.'

Julius set down his coffee. 'Well, the mines can't help you. I have one mine captain there, Tonkin, with a few men. He's there mainly to keep my mines safe, to stop bushwhackers breaking up the place and prevent the works from flooding. There's no prospect of moving any copper. The road isn't safe enough and besides, there's no market. The North has secure supplies elsewhere. I could sell the copper ten times over in the South, but the shareholders wouldn't allow it and there's no road to get it there.'

'What if I were to sell Comrie's share in the mines?'

'I wouldn't advise it. I was in New York two weeks ago. All the shareholders are sitting on their investments. The ore at Ducktown is good but when the war ends, it'll have to fight for its place in the market. Even if I could find you a buyer, they would pay you a fraction of the value from before the war.'

'And all Comrie's valuables are hidden in the mine beyond reach. I can't even sell those.'

'A mortgage perhaps?' Julius asked.

'The bank wants to lend to businesses that will make a quick return, not against a property way up in the hills.'

'And the wealth that was in the slaves is gone too.'

Clara said nothing. That wasn't something she could bring herself to regret.

Julius topped up his coffee. Clara was yet to reach for hers.

'The Duke,' Julius said, 'your father, he's invested in Comrie before now.'

This she couldn't explain to Julius: why she had to manage without her parents, how they had forgotten her as soon as she left England. 'I don't want my father taking a further interest. I didn't come to America just to send begging letters back home. Comrie has assets. It's cash flow that's the problem, labor costs that we have to adapt to.' She sat forward. 'I do have one idea.'

'Go on.'

'Before the war,' Clara said, 'Comrie drew income from cotton interests further west. I've seen it in the ledgers, but it all dried up when the Union took Nashville two years ago.'

'I recall.'

'There are two plantations. Neither that large. One is inland from Memphis and the other south of Franklin, Williamson County. I wrote to them late in the autumn and again since, but there's been no answer. I could sell those, or one of them.'

'We'd have to get an agent out there.'

'Could I not go?'

'Alone? Trenholm would skin me. There's no telling if the tenants are still there. You might have to re-establish your claim.'

'I brought what papers I have.'

'Well, I'm treading water here. I could go for you?'

Taylor's ghost loomed large, waiting for her at Comrie. She sat forward. 'Julius, I want to come too. Comrie will survive without me.'

Julius smiled and nodded. 'I'll see to the train tickets.'

'Not the train again. Let's take the river. There's no rush.'

Spirit of Kentucky, Ohio River – March 1864

Once the *Spirit of Kentucky* was clear of Pittsburgh and had followed the Ohio's first big turn into the west, Tod climbed the steep steps to the pilothouse and introduced himself to Captain Crestwood, then asked to tally the arsenal's paperwork with the manifest.

That done, he checked on the cargo as best he could. The *Spirit* was not the biggest of paddle-steamers with just the two decks, the lower one given over entirely to cargo. Most of the munitions were inside, but some crates were stowed in the March air on the side and front decks in between neat stacks of cut lumber. Tod helped the crew pull sheets of tarpaulin over the boxes and secure them against any prospect of rain or river spray. The lumber had been securely roped but was otherwise left to the elements. He leaned on the starboard rail and wondered at how deeply ingrained was the impulse to do a good job. He couldn't help himself.

It was too dark to inspect the cargo inside, but he was up at first light the next morning. It was wall-to-wall in there with narrow crate-lined alleyways made up of square pine-boxes, or squat fresh-cut munitions chests with rope handles at either end. Everything was stacked to the ceiling, making it hard to read the numbers stenciled onto the wood. It was so tightly packed that he couldn't check every last one, but he ticked off what he could.

He spoke briefly with the second mate about keeping any lanterns away from the munitions and received a flat look in return. 'Say, I've been up and down the Ohio carrying army cargo these three years and that's never once occurred to me. I'm sure glad you came aboard.'

Tod said he was only doing his job. Of course, an accident would do just fine as far as the Confederate Army was concerned. They would be one soldier down, but that was a good trade. He'd see if he couldn't get them a better deal. He still had his fuse and, if he had his way, the *Spirit of Kentucky* would be blown from bank to bank. It might not be the whole Union munition works, but he was damned if he was going to deliver its crop right into his home state.

He took breakfast alone, then found himself a man at leisure. He explored aft, passed the coal galley and looked in on the hellish engine room. Three men, coated in black dust and sweat from the waist up, paused their spadework to stare back at him. He nodded and left. He didn't like to seek out company, not given his intent. The upper deck was left entirely free of freight and was equally devoid of passengers.

If he smoothed out the twists and turns of the Ohio, he guessed that they were on a southwesterly course. Mid-morning, they passed Parkersburg on the port side and he began to wonder how far south the river might go. He visited the pilothouse again and asked if he might take a look at the charts. Captain Crestwood, who looked about as naval as a Dakota fur-trapper, was obliging enough and pointed out where they were. The charts hadn't caught up with the war so the port side showed as Virginia rather than the newly formed traitor state of West Virginia. Ohio was on the starboard side. The Captain said that they would pass Huntington late today before the river swung to the northwest.

Assuming his regiment was somewhere in northern Georgia, Tod figured if he was a crow, then he would be as close this evening as he would be in Memphis four days from now. 'Do we stop in Huntington?'

'Would you like us to?'

'Just curious.'

'Unless we're flagged, we generally only stop if we have something or someone to offload. There's nothing and nobody for Huntington.'

If they put in anywhere along this stretch, he could light the fuse, stroll away and let the boat blow up behind him, but the trek south through Virginia into Tennessee would be mountainous and solid Union. He'd do better to stay on until they were further down the Ohio and closer to Memphis. The Captain asked him where in Tennessee he was from. Tod answered briefly then went back outside to avoid further questions.

His problem here wasn't so different to his plight at the Allegany Arsenal in as much as he needed to work out how he might survive the blast. The obvious option was to jump into the Ohio but, looking at the cold current and the running weight of steely water, his chances of reaching the bank were slim. Maybe that was as it should be; it felt unfair to make the event devoid of personal risk when so many others would die as a result.

The next day, when the woman came aboard in Cincinnati, he told himself that it changed nothing at all. My, she was pretty though. It was a trial not to stare so he gave up trying. He was at his favorite spot on the upper deck starboard rail, close to the bow. When underway, it meant he was forward of the tall smokestacks and further still from the churn of the paddles. Just now, the *Spirit of Kentucky* was one of a long row of steamers with their bows moored up to the Cincinnati landing. It meant he had a prime view of her walking up the narrow swing stage. She managed to do that with the carriage and grace of a bride walking down the aisle. Behind her was a dark-haired jowly businessman who Tod instantly decided was more likely to be her father than her husband. The woman had a close brimmed hat so he had a clear view of her face. She wasn't as pale as was fashionable, if you liked pale. He'd always preferred girls that spent their time in the free air. Without thinking, he stood tall and squared his shoulders.

The Captain must have spotted her coming as he was down there to greet her. He swept off his cap, reached up for her hand and helped her step onto the main deck. She looked happy to be coming aboard. Tod wished at that moment that the *Spirit of Kentucky* was his and that he was there to hold her hand. The woman looked up to survey the vessel, evidently found Tod in the view and blessed him with half a smile. He felt like he had taken a minor wound in combat. There was an urge to retreat to the stern, but instead he met her eyes and lifted his hat.

Once they were out on the river again, he thought it best to avoid the upper deck: a woman that pretty could addle a man's mind. He had a job to do, and besides, she had company. He busied himself within the press of cargo, ostensibly satisfying himself as to its wellbeing. There was no powder magazine to blow. Instead, when the time came, he planned to open up a box of ammunition. From a few torn cartridges he could make a small pile of powder. Then he could run his rope fuse into that to flare the box. The fire would spread too quickly for the crew to have any chance of dousing it. There were several boxes of case shells nearby. Each shell carried a burst charge. Once the fire reached them, the whole boat would go up, pretty lady an' all. Could he live with that? No one would know except him. If he made it to either bank, he would simply be the lucky survivor of an unlucky accident. He'd spent too long at the arsenal thinking of the women's safety and missed his chance. Here there was only the one to set against all the Confederate soldiers that might be spared. That word, 'might', was at the crux of things.

Captain Crestwood sought him out late afternoon and asked if he would join him and their only two passengers for dinner. Tod tried to think of a good excuse but Crestwood didn't wait for an answer and asked him to get there for seven. He had no other clothes so had to make do with a wash in his cabin, all the time telling himself what a bad idea this was.

When he arrived in what passed for the dining salon, Crestwood introduced him to Clara Ridgmont, who sat to Tod's left. Her friend and 'business associate' was called Julius Raht. Clara was every bit as beautiful close up, her dark hair held captive in a fine net. She was so striking that after Tod introduced himself as Luke Edwards, he felt scruffy all over again. He apologized for his attire, citing the lateness of his sailing orders.

The conversation that developed put Tod in mind of his Latin oral exam at the Harpeth Academy. There too he had inquisitors who seemed determined to throw him off balance. Here, for no good reason, his past appeared to be more of interest than anyone else's. The Captain tended to veer toward precision and Clara more to the personal.

'What is it that you do, Mr Edwards,' asked Clara, 'that meant you had such late notice to come aboard?'

Tod enjoyed the English accent. Clara had a bearing about her, like she didn't belong on a common paddle-steamer.

'I work at the Allegheny Arsenal in Pittsburgh, ma'am, in the quartermaster's employ. I'm aboard to see that Captain Crestwood delivers our cargo safely to Memphis.'

Clara looked mildly alarmed. 'Are we sailing on a tinder box then, Julius?'

The Captain answered for him. 'Ma'am, it would be hard to find a boat that doesn't carry at least some munitions to the war. We're skilled at it. And we have Mr Edwards along to keep an eye on us.'

Tod had a sudden and unwelcome image of her pretty face blasted from that shapely neck.

'Are you from Pittsburgh?'

'No, ma'am, I'm from Tennessee.'

'You didn't side with the South?'

'Careful,' said the Captain, cutting into his pork. 'I've pried before into Mr Edwards' past. He's apt to leave the room.'

Being defensive would only make things worse. 'Forgive me, Captain, but we're going to dock in Tennessee. Having people know I fought with the North might prove unhealthy. If you'll all mind who you mention it too, I'm proud to say I was with the 2nd Tennessee Volunteers. I served a year as assistant quartermaster.'

Tod noted a shared look between Clara and Raht before she said, 'If we're sharing regiments, my husband was colonel of the Hiwassee Volunteers, raised in Polk and the surrounding counties.'

So, she was a Southern lady, or at least married into a Southern family. Should that make a difference? Tod knew the regiment. They had fought at Chickamauga. He thought he had heard of the colonel, a reckless leader by all accounts. He was about to comment but realized as Luke Edwards he would never have been there. 'Your husband is no longer their colonel, ma'am?'

'He was killed.'

'I'm sorry.'

'Bushwhackers. Close to our home.'

'That's a poor way for a soldier to meet his end.' Perhaps that explained it, a certain unsettled distress that she seemed wrapped in. She wasn't in mourning clothes.

Raht intervened. 'Is there such a thing as a good end?'

Tod considered for a moment what he might once have written for the *Chattanooga Daily Rebel*: carrying the battle-flag gloriously in front of the line, a doomed cavalry charge into a thicket of muskets. Clara didn't seem the sort to be impressed by romantic sacrifice. 'I guess not,' was all he said.

'It's a shame a greater part of Tennessee didn't fight for the Union,' continued Raht. 'The war might have been over by now.'

Tod wondered on Raht's loyalties. He spoke with a Germanic accent. Perhaps the Captain had not wanted to be left alone among Europeans.

'Where was it you said you were from?' asked the Captain. 'Franklin, wasn't it?'

'Really?' asked Clara.

Those wide eyes were dark as polished walnut.

'I have some land south of there,' she said. 'Julius and I are going to visit after we've seen another plantation near Memphis.'

That meant she would remain aboard for the whole voyage. 'Whereabouts? Your place near Franklin, I mean.'

'Spring Hill. I couldn't tell you exactly where. I've never been.'

Tod couldn't help a broad smile. 'That's close to home. Not a day's ride. Good land too. Better suited to potatoes than cotton in my opinion.'

The Captain swilled his wine. 'I thought most of the loyal Tennessee regiments were from Eastern Tennessee?'

Tod backtracked. 'That's right, but the east doesn't have a monopoly on loyalty. I had to leave the state to join up. We were mustered in Camp Dick Robinson, Kentucky.' He hoped that would satisfy the Captain.

'You could go home now.' said Raht. 'The Union controls all of Tennessee.'

Tod wore what he hoped was a wistful look. 'As I said, I don't think that would be healthy, even with the Union there. I fear I've seen the last of home.'

'War scatters us all,' said Clara, 'if not our homes then our lives.' She put down her wine glass and lightly touched Tod's arm. A buzz ran through him. He met her eyes. A bell sounded from the engine room. 'America is a good place to find another home, Mr Edwards. We all have to find some new beginning.'

The Captain was attending to his food, but Tod saw her touch didn't go unnoticed by Raht. Perhaps this was what English ladies did. It had been a mistake to come to dinner.

*

Clara lay flat on her bed in her state room. She looked up at the low ceiling and enjoyed the steady drift of the boat. She should get ready for bed. After the meal and the wine, it was pleasant to lie here but know that she was moving again, that the world, and more especially her life, had at least some prospect of change. And she was the impetus, she was the one who had decided to come away to Cincinnati and she was the one who persuaded Julius to come west with her. It was even her idea to take the river rather than go by rail.

She was grateful to Julius for not introducing her as the Duke of Ridgmont's daughter. It would have made dinner a much tighter affair. As it was, she had gotten to know Luke as much as he would allow. He was a strange one: he had the air of being lost but at the same time self-assured, but then he'd given his reasons.

It was a good thing that Mitilde and Moses had gone home. When the prospect of a river trip was put to Mitilde, it was as if she'd been asked to sail to the other side of the world rather than to the far end of Tennessee. And although Julius insisted on paying for Clara to travel in comfort, the cost for two lesser cabins would have been an imposition, so she'd suggested that they go on back to Comrie. Once Julius promised Mitilde that Clara would not travel alone, she was content to go – even glad of it, Clara thought. No doubt Mitilde would be worried how things might have moved on at Comrie without herself and Moses there to steady the ship.

The first thing Clara did after she'd seen them onto the train was to go back to the house and change out of her mourning clothes. Mitilde would have given her a hard time. When she emerged in her traveling dress, Julius had smiled and said she'd looked wonderful.

There was no prospect of sleep. She sat up. Pleased as she was to be away from her responsibilities, this trip would inescapably circle back to Comrie. Taylor's ghost would be waiting for her. She'd not so much escaped as been given a furlough, like the soldiers, only hers was to come *away* from home. She checked the shelf of books above the dresser but her finger ran along the spines without settling. There was a decanter which she sniffed in the unlikely hope it might hold sherry, but it was a sweet-smelling whiskey. She put her shoes back on and stepped outside.

The cold river air brushed her neck and she wrapped herself in her shawl. She was drawn to the rail purely by the pull of the stars. The night sky was wholly clear. The *Spirit of Kentucky* carried running lights fore and aft but that was all. There was no moon and the river wore the starlight as if it were black metal. The churn of the covered sidewheels rode over the sound of the engine, as if the ship was powered by its own will, a white wooden ghost on the river.

She walked toward the bow, into the light breeze manufactured by the boat. It might be warmer closer to the funnels. When she got there, she almost tripped over Luke who had evidently had the same idea. He rose to his feet and his silhouette took off its hat. 'Ma'am,' he said. 'Sorry if I startled you. I was away in my thoughts.'

'It's fine. Just so dark. Is the smokestack warm?'

'Yes. Yes, it is. It has an outer casing so you can't burn yourself.'

The second smokestack was a few steps away. 'Then perhaps I'll take the other one.'

'Alright, but the deck is cold. I had to get a blanket. You can share it if you like?'

She could have easily fetched her own. 'If I'm not imposing?'

'No, not at all.' Luke bent and rearranged the blanket.

She waited and tried to see beyond the bow light, thoughtful that Julius might step out or if the night-crew had any business on the upper deck.

'Here.' Luke helped her to sit down with her back against the warm casing then took station at right angles to her.

Beneath her shawl she tucked her hands under her arms. She cast her voice over her shoulder. 'I not sure that March is the best month for a riverboat trip.'

'Perhaps,' said Luke, 'but you need the winter to see the stars this bright.'

'Have you traveled the river before?'

'I've rafted on the Cumberland as a boy, but I've never been on a steamer.'

'Then it's a new experience for both of us. I sailed the Atlantic, but I prefer the river. At sea it felt like you were getting nowhere. This is better. We're moving so fast.'

'That's the dark fooling us. We run at half-speed through the night.'

She half turned her head to see the outline of his face and his breath misting out into the night. 'Are you sure I haven't disturbed you?'

'Not at all, I was just worrying what to say if Mr Raht should happen along.'

'That we are just sharing what warmth there is. What were you worrying about before I arrived?'

'Do I give you the impression of being worried?'

'You give me the impression that you like to keep your thoughts to yourself.'

'Dinner felt like a mild interrogation.'

Clara laughed. 'I'm sorry. It's a long time since I've had new company.'

'Our captain was nearly as bad.'

Luke was busy tying something. 'What have you got there?'

'It's just a bit of old rope. I was practicing my knots. I can tie them fine. It's untangling them I have trouble with.'

Clara thought she might be asking too many questions, just as at dinner. She let the silence stretch out. She recalled sharing the stars with Shire on a cold night at Ridgmont one Christmas Eve. That was a lifetime ago. They were barely the same people anymore. She wondered if his regiment was still only a half-day ride from Comrie. The bow struck a river-log and she jumped.

'You really want to know?' Luke asked.

'Know what?'

'What I was thinking.'

'I would.'

'I was thinking that this might be a better way to be. This work I mean. Sailing the river year on year.'

'Better than what?'

'Better than war, better than making bullets. It's sure better than walkin'.'

'You did a lot of that in the army?'

'More than you could imagine.'

'Have you ever thought to go out west, out beyond the war?'

'The war has its fingers everywhere, so I've heard.'

'Sometimes,' said Clara, only realizing what she was saying as she said it. 'Sometimes, going somewhere, it's like a substitute for home.'

'I don't take your meaning.'

'Like when you keep yourself busy in order to stop thinking. As long as you're moving, then there's the possibility of change.'

Luke drew up a leg and faced toward her. 'Now I'm inclined to interrogate you, only I'm too much of a gentleman.' He might have been wearing a smile in the dark, she couldn't quite tell.

'Does it bother you that you might never be able to go home?'

He turned away and looked out into the night. 'If a man goes against his own people, his own friends, then I'm not sure he has the right to be bothered about much at all.'

It was an odd answer. 'This funnel doesn't warm all of me,' she said.

113

'What you need is whiskey.'

'I have some in my cabin.'

'You're quite a surprising lady.'

'Help me up.'

The lamp was low in Clara's room but enough to find two glasses and pour by. Luke waited outside and she took the drinks to the door.

He was rubbing his arms. 'It's cold away from the smokestack.'

He took the whiskey from her and his fingers brushed hers. He didn't feel that cold. 'Shall we go back?' she said. Maybe the mistake was phrasing it as a question.

'Is it warmer inside?' he asked.

*

Tod had no idea what time it might be. He held his shoes and his hat under one arm and closed the door as gently as he could. The stars were still out. The riverboat overtook a patch of infant mist out on the water. He walked softly back to his cabin and sat on his bunk wondering, marveling, at what had happened.

It wasn't his first time with a woman, far from it. Before the war, there were girls in Franklin as easy with their virtue as he had been with his. His brother, Moscow, had once taken him aside to give him a lecture; told him he was gaining the sort of reputation that the family could do without. None of those girls had been anything like Clara. It was as if she had never made love before but at the same time knew a great deal about it. He was used to taking the lead, but Clara had told him to slow down or to speed up, lay like this, hold her just so. The first time he was spent she waited hardly any time before climbing above him, kissing and encouraging him to take her again. And they had been so reckless; she had *wanted* to be reckless. It was only after she was finally satisfied that he'd been able to lie beside her in the dim lamplight and run a flat hand over the curves of her hip and breasts, until the cold had reached into the cabin and they'd drawn over the quilt.

When he reached his own bunk, everything else – his regiment, the war, even his home – had no more weight in his heart than a seed of crack-grass. He knew it was only some temporary bliss, brought on by the act, but he also knew there were two more nights before they reached Memphis.

He swung off his bunk and stepped barefoot outside into the night once more. Going to the rail he leaned out a little way and let his waxed fuse slide from his hand and away into the cold Ohio. He was damned after all.

PART II

Cleveland, Tennessee – April 1864

Shire was on watch. Not for Rebels but for officers or, worse, the company chaplain. He sat on an empty ammunition crate not a yard from the tied flap of his tent, soaking up the April sun. Inside, Tuck, Mason and Cleves played dice.

Tuck called out to him with his languid Kentucky drawl, 'You know, you could try to be less obvious. Nothing proclaims a game of dice more loudly than a lookout doing nothin'.'

Shire would like to have played too, but his pay had been docked by the Colonel. So had Tuck's come to that, but he didn't ever seem short. 'Maybe I should go grab some branches,' he called back, 'build some cover.'

'Don't get clever. It don't wear well on you. At least put your nose in a paper or a letter.'

'No mail from England,' said Cleves. 'Shire don't get no letters.'

That was true enough; not from England and not a one from Clara in the weeks since he had left Comrie, but then he'd sent none either. He went inside for a cloth and his rifle, brought them back out and started cleaning. 'Why do you need a guard anyway?' he said. 'There's no money changing hands.'

'Shows how little attention you pay,' said Tuck, 'which is a matter of some concern in a guard. These caps are mere tokens. Mason's keepin' a book, so that when we're flush again, Cleves can pay up.'

Shire glanced inside. They made an odd threesome.

Mason was as thickset as a siege mortar. By contrast, Cleves, absently picking lice from hair raked back above his pockmarked face, was skinny as a musket barrel. And Tuck, well, Tuck was an overlong bean-pole sat with his knees up under his chin. Each had their pile of pretend money: copper percussion caps barely bigger than dried peas that would be swept from the box-table should Shire sound the alarm. 'From the look of things, you'll both be paying out to Mason.'

'Corporal Mason,' said Mason with a sideways smile.

'It'll be Private Mason again if Captain Elmer catches you.'

'Which is why you should be facin' outward rather than inward,' said Tuck, waving a hand, 'or you'll be in the stew too.'

'Why? I'm not playing.'

'These are your percussion caps.'

'Hey!' Shire stood up.

'It was the nearest box to hand.' Tuck threw the dice and Shire sat slowly back down. He had few enough possessions in the world without Tuck and Mason making free with what he had. Caps were the smallest tools of his trade. Fighting was his trade now, he supposed. Who'd have thought, but it was hard to see it any other way.

Mason made a good corporal. A one-time lawyer, he was slow to anger, but the biggest man in the squad. Shire had seen him dole it out when he had to. He'd once confessed to Shire, if 'confessed' was the right word, to being one-eighth Indian: Iroquois. If the recruiting sergeant had suspected, back before Christmas of '62 when the regiment was formed, then he must have turned a blind eye, perhaps thinking, Indian or not, they could use a man his size. Mason won another roll and laughed over the curses from Tuck and Cleves.

Shire's current assignment at least gave him license to watch the camp. They had pitched here two days ago, having moved no more than a couple of miles, consequent of some high-up army re-shuffle. All was well ordered, street after street of clean new tents, white or cream. Rations were in full measure, he had new shoes, a new cartridge box and the first bar of soap the army had given him this year.

The blurred aroma of woodsmoke and tobacco overlay the comforting smell of fresh leather. The order and contentment of camp should have conferred on him a sense of security; it did up to a point. The tents stretched away beyond the 125th Ohio: the whole of Harker's brigade was here, and somewhere about was the rest of the second division. When the 125th arrived, they had marched past General Newton, their new division commander. It was all preparation for more fighting. The roads for their short hop two days ago had been dry, the march so easy that it barely troubled his healed wound. There was no excuse for the Union not to restart the argument. What were the chances he would outlive this summer?

An officer, dressed in a spotless uniform, trotted by on a fine gray mare that would have been overweight by last year's standards. Shire remembered he was supposed to be on watch, but the man had passed by beyond the Union and regimental flags that were staked out and waving up the slope.

Cleves' comment about letters irked him. There was no one left in England. Although he was the one who had come away to war, it was Father and his friend Grace who had died. Mother was no more than a childhood memory. There was no one but Clara. If he *did* write to her, he could only imagine saying too much or nothing at all.

He considered that maybe he should keep a diary this year, in lieu of writing letters. Many men did. It would be for himself, his private thoughts. But right away a stab of honesty revealed to him that he'd be obliquely writing it for Clara, hoping one day the chance would come to leave it absently by her chair, or maybe bequeath it to her should he be killed. She'd read it and know that he loved her to the boundaries of his heart. No, it wouldn't do. He had to start thinking only of himself, wholly alone in the world.

The day after he had left her naked and willing in his bed – a point he tried and failed not to dwell on – he had avoided her altogether. He'd taken himself away early to sit by the fast river, the Ocoee, that cut its way out of the hills south of Comrie. He'd tried to work out where things stood, but it proved impossible without talking to Clara. He was back at Comrie by late morning, seated on the porch trying to settle on the right question to ask when, bizarrely, the familiar conjoined marshal outline of Colonel Opdycke and Barney appeared at the bottom of the meadow. He'd rarely seen the Colonel off that bay horse; it was hard to imagine one without the other. They started up the switchback drive with Colonel Moore and Sergeant Ocks trailing behind.

Shire had felt a strange sort of excitement; like he was a child again and a favorite uncle had come to visit. He collected his hat and called to Clara. It had felt wrong to stand to attention with her next to him, but what else could he do? His worlds had collided. The day was warm and Clara had coffee and lemonade brought to the porch. She invited everyone to sit, but Shire stayed standing with Ocks. The Colonel didn't look right in a rocker; that small clipped beard and straight soldier's back seemed at odds with the chair's intent. He came directly to the point. 'Please forgive our unannounced arrival, Lady Ridgmont. Private Shire is still technically on a charge of desertion, as is Private Tuck. Sergeant Ocks explained to me some time ago that there were mitigating circumstances, and both soldiers have strong fighting records, real strong. But this is no light matter, and I need to be satisfied, able to fully justify any leniency to my superiors.'

'I understand, Colonel. And please, Mrs Ridgmont will do fine on this side of the Atlantic. What would you like to know?'

'Why was it my men believed you to be in such danger that they could not delay? I'm told that your husband was a Confederate colonel and was killed here.'

Clara looked pained. 'Colonel, the war may have passed by Comrie, but I still have to live amongst my neighbors. My husband, by most reasonable definitions, had gone mad. I have no doubt that he would have killed me, and if Shire and Tuck had not come, he'd have taken all the Negroes away with him to the south. He'd have killed them too rather than leave them in the Union.'

'Why would he want to kill you?'

Clara glanced at Shire. 'You must have asked Shire and Ocks the same question.'

'They tell me it was a matter of honor, and that their own precludes them telling me.'

She'd colored then, whether in embarrassment or gratitude, Shire could not tell.

'My husband betrayed me in a way so complete that he would see me dead rather than have it known. If, Colonel, the precise nature of that betrayal would save Shire and Tuck from punishment, I would share it privately with you, but is it not enough to have my word? In the end it was Sergeant Ocks that killed my husband, but without Shire and Tuck coming to Comrie precisely when they did, I would be dead in my husband's place. And there are five more Rebel soldiers buried up in these hills on account of them.'

Opdycke took a slow sip of coffee, threw the merest glance at Shire. 'The punishment we are talking of is a firing squad.'

'I made a mistake, Colonel,' said Clara. 'I married an evil man. Your men rescued me from that man. I will always be grateful to them for that.' In what Clara said to the Colonel, Shire heard her goodbye to himself.

The Colonel thought on it a while. 'Then perhaps if I could see the grave. That would be enough. Is it a steep climb?'

'We moved him a few days ago, laid him with his family. Shire can show you. I'll see to some lunch.'

'I'm afraid I must decline. I don't like to leave the regiment alone too long. When Private Shire is fully healed you must return him to us. If we're not going to shoot him, we'd like him back.'

'He can ride with you today,' Clara had said. 'I can send someone along to bring back a horse.' She hadn't even looked at Shire. He'd just gone to collect his things like some abruptly dismissed footman.

He was drawn away from the stinging memory and back to camp as the regimental band struck up the *Battle Hymn of the Republic* somewhere among the forest of canvas. Last year, in a perverse sort of way, he'd fought the war for Clara, fought to reach her. What was he fighting for *this* year?

'Private Shire.' Ocks called ahead as he paced up the hill like a determined bull. He was only a few tents away. Trailing behind him was an officer and two privates under load.

Shire scrambled to his feet. 'Morning, Sergeant Ocks,' he said over-loudly and angling his greeting back into the tent. It had the desired effect: hurried movement, whispered profanities. As Ocks arrived, Shire cast a glance inside. Mason

124

was prone on his mattress; Cleves held a pocket Bible. Tuck stepped outside and scratched the back of his long neck.

Ocks looked inside too. 'Keeping company with Cleves, are we? If he's conducting Bible study, he might want to hold the good book the right way up.'

Shire understood his fellow Englishman had called ahead to give them time. Ocks knew the score better than most. The officer with him wore a stiff frockcoat with a shiny single row of buttons up the breastbone, the epaulettes of a second lieutenant on his shoulders.

'Out you come, you two,' said Ocks. 'All to attention now. We've a few more recruits from Ohio and some will join company B. This is our new second lieutenant, Mr Wick. These packhorses are Privates Hubbard and Corry.'

Wick looked the wrong side of thirty and the young privates made Shire feel ten years older. They were overburdened and overfed. Hanging from Hubbard's pack was a tin wash basin, a none-to-small shaving mirror and some sort of fancy utensil set. None of that would survive his first serious march.

'Hubbard in this tent, Corry in with Cleves,' said Ocks. 'Now, let's give Lieutenant Wick our best salute.'

Why didn't Ocks introduce this man on parade?

'Which two are the deserters?' said Wick.

Shire's salute wavered.

'Wipe that smile, Cleves,' said Ocks, 'or I'll wipe it for you. Sir, the Colonel made his decision on that. They were docked three months' pay. He didn't judge it desertion, otherwise I'd be presenting two corpses.'

'Which two?'

'The tall one's Tuck, this one's Shire, as English as I am.'

'I had no idea we needed the English in this war.'

'Well, maybe that's because the war is new to you, sir. You'll get used to us.'

Shire felt Wick's eyes resting on him despite the not so subtle insubordination from Ocks. The man's face was overlong; his nose kept to scale and his kepi hat sat awkwardly on unkempt hair. There was something benign in his speech, like a consoling preacher, that was at odds with his words. He took a step closer to Shire.

'We should be glad of the help, should we not, from a country that has seen the light of abolition?' A wide smile abruptly lifted Wick's face, as if it had been yanked up by strings, raised by some burst of benevolence. 'But not deserters. We'll have less of that.'

'Perhaps, sir,' said Ocks, from behind Wick, 'you might want to see them fight first. Maybe do a little of that yourself.'

The smile swiveled to Ocks then disappeared altogether. 'Are you always so free with your opinions in front of the men, Ocks?'

'Sergeant Ocks, sir. Let's keep it all right and proper, shall we?' Ocks towered above Wick. 'It's a funny thing the line between a sergeant and a second lieutenant. Most junior officers are a deal younger than yourself, and more often volunteers than through the draft. We'll have to make do, won't we? Shall I stand these men down?'

Wick faced Shire again and the smile snapped back. 'Shouldn't this man have his hat, Sergeant? I think I'd like a hat with my salute.'

'Fetch your hat, Shire.'

Shire reached into the tent and collected it from the table. There was a curious weight to it, but he flipped it on in a hurry. A waterfall of percussion caps washed over his head, bounced from his shoulders and into the grass. Cleves stifled

126

a laugh. Mason and Tuck moved to help gather them up.

'No!' said Wick, stepping forward to tread the caps into the soil. 'Let him be. Bring these to me later, Private, every one spotless. Not a speck, mind.'

Shire stood to watch Wick leave. The man had his sword strapped on all wrong. It impeded his walk.

'He's a funny fish,' said Cleves.

Tuck smiled like a man who knew Shire loved him enough to forgive him forever and a day. 'Sorry.'

Puppy faced Hubbard stood close like a schoolchild waiting for instructions. Shire had seen peddlers with fewer goods than Hubbard had hanging from his pack. Tuck would have them sold off in no time.

'What are you waiting for, Hubbard?' Shire said, 'go on inside.'

Shire bent and collected what caps he could see. He didn't need to find them all. It wasn't as if the army was running short. He'd visit the quartermaster for a new box later and take those along for the curious Mr Wick.

Cleveland, Tennessee – May 1st 1864

Emerson Opdycke, colonel of the 125th Ohio, hand on hat, hastened through the sudden warm rain. His regiment, his 'Tigers' as they'd been christened after last year's battles, hurried too, lest they become sodden tigers. Men who he'd seen stand shoulder to shoulder and brave a hail of bullets, scurried for cover, crowded under canvas. A colonel shouldn't be seen to run, not even from the rain, but he walked as fast as he could, careful of the abandoned campfires and the guy ropes.

Wet or not, the day would hold out a better prospect without the hangings. Better if the two souls were taken somewhere out of sight and shot. Then his regiment would have to suffer no more than the damp echo of the rifles. This show execution, with half the division ordered out to witness, couldn't fail to subdue the men.

He reached his tent and slipped between the flaps. Inside it was crowded. He hung up his cap and removed his sodden greatcoat. The tent had a festive air, as if it were a few days before Christmas rather than the first day of May. Harker, smiling like a schoolboy, sat on Opdycke's cot with Private Gartner measuring him for new cavalry boots. They were visitors. Wavy haired Moore – his bushy sideburns an inch short of the collision that would qualify them as a beard – shared Opdycke's tent. He was repacking a recently arrived box and listing the contents aloud: dried and canned fruit, hams, dried beef, horseradish, green apples and wine. Moore was nothing if not generous; Opdycke felt certain he'd share the bounty.

He needed to pack too, prepare his surplus baggage to go to the rear. Orders had come early today that they would move tomorrow. It was inevitable; the only way to win the war was to fight. This would be his third summer of fighting. Amateur soldier or not, he knew his business, knew he was good at it.

His heavy winter coat could go once it had dried, his woolen socks and drawers. He spoke over his shoulder to Moore. 'Your wife is a wonder, to have prepared us such a treasure box when she had her own delivery to think of.'

'She is indeed,' answered Moore, 'but I don't see your name alongside mine on the address, so less of the us, if you please.' He could hear the smile in Moore's voice. News of Moore's new son had arrived a few days ago. A cameo of Tine, Opdycke's own son back in Warren, racing alongside Opdycke's departing train, head up and little fists pumping, played out for the hundredth time.

To distract himself he teased Moore. 'I'm sure you'll want General Harker and I to help you celebrate.'

'Now Emerson,' said Harker, 'you know I'm not a general, not yet. The confirmation isn't through.'

'It's only a matter of time.'

'Nevertheless, this remains a tent of colonels. My apologies, Gartner. Three colonels and one worthy private.'

'All measured, sir.' Gartner stood up and put away his tape. He handed Harker a slip of paper, saluted to no one in particular, and hurried out into the rain.

It was preposterous that Harker still had the rank of colonel when he'd headed a brigade since before Chickamauga; a distinguished brigade at that. The army could be so slow.

'Do you have your bootmaker's address, Emerson?'

Opdycke held out his hand. 'Pass me your measurements. I'll write it on the back.' He'd used the city bootmaker himself while home in Ohio during the winter.

'Curious, isn't it,' said Harker, 'that I should make the order to Cleveland, Ohio, from Cleveland, Tennessee.'

Opdycke supposed it was. 'We might be halfway to Atlanta by the time they arrive.'

'All the way, if the reports of Johnston's army are to be believed.'

Opdycke had heard the same rumors repeated last night when Harker took the regimental commanders to meet General Newton, new head of the 2nd Division within the Army of the Cumberland's 4th Corps. The Rebel army faced mass desertions, it was said. All that was needed was a firm push and the whole Confederate house would cave in. 'I've never doubted that right will win out in the end,' said Opdycke, 'but they've turned us around before now.'

A blue and blasphemous order, barked by some sergeant, carried into the tent. The men should know better; they needed God on their side. Opdycke pushed open the tent flap and looked out into the rain but couldn't spot the culprit.

Harker pulled on his old boots and came to stand next to him. 'Come now, the situation is vastly changed. Sherman has three fine armies at his disposal. Poor Joe Johnston has only the one.'

'Johnston will be a canny general, I think.' Opdycke had made a study of these things, as if he was to be the general rather than the fresh-faced Harker, seven years his junior. Harker was an army professional though. As a volunteer soldier, Opdycke couldn't expect to be advanced ahead of West Pointers. Harker deserved it. 'And Johnston's on home turf,' Opdycke said.

Moore called over. 'It's a civil war, Emerson. We're all on home turf.'

'You might want to explain that to the two souls we're soon to watch depart. Brave men.'

'Bravery doesn't trump stupidity,' said Harker. 'I got the whole story from Wagner.'

Opdycke knew only that two Confederate spies had been arrested over in Wagner's brigade yesterday.

'Rode into camp bold as brass,' continued Harker, 'said they were army inspectors come to look at our dispositions. Their papers all looked good, Wagner said, so they knew what they were about. He let his adjutant give them a tour of the 2nd brigade but sent a rider over to General Thomas to check. Thomas knew nothing of them so Wagner had them arrested and searched. One of them had his saber engraved as a colonel in the Confederate Army. C.S.A. etched right there on the blade. Now if I was to ride into an enemy camp, I think I'd have the sense to leave that behind.'

'Shows they must be pretty desperate,' said Opdycke. 'That or they have a surfeit of colonels.'

'Much like this tent,' said Moore.

Harker checked his thin moustache in the hand mirror. 'Thomas said to get them up in front of a drumhead court-martial today and hang them before the sun went down.'

'Why do our men have to watch?' asked Moore. 'It's not like they're deserters. What good will it do?'

'Perhaps if we make a show, the news will get back to the Rebels,' said Harker.

Opdycke agreed with Moore. The men were well supplied and organized and he had them in good spirits. The hanging was hardly going to help.

Harker changed the subject. 'How are your new recruits, Emerson? Have you got them bedded in?'

'Everyone's got a home. We've parceled them out into

established companies rather than have them form their own.'

'Best way,' said Harker. 'Let them learn from the experienced men.'

'It's put us over five-hundred strong again.' Opdycke was grateful for the replacements, but he knew Harker well enough that he could speak plainly. 'Sir,' he said, to get Harker's full attention, 'these new men, most have come through the draft.'

'I know, Emerson.'

'It's a different path. I haven't had the time with them. I don't know how they'll fight.'

Colonel Moore lifted his box of produce onto his cot and sat next to it. 'It's not like all the originals were here on principle. You know that. At least half joined because they had no better option. It didn't stop you building a fine regiment.'

'I prefer poor men,' said Opdycke. 'The army is a step up for them, a place where they can belong. There's a good number of abolitionists with this new batch.'

Harker patted him firmly on the back. 'Aren't we all abolitionists, Emerson?'

'That we are, sir. Here in God's name, but we're not zealots.' He was suspicious of men who were pious about the war but who had to be drafted to take their part. 'There's one lieutenant, name of Wick, the men voted for his rank back in Ohio. He's been preaching to them away from the chaplain as if he's John Brown exhumed.'

'I understand, Emerson, but if what General Newton told us is true, they'll be action again soon. You can see how the abolitionists fight then. Your veterans will take care of them.'

*

Shire couldn't see the point in being here, neither could Tuck. 'All these soldiers,' Tuck said, 'we could be gettin' ready to move, out on drill with the new recruits, workin' the round edges off young Hubbard. Instead we're waiting in the rain to watch this sad scene.'

Ocks barked at him to keep quiet.

Shire would sooner be anywhere else. The division was set out by brigade and regiment on three sides of a square in a sloped field. At the low open end was a cherry tree with two ropes thrown over a long bough. The nooses hung above a flat-bed wagon hitched to two mules. Beyond the wagon, two pine coffins waited, their lids resting on the grass. The 125th was placed at the floating end of one line with Company B on the extreme left. Shire was the last man in the front rank, which meant that he was closer to the hanging tree than any other man. He wished he'd feigned sickness.

The last hanging he'd seen was in New York, a mob lynching. As a reminder of that day, he carried a tear-shaped burn on his cheek. It had endured rather than faded, as had the horror, as if it had taken up residence within the scar. He'd witnessed no end of battle and hospital death since, executions too, but those were by firing squad for desertion. That seemed a more soldierly way to leave the world. Maybe what unnerved him today was the thought that, but for Colonel Opdycke's rare leniency, this ordered crowd might have been here to watch himself and Tuck being led out to die.

As if drawn by the thought, the Colonel's horse, Barney, appeared beside him with Opdycke on board. Shire pulled back his shoulders and lifted his chin.

'At ease, Private Shire,' said the Colonel, 'this will be an uncomfortable watch as it is.' The Colonel let Barney crop the grass but pulled up his head at the sound of the first short drum-roll.

Behind the drum the two Rebels were led into the field and down the slope. Their march was firm and steady, all things considered. Shire imagined the sudden sight of the noose, feeling it on your neck ahead of time. If it were him being led to that death tree, he would run screaming from the field, let a liberating madness claim him rather than suffer cold, contained fear simply to hold on to his honor.

The prisoners stepped up onto the wagon and their hands were untied so they could embrace and say farewell. From his close position, Shire couldn't quite catch what they said above the rain. He thought he heard the words *better, children* and *God*. The provost marshal tied a linen cloth over their faces, then placed and adjusted a noose over each head. He stepped down and lifted his sword. When he cut the blade through the wet air the drum fell silent and the mules were hurried away. The prisoners swung free. There was no sound other than the rain in the grass and the creak of taut, wet rope.

There being no merciful drop, the men began to struggle, so close that they kicked into each other. The provost hadn't retied their hands and one prisoner reached above himself to grip and pull on the rope, drawing out his suffering.

Shire looked away to the lines of men, every one of them subdued; like him forced to live the moment in vicarious horror. Here was their old friend, death, let back into the world beside the promise of spring.

Long minutes passed. The men danced and swung in the rain. Barney twitched and Shire heard the Colonel mutter an oath. The cloth slipped from the face of one man and the rope began cutting up under the chin, the eyes beginning to take sight of another world.

Mercifully, the man further from Shire ceased to fight and hung limp at last, disturbed only by the protracted struggle of his friend. The ranks of men became unsettled: Hubbard, next to Shire, looked to the ground; Tuck, beyond him, whispered, 'Dear merciful Lord.' Along the line men moved hands over their eyes. Another long minute passed and the dance of death went on.

The Colonel jumped from his horse and handed Shire the reins. 'Damned useless provost marshal doesn't know what he's doing.' He marched away behind the lines with many eyes in pursuit. Shire saw him speak sharply to the brigade commander, Colonel Harker. A staff officer trotted over to General Newton and quickly returned. Opdycke marched briskly back toward the regiment and called ahead. 'Captain Elmer.'

'Sir.'

'I have permission to end this suffering. See to it.'

Whether Opdycke had intended Elmer to do something himself wasn't clear, but Elmer was close to Lieutenant Wick and spoke quietly to him. Wick stepped out from the line and scanned the front rank. His eyes found Shire and he smiled. Shire lamely held up Barney's reins. Wick looked disappointed but settled on Hubbard. 'Come with me.' Wick started toward the cherry tree.

Hubbard shouldered arms – badly – despite there being no order. He ran after Wick to catch up. When they reached the hanging tree, Wick took Hubbard's rifle and dropped it to the grass. Wick had a side arm, thought Shire. He could end it all with a bullet. Instead Wick pushed Hubbard toward the kicking feet of the Rebel. Hubbard looked to the crowd, as if *he* was about to be executed. His eyes connected with Shire.

Wick tried to still the feet. Hubbard gripped the man by the knees and hauled down. The body straightened, the arms again reached desperately for the taut rope. Hubbard put in all his young weight until he swung clear of the ground. There was a loud crack, as if someone had used a heavy boot to snap a thick, dry branch. The army shuddered. Shire let out a long-held breath. Private Hubbard fell to the ground. The Rebels were inanimate at last, two strung pheasants, twisting slowly in the rain.

Comrie, Tennessee – May 1864

At the top of the wooden stair that spiraled up from the cold hall of Comrie hid a high, vaulted attic. Its low wooden door could be pulled closed quietly with a knotted rope. Clara never had cause to spend time here, not until Matlock arrived from England. Inside was a dusty window set into the gable with a low seat. It looked out above the trees and along the hills to the south, so in the daytime there was rarely the need for a lamp. If she took her shoes off to climb the stair and sat quietly at the window, no one knew she was here. She could disappear for hours on end; from Hany, from Cele, but most of all from Matlock, an unwanted emissary from her former life.

The attic hadn't been scoured like the rest of the house before the Union Army came. There was nothing of any real value save perhaps the rocking horse, although she'd not yet explored all the crates and trunks. She preferred to sit and think. Even the worth of the horse would be largely sentimental, meaning it had devalued to nearly nothing after the death of Taylor and his mother. She reached out to stroke the soft mane and tail, both fairytale long. It was a lovely thing: a dappled palomino with a faded red saddle and bridle, its legs stretched out to meet the varnished rockers. Cele would like it of course, it was practically hers by right as Taylor's little black daughter. The jarring spite that answered that idea made Clara close her eyes in shame.

Matlock was at Comrie when she returned from Spring Hill. She'd persuaded Raht to dally, not wanting to hurry back.

Matlock had been waiting a full ten days, Mitilde had said. He'd arrived ahead of the letter that announced his coming. Hany had taken Clara to find him in the near empty study. He was nose deep in this year's ledger. It was odd to see him here in his Ridgmont clothes. She recalled he'd always been well turned out, somehow dressed above his station as head steward to Ridgmont, almost as if he was nobility himself. His attire was a reassurance to him perhaps, tailored armor for a weak man. He'd aged well. In fact, seeing him afresh, she realized he could have been a handsome enough man if the ugliness of his dealings through the years hadn't leached the warmth from his skin.

Belatedly, he stood, ledger in hand. To say he had been waiting was not strictly accurate. He explained he was here on the Duke's business and had made an inventory of the Comrie livestock, 'such as it is', and also of goods and tools in the stables and the farm buildings. He'd been down to Cleveland to visit the bank and brought in some lawyer from Chattanooga to have Comrie valued. His overt activities had stirred the unsettled pot at Comrie enough for two more young families to leave.

She tugged the ledger from his grip and saw he had made copious pencil notes in the margins.

Matlock said that knowing of her misfortune her father assumed that she would want to return to England since the Union had come and the way was open. That would mean selling all her assets here. There was a debt to the Ridgmont estate that needed to be settled. When she assured him that she was long past acting on her father's assumptions, he'd suggested she must be tired and that they could talk once she was rested and more rational.

Of course, it had been too late to tell Hany to keep her

mouth shut; Matlock knew all about Shire arriving last year and Taylor's death on the hill, and of course he'd always known of the false marriage, complicit as he was. She'd written to Julius to thank him for his company on her trip and found herself writing of Matlock as well and what an imposition it was that he was here.

At the base of the rocking horse, where its arc rested on the ground, the rockers were connected by the same varnished wood to give the horse some strength. Clara reached to one end of the cross-strut and felt for the secret drawer. You had to press it just right to spring it free. Inside was a single sheet of paper, doubled over twice to fit. She unfolded it. Its edges were worn and there was a hole through one of the signatures, but the other was clear. Isaiah Matlock, witness to the wedding of Taylor Ridgmont and Grace Rees, 'spinster of this parish'.

Shire had given up so much to bring this license to her. With him, it had endured long marches and hard-fought battles. All to prove her husband was a liar and a cheat and that, perhaps, she had never been legally married at all.

What could Matlock do? He couldn't sell Comrie without her consent, but it was easier to hide in the attic than confront him and his knowledge of her past, easier to sit and look out over the hills and think of Luke.

It was odd to have spent such an intense time with him, three long nights of passion, and yet not truly know him at all. During the day, steaming with the current, Julius was ever on hand and she barely risked a glance at Luke. At dinner they let Captain Crestwood and Julius lead the conversation. They could have whispered of their lives after their lovemaking, wrapped into each other in the cool darkness, but they never did, understanding they both had secrets to guard and that there was never any question of a shared future. They would lie together until the afterglow faded and then Luke would pull over the blanket. Inevitably her hands would stroke and tease him and they would make love again to the slow churning rhythm of the paddlewheels. Each bout of love, each aching kiss, pushed Taylor deeper into his grave.

She felt no shame, only a vindication that she would never be able to share. She had been right. If not gone altogether, Taylor was a full step further away and she had started to believe she could find a life beyond him. She just needed to make her own decisions. If it had been Shire rather than Luke, it could never have been so good: their shared past would have weighed in the moment, demanded a new understanding and commitment. That realization was almost enough for her to forgive him.

Her public goodbye to Luke, at the head of the gangplank in Memphis, was constrained to no more than a nod of the head. Her true goodbye had been as they descended the Mississippi before dawn. For a few days, she'd believed all she carried away from the river was a cure, an escape from Taylor, and a new blushing knowledge of the many acts of love, but when she came with Julius to Spring Hill, she wanted to go beyond the plantation and on the few miles toward Luke's home town of Franklin.

The letter Luke had asked her to carry gave her the excuse. He'd merely asked that she get someone in Spring Hill to deliver it when they were next in Franklin. It was addressed but with no name. She suspected Luke hoped she would deliver the letter herself. It was also unsealed, but she resisted the temptation to read it.

His home was on the fringe of town, a farm shaded by tall cedar trees. The house wasn't overlarge, but was smart with a red-tiled roof and stepped gables. Julius waited in their hired carriage and she approached the door with the letter. Her knock precipitated a commotion within and the door was pulled open by a host of children, the oldest girl no more than eight or so. They were all struck dumb at the sight of her.

'I have a letter. For your father perhaps,' she said. 'Is he home?'

'He's in the fields,' said the girl and took the letter. 'I'll make sure he gets it, ma'am.' And she closed the door.

Julius was waiting. Perhaps it was for the best. They'd started back south. She'd felt a strange echo then, as if this was a place that hovered on the edge of her first memories, as if the flat fertile fields they crossed on the long straight road that led back toward Spring Hill were waiting for something. Maybe it had been mere wistfulness that she was riding away from Luke's home having understood nothing more.

A few days later, after they'd decided the better property to sell was the one nearer Memphis, Julius had accompanied her all the way back to Cleveland. He arranged for a carriage to take her up into the hills and home to Comrie, while he waited for the next train back west. Climbing the switchback drive, she remembered feeling elated, triumphant even, ready to take the helm at Comrie and perhaps help other futures as well as her own. When Hany ran into the shingle circle to tell her a 'Mister Matlock' was here and how he was 'makin' notes and numbers fit to sell the place', all her new certainty had dissolved. And now here she was, Lady Clara Ridgmont, alone in an attic, afraid to face her father's steward, a mere clerk.

She refolded the license, put it back in the secret drawer and clicked it shut. Sitting at the window seat, she pulled down the head of the rocking horse so they could touch foreheads. 'You'll keep my secret, won't you? But it won't do,' she said, 'hiding in here.' She stood and brushed the attic dust from her dress. 'We can't let him have the run of the place.'

Dalton, Georgia – May 1864

The commissary wagon wobbled away from Tod and back up the rutted track toward Dalton. He started to sort through the boxes and sacks he had just helped to unload. There was half a wagon load more waiting at the division depot, Morris had said. Tod had sent him straight back to collect it, lest it get spirited away, though there was less of that these days. He was left with this assorted pile. There was sugar, flour, a little coffee, the usual hunks of hairy bacon and even tobacco and whiskey. He couldn't fault the variety, only the quantity.

He'd been back with the 20th Tennessee for two weeks. It would be entirely incorrect to say it felt like he'd never been away, or that things were as he had left them. His absence was populated with such a confused mixture of experiences: under guard in Louisville, the prison on Johnson's Island, his escape from the train and time with Luther's family, working at the armory in Pittsburgh, on board the *Spirit of Kentucky*, and then the adventure from Memphis to re-join the army here in Georgia. But all of those recollections vied for a distant second. The most telling place he had been was naked in the cold dim light of a paddle-steamer cabin, wrapped over Clara, propped on one elbow with his free hand rhythmically pulling her lower back up to meet his efforts; or beneath her urgent labors, the slat-filtered stripes of a thin moon animating the sway of her breasts above his lips.

A bottle of whiskey slipped from his hand. He only just caught it.

'If you're plannin' on casting that aside, I'd be obliged to you for first letting me kiss the neck a few times.' Waddell sat bent over on the short end of a box-crate, whittling on a twisted stick like his craft might yet fix the world.

Tod called over to him, 'The salt pork needs to be cut into rations if you're done shaping that wood.'

'I ain't never done.' Waddell carried on as he was, Tod's rank counting for nothing. He had slotted back in as the assistant regimental quartermaster but, as before he was captured, there was no one to be assistant to. Morris was the quartermaster sergeant and had managed with Waddell in Tod's absence, though Waddell wasn't much use at all unless you wanted a walking stick whittled to resemble your worst nightmare. In the fall Tod and Morris used to have young Boyd to help, a more willing pair of hands, but the boy had faded and passed away late winter they told him – nobody could say what of exactly.

Waddell, Tod had learned, was a Mississippian and put in with the 20th Tennessee after his own regiment was decimated. He'd been sent over to work with the quartermaster as a semi-invalid on account of a sniper bullet that had taken off his smallest right toe. There was still a tell-tale hole in his boot. Not that the man couldn't put a fast mile behind him when he had to. Tod had seen him do that, but also noted Waddell preferred the relative comfort of the wagon, preferably with his feet hanging off the tailboard.

Unprompted, Waddell said, 'It's a different army you've come back to, for sure. General Johnston, why he started out shooting more men for desertion than Bragg ever did, as if he was minded to apply for a position on the other side, but he got the food coming in alright. One day he gave us a double ration. A little tobacco and a couple of hits of whiskey and we're all ready to get shot at again, easier to persuade than a fifty-cent whore. But you, Captain, you're a man of learning. You should've known better. You, sir, should've stayed away.'

Tod wouldn't rise to the comment; he'd heard it often enough since making it back.

They were set up a short stone's throw from camp. He never liked to sort the supplies with the soldiers milling about; it depleted his stocks before he could call the men over by company to hand them out. The camp itself had an air of permanence. They had been rooted here, along with the rest of Bates' Division, between Rocky Face Ridge and Dalton for the second half of the winter. The regiment's tents were dirty and sagging, but if you glanced inside, many of them looked as snug and orderly as a country kitchen. He watched two soldiers, beards long, shirts hanging loose, leaning on a tent pole and jawing like they were neighbors of twenty years.

To the northwest was the long and high Rocky Face Ridge. It was colored white with dogwood blossom and there was a deep notch where the rail line ran through up to Ringgold, though it was no longer of use to anyone. The engineers had filled in the culverts to the railway ramp and extended it to act as a dam, so on the near side Mill Creek had become Mill Lake. This then, was the ridge that General Johnston had chosen to defend.

Tod tried again. 'You know, Waddell, I'll hazard that the men are more interested in these rations than they are your walking sticks.'

'I'm building up a supply. I'm spectin' a rush on demand any day now.'

Tod unwrapped the trotter end of a pork joint and pulled his head up and away from the stink. 'Why not crutches then? We'll need those before we'll need walking sticks.'

Waddell stopped whittling and put his head to one side. 'A whittled crutch? More wood to work with I guess, but there's no tradition in it, no history. My pappy would laugh at me from on high if I whittled a crutch. 'Sides, a crutch is transitory. Once a man is mostly fixed he throws it away. A walking stick you hang on to, keep in the corner for the winter, by your chair to help you up, that's why it has to be a fashioned thing, somethin' to 'preciate.'

Tod doubted that any of Waddell's sticks would be much of a comfort to anyone, not with their particular subject matter. A few days ago, when Waddell was busy handing out tobacco – the only useful task he seemed to enjoy – Tod had taken a closer look. He'd found upward of a dozen sticks, tied together, but each so warped that the bundle sat awkwardly, like each stick was trying to wriggle away from the next. He couldn't deny that it was skilled work, but they were carved so darkly: snakes and alligators, lizards and frogs, their half-forms raised from the smooth wood like they might be from a dead-water swamp, they climbed up the sticks, one creature tailing another. He searched for a single redeeming example but found none. Death was a recurring theme. There was a hanging; there were dead twisted recumbent forms of men, sometimes with a battle-name etched above them echoing the long and bloody history of the regiment: Chickamauga, Stones River, Shiloh. The grips were usually a death-head or a skeletal hand. The sticks reminded Tod of sketches he had seen of the preternatural totem poles that the Pacific Indians raised. It made him wonder on Waddell's ancestry. He had the same creased look around the eyes as so many old Indians had, like fine rills and tributaries across a mud flat. It would be hard to guess at the man's age; he could be anywhere between forty-five and seventy. His moustache and sideburns were flecked gray, as was the long hair that escaped any which way from under his kepi. If Waddell chose to lock eyes with you, it was like looking into the soul of a recently bereaved buzzard.

'How was it you ended up in a Tennessee regiment anyway, Waddell? There must have been plenty of Mississippi outfits short of men.'

'They weren't particular where they put me.' He bent close to his wood to shape out a snake eye. 'But I didn't mind. If you ask me, those Mississippi boys 'r over gloomful.'

Tod shook his head and went back to sorting. There was only the one box of cartridges. Without any fighting, there was no call for them. It was enough to remind him of Pittsburgh. He wondered how it would go down if he waited until Morris was back and then said, '*Hey boys, here's a tale. When I was on my way back, I fell to working in a Yankee munitions factory. I don't like to brag, but I think I was pretty useful to them. Not only that, I boarded a paddle-steamer to help ship the arms down the river and when we got to Memphis made sure every last box was offloaded safe. So, chances are, when the shooting starts up, the balls and shells coming at us will be old friends of mine. Isn't that a hoot?*'

He shouldn't let it prey on his mind. God had been against his plans for violence; He'd sent a peacemaker and then a lovemaker to intervene. Once again, Tod saw Clara climbing the gangplank in Cincinnati and then descending the same one in Memphis. He could have come clean, could have told her everything. Maybe then she'd have found a way to steal him back to her big old home in the hills, park him in a bedroom and visit him twice daily until the fighting was over. He'd have prayed for a long war.

It might be she knew all about him by now. Since she was going to Spring Hill, he'd given her an addressed letter and said most anyone around there would be able to get it to his family in Franklin. It wasn't sealed. If she'd opened it, she'd have found it signed Tod rather than Luke. The contents were necessarily circumspect, enough to let his family know he was alive and planned to rejoin the fight, but if she delivered it, and he suspected that she would, then his father and Moscow would no doubt invite her in and want to know how she came by it, where she had seen him and so on. Then things would unravel. He was content with that, even hopeful that it had happened. While on the boat it went unsaid, but was understood, they were together for comfort, and both in sore need; where their own particular problems hailed from wasn't part of the deal. When he dwelt on it though, it seemed obvious that, whatever Clara's need, it greatly outweighed his own.

His time with Clara had been so overpowering that when the *Spirit of Kentucky* had finished unloading and the Union Quartermaster had checked and signed for all the munitions, he'd found himself flatfooted as to a plan. As an employee of the Allegheny Arsenal he had reason to be where he was but getting through the lines to the shrinking Confederacy was another matter. After a few careful saloon conversations as to where those lines might be, he used his railroad pass to board a train to Corinth. He got off a couple of stations beyond the city on the line to Decatur, making sure he stayed short of the Tennessee River. Turning his back on the howling temptation to visit home, with all the risk that would have entailed, he moved away from the station, waited until dusk and then slipped south into the woods.

A single man walking the country alone would attract attention, and there was no cover story that would save him if he was questioned, so he laid up in the day and made his way by night as best he could, figuring to aim roughly along the line of the Mississippi–Alabama border. The woods were busy warming into the spring; as long as he kept moving in the dark it held the worst of the night chill at bay. One night it was too wet to move anywhere. He waited out the weather below the exposed roots of an old poplar that stood precariously on a head-high sandy cliff. Thoughts of Clara tussled with memories of the war and won.

On the sixth day he began to run low on provisions he'd bought in Memphis. He had no idea where he was. He came across a tall, square timber cottage raised high off the ground on corner stone pilings. There was no cleared ground, just a hog and a scratch of chickens. He hollered from the woods rather than risk a dose of buckshot. An old woman came out. She seemed less wary of him than he was of her. He asked if this was Union or Confederate territory. She said she didn't rightly know and that it wasn't land worth fighting over. She pointed him south and gifted him a slippery chicken thigh and a hunk of ryebread.

It was in his mind that the Confederates were as likely as the Union to take him for a deserter and hang him. He had no proof in his pack to deter them. So, when he spotted a gray squad of cavalry trotting along the first wide track he had seen in days, he stepped out from cover in an attempt to claim the moral high ground. They hauled up and no one pulled out a gun or a saber; they knew they had the legs on him. There was a thick rope coiled on one trooper's saddle pommel that looked like it was kept ready.

Tod declared his rank and regiment. The lieutenant kept quiet and let Tod get out the bones of his story. 'Well,' he said, when Tod was done, 'we hear all sorts of tales. Usually we hang the fellas heading north and take a second look at those heading south. Corporal, which way's this track headed?'

'East.'

'That's bothersome. Captain Carter, suppose you tell me who the colonel of the 20th Tennessee is?'

'Do you know the answer?'

'That's not an encouraging reply.'

'Thing is, I was taken at Missionary Ridge last November, and we'd been through a few colonels before then. Joel Battle was the colonel who fought at Shiloh, but he was captured and sent to Johnson's Island where I ended up. After that it was my brother Moscow Carter but he was captured at Fishing Creek. Colonel Benton Smith led us at Chickamauga but was injured, and at Missionary Ridge it was William Shy. He'd have to be my guess as to now, but the honest answer is I don't know how things stand. My intent is to get back and find out. Otherwise I could have stayed in that thicket and let you pass by.'

'Well, if it's a lie it's a commendable lie as it tends toward detail. I guess you can double up behind my corporal and come back with us. We'll get a wire off to your regiment best we can, but I'm afraid if they don't give us a sound reply we'll just have to hang you later rather than now.'

'Later is preferable to now,' Tod said.

Once they were back in camp the telegraph became superfluous. There were a few old hands who knew of Colonel Joel Battle and of Moscow Carter. Some had even read Tod's past dispatches as Mint Julep in the *Chattanooga Daily Rebel*. He was given papers and put on a train down to Mobile and then came back to his regiment by way of Montgomery and Atlanta. As no telegram had announced his coming, he had the pleasure of walking into the regimental camp past old astonished faces and right into the Colonel's tent to declare his return to duty. His guess at William Shy turned out to be accurate. After handing him a large whiskey and hearing Tod's story – abridged – Shy lifted his glass and said, 'That's a long road to travel. I'm not so sure I wouldn't have stayed in prison myself. You're just in time to let General Sherman take a bead on you.'

Tod lifted a box of crackers from the ground and turned to stack it on another. He was surprised to find Waddell stood no more than a sour breath away, looking right at him with one eye in particular. 'Captain Carter, can I ask you a straight question?'

'Sure.'

'I mean like you weren't my superior nor nothin'?'

'Could you stack some boxes while doing the asking?'

Waddell held up his whittling knife like he was quoting from it, like it was an open Bible. 'What was it that made you think you needed to come back?'

Tod had been asked this any number of times in the last two weeks, but usually by way of a joke. Waddell wasn't the joking kind so Tod found himself searching for a deeper answer.

Waddell didn't wait on it. 'I figure it can't be obligation, not if you take your brother as an example. He was colonel of this regiment they tell me, before I was thrown in. Captured but paroled. So he's retired from the war, sitting pretty at your home in Franklin. It's as good a precedent as a man could want. Yet you loop round a thousand miles or more to join us in this shitty predicament. It makes no sense to me, Captain Carter. I hear half the men say you're a hero, but I'm inclined to side with the other half.'

Tod sat on a box and tilted up his hat. There was a simple answer to this. His brother Moscow was a widower. Their father was widowed also but there were still children and grandchildren at home. Moscow had been in the fight but now his family were in an occupied town. Father was getting older. Moscow's place was there. Tod said as much, but Waddell stood there and dragged his wad of tobacco from one cheek to another. He wandered back to his whittling spot and selected a fresh stick, fingering the shapes it presented. Tod turned his head at the squeak of a wagon and there was Morris coming slowly toward them.

It had been straightforward enough when he was waiting to be thrown from the train. He'd had more or less the same argument with his friend Wrigley: it was a matter of patriotism, loyalty to the cause and his regiment. How could he stir his readers' blood with his writing and then sign a parole and take himself home? Moscow was older. What if Tod was put back on that train today, having met Luther, having seen the power of the North and after laying with Clara? He wasn't sure he'd gripped an answer but Morris was nearly upon them. 'I guess,' he said, 'before I escaped, I never once truly considered that I had any other choice than to come back and fight.'

Waddell squirted a stream of tobacco juice.

Morris pulled up the horses and stood up out of his seat to stretch and scratch at his belly. Before he could climb down, there was a distant ripple of rifle fire. Tod stood too and, like Morris, looked to the northwest, up onto Rocky Face Ridge. That was too many guns for a firing squad. A few seconds later and they sounded again to be followed by the deep report of a single cannon, a sound Tod hadn't heard since Missionary Ridge. It passed right through him, sounded inside his gut.

'Best turn the wagon around, Morris. Looks likely we'll need more cartridges.'

Rocky Face Ridge, Georgia – May 8th 1864

Opdycke kept the light from his lantern low so as not to wake Moore. He bent over his desk and scratched a letter to Lucy. Harker was expecting him at five and they were to move at six; where to, he didn't yet know. All this he told Lucy; he never kept anything back. He knew she wanted to hear of other friends from Trumbull County or beyond. News was precious at home, and as colonel of the regiment he had a duty to share it. He wrote how yesterday they had fought at Tunnel Hill where the railway passed through a low ridge. It was a skirmish only, the Rebels fading away. The regiment was barely involved. Beyond was a greater ridge, two miles distant. There was always another ridge. This one, named Rocky Face, was higher than most. *The scenery is very fine*, he wrote, *and the foliage well out. The bugle sounds. Moore is rousing and I must go and see Harker. My love to Tine.*

He walked through the dark but waking camp. Men blew life into fires, set water and coffee to boil. Harker's brigade headquarters wasn't far from the 125th. He'd stretch his legs and rest Barney's.

Despite the hour, he found Harker dressed smart enough for parade and pouring over a map spread on a trestle table. The map's corners were weighed down by red Georgia rocks. No other regimental commanders were present, only Harker's aide-de-camp, who handed Opdycke some coffee.

'Morning, Emerson.' Harker looked up, smiling. 'Are you well rested?'

'Is anyone well rested at five in the morning?'

'Perhaps not.' Harker had the air of a boy up early for a fishing trip. 'Rested or not, I have work for you today.' He held Opdycke's gaze. 'Real work, Emerson.'

Opdycke drew closer to the map.

'I've been with Newton. He shared Sherman's plan.' Harker tapped the map. 'Before us is Rocky Face Ridge. It runs away north and south but much further to the south. We are here, in front of Mill Creek Gap. The enemy is dug in on either side. Sherman will use his three armies. Schofield will enter the valley beyond the ridge well to the north. Thomas, meaning us, will pin the Rebels before us and press their front. MacPherson will take a wide arc to the south and try his luck at gaps further down. If Johnston doesn't pull back quickly, we'll bag him. Understood?'

'Understood, but MacPherson has the smallest army. Johnston will look to isolate him.'

'Which is why we must keep him pressed here. Our brigade is to attack north of the gap and the 125th will take the lead. I want you to feel your way north until you think you are beyond the Rebel front then get up on top and attack them down the spine of the ridge.'

'With only one regiment?'

'If the guide is correct, the top of the ridge is narrow. You'll barely be able to attack much more than a company at a time. Keep it hot. We can't be too tentative. Rotate the lead company. It'll be a while before we can get cannon up to support you. The brigade will come on behind. I want you to establish a signal station. There will be attacks south of the gap at the same time. Alright, Emerson?'

'Alright, sir.'

Harker moved the rocks and folded the map. 'Take this, I have another. And Emerson.'

'Yes, sir?'

'Put the men in hard, but not you. It's likely to be a long campaign. I can't do without you.'

Opdycke knew that Harker would lead a charge himself given half a chance. 'I'll have to see how I find things.'

*

Shire lay on his back in his tent, one hand under his head. It was sometime before reveille, but there were stirrings outside. The dim glow of shallow campfires filtered in. He could see the untidy outline of Tuck's hair. A lantern was carried by and the pyramid shadow of their stacked rifles traveled across the canvas. Mason snored lightly. There was a sharp crack and Hubbard, lying close to Shire, jumped like he'd been pricked with a bayonet.

'It's alright, Hubbard. Just someone breaking wood,' said Shire.

'Sorry,' said Hubbard. 'It caught me half awake. Startled me.'

Shire wondered if Hubbard had managed any sleep at all. 'Time to get up anyway.'

Hubbard rubbed his upper-arms. 'You think we'll fight today?'

'Perhaps. Sometimes you don't get much notice.' Probably best that way.

Another noise outside, a spoon dropped into a skillet maybe, nothing more, but Hubbard jumped again. 'Sorry,' he said.

'Hell,' said Tuck from his dim corner, 'if we do fight today, we'll have to ask everyone to shoot quietly, otherwise you're going to run low on apologies.'

Tuck could have been gentler; the boy didn't need to be made fun of. Wick could have picked out any one of them at the execution. Shire was sure it would have been him but for the fact he'd been holding the Colonel's horse.

Either Hubbard was naturally jumpy or the hanging had unhinged him. It couldn't be easy for the boy to carry that memory: to feel the jolt of a life ended and know you were the cause. A fight might do him good, give him some more grim memories aside from the hanging.

They hurried through breakfast. There was a snap to the orders barked into the dawn twilight that made Shire believe this would be a long day. He buckled himself tightly, checked on his cartridges and percussion caps. From up the slope he could hear a communal prayer. Lieutenant Wick was officiating in the deeper dawn shadow of a Georgia pine, a score of men around him.

'Are those Company B men?' asked Tuck, squinting.

'A few of them,' said Shire.

'They would do better to look to their rifles. There's a fighting scent in the air. It's a little late to get the Lord on side.'

Shire nodded at the crowd. 'Not for everyone.'

Private Dana came forward of the others and knelt in front of Wick who flicked water from a mess tin onto the boy's head. 'Accept this child into your heavenly grace. Let him live and die in your Holy Spirit.'

Tuck sipped his coffee. 'Here comes trouble,' he said.

Captain Elmer strode up to the congregation, Sergeant Ocks close behind. They pulled their way through the crowd. Dana came to his feet. Elmer knocked the canteen from Wick's hand. 'You think this is a Sunday school, Wick? These men need to get ready.'

'They come to me, Captain. I prepare them.'

'That man doesn't know when to quit yacking,' said Tuck.

Ocks pushed Company B men back to the tents.

Shire turned away rather than watch further; there were too many men staring. A few days back, Wick had virtually ordered him to come to prayer meetings but he'd demurred. 'Let me baptize you, Shire, bring you into the fold.'

'I'm already in the fold, sir. We have fonts in England too.'

The familiar wide smile had shot across Wick's face. 'Old countries and old Bibles. It would be a new birth here in the name of abolition. You can go to your maker in peace.'

Shire explained that he had no inclination to meet his maker any time soon.

The light was up but the sun hidden somewhere behind Rocky Face as they tracked out of camp, Company B in column and bringing up the rear. Shire had Hubbard beside him. The Colonel moved them quickly through the woods and swung them north once they neared the base of the ridge. The shooting started a half hour later but was directed at the forward company. Hubbard, working up a sweat, twitched or half-stumbled with every shot. To Shire it seemed nothing more than sporadic and hopeful musketry, but the sound was enough to make him think again on what Wick had said. Was he ready if death arrived today? War had made him at once more earnest and more despairing about the Lord. This would be his first fight since Dandridge. He wondered which self would turn up: soldier Shire or schoolteacher Shire? Maybe it wasn't too late for a prayer. He whispered one through his laden breath as the regiment angled right and started to climb obliquely up the slope. Cleves muttered something disparaging about fighting the whole goddamned war uphill.

High as the ridge was, it was only lightly defended this far north. In short order Company B was atop the boulder-strewn narrow spine and repointed to the south to follow the rest of the regiment. Looking down and east Shire could see into a wide valley and in the distance what he supposed to be Dalton. A rail line stretched from the town toward the ridge. He could hear gunfire down in the valley, and here and there glimpsed a rush of cavalry.

Ahead, along the spine, the rifle fire intensified and companies were rotated to the rear, pushing Company B closer to the front. Injured men sat propped against trees or rocks, there was the sight of blood, shockingly red despite past battles. One body was rolled face down. Shire's heart pumped with more than exertion. He remembered last time out, at Dandridge, where he was hit. Before that day, some unreasonable part of him had understood that he was to be spared, protected by fate from bullet and shell. That helpful belief no longer held any water; he'd seen the color of his *own* blood to be as bright as everyone else's, heard the remains of the guilty lead that was pulled from his leg drop into the surgeon's metal bowl. He had a new insight on fear.

Another company melted behind them, some of the men wide-eyed, others limping or supported. They passed into a thicker stand of trees and the canopy twitched, dropped dismembered twigs and bullet-shaved leaves. He passed a big man sat out of the way pulling a boot free that was dripping blood and was shocked to see it was Ocks. He stepped out of line to help, but the big sergeant swore at him. He got back in place beside Hubbard and hurried him along.

He had thought his second year of war might be easier but inside the same gut churning dread was back. The morning wore on and the regiment slowly pushed its way south, Company B ever nearer the front, nearer to the crackle of rifles. A fresh breeze whipped gunsmoke off the ridge ahead. The slope on either side was so steep that there could be no flanking move, just a direct nose-on-nose fight with stubborn Rebels. His squad reached a cleared plateau ahead of the rest of the company. The ridge widened and they could see enemy works: a stone wall five to six feet high. Shire ducked behind a boulder with Tuck and Mason, Hubbard hid himself behind a waist-high bush.

'That's about the shape of our luck,' said Tuck. 'We ain't seen a wall or a trench all day.' The rest of the company was catching up. Looking further back, Shire glimpsed flags from the 64th Ohio and the 79th Illinois advancing to join them.

Lieutenant Wick bent behind a neighboring rock, pistol in hand, eyes wide. He called to the few men who were up. 'Prepare to charge that wall.'

Shire looked around. There were a lot of fresh faces, acolytes from Wick's prayer meetings. Some drew bayonets without the command. Hubbard tried to load but his hands shook so much that the powder missed the barrel. Shire wished Ocks was here.

A bullet fizzed off the rock above them. 'Lieutenant,' Mason called, 'we should wait until the company is all up, go in with what's arriving from the rest of the brigade. We can't take that wall alone.'

Wick's face pulled into the smile that Shire had come to hate. 'It isn't given to us to choose the moment, Corporal. *Teach us to number our days, that we may present to You a heart of wisdom.*' His prophet eyes picked out Shire, reached in and unwrapped a deeper fear. 'Time to make amends, Private Shire.'

'Sir, we must wait,' shouted Mason.

'Charge, men! Charge the slavers.' Wick rose as if to lead

but let a dozen men come past him. Shire rose too. How could he disobey Wick under fire with all that had gone before? He'd be called a coward as well as a deserter.

Tuck yanked him to the ground. 'Get the hell back down. You want to die for a zealot? Hubbard, stay where you are!'

They heard a powerful volley from the wall and Mason chanced a look. 'Damned fool. They're all down. If they're not dead already they will be if they stand.'

More of the company joined them from the trees, Captain Elmer among them. 'Who ordered those men forward?' There was no time for an answer. The 64th Ohio sounded its own charge and the Illinois boys went with them. Elmer dragged Company B together and they went in half a minute late. It was a slow disjointed charge; men vied for the cover of scrub and rock. The other regiments drew the Rebels' fire and Shire made good ground with Tuck and Mason, Hubbard in behind. They found Dana sitting up, only winded it appeared until he took his hands from his chest and showed them the blood. He held them cupped up to Shire like a young boy who had found a small lizard or a polished rock. A ball slapped into the dirt beside them.

'Lay back down, Dana,' Mason said. 'Until this hail passes.'

Wick was suddenly there. 'I'll tend to him,' he said. 'The boy is spent. Let me take him to the Lord.' He helped Dana to stand and walked him away as if braving nothing more than light rain.

Shire hugged the ground to endure a fresh volley. 'Wick should stay. He's our lieutenant, he can't just leave.'

'Let him go,' said Tuck. 'We're better off without the crazed bastard.'

'Dana was lung-shot,' said Mason. 'I'd sooner stay here than spend my last minutes with Wick.'

Union weight began to tell; the Rebels' fire became piecemeal rather than combined. Mason led them on, dragged them forward past the detritus of Wick's charge: dead and dying men, faces Shire knew, men who might have poured him a coffee but yesterday, men he had dealt cards to.

They got off a few shots lying prone, stretching in the dirt to ram the ball home and firing into the smoke that masked the wall. What would they do if they got there, thought Shire? That wall was as high as a man and there was a ditch before it. They had no ladders; they had no cannon to make a breach. Colonel Moore appeared, on his feet, sword drawn, waved them on, pulled Hubbard up from the ground and pushed him forward. Around them men stood and started to run.

'Here we go then,' said Tuck.

Shire stood and found himself alongside Moore, the only man not crouching as he ran. 'Almost there, boys, almost there.' Ahead, Corporal Calvin spun and at the same time Moore flinched. Calvin dropped to his knees, his jaw shot away. Moore reached to his lower back only to pull a wet and bloodied ball from inside his jacket. 'Dear God,' he said to Shire, 'I believe this passed through Calvin.'

They never made it to the wall. The Rebels must have brought up more men: their fire strengthened. Along with everyone left in the fight, Shire backed away, relief flooding through tired limbs, thankful today's ordeal was over. He managed two more shots to help keep the Rebel's mindful. It had been a brave charge, but the regiment's drive along the ridge had hit the buffers.

They stayed up on Rocky Face for three more days, picking at the Rebels, hauling cannon up the slope on the first night. On the third day a cold drenching rain came on and it was a blessing to be called off the ridge on the fourth.

The Rebels abandoned their lines the day after, outflanked miles to the south by MacPherson's army. Shire wondered why the 125th couldn't have just stayed in camp. He found a hospital orderly and persuaded him to come and change the dressing on Ocks' foot, Ocks complaining all the time that it was no more than a scratch and that he could use it just fine. The orderly told them around fifty men were lost or injured from the regiment. Dana was dead, they learned, but Calvin alive, despite his head wound.

'That's the trouble with us being up to strength,' said Tuck, picking at his stew, 'and ownin' a reputation to boot. We're always liable to be put in when there's a fight.'

Shire looked over to where Wick had found another tree and was leading another prayer. Hubbard was there. Shire was cold and tired. A big ridge, a small wall; what was it all for? It did no good to ask when you had no choice but to fight.

Comrie, Tennessee – May 1864

Matlock stood in his box-room and fretted once more over how little there was he could do. He looked out through the meagre window to the north. The late afternoon sun was on the hills, but his window was, as ever, in shadow. If he were back at Ridgmont there would be invoices to challenge, payrolls to squeeze; barely a week ever passed without there being a dismissal to enact or at least threaten.

When he had arrived at Comrie and found Clara absent, he'd insisted that Mitilde place him in one of the better rooms. The one he'd chosen had belonged to Emmeline, Taylor's mother. She was dead so why shouldn't he make use of it, even if, like all the others, it was largely devoid of furniture? At least it had a high comfortable bed and a commanding view, but when Clara returned, after her strained welcome, he had come upstairs to find Mitilde and Hany moving his belongings to this smallest of rooms, barely fit for a child.

'I done told you, Mr Matlock, the room weren't 'propriate,' Mitilde had said, stripping the sheets. 'But you ain't one for listenin' overmuch. It's a ladies' room to start, and right next to Miss Clara. What's more, it's a deathbed and the year ain't turned full circle. We want death to clear out.'

He could compose a letter to the Duke, but what to tell him? That his daughter was obstinate, that any assets sold now would fetch a low price, that it would be hard to find a wealthy buyer who wanted to live this far from civil society; although to Matlock's mind, that applied to every bit of America he had seen thus far. The truth was, it was he who was desperate for a sale rather than the Duke, and that without one soon, his own 'appropriation' of the Duke's assets would be forced into the light.

He collected his hat and took himself downstairs, wondering where Clara had hidden herself today. It was like living with a skittish ghost. He would trail her perfume to an empty room or, when entering the study, see the tail-end of a dress depart the opposite door.

He let himself out the back door and glanced through the pane into the kitchen where Mitilde's black face looked up at him. Not openly hostile – not quite. Mitilde was one to watch. Comrie's time might be passing, but she had a stake in it. What made things so impossible was he held only that authority which he assumed, and that was paper thin. At home, as steward to the Duke's estate at Ridgmont, he was empowered above the entire staff: the hall-boy, the housekeeper, the head gamekeeper, they all answered to him. He oversaw the Duke's finances, dealt with his correspondence, knew where he kept his most private of letters. Secrets were power, after all. Here, he had only the one secret to spend.

May Day would have come and gone back in Bedfordshire. Confirmed bachelor though he was, it didn't mean he couldn't stand one step behind the Duke's family and appreciate the procession or the maypole dance. When the men of Ridgmont tilted their heads and tugged forelocks for the Duke, Matlock was in his orbit, a shareholder in their respect.

Clara dismissed his assertion that he was acting in the Duke's stead, brazenly stating that she no longer recognized her father's authority. She had always been willful: a noisy young girl running around the halls and patterned gardens of Ridgmont. It was often the way with the last child, he believed, so much so that he declined to hire staff if they were the youngest. They lacked a sense of responsibility. Perhaps that was why the Duke had been happy to let Clara come away to America, to invest her here with Taylor and then forget her. There had not been the merest suggestion that he might come to see to the welfare of his daughter, to look over his various assets after the Union had swept south and liberated some, burned others. No, it was all left to Matlock. He'd had to propose the task himself, despite his distaste for travel; the estate's assets needed to be assessed, liquidated if necessary. Of course, it suited his purpose that the Duke wasn't here. He at least had the whip hand, even if it lacked a whip.

A young black couple ambled uphill from the springhouse, the boy carrying a hoe lazily in one hand and troubling the giggling girl for the milk churn she was protecting. Matlock recognized Hany, Clara's supposed maid, though she rarely seemed in attendance. 'I ain't needin' your help,' she said. She smiled all the same. The pair bumped hips, but then saw Matlock and straightened up. They passed quietly by before their laughter started up again.

Matlock watched them walk on, another couple almost ripe to leave Comrie. He'd helped two on their way already: one pair with nothing more than a few encouraging dollars and another with the promise of a position in New York that didn't exist. Why shouldn't they be pushed out into an unsure world? It wasn't so different to him having lo leave the safe authority of Ridgmont to cover the missing funds in the Ridgmont finances, funds that, with a share in the Duke's blood – generations old and a bastard's share though it was – he had justifiably appropriated. It wasn't his fault that his subsequent investments had foundered. His conscience didn't trouble him. He was kin, even if the Duke had never overtly acknowledged it. Matlock's grandfather was the true bastard and, in some odd form of compensation, had been given the stewardship of Ridgmont. Matlock's father and then Matlock himself had simply followed on, a lineage of servants to the true bloodline of which Clara was a part. He wondered if she even knew they were cousins. He must bring her to a point of decision, the right decision, otherwise he was wasting his time. She had already made a sale of some estate in Western Tennessee for no other purpose than to keep the foundering ship of Comrie afloat.

He came further into the yard and looked up the steep hill that was crowded thick with trees and loomed over Comrie. It was nothing like the gentle landscape of the Ridgmont estate, where the trees were carefully spaced in the grounds to please the eye. Why in God's name would Clara want to stay here?

Moses ambled across him, carrying a pail, touched his wooly gray head by way of hello. He was another one to keep an eye on. He might totter about the yard feeding the hens and the horses, but the other blacks followed his lead. Moses and Mitilde, if he could get some sway with those two, it would be a start. 'Mr Moses, have you a moment?'

'I got plenty o' those,' said Moses. 'More 'an I used to, as a fact.'

'You always seem to be doing something.'

Moses shuffled back toward him. 'I wouldn't want the devil to find me at ease.'

'But you used to be busier, before the war?'

'Master Taylor was here then. The mines were open and the Copper Road busy. The war's knocked the wind out of the place.'

'Without a master, it's hard to see a future.'

'Without a master, at least we don't see the lash. Don't be thinkin' I'm wantin' to go backward.' He half closed one eye and tilted his head. 'Why d'you want to sell Comrie out from under Clara, anyhow? I don't see your dog in that fight?'

'I work for the Duke, Clara's father.'

'I know who the Duke is, though he ain't never come near Comrie. His daughter though, she's suffered here. Suffered and endured. That ties you to a place, Mr Matlock.'

'I imagine it does. Before the war, there must have been more livestock, more horses?'

'Plenty more.'

'Did the army take them? Is money owed to Comrie?'

'Hah. You run out of things to add up? Now you wanna count what's not here as well as what is. You can't sell what used to be. Otherwise you could sell me, and every black face here. These days I ain't worth a silver dollar and that suits me fine.' Moses turned again, talking as he walked away. ''Sides, anything that got took, got took by the Confederacy. And neither you nor Miss Clara is ever gonna see a bent dime out of that business.'

Too on edge to settle, Matlock took himself down the first small field to the north, threading his way through a handful of curious wet-nosed cattle, to where three headstones stood just in under the trees. He stood beside them and addressed Taylor's grave.

'Well, how did you come to this? Young Shire certainly got the better of you, didn't he? Now here I am to tidy up your mess. The problem is, I'm not sure I can. All I have is the same secret that killed you, that Clara never lawfully married you in the first place, and that her inheritance is down to your past deceit and mine ongoing.'

Perhaps he could persuade Clara to dine with him tonight

and try again to get her to see reason, to come home to England and leave these dark hills to America's future. She might be soiled goods, but the Duke could spend her again. Evening crept in among the trees. He indulged himself, imagined a fourth grave in the shade. Then everything, Comrie, the bank interest, the mine shares, it would all come back to the Duke, back to Ridgmont.

'There's nothing to do but stay. Something has to give, and if I go home with nothing for the Ridgmont coffers then I may as well be dead too.'

He turned to leave only to see Clara come in from the light. She carried a basket of flowers. How long had she been there? She wore a startled look but that could be feigned. 'Matlock. Are you alone? I thought I heard a voice.'

'Yes. Alone. Just thinking out loud.'

Her eyes touched Taylor's grave. 'I hope you weren't speaking to my husband. I doubt that he's any more trustworthy now he's dead.'

'I was showing my respects. We had some common interests when he came to England.'

'Indeed. I think I was one of them.'

'Yet you've brought flowers.'

Clara brushed past him and knelt down at the central grave. 'For Emmeline. She used to tend William's old grave, her better son. I'd sooner lay a dead dog over Taylor.'

He watched her place the flowers against Taylor's mother's headstone. 'I wonder then why you stay, in a place that holds so many troubled memories?'

She stood and brushed at her dress. His distant cousin had lost none of her looks, quite the opposite if you preferred weathered beauty to pale. Most men would have been more than content with the prospect of Clara for a bride, but then

Taylor was ever selfish in his wants. Grace, that plain vicar's daughter, had been his undoing.

'Do you imagine there are happier memories waiting for me at Ridgmont? Would I look out over the grounds to the church where he wed Grace?'

Did she expect him to cast his gaze away or to look down, embarrassed at the airing of their secret? It was good that she would talk so directly. They might get somewhere. He kept his eyes firmly attached to hers. 'I'm sure you would not be at Ridgmont overlong with a beauty such as yours. The Duke would find a match. There would be another grand house, a home away from here and away from Ridgmont.'

He thought he saw her wonder at that, a new safer future, but then the door slammed shut.

'I'll make my own future. If my father wanted to discuss it, he should have come instead of you. Maybe then you would have been a topic of conversation. How you colluded with Taylor in his secret wedding to Grace, then without a word let me away to America to marry him as well.'

'There was no collusion. You forget there was a child due, since sadly lost. There were interests other than yours. Taylor played the hand, not me. I had no expectation he would go on to marry you.'

Her chin lifted. 'That is a barefaced lie.'

'And then there was the war. We had no news of how things stood here.'

'Who is *we*? You do your work alone.' She paused. 'I have the wedding license. Shire left it with me. I have it with your name clear and bold. It would be the end of all your schemes, wouldn't it, if that was to fall into my father's hands?'

'You would not wear the shame?'

'The shame would be an ocean away.'

He moved behind Taylor's marker, placed his hands on the cold, smooth stone. Why would she threaten this? It risked everything for her as well. Maybe she wasn't sure of the date that Grace died, didn't know if her wedding was legal or not. 'Is there nothing you wish to ask me?'

Clara picked up her basket, arched an eyebrow. 'When can I expect to be rid of you?'

'The date of Grace's death, perhaps? Shire couldn't have known it. He was already on his way to save you.'

'Ocks was still in England.'

'Not at Ridgmont. I'd sent him away. Are you not curious? You must know it was close to your wedding date. Everything hangs on that.'

'You could tell me any date you wanted.'

'It was your wedding day, the exact date.' He looked for a reaction but her face was set hard. 'You should be thanking me. After the Vicar died, I covered your tracks, or at least Taylor's. The gravestone reads a day earlier, as does the parish record.'

'Then I've no need to worry.'

'It's enough to blind a trivial enquiry, but not a court of law, not if I was to tell the truth.' This was his chance. There was no point in leaving anything unsaid. 'Then everything would unravel. Heaven knows who Comrie would belong to then, certainly not a false widow. It would be more prudent to sell everything now, to bank the money and come home.'

Clara stepped away but then stopped and turned. 'I have no reason to believe you, but if it were true, then we are both held to the same secret. You would be damned with me, by your own signature. So you can do nothing and Comrie will remain mine. Stay if you wish. Stay and watch me make Comrie my home. Not Taylor's, not Emmeline's, but mine.'

Matlock remained in the trees and watched her walk up the field toward the house. His chest was tight and his fingers ached from gripping Taylor's cold gravestone.

Resaca, Georgia – May 14th 1864

Tod stood in the filtered-light of the Georgia pines. Morris was ten paces to his left and Waddell ten to his right. It wouldn't do to have one shell find its way down through the branches and account for them all. Who then would guard the horses and supplies? Who would fetch and carry for the regiment? The 20th Tennessee was before him, down the slope in line of battle and facing out from the fringe of the woods. Over their heads Tod could see the blue army across the small valley, almost a ravine. The Yankees were mostly hidden in trees of their own, but a double line of skirmishers and then a solid rank two deep was advancing down the slope to the creek. The ground was wet here in the woods, the musk of pine straw mixing with that of men and horses; it must be slick out there.

He hated this part of his duty. He wasn't fool enough to want to be in the front line, but he needed to fight, not stand at the back guarding the ordinance, waiting with the surgeons and the camp cooks. Sure, he'd done his bit since they left Rocky Face Ridge: they had moved quickly with the supplies ahead of the regiment, they had foraged for fuel, collected and distributed the rations and re-armed every man. All this time they'd had to be ready to move again, but here, near to the town of Resaca, General Johnston had stopped the whole army. Close behind them was the Western and Atlantic. They couldn't give that up to Sherman without a fight. Railroads mattered; railroads and rivers.

He could see Waddell scanning the ground, even in battle

looking for whittling wood. Tod's own hands were busy with his pistol, checking the chambers were full, searching for certainty. Waiting was hard.

Before the Union kicked things off at Rocky Face, he had thought to do some writing. He used to relax that way. Waddell carved his sticks and Tod fashioned his words. It wasn't so different, bringing something out of nothing. He'd gotten as far as getting out some paper and dipping his pen but hadn't so much as written the date. Held in mid-air, the pen dripped once and then he'd put it all away. Writing for the *Chattanooga Daily Rebel* had come easy early in the war. Any amount of patriotic hyperbole used to write itself, but now there seemed some deeper contract with honesty. When did that happen? Somewhere between Missionary Ridge and Memphis, he imagined. Somewhere near a certain farm in Pennsylvania. If he was to write today, it would be from an older heart.

This close to the edge of the forest he could look ahead and see the blue lines advancing, but if he looked to the right or the left the depth of trees obscured his view. They were long lines. Both armies were in force today. Tyler's Brigade, the home of the 20th Tennessee, was supporting the Kentuckians in Lewis' Brigade who were in front and out in the clear.

There was a roar as the Union climbed out of the creek and came up the slope. They stood to fire one volley but didn't get within fifty yards of the Kentuckians, melting back before the Rebel reply. White smoke trailed up to the gray sky and filtered into the woods to bring on a false dusk. Sulfur touched Tod's tongue.

The men had plenty of ammunition. Sixty rounds apiece. It was early afternoon and his regiment hadn't fired a shot. They wouldn't need more cartridges today. He should be allowed to go forward. He considered finding Colonel Shy to request as much, but there'd be no thanks for the interruption. He caught himself checking his pistol again, cursed under his breath and thrust it into its holster.

*

Opdycke sat astride Barney and raised his field-glasses to look across the valley. The 125th had been pulled out of reserve and were to go in with any number of other regiments, most of them to his right. The ground to his front didn't look good. There was a muddy ditch of a creek down between the lines, then a wet grassy slope up to the first works which the Rebels had abandoned after the last assault. No doubt that was planned. It was little more than a line of piled logs, enfiladed by the stronger second line further back. The men would want to stop at the logs but he would have to keep them going. There was a thin tide line of bodies where the first assault had been hit hardest; a few men were painfully crawling their way back.

This fight was the cost of not bagging Johnston when he retreated from Rocky Face Ridge the night before last. McPherson had failed to get behind him further south so now here the Rebels were, their whole army by the look of it, concentrated and entrenched.

The cannon-fire stopped and the bugles sounded away down the line, their marshal call spreading toward him until the 125th buglers behind him joined the fray. He drew his sword, arced it through the air until it pointed over the valley, nudged Barney into a walk and shouted, 'Forward, march!'

Sending his men into battle always stirred the blood, but at the same time, he could have wept. It wasn't so different to the feeling of saying goodbye to Lucy and letting her slip from his arms at Warren station. He let the ranks overtake him, their company officers in advance. The sergeants dressed the lines. Captain Elmer of Company B saluted as he went by. There were privates Shire and Tuck in the second rank, stepping out as well as anyone. That Englishman had his own grizzled edge now, his scarred cheek showing through his stubble, as if he was a frontier woodsman rather than a teacher from the English shires. Opdycke was glad he had spared the two of them and hoped God would do the same today.

Confederate cannon opened up but fired short, pelting the front line with no more than wet earth. A rogue shot flew long and he twisted in his saddle to watch. Harker was back that way with General Cox. No time to worry over that. They all had to take their chances.

The slope was too steep for the double quick so he held the pace steady. The skirmish line reached the creek and it was boggy on both sides. Barney muscled through the rank mire and worked on between struggling men to reach the upward slope. Opdycke was to the fore again. Cannon-fire roared in front and behind, their thunder intruding from some greater world. A volley from the second line of works spat into the mud behind him. Two men fell. Barney twitched an ear as a ball fizzed by. Better to dress the line here once the men were over; the Rebel muskets would only do more damage if Opdycke waited until they were further up the slope. It was amazing how ordered his thoughts could be in such a place, how measured. What life experience had shaped him this way? To his right other regiments tilted their flags forward. Men roared and charged the Rebel line. Opdycke shouted at the captains to hurry the men. Three companies were over.

That would have to do. He wheeled Barney and rode up the hill toward the abandoned logs. A second volley from the Rebels exploded and the bullets cut the air above him. He berated himself for clinging to Barney's neck, forced himself to sit erect. At the logs he steered Barney obliquely and found ground to jump. Once over, he waved the men on, encouraged them to leave the false safety of the thin barricade. Another volley. He felt a hard slap on his left arm and lost his one-handed grip on the rein. Barney spun. Opdycke felt himself begin to fall but hands reached up to catch him, lowered him slowly into the soft, wet grass. Men ran past. He looked into the shining brown eyes of the private that held him.

'You're hit, Colonel.'

'Let me stand.'

'Better not.'

He rose anyway, fighting off the soldier. His arm burned hot and he looked down to see blood pouring from his sleeve and over his hand. The world turned and everyone in it, every soldier, Barney, trees up the slope. All rose as one. The ground felt warmer this time, the smell was of summer, the grass a comfort. The screams and the guns faded away as if the battle had passed over the hill.

*

'Here they come again,' said Morris. 'Why won't they give it up?'

Tod might have answered but for the Union cannonade. It fired over the lines and into a Confederate battery, scattering men and metal alike. The Union infantry was thicker this time, three deep – enough to flank the Lewis Brigade. Shouts and bugles under the cannon-fire summoned Tyler's Brigade and the 20th Tennessee to step out of the woods in support. Tod followed with Morris and Waddell as far as the trees' edge. He could see more of the lines from here, stretching north and south: a battle seen sideways.

To his left and in the open was the brigade quartermaster, Linden. Why was he clear of the trees? He stood close to his men and stacked supplies in a small hollow that afforded some protection, but it was only a stone's throw back to the greater safety of the woods. Someone should order the fool to reposition.

Across the valley a six-strong Union battery fired from left to right, one after the other, as if counting time, their shells exploding above the gray lines. The Confederate Army was feeling the heavy press of the Union but Tod considered that he knew its true weight more than most. He had inside knowledge. A shell burst high in the trees, dropping branches and pinecones onto the damp forest floor. Tod recalled Pittsburgh's underground stores piled high with boxes, a half-dozen shells in each. He saw a Yankee horse stumble and throw its rider and remembered the acre of saddles he'd seen unloaded on the wharf in Memphis. Waddell might curse at the sight of twenty Union cannon lined up on a ridge across the valley; Tod imagined fifty more outside the Pitt Foundry waiting to be loaded aboard a steamer. If half the Southern men fighting today had seen what he'd seen, the army would dissolve overnight.

Maybe he did them an injustice. There was some dumb comfort they all shared: that, come what may, they could rely on each other to stand stubborn as an army of mules and make the Yankees pay for each ridge, each river. General Johnston might have given ground when they were flanked on Rocky Face Ridge but there remained that obstinate

Southern pride, as hard and sharp as newly cut flint.

The 20th was engaged. After a punishing exchange of volleys, the Union infantry backed away, but only to allow for an intense artillery barrage. Several batteries concentrated on the two Rebel brigades. He'd never seen such heavy fire. The Union lines were lost behind the cannon-smoke but almost every other second there was a detonation. A shell struck close and to his left, so close that Tod flinched and looked out under a raised arm. Morris was alright, but beyond him, in the hollow, Linden and his men were all down, half their neatly stacked cases of cartridges destroyed or burning. Tod ran down the slope and into the middle of the wreckage, Morris and Waddell with him. Linden was headless, recognizable only by his uniform. Two more lay dead next to him. Others tried to stand. The cartridge boxes burned like a steel furnace. They helped pull the living men away as more shells rained into the slope either side of them. The rest of the munitions would burn unless they were moved, and they weren't as blessed with supplies as the Union.

Tod was in the fight now. He shouted over the rolling din at Morris, 'Get back over to the regiment. The first company captain you find, tell him I want three men. Just three. If he argues, tell him he'll have no ammunition tomorrow unless he sends them. Go!' He turned to Linden's battered men. 'We have to get these boxes into the woods. There's no time to bring a wagon up. Grab a box and get it into the trees.' Waddell was down in the hollow, skirting the smoke and the fire to carry the first box out. Tod sent one man to grab a rope handle and share the load. This would be quicker if they worked in twos.

Awash with energy and intent he got down there himself with one of Linden's men and grabbed the box nearest the blaze. The shells rained in. They found Waddell in the woods and Tod ordered him to take his box in a little deeper. His father spoke to him. *'If a job's worth doing, it's worth doing well.'* What a curious place to find Father. They ran back to the hollow and the falling shells. Morris returned with three privates from the 20th. Tod put them to work, focused himself on nothing but this, oblivious to the armies clashing up and down the line.

*

Opdycke awoke slowly to a familiar voice but a less familiar face. There was a flurry of cannon-fire. The face came into focus against a moving gray sky and he recognized the surgeon from the 65th Ohio whose name escaped him. The surgeon wasn't speaking, just wrapping a dressing painfully tight around Opdycke's upper left arm. The voice was Harker's. 'You awake, Emerson?' Harker appeared next to the surgeon, as if Opdycke was a newborn in a crib. 'Brandy for the wounded.'

With their help he sat up. Harker passed him a hip-flask. Opdycke took a pull.

'You've been out for a while,' said Harker. 'Did you know that you had a hidden talent for bleeding?'

'The attack? My men?'

'All over for now. The Reb's were well dug in. We couldn't take the position. The artillery's been doing some damage since. Johnston might regret staying. There's talk of a flanking move around the Rebel right. So he'll likely be forced to leave anyway.' Harker retrieved the flask and took a pull himself.

'I thought that was for the wounded?'

'Nicked by some shell casing. Nothing much.' Harker

held up a dressed hand. 'I was with Mahon and Cox. No limbs lost but Mahon was out cold. If you're alright, I need to get back.'

'I'll come with you.' He managed to stand.

Harker helped. Ignoring the surgeon's objections, they walked slowly through the noise of the cannonade to where the 125th stood in the front line. The Rebel guns weren't replying. The men cheered his return and he asked Moore after Barney.

'Last I saw,' said Moore, 'Private Shire had him. After he saved you from falling.'

Later, when the cannon finally fell silent and darkness hid the far side of the creek, Opdycke sat against his saddle and awkwardly scribbled a few words to Lucy. He didn't want her hearing of his wound from anyone else. These things got exaggerated. *Four killed from the regiment*, he wrote, *thirty-eight wounded, many mortally no doubt.*

He put down his pen and stretched the fingers of his wounded arm. Should a dressing be this tight? That was two hard fights in a week. His regiment had bled more than he had.

Georgia – June 1864

The storm had passed over. Shire watched a scatter of stars race between shredded, moon-chased clouds. Tuck sat next to him on a damp log. To his right, Mason stirred and stretched his great hands toward their frugal fire. Thinly sheened empty black skillets lay beside it. Earlier, Shire had cooked his thin strip of pork as slowly as hunger would allow, trying to hold the fat in the meat. The big Indian looked tired, he thought. They were all tired. Strange that he should think of Mason as an Indian. It was only one eighth; it should hardly define the man. 'Hey, Corporal,' Shire said.

Mason dragged open an eye.

'Do you think that storm counted as a wash?'

Mason managed a one-eighth smile. Perhaps it was the Indian. 'It bounced the lice from my hair. I never saw rain that heavy.'

The air had been warm during the day despite the rain, but a chill had crept in with the darkness. A rifle snapped far away. Out of habit, Shire glanced beyond Mason to where Hubbard lay with his head on his blanket-roll. For once the new recruit hadn't jumped. Shire couldn't see if his eyes were open, the sockets shadowed in the firelight. 'You want some coffee, Hubbard?'

There was no answer. Nothing unusual in that. Shire picked up a rag and reached for the coffee pot, feeling the damp weight of his sleeve. It had been dry enough when they came south after Resaca, the roads dusty though they followed the railway track for most of the way. For the most part the country was forested with only occasional clearings. The ridges, although lower, were never-ending. Each one was good ground for the Rebels to turn, make a stand and slow them up, send a few more Union soldiers home or to their grave.

Shire liked to know where he was, it mattered to him. Captain Elmer would oblige if you asked him at the right time. They had come down past Calhoun, then Adairsville and, after four hard days, to somewhere short of Kingston, all the time moving further from Clara. Maybe that would make things easier; heartstrings could only stretch so far. Kingston was the last day he'd had a wash, though he hadn't undressed. He'd had nothing else to wear. They'd all simply waded into a creek and soaped their clothes, rinsed off the sweat and the dust, then lain down on the grass and asked the Georgia sun to do the drying.

The wounded were sent up the tracks and, for a few days, the killing stopped. It was peculiar, that first day without death. Like someone was missing. No one wanted to start south again, but they were kept busy. The trains arrived two to an hour. Kingston was turned into a base of supplies: wagons, boxes and sacks everywhere you looked. The regiment was given twenty days' rations. Ocks had said they were in for a rough time if Sherman was thinking in terms of twenty days.

Since they had left Kingston, he had no idea where they'd been. Captain Elmer was always busy and Shire had other cares. The pressing matter of staying alive ranked ahead of geography or considerations past and future. Even the idea of Clara was held static. There was no space to rework the past or indulge emotions that might color an already black day. The storms had started. They had fought every day, the enemy never more than a chance shot away.

He should sleep. If he'd had a tent, he'd be more inclined to, but there'd been none for a week. Evenings, if they weren't marching or fighting, would be spent pulling brush or deadwood into a poor excuse for a shelter. Sometimes he tried to think beyond the war, but it was akin to being swept helpless and drowning down foaming river rapids while wondering how you might later spend your evening.

Tuck shuffled closer along their shared log. 'You know,' he said, 'on the march today, I made what you might call an approximation. Since this campaign started, I've fired over three-hundred rounds. At least that many. And, if I'm plain honest, I ain't clear I've hit a Rebel yet.'

'Truly?' said Mason, straightening up. 'And we used to think Shire was a poor shot.'

'It's likely I have,' stressed Tuck. 'Only with all the smoke and the rain and the brush, who can tell? I could be the best or the worst shot in the regiment.'

Shire preferred it that way. He usually closed his sighting eye after he fired, as much to spare him the knowledge as to avoid the sting of his gun-smoke.

'Is it so important to know you've killed a man?' Hubbard said in a flat tone from the edge of the firelight.

'It irks me, is all. I'd like to know I've put someone out of the fight. That's one less to shoot back. He may have had two or three Union boys in his sights for the future. Maybe you. I imagine that if I've hit three or four Rebels, I could have saved a whole Union squad by now.'

Mason collected the coffee pot, not bothering with the rag. 'The problem with that line of thinking,' he said, 'is that if there's a Rebel over there of the same mind then, pretty soon, you can reason that if we all killed each other, no one would get killed at all.'

Tuck held out his mug. 'Don't confuse the matter just to make me look stupid.'

'Why would I need to do that?'

'My wider point is,' said Tuck, 'that I would feel better knowin' I'm making a difference rather than just churning the same mud as they are.'

Shire supposed Tuck was right. It was a war after all, but what sort of man would he be if he measured success by death. 'We're moving forward, aren't we?' he said. 'Every day we're getting closer to Atlanta.'

'I guess,' said Tuck. 'Johnston can't help but back up. It's like three men herding someone up a narrow alley. Each time one gets around his side, he has to take a backward step.'

Mason stood, took on the air of an officer. 'If you'll excuse me gentleman, I'm going to retire to my thicket.'

'Make sure you check it for Georgia critters,' said Tuck. 'I heard Tom Brown sat on one yesterday and had to go visit Doctor McHenry.'

'That so?'

'Doc said he would live out the year, Reb's allowing, but there was nothing he could do for the scorpion.'

Mason left. Tuck got out his pipe and tapped it firmly on a stone to get out the dregs. Hubbard sat bolt upright as if he'd been snake-bit.

'You want a little whiskey in your coffee, Hubbard?' asked Tuck. 'Might help you relax.'

'Lieutenant Wick says it's a sin.'

'I guess he's the man with the list.'

Shire went over and collected the mug from Hubbard's side. All this talk of death wouldn't help. He poured in the coffee. Tuck generously topped it up from a bottle spirited from his coat.

'Here you go, Hubbard,' said Shire. 'Come and sit closer to the fire.'

Hubbard took the mug and Mason's spot. Shire noted how the puppy fat had vanished from his hands. Hubbard sipped his coffee and winced.

Tuck laughed. 'It's whiskey laced with coffee.'

'It'll help you sleep,' said Shire.

'I ain't ungrateful,' said Hubbard. 'Sleep is better, I guess, but not always.' He braved more coffee. 'Sometimes I dream about a rope we had over the river back in Orwell on my cousin's farm. You could swing out and let fly into the water.' He showed the merest hint of a smile. 'I struggle to recall what that felt like. It ain't so long ago. In my dream I can never let go, I just swing out and back until I look up and then I'm holding onto that Rebel again and I know it'll come, the give, the crack. Whatever it is you call it when you feel a man's neck break. There ought'a be a word for that. Maybe I'm best placed to invent one.'

Shire considered that, since the execution, Hubbard would have seen countless more men die. Surely the weight of those images would in time push the hanging into the past, but then what sad form of hope was that: wishing for new horrors to paint over the old? 'You were following an order,' he said.

Hubbard looked away. Shire sent a pleading look at Tuck, hoping he might do better. Tuck sipped at his bottle. 'Why d'you pray with Wick?'

Shire didn't think that was the angle to take.

Tuck ploughed on. 'He's the man that asked it of you when all he had to do was take out his revolver. And now, whenever we're stopped for more than two minutes, you're off with the other disciples to Bible class. There's more godliness in my left boot than in that man.'

Hubbard turned his head. Shire could see his wet eyes by the firelight.

'I've forgiven him that. He was following orders too.'

'Then forgive yourself,' said Shire. 'What does Wick have to offer you?'

'The idea that there might be somewhere after this,' said Hubbard, 'somewhere better.'

Tuck came around Shire to kneel in front of Hubbard and put his hand on the back of the boy's head. 'Listen to me, Hubbard. If I were that Rebel, I'd wait a long time by the gates, checking the lists, watching out for you if I had to wait a full lifetime, so that when you stepped into paradise, I'd be the first man to you. I'd thank you and put my arm in yours, show you around, take you for a drink. It's only a memory, Hubbard. Let it fade.'

Hubbard looked as if that was his only desire. 'How can I,' he said, 'when I feel that man's neck break every time you tap out your tobacco pipe, or when a wagon-wheel rides over a rock, or when I click the trigger back on my musket? It never goes, Tuck, not asleep and not awake. There is only one time. When I kneel down and give my soul to God.'

*

Opdycke attempted to get Barney's bridle on one-handed but failed again. He threw it to the ground. Barney watched on patiently. The dawn sun filtered through the trees.

'Let me do that for you, sir.' Captain Elmer was acting as his aide-de-camp while he was incapacitated. He picked up the bridle, stepped to the other side of the horse and slipped it on. 'I'll take him for a drink.'

Barney looked worn down, thought Opdycke. Not for

186

lack of forage; he just needed a rest like everyone else. He shouldn't have shown his impatience.

Harker was shaving nearby. 'You should be in a hospital tent, Emerson.' He dismissed the guide he'd been talking with.

They'd had this argument. 'I can't do a damn thing with it. It doesn't hurt. I'd happily suffer some pain if I could get the use of it.'

Harker teased him. 'The received wisdom is that rest is the best way to heal.'

'Well, that's not the wisdom I intend to receive. The wound is more likely to fester in the foul air of a hospital tent.' It was better to be out, despite the frustration, using his wits and his energy. 'Elmer makes up for my arm. Dr McHenry says it's healing well.'

McHenry had said something more than that: how it had narrowly missed the bone above the elbow and come within a quarter inch of a vital artery, but good fortune was no reason to lie in bed.

'I was with General Thomas last night,' said Harker. 'Sherman was there.'

'You truly do move in the higher echelons these days.' Opdycke hoped he hadn't let out any bitterness.

'Sherman congratulated me on having one of the best brigades in the army.'

'Truly?'

'He mentioned the 125th.'

Opdycke hoped to hear his own name, but it didn't come.

'He said these flanking movements are getting us ever closer to Atlanta. Only thirty miles away, but the objective remains to destroy Johnston's army. He expects a test soon. He wants us to be ready.'

'Does the information in my reports not get passed on?' Opdycke heard the curtness in his own voice. 'We've lost more than a hundred men since the campaign started. Last night it rained as if it was the end of the world. We're on half-rations, living in the dirt and the mud. Does Sherman not see that as a test?'

'We're all tired.' Harker wiped the soap from his face and walked over. 'Emerson, did you know that Major Hampson is dead?'

'James Hampson?'

'Yes.'

'I hadn't heard.'

'Sharpshooter.'

He would need to put it in a letter to Lucy.

'Sherman says that every time we move around him, Johnston merely falls back to the next line of entrenchments.'

Was that all Hampson was due: a simple aside and then it was back to tactics?

'Sooner or later we're going to have to try our luck and go straight at him, a direct assault.'

Two echoed shots mixed in with the birdsong.

'Isn't that what Hooker's just done?'

'On a small scale.'

'Seventeen-hundred men lost.'

Harker looked past Opdycke to make sure Captain Elmer was out of earshot. 'It's going to get worse than that. You know it is. The point Sherman made, after he mentioned the 125th, is that when we go in hard it's no use putting green regiments in the lead and hoping for the best. When the time comes, Thomas will have to put Newton in, and he's going to put me in, and I'm going to put *you* in.' Harker walked to collect his jacket from the camp chair. 'So do you think you can manage that with one arm? Because if you do, I'm giving you command of the demi-brigade.'

That meant commanding three other regiments as well as his own. It meant leaving the 125th to Colonel Moore. What if a sharpshooter got Moore? Who would lead the regiment then? 'I'll go where I'm ordered, Charles, you can't doubt that, but if my regiment is going to be tested, if we're going to be spent, I want to stay with them.'

Harker slipped on his jacket, began to button it up then stopped halfway with his arms wide and surveyed the stains and the mud. 'I look like I've been digging trenches all night, 'though Sherman's not one for boot polish if his appearance was anything to go by—'

'Charles,' interrupted Opdycke, 'I'm asking to stay with my regiment.'

Harker half turned away and attended to his buttons again. 'I'm sorry, Emerson. I can't do that for you. We split the brigade at Missionary Ridge and it worked well. We have too many regiments. I can't manage them all.' He turned back and smiled his young smile, patted Opdycke on his good arm. 'Hell, Emerson, you're more of a general than I'll ever be.'

*

Shire leaned his shoulder and his face against a pignut hickory tree, his only company. The roughness of the bark pricked his cheek and helped to keep him awake. Down in the damp mulch he had rucked out a scrape not fit to be a shallow grave. He was supposed to reside there, look out into the dark world as if he were an unsure fox cub, but if he lay down sleep would claim him, and that was tantamount to desertion. Standing kept him awake. He could see no further than the next tree so how could the Reb's see him? To his rear he could hear the company digging deeper rifle pits; in the darkness they sounded closer than he knew them to be. He'd have preferred that work, tired as he was. There would be company, maybe food.

Wick had sent them out alone rather than in pairs, so hidden twenty paces to his left was Tuck. Hubbard was out to his right. 'Solitude is good for the soul,' Wick had said. Shire was inclined to agree as far as the first hour was concerned, but after that, after the half-moon set and the darkness tightened around him, his soul needed company. Otherwise, Clara came calling. He recalled picket duty on the march to Chattanooga last year, sitting with Tuck, nipping whiskey and sharing stories in the sure knowledge there wasn't an enemy within twenty-five miles. Here, he would bet his last quarter against this hickory's roots, that in the woods downslope from him, there were a dozen or more Rebels within rifle range.

It was June they told him. He had no idea where he was. They'd not seen the railroad since Kingston. Their marching roads had become tracks and then barely more than two-man paths. Place-names occasionally bubbled out of overheard conversations when on the move: Dallas, New Hope, Pickett's Mill, but he'd not seen a single dwelling to attach to any of them. He'd not eaten since first light yesterday. His hands started to tremble, as they had on occasion the last few days. He clutched them together as if in deepest prayer but it was no use; he had to let it play out and pass in its own time. How would he load his rifle if this came on in battle?

The rush to reach here during daylight had been unorthodox. With Captain Elmer away, Lieutenant Rice had the company when it was ordered to skirmish forward and find the Rebel front. The snap, snap of rifle fire in the woods suggested that front wasn't so distant. Rice had more or less said, 'Every man for himself.' Shire had come down the slope in a series of tumbling runs from tree to tree, dodging bullets and heedless of his comrades until they had bunched at the low point behind a felled hemlock. From there they organized a reply to the enemy fire until it was suppressed enough for them to try the uphill leg. Once on top, the trees thinned and like everyone else Shire could see the enemy breastworks a couple of hundred paces away over the next Georgia gulch. They waited until dark to start digging the pits. Then Shire had been sent out to this lonely post.

He tried hard to suppress thoughts of the future; where was the return, given he might die tomorrow or the day after? But it had become more alluring than the past. Conceding ground, he allowed himself to think on *how* the future might be rather than *what* it might hold. He wondered how the horror could be put aside beyond the war. Would time and the weight of new experience eventually tell or would death and the war haunt him like it did poor Hubbard? At some deeper level he encountered a question about his will to go on. He felt he was the master of it, but it was there nonetheless.

An owl, borrowing its light from some secret store, ghosted out of nowhere and straight toward him. He froze and gripped his gun. The bird rose silently into the trees and was gone, leaving only a faster heartbeat behind. Once he settled, Shire was glad of the sighting; it punctured the night, brought him fully awake and reminded him of a dusky adolescent walk with Clara back in England. Here she was again. His faster heart ached and he laid his head back against the tree as if it was his mother.

'Are you communing with nature, Private Shire?'

The voice was sudden and close. He spun, levelled his

bayonet. 'Lieutenant,' he whispered, 'more warning if you please, sir.'

'I can hardly blow a whistle,' said Wick. He made no effort to keep his voice down.

'A quiet word then, and from a little further back. Our nerves are taut and our guns loaded.' Shire wondered if it would be such a bad thing. They would all be safer without Wick.

'Anything to report?'

'Nothing but a barn owl.'

Wick's tall face was on the very edge of the ambient light, like a mask pushed through pale cloth. No hat. 'Give me your canteen.'

'Sir?'

'There's too much whiskey in this regiment.'

Shire lifted the strap over his head and handed over his canteen. He'd hardly taint whiskey with Georgia creek-water. Anyway, the whiskey had dried up a week ago; not even Tuck could lay hands on any.

Wick pulled out the stopper and sniffed. He stepped closer, passed the canteen back. His smile bloomed out of the darkness. 'How is your soul, Private Shire? I've not seen you at our prayer meetings.'

'I attend the chaplain.'

'No more than choir practice.'

'It suffices for me.'

'Will it suffice when the Lord calls you to him? Singing is not repentance.' Wick was so loud; the Rebels would shoot at his voice.

Shire edged behind his tree. 'Music is communion enough for me.' He looked at that smile and imagined a single shot tearing it away. How many times had Wick thrown them in without a soldier's care? There had been men lost almost every day. Any private in the company would make a better lieutenant. 'I should be watching my front.'

'Turn then. I'll wait a while.'

Shire set his gun at port and turned his back. He sensed Wick take a step nearer.

'Do you have thoughts of slipping into the night?' Wick whispered. 'How easy it would be to give yourself to the enemy.'

It wouldn't be easy at all. There'd be a bayonet in your gut before you got the chance to give yourself to anyone. 'You mistake me, sir. Sometimes, I think deliberately so. This was my regiment before it was yours.'

'But my country.'

'Throw us out then, all of us. The Dutch, the Irish, all the Catholics too. Then you can have a pure army, a smaller one mind, but a pure one. Is that what you want?'

'I want to know my men are soldiers of God and ready to meet him.'

You might have heard less earnestness in a man's dying wish. He turned his head to look into Wick's eyes. He was as close as a lover, as benign as a saint. 'You're preoccupied with death,' Shire breathed, 'at least as it pertains to us. In all the fighting we've done, I've yet to see you fire your pistol.'

The smile broadened still more. 'I'll let you into a secret, Shire. It's never loaded. My duty is to send the men forward. Every death pays the price.'

'What price is that?'

'For the slavers' long reign. We're as guilty as they are.' He nodded into the night. 'We put our names to the document that condoned it. These long years we've been deaf to the cries, blind to the suffering. John Brown saw it, saw that we needed to pay.'

Shire felt his gut churn. 'You waited though, waited for the draft.'

'God's hand. I let Him decide. He chooses who He will take, but He won't take me. Not yet. He has work for me.'

Shire wondered at this man's deeper past, at what ill path had bent him this way. He felt Wick's cold hand wrap over his own that was gripping his rifle barrel. 'I see that He will take you soon, Shire. There will be a great slaughter. It would be better if you were prepared. None of us can be spared the shame.'

Shire couldn't help but ask himself the question. What was *his* own shame? Where was *his* guilt? The answer escaped from some vault inside and bled through him like cold sap. If he'd never come to America, to Clara, he could have looked after his father, at the very least been there when he had died. Instead, he'd abandoned him to follow a self-indulgent love that was hopeless from the very start.

'You know, don't you, Shire? We have all brought ourselves to this end.'

A single cannon sounded. How far away Shire couldn't tell but he jumped and Wick's hand tightened on his. Then came a distant roll of musketry followed by a cannonade that shook the earth and the trees. Shell arcs raced each other across the sky and burst so that the forest was cast again and again in silhouette, so bright that Shire could see the red Georgia clay heaped to hold the Rebel breastworks in place across the gulch. Flash upon flash was followed by the rolling thunder of cannon. He watched in awe, Wick holding onto him and seeming no more troubled than a harbor wall in a storm.

'He comes, Shire. What are we to His wrath?'

A bullet struck the hickory tree a hand-span from Shire's head. Ripped splinters stung his cheek. He pulled his hand from Wick and ducked behind the tree. Two, three other balls fizzed by – hot white streaks. Wick stayed out there, lifted his arms high. 'It is the rain of God.'

Shire stepped out and grabbed Wick, hauled him back toward the tree and they fell into the scrape. The cannonade ceased and it was dark and quiet once more. Shire was breathless and struggled to stand. A hissed whisper came out of the dark, 'Shire.' It was Sergeant Ocks. 'Where are you?'

'Here.'

Ocks' bulky form was briefly lit by a last flash of light. A final cannon boomed. Wick was back on his feet.

'Lieutenant Wick,' said Ocks. 'No need for you to be out here. Private Shire knows his business.'

'I'll leave him in your charge then, Sergeant.' And he was gone.

'You alright?'

'I'm not sure.'

'What was he about?'

Shire wiped himself down as if he had been touched by the devil. 'He was out collecting souls.'

Columbia, South Carolina – June 1864

The Columbia Dancing Band struck up a polka. Officers collected their partners and took to the floor. For a few blissful seconds, George Trenholm forgot the war. Reverend Porter strode toward him outside the fluid boundary of bouncing satin, narrow beard on his thin face, his hand preceding a warm smile. Trenholm removed his cigar and embraced his old friend. 'Thank you for the service, Toomer. They'll be missing you back in Charleston.'

'Not at all.' Porter leaned closer to be heard above the hubbub. 'What would a Trenholm wedding be without me?'

'Can we call it a Trenholm wedding? Emily is a Hazzard now.'

'We're in your home, aren't we?'

'Ashley Hall and Charleston will always be my home. De Greffin is a wartime necessity.'

Porter toasted the ballroom in general, its paneled ceiling, the low-slung chandeliers. 'I have to say, George, your necessity is any other man's dream.'

Trenholm cast an eye over the curled and bouncing hair, above the brushed uniforms, as if viewing De Greffin for the first time. It wouldn't do to host Emily's wedding anywhere less splendid. There were probably other houses more to his taste that he might have chosen if he'd had the time. De Greffin was intended as a bolt-hole for his family, a place of safety, but more and more it was used by friends made strays by the war. Owning a retreat inland was pragmatic: the Union Navy was too close to Charleston. De Greffin was well-placed. He could travel here to be with Anna when circumstances allowed, and from nearby Columbia he could take the train to Richmond or Atlanta, wherever he was needed most. He'd enlarged the estate, buying three and a half thousand acres. It made sense: no one knew what shape the future would take.

'It warms my heart to see the young people enjoying themselves,' said Porter, 'putting their cares down for a while.'

How long a while? One day? Trenholm wondered if he'd been right to let Emily marry when the enemy was at the gate. There was every chance she'd be a widow before the year was out. He looked for her on the dance floor but could find no white wedding dress among the kaleidoscope of hooped skirts.

'Did you ever wonder how ladies can dance so elegantly with dresses that heavy?' he said. 'They must have hindquarters like mules under all that cloth.'

'Ha. I don't think you should challenge them on that, but there's certainly a great weight of lace on show. It's a wonder in these times.'

Colonel Wright joined them with a face fit for inspecting troops rather than celebrating. Trenholm made the introductions. 'Toomer, this is young Colonel Wright who is in charge of the Atlanta defenses. Colonel, Reverend Porter is a long-time family friend and a shoe-in for marrying my daughters.'

'We were just admiring all the lace,' said Porter.

'There's a lot to admire,' said Wright. 'Wherever did you find everything?'

'In truth, this is a British wedding,' said Trenholm, thinking that Wright didn't look over-comfortable with the opulence. 'From the material for the bridal dress to the sugarplums. All shipped out of Liverpool. We can still get the occasional boat past the blockade. Lace and sugar, rifles and cannon.'

'But no copper, I imagine?'

'No. No copper. Though your invite isn't entirely social.' Trenholm looked pointedly at Porter, who failed to take the hint.

'Are you not nervous away from Atlanta,' Porter asked Wright, 'or are our defenses so well set?'

'We're moving what production we can out of the city, in case the worst should happen, some to Augusta, some to Columbia, so I am able to mix business with high society. General Johnston appears to have Sherman stalled around Marietta. Hopefully, he'll keep him there until after the election. And I have business with Mr Trenholm, I believe.'

Porter remained unmoved. Trenholm shared a smile with Wright. The polka ended in gloved applause.

'Sending campaigners home,' said Porter out of nowhere.

'Sir?'

'What Johnston is doing. I overheard someone calling them campaigners, the Union dead or wounded, that each one might persuade a family in Pennsylvania, Massachusetts or Ohio to vote for McClellan and peace. There are plenty being sent from Virginia. So sad.'

Trenholm doubted bereavement had that effect. Once a sacrifice was made, why undermine its intent? He scanned the room for his younger boy, Frank, who'd been promised a place under John Bell Hood's command. Frank had been itching to get the uniform in time for the wedding, but Trenholm had written to Hood and asked him to defer the enlistment a month or two yet. At the ceremony Frank had looked morose in his Sunday best.

From behind Trenholm a clump of bachelor officers attempted to start a chorus of 'Dixie' but abandoned it when the band began a slow waltz. It was a small miracle that he and Anna had not had to suffer the loss of Frank's elder brother or any of their sons-in-law: they were all under arms. Why risk Frank as well? 'I'm not sure the Yankees are as charitable as you, Toomer. You have a soft heart.' He nodded to the dance floor where he found Emily, waltzing with his newest in-law, their arms stretched to join above the wide bell of her wedding dress. 'Captain Hazard – my son gained today – his cavalry company has been defending the Florida and Georgia coast. They've been called to Atlanta in anticipation of Sherman's arrival. If McClellan doesn't win the Presidency, I doubt Columbia will be safe for long. I'll have to find my family yet another home. Toomer,' he put a hand on the reverend's shoulder, 'will you please excuse us?'

'Of course.'

Trenholm watched his friend disappear into the lace and the gray. He captured two glasses of wine and maneuvered Wright outside to the lawn, nodding and smiling to well-wishers all the way, but not stopping. They tactfully steered between couples enjoying the cool of the evening. The last band of red was dying in the sky to the west. Wright spoke as they walked. 'If my news is accurate, Mr Trenholm, you have more than one event to celebrate.'

It wasn't the first time he had heard that line today. 'Whatever can you mean, Colonel?'

'Is it a secret then?'

'If it is, then it's a poorly kept one. I daresay even Lincoln knows I've been asked to replace Memminger.'

'You've not accepted?'

Trenholm caught sight of Frank standing by the well, conversing with a brace of smiling cavalry officers.

'I have my interests to consider. Becoming Secretary of the Treasury isn't a part-time position, but my country comes first. I've asked for a little time. President Davis has indulged me.'

'I can't imagine anyone more qualified.'

'That's as maybe, but even the best doctor can't always save the patient. Our economy is lost unless the war ends. We have to hold Atlanta.'

'I wish I could say things have improved.'

'And the copper?'

'Stocks are lower than ever. There's nothing to be done.'

Trenholm looked again at Frank. He was taller than those cavalrymen. 'Alright then.' He pulled on his cigar. 'When you are back in Atlanta, I want you to get hold of some mules – two, three-hundred if you can. The best you can lay your hands on. None that are on the way out, they'll be worthless. Find some good men, men who are comfortable in the hills. They don't have to be army. And keep your ear open for a leader, someone that can act on his initiative. I know where we can acquire some copper. I'll come to Atlanta as soon as I can.'

'What have you in mind? I've scoured all of Georgia.'

Trenholm took a step closer to Wright and lowered his voice. 'Oh, this isn't anywhere as friendly as that. Not a constant supply mind, just a windfall that might keep you going until after the election. Or, as the good Reverend Porter put it, help us send a few more campaigners home.'

The Copper Road, Tennessee – June 1864

Clara crunched across the river-shingle circle at the bottom of Comrie's grand steps. Moses passed her bag up to George Barnes who carefully laid it in the back of the wagon. The canvas was down, there being nothing to cover. She reached to grip the cold metal seat-spring and hauled herself up. She wore the plainest brown cotton dress, practical for the journey. The day would soon get warm. Barnes moved his musket under the seat so she could take her place.

There was something holy about being out at this time of day. The moon was fading from gold to white and the sky graded from purple to the darkest blue. The forest still nothing but black.

'You get yourself settled, Mrs Ridgmont,' said Barnes. 'It'll be a long day.'

Clara had no issue with that. The days could be long as they liked if she could spend them away from Matlock. He was no doubt warm in his bed. He hadn't asked to come, not that she would have allowed it. Leaving Comrie empty any longer felt like an admission of defeat. If she could begin to find a new normal under the better banner of freedom, at least have the house set back as it once was, perhaps the 'staff' would settle and the slow bleed away from Comrie might stop.

The circle was just big enough for the triangle of the three wagons with four mules a piece. Moses passed up a basket of food that weighed more than Clara's bag. Mitilde must have been cooking late into the night.

'Are we set then?' asked Barnes.

A light showed at the top of the steps. Moses turned to look up. 'It's an early hour for our friend Matlock.'

Matlock was smartly dressed, stovepipe hat in hand, business-like, as if his day had an agenda. He put the lantern down but said nothing.

His meaning wasn't lost on Clara and she bent toward Moses. 'I grant him no authority. Do you hear, Moses? You take your own mind on matters until I'm back, you and Mitilde.'

'Don't fret, Miss. What's he gonna do all dressed up for the city. There ain't no city to speak of.' He smiled. 'We'll give him a heavy breakfast and put him back to bed.'

They couldn't have made it to Ducktown in a day if they'd started from town. Setting out from Comrie instead meant going out of the hills, cutting south and then in again once they hit the Copper Road, but it was still a shorter trip. When Clara hired him, Barnes said that the Halfway House, the long-used resting place for the copper haulers, was all closed up and there was no safe place to spend the night. They had to get to Ducktown by sundown.

By mid-morning they were back into the hills. The wagon jolted and swayed beneath her. The sun fought to get into the valley. Down to her right ran the Ocoee, as white and loud as she'd ever seen it. The wheel below her jarred in a pothole. She clutched at the seat, realized how jittery she was.

'My apologies, Ma'am,' said Barnes, bouncing in tune with the wagon and raising his voice above the water. 'The road is always worse after the winter. And now the turnpike company ain't collecting the tolls and seeing to the mending.'

Clara wondered how old he was. In past dealings she'd assumed he was well into his middle years but, sat close to him, it appeared there was a younger man beneath the whiskers and the worn wool coat. 'I'm fine,' she said, 'as a shareholder, I should apologize to you.'

Barnes chuckled. Laughter seemed to bubble up in him. 'I guess so, but we're the only souls to take tolls from. We'll just have to endure the road.'

Between them on the seat was a fiddle case. Clara had never known Barnes to be any more than arm's length from his instrument. It occurred to her that she'd never met Mrs Barnes and wondered if he held her so dear. He'd played at Clara's wedding, but well before then she'd danced to his tunes at the Halfway House. She'd seen him play on this very road on the day that she met him. Maybe it was the hoarded wisdom of the songs that made him seem older. She nodded at the fiddle. 'Would you care to play for the mules? I could hold the reins.' She leaned closer and whispered. 'They would never know.'

'I wouldn't like them to take advantage of you. They have a way of tellin' who's at the other end of the leather. Sad as I am to decline to play, I don't think we should draw any more attention to ourselves than we're obliged to.'

Clara considered that three wagons creaking their way along the only road for miles around would be hard to miss for anyone within fiddle range. She looked over her shoulder. The driver behind tipped his hat. He drove alone as did the youngest man who brought up the rear. They were all she could muster, three wagons and three men. She'd have used the wagon from Comrie as well but she no longer had her own team of mules. With the mines closed and the muleskinners out of work she'd expected more takers, but so many were away in the war. Those left were disinclined to take to the empty road. Too many dark stories crept out of the hills. She supposed Taylor's story – her story – was one of them.

She looked across the river – wide and busy tickling the shallow stones – up above the mossy boulders to the steep hills. Even in early summer they threw a cold shadow onto the road. 'Why did you decide to come, Mr Barnes? Almost everyone else turned me down.'

'Well,' Barnes said, 'you appeared set on it, and I wouldn't want you out here with people you didn't know. We have to claim the road back sometime. It's my living. People need to feel they can use it again. The sooner that's the way of things the sooner the mines and the Halfway will open up, but like I said when you asked me, it might have been safer to try this at the other end of the summer.'

Clara didn't mind the risk. Quite the reverse. When the furniture was safely back and Comrie the more presentable for it, then it would be down to her. Mr Barnes had his musket; the other drivers were armed too.

Three wagonloads were a start; she had a mental list of what she'd like to recover first. A second trip would be easier. More hauliers would come along once they saw it was safe. The four of them were pioneers as Barnes had said. Raht was a shareholder in the turnpike company too. She had written and told him she was going to recover the furniture, not waiting for an answer. She would write again and find out the names of the other shareholders, ask him what could be done. Men would be glad of the work.

The road pulled away from the river and into the deeper dark of the woods. The water quieted enough for her to hear the breeze brushing through the canopy. The road cornered and ended abruptly at a pontoon that edged into a stillwater back-creek that hosted a crop of duckweed from bank to bank. Clara recognized the spot. A copper bell, a bluer green than the duckweed, hung from a post beside the road. A rope left the pontoon and disappeared into the water. It could be seen rising again onto a flatboat across the other side. An oversized rat fought its way through the weed and raced up the far shore.

'Our luck's out,' said Barnes. 'Or at least young Calvin's is. Calvin,' he called to the last wagon. 'Get up here... and bring your swimming arms.'

Calvin came along, uncomplaining, and stripped to the waist, tall and skinny as a sapling. 'At least no one's cut the rope,' he said. 'Would you mind, Mrs Ridgmont? I don't want to get my pants wet.'

Clara wondered how he'd escaped uniform but twisted in her seat and faced away. She heard Calvin wade in and whisper, 'Sweet mother of God,' which she took to mean that even this far into June the forest air had failed to warm the water. She imagined what must have happened here last autumn. The ferryman, McGhee was found dead outside his house the same day that Taylor arrived at Comrie – the same day *he* had been killed. McGhee had a son, a simpleton. The boy had ferried her across more than once in the past, not an ounce of malice in him. His body had washed out of the hills a few days later, the attentions of the catfish not enough to hide the wide bullet wound in his chest, so Hany had ghoulishly related. No one said directly to Clara that it had been Taylor and his men; no one had to. Taylor had held a grudge against McGhee for refusing to sell his rights to the ferry to the turnpike company.

'Calvin's back and decent, ma'am,' said Barnes.

It took a good hour to get everyone over, the flatboat only big enough for one wagon at a time. Clara stayed in her seat when it was their turn, watched the duckweed lift with the rope as Barnes pulled them across. As they rode away Clara couldn't help but glance back. In her mind's eye, Taylor stood laughing in the road, pointed a rifle at her and took a slow, cruel shot.

Soon afterwards they approached the Halfway House. The scattering of homes along the road were all abandoned, their windows boarded up or broken. The fields beside the Halfway were unploughed and the grass gone to spears, weeds beginning to win out. The long, white wooden inn, which used to be the busiest place on the road – the meeting place, the dancing house – was empty and silent. The door hung loose from its hinges. Barnes stopped long enough to check inside and then set the door right as much as he could. 'I've played more times here than I care to remember,' he said, then nodded. 'It'll come again.' He climbed back up. 'Best we press on. It's empty, but there's a recent fire in the hearth. There might be no one to serve the whiskey, but someone's been using the inn. I don't care to think who.'

The road got worse as the day wore on. A mule brayed in alarm behind Clara and she turned to see. Calvin jumped from his seat, spade in hand. He chased after a twisting brown rattler and beat it until it was still. The mule wasn't bitten so far as they could tell. It became obvious they wouldn't make Ducktown before nightfall. Barnes gave the reins over to Clara. He lit a lantern and took it on ahead. The lead mule followed him like a faithful bloodhound. The road steepened and rose away from the river. Clara prepared herself for the remembered stink of sulfur, but there was only a hint of it out there in the dark. The trees died away and at last they reached the mines. By the light of Barnes' lamp she could make out a cold blast-furnace and then a quiet and empty millrace. They passed any number of houses boarded and empty just like the Halfway until they reached one with a single lit window. She heard a door open.

'Who the hell's there?' And then, 'Is that George Barnes? Glory hallelujah, it is. Did you bring your fiddle, George?

Comrie, Tennessee – June 1864

Matlock paused on the checkered stone floor in Comrie's hall and tried to hear above the summer rain that peppered the double-door. Somewhere above him was a rhythmical creaking. He could hear laughter. He wondered if someone, some couple, had stolen into the house, but there were so few beds beyond his own and Clara's. The rhythm was as steady as a clock pendulum; there was no passionate acceleration, which he seemed to recall was the way of things.

What could he do? Threaten to tell Clara? In her absence, each slave couple – as they once were – could abandon their huts and take a room for their own sordid pleasure; he could only listen or leave. Two wasted months in this wilderness and his authority counted for nothing.

He carried his sour coffee into the small hunting room, which had been allowed to keep its trophies and furniture. Before she'd left on her meaningless foray to the mines, he had goaded the elusive Clara as to why the room was left intact. Did the animals mounted on the walls or the worn leather chair hold some attachment to Taylor? He remembered her level gaze as she replied, 'I was expecting the house to be burned to the ground. It was a happy thought that this room would burn as well. Please make use of it if it keeps you from me.'

He sat. The decanters held no more than a residue of some brown spirit. There was nothing to commend the room except the absence of an echo, but he could still hear that persistent creaking. The rain driving against the window made him feel cold. He doubted that Mitilde or Moses would oblige with a fire.

Perhaps it really was time to write to the Duke; to tell him that his daughter was belligerent and closed to reason, that only if he came himself could she be brought to heel. It would be an admission of defeat; there was no denying that, but he could linger in New York and await the Duke's reply. It would be preferable to witnessing Clara's return. He imagined her hanging each picture like a permanent flag. Yet the Duke had never shown any inclination to come to Comrie. The likelihood was that if Matlock left without a sale, there would come a day of reckoning at Ridgmont. He couldn't hide the losses forever. It was maddening: forced to stay here with no power to affect an outcome.

He would write, but only to advise of his necessity to stay longer, and to ask the Duke to write by return and urge his daughter to sell. He gloomily calculated how long a reply might take. What if the Duke was away from Ridgmont? He roused himself to go to his room.

On passing through the parlor, he saw through the back-window two blacks, both men, racing through the rain toward the huts. He stepped closer. Women and children were spilling outside. The men rushed them away into the woods. He hurried to find Mitilde in the kitchen. Above him the creaking had stopped. There was no sound other than the rain. He opened the back door and a sudden wave of horsemen boiled around from the side of the house and filled the yard. He glanced through the open kitchen door. No Mitilde, no one at all. He took a step back into the cover of the hall and looked on. It was too late to run.

Riders in oilskin ponchos dismounted from steaming horses and into the shallow mud. Orders were given but no guns drawn. Some walked to the slave huts, others to the detached kitchen. They must be Union. He was safe if they were Union. The kepi hats on show were an indeterminate color in the rain. Why would the blacks run?

A big man strode directly at him, took off a cavalry hat with a soaked feathered tassel wrapped around one side. He called over his shoulder, 'Come find me when you're done.' He walked inside and past Matlock without breaking stride, a wealth of red hair tied at the back. There was nothing for Matlock to do but follow into the hall where the man tossed his gloves onto the stone bench. He untied his cape at the neck, sweeping it away to reveal a greatcoat that, though its buttons were dimmed and its cloth was stained, was distinctly gray.

Wanting to do nothing but run the other way, Matlock followed him into the parlor. His visitor surveyed the empty room and held his arms wide. 'Is there nowhere a man can take his ease in this house?'

'Through here.' Matlock led him into the hunting room where the soldier pointedly checked the empty decanters. Matlock stepped back as an evil looking long-barreled pistol was drawn from its holster only to be set carefully on the side-table. The soldier wearily sat down. For the first time, he looked Matlock in the eye. Matlock wished with all his heart that he'd taken Clara's advice and was on a ship bound for England. 'You have scared off the blacks,' he said, as evenly as he could, 'but there will be coffee in the kitchen.'

'They your blacks?'

'I was under the impression they're no longer anyone's.' It sounded a little bold, or a poor attempt at humor, but it was the best he could manage.

'I'm more interested in the coffee than the niggers.'

It was an excuse to leave. 'I'll do what I can.'

He clutched Matlock's forearm, wrapping it completely. 'This isn't your home, I'm guessing.'

'It's not. I'm from England.'

He let Matlock go. 'Whose home is it?'

'Lady Clara Ridgmont, widow to the late Taylor Ridgmont, a Confederate colonel.'

A second man entered the room and brushed past Matlock. 'Everyone's skedaddled, Captain Bowman, sir, 'cept this fella. Huts are mostly lived in. Kitchen and the smokehouse are well stocked. There's only the one horse.'

'Our friend here is from England.'

The new man turned to stare at Matlock as if he were a zoo exhibit. 'That so? Funny what you find, ain't it?'

'You reckon that counts as Union?'

'I reckon it might.'

'It counts as neutral,' said Matlock, more forcefully than he'd intended. 'I have nothing to do with the war.'

The rhythmic squeaking from upstairs started up again, all the louder now the rain outside had eased. Bowman's eyes rolled upward. 'Someone you want to tell us about?'

'I don't know who that is.'

'See to it, Grady. What's your name, Englishman?'

'Matlock. At your service, sir.'

'Ha! At my service. I'll be damned. What are you, Matlock, some sort of butler? But I have some sympathy with you. I'm only loosely associated with the war myself, these days.'

Matlock eyed the uniform.

Bowman looked down at himself. 'Oh, this? Call it sentimental. They don't make uniforms for irregulars. The thing is, Matlock, it's hard for anyone to divorce themselves entirely from the war. You know who General Wheeler is?'

'I don't.'

'You don't know much, do you? General Wheeler is in charge of the Confederate cavalry. I don't report to him, not strictly, being under my own steam, as you might say, but he's let me know he's happy for us to raid up this side of the Georgia line to see what we can find. He wants us to discourage any backsliding.'

'Backsliding?'

'Loyalty, Mr Matlock. It's everything in a civil war, wouldn't you say?'

'I have no loyalties here. I—'

'For example. Yesterday we were north a ways, up near Benton. We found two boys riding to town, on fine horses, mind. Once we persuaded them to talk, they conceded they'd heard of a cavalry company being mustered and were on their way to offer their services to the Union Army. Can you credit that? We took their horses and left them there to rest a while.' He patted his gun. 'You heard any such talk, Mr Matlock?'

A soldier trod mud into the hunting room to bring Bowman coffee. There were cries and squeals from upstairs.

'As I said, I don't concern myself with the war. I'm a man of business, here to help Lady Ridgmont.'

'Business, now. Well, I'm interested in business. Any that's to my advantage.' He drank his coffee and waved a hand for Matlock to tell more.

'I'm here to affect Comrie's sale.'

'Poor time for a sale, middle of a war an' all. Where is this… Lady?'

'She's gone up the Copper Road. Her furnishings were hidden in the hills before the Union came.'

'Where in the hills?'

'Ducktown. In the mines.'

Bowman stretched out a leg, rubbed some life into his

thigh. 'That's not much use to me. My men can't eat curtains and carpets. And I can't spend them. It's a careless lady who would head into these hills, though.'

There were footsteps and sobbing outside the door. 'Go on in.'

Hany was pushed into the room with Cele on her hip. She backed away as far as she could.

'Whoa,' said Bowman with a red whiskered smile. 'What have you found, Grady? Two pretty little things.'

'They were in the attic.'

'Anything of value up there?'

'Only if you're partial to a rockin' horse. Perdy one, though. The little girl was riding on it like she was charging the line.'

Cele was clamped to Hany who, eyes wide, stroked her child's hair. 'I's sorry, sirs. I didn't know you was here. Miss Clara, she doesn't know. We play when she's away. Ain't no harm done. I didn't know you was here.'

'Let her to me,' said Bowman. 'C'mon, now.'

Hany eased Cele to the floor. 'Go see the man.'

Cele walked slowly across the room.

Hany held busy hands to her chest. 'I don't think Miss Clara would mind, not really.'

Bowman lifted Cele onto his lap. 'Your mother sure can talk. Tell me, when you was riding the horse, was you Union or Rebel? You're not sure? No matter. There's a lot of that about nowadays. Say, Mr Matlock, this one is paler than her mother. You sure she's not one of yours?'

Matlock had never noticed before. He shared a look with Hany and, beyond his own fear and that in her eyes, he understood. She had no husband. The child must be Taylor's. 'I've not been here very long,' Matlock said.

Bowman relaxed back into his chair, leaving Cele to balance. 'New as you are to these hills,' he said, 'do you have anything you can tell me to my advantage? I mean, we will eat your hams an' all, but I confess, it's not all I'd hoped for, two pretty niggers and a "don't know" Englishman who's barely worth a bullet.' He reached for the gun.

Matlock cast about the room. The brown bear, jaw wide below glass eyes, provided no comfort. On the sideboard he spotted a single, worn, red cent. It was all he had to offer. 'Money,' he said.

'Where?'

'The bank, down in Cleveland.'

Bowman lightly circled his pistol barrel in the air. 'Not much use there.'

Hany wept into her hands.

'I can get it, if you help me.'

'You asking favors of the man pointing the gun? I'm impressed, Mr Matlock.'

Matlock guessed at the right number then doubled it. 'Six-thousand. I can get you six-thousand dollars.'

Bowman looked at Grady who whistled and tilted his hat back. 'Lot o' money, Captain.'

'A condemned man can promise what he likes, but I'll play along.' In mock politeness he said, 'What service is it you require of me?'

Matlock nodded at Hany. 'It would be better if she was to leave.'

'Don't draw out my time.'

Matlock glanced at Hany who was holding a finger to her lips, her eyes fixed on Cele.

'Lady Ridgmont,' he said, 'her interests are not aligned with mine.'

'Oh, my.'

'It's dangerous in the hills. If she were not to come back…'
Hany was still looking at Cele.

'… things would go better for me.'

'I think I want to hear you spell it out, Mr Matlock.'

'Very well.' Matlock drew himself up, or maybe he imagined he did. 'I need this sale. For my own sake. Lady Ridgmont is not of the same mind. Ride to the mines, Captain. Find her and dispose of her. I'll need ten days to get the money.'

Bowman cocked his gun beside Cele while he considered, then leveled it at Matlock. 'And come back to find you gone. Where's my security, Mr Englishman?'

'I could run,' admitted Matlock, 'but if you return and burn Comrie, I'm ruined anyway.' It was the simple truth.

'Ruined is better than dead.'

'Not always. A matter of trust then.'

'Amongst thieves… You and I. It's a strange brand of trust, is it not, Mr Matlock? What d'you think, Grady? Can we keep busy in these hills for ten days?'

'Hell, I'll stay all summer for that pay.'

Hany took a step away from the wall and stared at Matlock. 'What is it you're saying? You can't be saying that.'

'My apologies, Mr Matlock,' said Bowman. 'I see now it was a delicate matter.' He swung the gun onto Hany and shot her low in the chest. The blast in the small room was obscene. Hany was thrown back against the wall, then slid down to sit slouched like a rag-doll, blood pouring down her brown dress to pool in her lap. Her eyes closed, but the blood continued to flow.

Cele wailed. She jumped from Bowman and ran to her mother. Bowman clicked back the hammer once more and aimed at the child. Matlock closed his eyes and waited for the shot.

'Too much for you, Mr Matlock? Well, let's leave her to her own kind then.' He stood. 'Don't cross me Mr Matlock. I'll burn this place root cellar an' all and maybe find out a little about this Duke, write him a polite note about his loyal butler. We'll let you keep your one horse to collect the money. C'mon, Grady. We have an errand for our new English friend.'

Matlock was left with Cele. The child wailed and paddled in the blood, tugged at the sleeve of her mother's dress, turned her face to him and wordlessly asked for help. He edged around her and out into the hall, desperate for clean air. From the back door he watched Bowman's men mount up. Full sacks were tied to their saddles. One of them gnawed on a ham. The rain swept in again. Bowman lifted his hat like a gentleman and, with his men, splashed his way out of the yard.

Matlock left the house and hurried to saddle the horse. There was no reason to witness what would follow. He shook so much that he was still struggling to tie the girth when Moses appeared out of nowhere. Mitilde was close behind, naked dread in her eyes.

'I have to ride into town,' Matlock said, 'tell them what's happened.'

'What *has* happened?' asked Moses.

Mitilde raced into the house.

'She wouldn't stop talking,' Matlock said.

From inside came a run of screams, as if Mitilde was being beaten. Moses rushed to find her. Matlock finally secured the girth, climbed onto his horse and hurried away down the switch-back drive.

Brush Mountain, Georgia – June 1864

Tod had a moment to himself. There were any number of smooth exposed rocks among the trees. He chose one as a cool seat and took a pull of tepid earthy water from his canteen, glad not to see its color. Musket fire cracked randomly far away in the woods. It might as well be birdsong; you barely noticed it unless it stopped. He beat away a rash of storm flies.

Waddell and Morris were with the squad detailed to Tod for the day. He had sent them up the slope to find wood and build a pile for the regiment to draw on when it arrived. Every day the same job; this wasn't what he had returned for: to be in charge of the wood collectors. The tar sheets lay ready to pull over whatever they found; no sense in it getting a new soak when the storm broke.

He picked up Waddell's latest walking stick from beside the Mississippian's pack. That man didn't lack invention. This piece was as light in the hand as a riding crop and the shaft at its core as smooth and straight as a ramrod. Waddell had found some vine or dead and dried ivy stem then twisted it to fashion a snake that wound around and around. Tod turned the stick and the snake climbed. A band of copper announced the start of the handle; above it the serpent's body passed through the thickening wood. It arched back over itself so it was not unlike the guard to a saber. The snake's flattened pin-eyed face rested atop the stick like a dog's head in his master's lap. There was a smaller band of copper on the tip end too, no more than three-quarters of an inch. Where had

Waddell gotten the metal, and how in hell had he fashioned it to the stick?

His closer inspection was interrupted when the men returned. Waddell, dragging a large branch behind him, eyed Tod. 'You fixin' to make me an offer, Captain?'

Tod set the stick aside. 'Just admiring your craft.'

'My stock is low. That's the only one yet to find a home.'

Tod thought to ask about the copper banding but Waddell carried on. 'I been thinkin' maybe it's meant for me.'

'Your foot troubling you?'

'No. Truth is I'm quicker on nine toes than I was on ten.' He let go of the branch and took off his hat. 'I can't find new wood.'

'Truly? We've not been outside a forest for a week. And you've collected for the regiment every day.'

'You have to see the shape in it straight off. It's no good staring hopefully at the wood for hours on end. You either see it or you don't. And lately, I don't see it at all. It's gotten me spooked, like I've lost the gift. You reckon that happens when we're not long for this world?'

'That we lose our calling?' When did he last write? Not just requisitions or orders, actually sit down and write. 'You're tired like the rest of us. Something'll come to you.' Something low to the ground and evil, Tod thought.

He would have liked to help them chop the wood; the exertion might put him in a better frame of mind, but the major had warned him to keep a respectful distance between himself and the men. 'We're officers after all.' Instead he walked down to the breastworks. Here was another miracle fashioned from nowhere, not unlike Waddell's copper bands, and a repeating miracle at that. Every few days, somewhere away in the trees and out of knowledge the Yankees would extend their lines and threaten to flank the army. Then the order would come to pull back. Coming to expect it, Tod was ever ready and got a jump on the regiment if he could, or at least made sure he was in the van. They would march for a day, maybe less, and then be tucked behind a new set of works, like these in front of him, sprung new from the earth, as if Johnston had a pact with the devil.

He stepped down into the empty trench and up onto the firing step to peer out and down the slope. He lifted his arms as if he held a rifle and took a bead on an imaginary Yankee climbing up from below. Just once it would be good to fight, to line up shoulder to shoulder behind the thick safety of these high pine logs and let the Yankees spend their volleys chipping at the breastworks.

Their makers were long gone, the engineers and laborers spirited away and no doubt busy with saw and chisel constructing Johnston's next line.

He had come to see himself as merely associated with the regiment: behind the lines in a fight; ahead of them on a retreat; away from them collecting provisions. Once a week he might eat with the other officers. 'Here's the prodigal,' someone would call, if he found time to sit with them, a dual reference to the fact that they saw so little of him and to his long winter's journey back to the regiment. Was that all it had earnt him: a nickname that inferred that he'd been up to no good while he was away? If only they knew.

He should write home to Franklin. He'd heard that some letters were getting through; slowly no doubt and by circuitous and secret means. If his brother or father answered he might learn if Clara had ever paid a call, but what would he say about his duties? All the glory was owed to the fighting men, not the wood collectors. Nothing had come of his intervention at Resaca. He'd been passed over for the brigade quartermaster post after Linden's death, despite having the requisite rank. His half year's absence seemed to have moved him to the back of the queue.

There was movement to his front and for a moment, in the dregs of his imagination, he thought it was the enemy, but there was no Yankee blue, just a collection of faded brown. Colonel Shy rode at the head of the column. Tod climbed onto the breastworks as they passed below. He saluted. 'Afternoon, Colonel. There's good ground behind for settling in.'

Tired orders sounded down the column. The leading company wearily unslung their packs and dispersed among the trees.

'Thank you, Captain Carter, but we'll only stop to rest. Sherman's got a big swing on us this time and we're to fall back to the next line. It's ready and waiting, I'm told, at Kennesaw Mountain. I'll fetch up the scout and you can get on ahead.'

Ducktown, Tennessee – June 1864

An orange-tinged paste covered the outside of the window. It was thicker at the corners, arcs of collected grime and dust. The center was almost as opaque; Clara might as well have tried to look into a muddied puddle. She worked open the stiff catch. The sash window complained as she wrestled it upward and bent to look outside.

The view from her room in Tonkin's house was ample testament to why the windows were never cleaned. There was not a tree or a scrub-bush to be seen. The road they'd arrived on last night wound away through spoil heaps of raped red soil.

Ducktown, she knew, referred to the district rather than anything that could pass for a town. It was divided into divisions and each had its mine. Tonkin's home was in a village called Hiwassee, the only one nearby as far as she knew. She put her head out of the window to look at the neighboring houses and shacks. They showed no more sign of life than the ruined landscape. The air was far better than she remembered. The faint stink of sulfur pervaded but was not so overpowering. Gone was the smoke that used to thicken every breath and sting her eyes.

She heard movement below. Such a small house. She squeaked the window closed and made her way downstairs. The kitchen was empty but there were voices outside. She stepped onto the thin wooden porch. George Barnes and Tonkin struggled from their rockers.

'Mrs Ridgmont,' said Tonkin, tipping his hat. 'Let me get you some coffee.' He hurried inside.

'A fine day,' said Barnes.

How could any day be truly fine in this place? There was nothing more than high transparent strips of cloud to taint the blue sky, but even the frame of the heavens couldn't improve this sterile wasteland. Low rolling gray and a sweep of rain would suit it better. She looked beyond the closed dry-goods store and boarded up schoolhouse. There was a line of dormant roasting sheds on top of a barren hill. They'd all been smoking away last time she was here.

Tonkin returned with her coffee and apologized for the chipped cup. She'd met him on her first visit – a Cornishman, transplanted as she was. He had visited Comrie with Raht on occasion when they journeyed together between the mines and town. A strong looking man. She imagined mine work didn't suffer weaklings, but he looked a good deal older than she recalled, a lace of spidered veins across his cheeks and nose. She remembered his son had gone to fight with the Rebels at the start of the war. She would ask after him later; it wasn't a question for the start of the day. 'You aren't burning any ore, Mr Tonkin?'

'No, ma'am. We did last year when I had more men. It kept us busy, but after the Union took Chattanooga and Cleveland, there was no call for copper. More miners and families chose that time to leave. I sent my wife with them. I've only four men here. And you can't simply stop and start a furnace. We shut them all down and quit the roasting as well.'

'At least you can see the sky now.'

'There's that to it.'

'And breathe,' said Barnes. 'I never got used to the air.'

'I'd prefer the work,' said Tonkin.

Clara wondered how long it would take for Ducktown to revert to nature if the mines were abandoned, for the trees to creep in, for the soil to be of use. Or was it ruined until the end of time? 'You must miss your wife.'

'It's not the best place for a woman, just now.' He put his worn hands on the thin balustrade and gazed up at the sheds. 'She's with kin in Indiana, away from the war. I couldn't do my job right if I was worrying over her. Raht asked me to preserve the place. The equipment here'll be needed again one day.'

'I'm grateful to you for watching over my furniture.'

'It doesn't take a lot of guarding. It's in the Isabella. That mine isn't so deep and doesn't flood. There are a couple of natural chambers for storage which is uncommon here. Mrs Ridgmont, I'm glad you and George felt able to come but, truthfully, I would have talked against it.'

'We arrived safely.' She caught the glance that Tonkin shared with Barnes. 'Is there something more?'

Barnes tipped the dregs of his coffee over the rail. 'John – Mr Tonkin – was telling me some of the happenings. Ducktown might be empty but the hills ain't entirely. Some farms don't have a wagon or their mule's been stolen. Men are away or killed in the war. People ain't got no choice but to stay. There are deserters and shirkers clumped together and preying on the weak. To put it plain, there's been murder, ma'am. People I know. Sydney McLeod, Elam Stewart, Solomon Stansbury. All men that have danced to my bow, all killed not more than a few miles from this spot. And word don't always get out. I hate to think what these hills are hiding.'

'Has trouble come to the mines?'

'Some,' said Tonkin. 'We had a Yankee troop through in the fall. They were intent on burning up the place until I took their lieutenant aside and listed the shareholders that are Yankee generals. We got Confederate irregulars in the spring that robbed me of my horse. No matter that I have a son in gray. I argued that we were keeping the mines serviceable in case the Confederacy came to need them again, but with those kinda men loyalty don't extend beyond their horses' ears. Truth is, Mrs Ridgmont, I'm of a mind to come with you when you take the road back.'

Selfish as it was, Clara thought how that would leave Comrie's things unguarded. They couldn't pack everything on this one trip.

'Best we can do is be quick,' said Barnes. 'Could you write up a list, ma'am, of the things that matter? Then we can get to it.'

That wasn't what she had in mind at all.

'You sure you want to do this, Mrs Ridgmont?' Tonkin said yet again. 'If we bring up the wrong thing we can easily go back down. We're going to be at this all day.'

They were standing outside the shack that housed the mine-head. A narrow rail-track emerged between double doors and fed off down the slope to where a small, empty, wooden minecart rested by a spoil heap. Beside the shack a mule, not the fittest of its generation, stood ready by a whim to trudge its circle of sand and lower them into the Isabella mine. The animal's efforts turned a high drum via a crossbar connected to its harness. The drum, in turn, wound a taut and thick rope which stretched into the shack. 'I can't recall everything that was removed,' said Clara. If I come down, I can make the best choice. It will save time.'

That was all true enough. She didn't want to wait up here while assorted men brought her dresses or hats, some to keep, some to send back.

They were higher here. Down the hill were empty houses.

A dry wooden race, at least a hundred yards long and cradled by scaffolding, zig-zagged its way to a static waterwheel beside a cold blast furnace. On the neighboring hill stood the wooden church, abandoned and forlorn, as if it had taken its own vow of silence.

'George,' said Tonkin. 'Can you explain to Mrs Ridgmont what Mr Raht will do to me if he hears of this?'

Barnes was tuning his fiddle. 'Ain't my place to gainsay the lady. She's more gumption than me though. I've never minded hauling the copper, but lowering yourself into the earth, it's like knockin' at the devil's door.'

'Is it really so dangerous?' she asked.

'Well, no—'

'Then there's no need for Mr Raht to find out.'

Tonkin accepted defeat and held his hat out toward the shack. Clara led the way, following the narrow rail-track through the doors. Inside, enough sunlight filtered through a smeared window for Clara to see that the rope took turns around a smaller drum. It hooked onto a metal eye above a wooden cage large enough to walk a horse into. A cool breeze flowed out from the void around the edge of the cage. Tonkin lit a mine lamp. She belatedly noticed one of his men in the shadows. Outside she heard Barnes begin to play in earnest.

'You tend to that brake, Steffan,' said Tonkin. 'We have valuable cargo today.'

Clara ignored the clumsy compliment. She stepped into the cage and felt its sway. Boarding the sail ship in Southampton came to mind: another irrevocable step, a commitment. Tonkin joined her. Steffan eased the brake. To the creak of wood and rope, and the veiled and plaintive sound of George Barnes' fiddle, the ground rose up and swallowed them.

'It's not a deep mine,' said Tonkin. 'This is number one shaft. Not sixty feet.'

The cage was chest high and Clara gripped the edge.

Tonkin removed her hands. 'We rattle a bit in this shaft. Your piano is down below. It would be a shame if you lost your fingers. Brace in the corner. Like this.'

As the light from above died, the rock of the shaft borrowed the color of the lamp and shone yellow gray. She couldn't help but think of Orpheus. She hoped she would fare better.

'We called this stone gossan,' said Tonkin. 'It has some oxides but low grade. You usually find it above the ore proper. That's how we guess the ore's here.'

'You said this is number one shaft.' It was better to talk than watch the rock go by. 'There are more at this mine?'

'One other. It's shallower still. Other mines have more, but most of the work at the Isabella was done driving levels into the side of the hill. We sank the two shafts as it was the only way to reach the best ore.'

The cage struck hard and Clara almost fell. Tonkin shouted up the shaft. 'You could land us a little easier, Steffan.'

Steffan's voice echoed back as if he was close above them. 'Sorry, sir, ma'am.'

'Probably distracted by the fiddle playing. George will do that to you.' Tonkin hung the lamp on a hook in the wall. He picked up another from a row on the floor. There was a supply of matches and he lit the new lamp. She stepped out behind him onto a sandy, gritty floor and her steps echoed away down a passage. She tripped on a rail. There was a minecart just ahead like the one she'd seen above. It was no higher than her waist. Empty. The rails ran right up to the cage. Up above Barnes had moved onto a jig, the shaft multiplying him to a quartet. To her side was an oil-sheet pebbled with small stones and dirt. Underneath she found Comrie's squat square piano, resting like a tired dog in a hallway.

Tonkin stepped over with his new lamp. 'Seemed easiest to leave it here. Steffan can play a little. Sounds like a whole orchestra down here when he's in full flow.'

There was a folded camp-stool leaning on the wall next to a row of shovels and sledge-hammers. In her simple cotton dress she was pleasantly cool rather than cold. The sides of the tunnel were rough-hewn. For some reason she had expected something neater, smoother, like the inside of a vein. The ceiling was rib after rib of blue-black rock for as far as the light reached. There was a bloodlike taste in the damp air.

'It's not far.' Tonkin moved off, comfortably upright, with the new light. He left the other behind. Clara couldn't help but stoop with all the rock-weight above. She edged around the minecart and followed Tonkin and the sheen of the rails. There was an echoing drip, drip, out of time with Barnes. It was hard to tell, but she felt they were going gently downhill. They reached a junction. The rail split both ways. Tonkin took them to the right. The walls soon fell away and the lamplight climbed up to a higher roof.

On her left was a pile of what looked like loose rock, but it threw a dull metallic reflection, touched green and blue in places. It rose and spread until the heap was taller than Clara and stretched beyond the light.

'The other treasure,' said Tonkin. 'Smelted copper.'

Clara picked up a single piece, heavy as a full pail of water, at once pocked but smooth, like a rock at low tide.

'Most of it's from the early months of the war,' said Tonkin, 'when we were producing more than we could sell.

The rest is from when we had nothing better to do.'

'Why keep it down here?'

'That was Raht's idea. When the time comes to sell it, after the war, we wouldn't want to glut the market, but we could augment new production. It's not something he wants everyone to know. Your things are further on.'

They moved away from the copper heap and into another short tunnel that sloped gently down. The fiddle music died away to almost nothing. A short section of the ceiling was supported by timber. Until now, Clara hadn't noted its absence elsewhere. She tried not to fret over it. The tunnel opened into a second smaller chamber half full with boxes and assorted shapes covered by more oil sheets. Beneath one she found the smooth walnut wood of Comrie's dining table; here was the mirror from the parlor, the wall-clock, the chaise lounge. In her mind's eye she escaped the mine and saw Comrie as it would be: renewed, complete, ready for a new and better future.

It wasn't difficult to make choices. She tended toward the practical. Tables and chairs were needed; the chaise lounge was not. Curtains would keep Comrie cooler in summer and warmer in winter. She selected a few landscape paintings but left the portraits, pricked by the possibility that it was a family that she hadn't truly ever joined. There was a bed; she could take that, but it would leave much less room on the wagon for other things. They grouped a few lighter pieces to help Tonkin's memory and then he led her back to the shaft. There was no music now, only the drip, drip.

They stepped into the cage and Tonkin whistled up the shaft. There was no answer but the cage lifted away. Clara felt exhilarated to be rising up. It was as if she'd survived a shipwreck. They would take the furniture back; Comrie would turn a corner and face the future. She closed her eyes against the light as they broke the surface.

Steffan opened the cage but his face was nothing but fear. As he backed away, she saw a gun held to his head. There were two strangers in the shack. One spat tobacco juice and waved his pistol to encourage her and Tonkin out of the cage. The man lost patience, yanked her out and she was pushed through the doors into the sunlight. There was a sea of faces, beards, hats; men rimming the circle of the whim, horses behind them. She fixed on Barnes, his bow and fiddle held slack beside him, tears running freely. Before him was a body, a glut of blood soaking into the sand, almost touching the hooves of the mule. The name wouldn't come, obstructed by the horror. It was the young swimmer, from the ferry. Calvin, it was Calvin laying there, his still fingers at his skinny neck.

A red-bearded man, a big man, bent and wiped his knife in the sand and then on Calvin's trouser leg. He stood and smiled at Clara. 'He didn't want to join up.' Low laughter from the crowd. 'Boy that age should want to serve, don't you think?'

She couldn't find any words.

Tonkin spoke, his voice unreasonably calm. 'Are you regular army, Colonel?'

'I appreciate the flattery, I really do, but colonels are so distant, I find. Above the dirty work.' He sheathed his knife. 'I'm Captain Bowman. Who are you?'

'Tonkin. I look after the mines, keep them safe for the Confederacy. We're loyal, sir. My own son is serving.'

'Good. We could do with some loyal men. Who's your son with?'

'Nineteenth Tennessee. Second lieutenant.'

'Very commendable, Mr Tonkin, but we have to attend to those less faithful.' He waved a hand at the body.

The mule backed up, its hoof treading the blood. Clara tore her eyes away.

'That boy was from down in Bradley County,' said Tonkin. 'Union's taken hold there, turned his head. It's not that way here.'

'This fiddler...'

Barnes flinched as Bowman threw an arm around him.

'He tells me he's from Bradley too.'

'I can vouch for Mr Barnes.'

'I ain't asking for you to vouch for him.' Bowman left Barnes and walked to Clara. 'Just curious why he might be here? Is it on account of this lady perhaps? He bent down, put his hands on his thighs and pushed his coarse, red beard close to her face. 'Am I,' he said slowly, 'perchance... speaking to Lady Clara Ridgmont?'

'She's a guest of mine, Captain,' said Tonkin, 'and distressed. Best if I take her away?'

Bowman kept his stare on Clara but pointed an arm at Tonkin. 'Shut yer mouth.'

She forced herself not to turn her head, tilted it upward. 'I am Lady Ridgmont.'

'Huh,' Bowman smiled. 'You got the same purdy way of talking as your butler friend. You know, he ain't so fond of you.'

Clara reached back to England for all the arrogance she could muster. 'Are you in the habit of murdering young men for no reason?'

'Well now, I'd say that's one of those yes and no answers. Yes, I confess to being in the habit, but no, I always have my reasons. Some reasons are more profitable than others. Your friend Matlock tells me your things buried in this mine. I'd sure like to see that, pick out a keepsake or two. Grady,' he shouted.

'Captain?'

'You want to come on the tour? Mrs Ridgmont will be along and Mr Tonkin can lead the way.' Bowman grabbed and twisted Clara's arm, pulled her back toward the minehead. The circle of men broke up, some kicking their way into closed-up buildings nearby, breaking windows. Three men crowded Barnes and the other wagon driver. One pulled a pistol and barked at Barnes to play.

Inside she waited while Bowman looked over the workings – the drum, the brake. He cuffed Steffan and asked how old he was. Tonkin tried to talk again. Bowman struck him backhanded across the face.

The journey back down seemed slower. Grady leered at her the whole way. All she could think was that Calvin's death was down to her: she'd persuaded them to come into the hills. She'd been told it wasn't safe. Bowman was looking up the shaft. Tonkin held the lamp. In the half-light she caught a sideways look from him and he patted the air slowly to ask her to keep calm, to wait this out.

When they stepped into the tunnel, Bowman pulled back the sheet on the piano, tapped out a one fingered scale. The notes dissolved away into the dark. 'Reminds me of home,' he said. 'Ma's pride and joy. Our piano weren't so fine as this one. We should have brought your fiddler down, had ourselves a dance.'

As before, Tonkin hung the lamp and lit a second before leading them past the minecart and down the tunnel. Bowman filled the passage ahead of her. They passed the mound of copper without comment. At Comrie's pile, Bowman and Grady took more interest. They pulled away sheets, broke open crates.

'This is all heavy gear, Mrs Ridgmont,' said Bowman in

feigned disappointment, 'not much I could strap to a horse.'
He held up a portrait of Taylor's father.

'I could have told you that before we came down,'
she said.

'Well, we ain't in a hurry. Why don't you find me something
I might take? Something to help the cause.'

She tried to think what might placate him. 'There's a
silver teapot. Some china.'

'I'll take the silver.'

She had seen it earlier, but had to find it again, all the
while imagining Calvin's blood seeping down through the
earth above. Grady found a portrait and told Tonkin to bring
the light. It was of Taylor, painted when he was a newly made
colonel, before their wedding.

'Who's this fella?' asked Grady.

'My husband. Colonel Ridgmont. He was killed.'

'That's as well, Captain,' said Grady. 'Otherwise he'd
outrank you.'

'We're done with regular army. Hold him away from you.'

Bowman drew his pistol and shot Taylor through his
proud jaw. For a split second it was bright as day. The blast
sent Clara's hands to her ears. The bullet ricocheted off rock
and ceiling, went spinning around the chamber like some
demented firefly.

She hurried back to her task, found the teapot.

Bowman felt its weight in one hand and looked
appreciative. He raked through a box of china with his pistol.
'You lived a fine life, you and your colonel. Nice place you
had. I never saw the like in the hills. Would be a shame to
have to burn it.'

'Why would you do that? My husband was a Confederate.'

'Yet here you are consorting with turncoats, planning to

set up house again in the Union. Mr Matlock persuaded me against it, for now. There was some damage.' He placed a heavy hand on her shoulder in consolation. 'A slave. She had a young girl.'

'Hany?'

'I didn't trouble her for a name. We caught them playing in your attic on account of you being away. Thought you might appreciate us takin' a firm line on that?'

'What did you do?'

'Sad to say, I had to shoot her. Not the little girl though. That would have been harsh.'

The rock floor melted away and Clara sank to the ground.

'Don't take on so. Plenty of other niggers in the woods.' He tossed the teapot and caught it.

Bowman and Grady searched the boxes a while longer. If they took more things, Clara didn't notice or care. When they left, Tonkin held her weight and helped her to walk. They could hear Barnes playing above. It was a dancing reel but Clara could only hear sadness in the rhythm, desolation in the melody.

At the cage Bowman collected an evil looking spike from the row of tools. He took a lamp and said he would go up with Grady first. She was to wait with Tonkin. Bowman whistled up the shaft and smiled from within his lamp-lit red beard. 'We'll send it right back down.' The cage lifted away like the last ferry before winter.

Clara slumped to the floor and wept. Tonkin took the lamp from the hook and knelt beside her. 'That'll have to wait. Listen to me.' He put the lamp down and shook her. 'Listen to me! There ain't no reason for them to go up alone. If that cage comes back down the last thing we want to do is get inside.'

'But we can't stay here.'

'I doubt the killin's over. He has a cruel eye.'

'Is there another way out?'

'No, but they can't stay up there forever. Help me move this piano?'

'What for?'

'We need to put some weight in the cage, like it was us. The minecart ain't enough. Quickly.'

The fiddle sped up. She could hear whooping and hollering. The cage began rattling its way down to them. She made a guilty effort to put Hany aside. They removed the tarp sheet. The piano was on casters otherwise it would have been impossible. As it was, they had to move stones from under the wheels and navigate alongside the rails. The cage arrived plumb level with the floor. Tonkin opened it and stepped in, turned and strained to pull the piano inside. Clara pushed all she could and Tonkin edged back out to help. He closed the cage and whistled. The rope stretched and tightened and the load lifted away.

'We should back up. Hurry. Behind the minecart.'

The fiddle stopped playing. Two shots echoed down the shaft, then a third which was louder. There was distant laughing. Bowman's voice reached down to them like a god. 'Matlock sends his compliments, Mrs Ridgmont.' There was a sudden rising clatter like a train derailing through a tunnel, discordant chords from the piano, louder and louder, a sudden rush of air and a final breath-stopping crash. Wood and wire whipped through the air above them and they cowered together. The minecart shunted on the rails and pressed against her. They only uncurled once the last notes of disaster died away. Clara was swamped by dust. Tonkin stood and turned down the light. 'Follow me,' he whispered.

Kennesaw Mountain, Georgia – June 26th 1864

Opdycke stroked Barney's forehead then stepped away to bend and rip a tuft of grass. It could almost be called quiet in this pasture. 'Do you like this spot, my friend?' Barney was pegged out only a minute away from the regiment, but it was so peaceful, only the snap and echo of random rifle shots chasing through the forest. The fading evening lent a strange clarity to the trees; the scarcer the light the more precious they became.

He fed Barney the grass from a flattened hand and wondered if he should ride him tomorrow. Lately he'd taken to using Tempest more and more. Since the wound in his arm, it felt like the shared charm that he and Barney had worn all last year was gone. He feared to lose the horse more than himself. That shouldn't be true. A trick of the mind perhaps, to place the care due for himself into the horse. What would Lucy say?

The precise ground for the attack was unknown. They had pressed as close to the Rebel pickets as they could. Yesterday, he had gone as far forward as he dared with Harker and his staff officers. Through their field glasses they could pick out cannon on the heights, but the forest before them was impenetrable. It would be no different to what they'd become accustomed to of late: full of scrub and fallen trees, wide and wet ditches despite the let up in the rain and the warmth of the last few days. Exactly where the Rebel works were, he didn't know; no one on the Union side did. For once, would it be better to command on foot? Except now he had three regiments to watch over across a broad front.

He was taking his orders as much from Newton as he was from Harker. The division commander had chosen Opdycke to lead the heavy skirmish line ahead of the three brigades. That had scuttled Harker's plans to give Opdycke half of his own command. Instead, Newton had given him the 57th Indiana from Wagner's brigade and the 36th Illinois from Kimball's. Opdycke had insisted on taking the 125th from Harker. He didn't choose them on a point of honor, so that his own men might be given the most dangerous position. It was more a matter of trust. Depleted as they were, down to half the number that had climbed Rocky Face Ridge over six weeks ago, he knew they would do whatever he asked. And he would be able to keep an eye on Colonel Moore.

No, it was too wide a front to cover effectively on foot. He checked Barney's hooves, lifted them one at a time in the hope of a cut or a sore, anything that would allow him to leave the old boy behind.

It was apparent from Harker and Newton that this assault was born of Sherman's frustration. Before the recent dry spell, the long rains had slowed the Union Army and then stopped it altogether. This time, it was proving hard to get around Johnston who'd spread himself along the base of Kennesaw Mountain and the lesser hills that tended to the south. Somehow the Rebels had dragged cannon up on those heights and sent down their shells at intervals to deter the Union from pressing ever closer. It was obvious to Opdycke that they were holding back, saving their true firepower for a major attack. Tomorrow they were going to get one.

Sherman must believe the Rebel lines were stretched thin. Maybe he was right. A broad push on all fronts and the Union Army might find a weak point somewhere and then the great game would be over, Johnston's army destroyed. If only they knew where the weak point was. Johnston had been buttoned up as tight as a major general's jacket since the first shot of the campaign.

He put down a perfectly healthy fetlock. 'Fact is, Barney,' he said, 'we should all be resting.' It was true enough. Admire Harker as he did, Opdycke suspected the young general had been instrumental in ensuring his own brigade was at the sharp end, at the head of the strongest attack along the whole front, but the men were tired, overdue a break. They'd been chewed up in a fight only a few days ago: three killed, thirteen wounded. Lieutenant Collins had been only a few steps away. The shell fragments had passed right through him. His torso offered no more resistance than thin soup. He'd been left standing a second or two beyond his life's end. Opdycke had a score of such memories to keep at bay.

Yesterday, the brigade had been sent to the rear. Here at last was their due, a chance to wash, a chance to sleep a full night. Yet before the first hour was up, they were summarily sent back to the front to replace Stanley's men, who'd already been rested. It must have been Harker's doing. Newton hadn't said as much, but there was no other way of accounting for it.

Harker's command wasn't circumspect enough; it was one of the hardest things to master. You had to lead men by example, reckless example on occasion, but a good general knew when the odds were too long, the ground too poor, or his troops too damn tired. Harker didn't see it; not for his troops and not for himself. The mane of his white horse was burned by a shell the same day that Collins was killed. Harker had laughed it away. 'A miss is as good as a mile,' he'd said. Bravado was all well and good, but not when it endangered Opdycke's regiment. Maybe he should speak to

237

Harker directly; he'd done it often enough with other men, regardless of rank. Why couldn't he bring himself to do the same with Harker? Perhaps because it would be like scolding a favorite child.

He was hungry. The sun had died behind the trees and a blood-orange sky burned above the hills. 'I'm going to need you tomorrow,' he said, patting Barney's shoulder. 'The boys will want their lucky charm. Let's get through this next fight, me and you. He'll have to let us rest after this one. I'll talk with him then.'

Kennesaw Mountain, Georgia – June 27th 1864

The bugle invaded Shire's fragile dream, one he'd only settled into minutes before. He snatched at slippery images and thereby lost most all of them. Fragments remained: a row of worn boots, muddied and dusty but lined up like they were on parade without their owners. His father had been there. In his schoolmaster's voice, he had told Shire to count the boots by chalking a slate, but Shire hadn't known which pair to start with and whether a pair equaled one or two.

In the shallow scrape that passed for his bed he rolled onto his back, staying tightly wrapped in his blanket. It wasn't over cold; the blanket was to keep out the bugs. 'What time is it?' he asked the dark.

'Does it matter?' came the reply.

Shire sat up and brushed the night grit from his hair. He unstuck tired eyes and watched a burning splinter magically lift from the dull glow of the fire. The light bloomed. A candle. Where had Tuck acquired that? His friend squinted. He looked old, haggard. How must *he* look to Tuck?

'When did time last hold any meaning for us?' Tuck said. 'The trumpet sounds and we get up. It bears no relation to the old order of things. Seein' where that half-moon is pokin' through the trees, I'd say we're a couple of hours from dawn. Sherman must have plans for us today.'

Shire knew the showdown was coming. Everyone did. Yesterday, there had been a surfeit of colonels and generals moving in their own private cohorts with their field glasses ever in their hands. They were given a full ration last night, the first in weeks. There were sixty rounds stored in Shire's cartridge box. It hung on the wigwam of rifles that leaned against each other like tired old men.

A coughing Hubbard crept past Shire on all fours and fed the fire. Mason shuffled by and on into the trees. Shire heard his wet stream. Sergeant Ocks, buttoned up and booted, marched by at pace calling, 'Breakfast and light marching order. Quick about it.'

'Hey, Hubbard,' said Tuck, 'boil some water.'

'What for?' said Mason, returning and pulling his braces over his shoulders. 'We got nothing but crackers and dried beef.'

'Coffee,' whispered Tuck.

Shire felt a burst of excitement at the very word. Mason hunkered down between them. 'Truly? I ain't so much as smelt coffee in a week.'

Tuck produced a scrunched paper bag that looked like it held nothing at all.

'Where did you get it?' Shire asked.

'Humphries in C company got his canteen shot through, but the quartermaster was clean out. Humphries didn't have a dime but he had half a silver dollar that was his charm.' Tuck took his rifle from the wigwam and detached the bayonet. 'A man can't go into a fight without water, you might as well eat sawdust, so I told him I knew Westerman in the 64th. He has their quartermaster in his pocket.' He tipped the beans into a skillet and began grinding them with the bayonet socket. 'Westerman's a good trader, almost as good as me. Broken coin or not, it was good for the coffee as well as the canteen.'

'Humphries didn't oughta fight without his charm,' said Hubbard from the fire.

'At least he won't die of thirst.'

When Shire stepped into line a while later there was still no sign of the dawn. The coffee was a tonic but not much to set against the day. They marched into the dark. The collective stink of the men kept pace. Shire knew he was making his own contribution. Yesterday it had looked like they were to be rested and would get their first chance in weeks to clean and lay up, but they were turned around and pushed back toward the front before they had time to cook a meal. Mason had said that it would be best to get the big fight over with just so those who stayed earthbound could get a wash. There was more to it than that. Mason wasn't the only one wishing on a fight. Shire felt the same senseless logic as everyone else. After weeks of rain, the skin on his hands had begun to turn white and peel and was only now starting to heal. The overdue Georgia sun had been welcome at first but he'd since baked and blistered inside his jacket and his boots. He was tired of marching through this endless forest, his nerves stretched taut by the shell bursts and the bullets that grazed the warm air. 'Bring on the fight,' was the mumbled refrain in the regiment. 'Bring on the fight then let us rest.'

He was sweating though the sun was not yet up. He couldn't sense how long they marched, but eventually the moon went down in the west. They stepped into a cool mist that had settled into the trees and held the first luminous hint of dawn. For once his mind stretched beyond the war, reached out for some safe unknown home. He imagined himself a teacher again; how wholly peaceful a pursuit that seemed: to rise at the same time each day, go to common ground and simply talk, encourage, nurture. Where that might happen, he didn't know. He was never one for the big cities. Out west perhaps, a prairie town. Then he'd truly be an American by default. That one decision, to come to Clara's aid, would have redefined him utterly. He cut off his line of thought when he visioned Clara on a swept porch, smiling, her hand on the head of a young girl. Why should such hopes return to taunt him now, at the dawn of such a day as this? He wasn't that man, not today. Today he was a soldier, grim and dour, brave and terrified.

They passed regiments getting into order, overtook another that had been made to stand off the forest road to allow them to pass. This was more than just Harker's brigade moving. The whole army was making ready.

What if he took a wound again? Beyond the army hospital he had no refuge and couldn't imagine returning to Clara's charity. He wished that he'd stayed with her on that night, known *that* comfort at least. What if he lost an arm or a leg? It was common enough. He pictured himself sat on a muddy boardwalk, leaning against a saloon wall with his hat open for cents and dimes.

He side-stepped out of line to relieve himself then hurried to regain his place. He overtook Wick in the ethereal light as if brushing past death. That was the most likely future of all. That the war would end soon but that Shire would end sooner; today, perhaps. The thought wasn't as full of fear as it should be. The idea that the future was a simple transition, that the marching would stop, that he would hear one last bullet and then no more. Clara might receive a letter from the Colonel and eventually put him from her mind altogether. Then he would just be one more dead soldier and there would be no need to trouble over his opaque future.

The light was coming on, but the mist was so dense that men twenty paces ahead were no more than gray spirits, moving in and out of the world. The Colonel rode by so close on Barney that Shire could have stroked the horse's flanks. They were ordered to halt and then to fall out and rest. Shire unslung his canteen and followed Tuck. Wick was suddenly before him, eyes mad and shining, smile beatific.

'Do you sense it, Shire? God is among us. *To me belongeth vengeance, and recompense; their foot shall slide in due time: for the day of their calamity is at hand, and the things that shall come upon them make haste.*'

*

Tod followed Colonel Shy in the chill mist, waiting for his moment. The Colonel, buttoned up, beard trimmed to a point, was inspecting the 20th Tennessee's works and, Tod thought, was taking his time about it. Shy talked to men directly, dispensed plugs of tobacco. More than once he accepted a mug of coffee, no doubt awful and made from many-time-beans. He didn't complain. He looked out over the head-log and across the killing ground to the trees and the men looked with him. 'They will come today,' he said. 'I can feel it.'

Tod could feel it too. It made sense. The weather had dried up, the Union army had closed in tight to their lines and, only days ago, General Hood had checked a move around the left wing. If ever Sherman was going to try a head down, straight on assault, it would be now. And this time, Tod didn't want to be in the back row.

These were the best entrenchments he'd yet seen. Long stripped logs held in place by solid posts on the near side with a thick sloping rampart on the other. Clean and fresh wood, the smell of a newly built barn. Shy moved through a communication trench to glad-hand the next squad. Tod rehearsed his argument. *We are well set, sir*, he would say. *All the men are provisioned with forty rounds. There are ammunition boxes behind each company should they need more. Rations have been distributed and canteens filled. Water butts are placed next to the ammunition. The regimental wagons are to the rear and well situated to get onto the Dallas Road should we need to pull back. I have spoken with every company captain and they need nothing more. That being so, sir,* he would finish, *I formally request permission to take my place in these works with the men.* He'd even found himself a rifle.

What he was less inclined to say was, *I have to fight, sir. This Amish fella I met in Pennsylvania, name of Luther, he's living in my head and whispering thoughts of peace. If I don't fight this time, well, sir, I might just come to think myself a coward.*

He fully expected Shy to push back. *I can't spare you, Captain Carter. I need you behind the lines to cover all eventualities.*

Shy climbed out of the trench and acknowledged Tod. 'What is it Carter? You've been idling close to me like you want to marry my daughter.'

Tod took a breath. 'I wanted to report, sir. We are well set—'

'Colonel!' A call from up the hill. A staff officer from brigade walked down toward them.

Tod hurried on. 'The men are provisioned with forty rounds—'

Shy straight-armed him. 'A moment, Carter.'

'We've been asked for help,' said the staffer. 'Up the line a way. Our batteries on the heights, they don't have enough shells for a long exchange and it's the devil's own job to carry them up there. There's no road, barely a path. They had to drag the cannon up there by hand in the first place.'

'What do they want me to do?'

'The General's asking, if there's no sign of movement to your front, can you spare half a company?'

Shy looked irritated. 'It's quiet now, but that's not how I see the day playing out.'

'I guess the gunners are thinking the same, sir. Better lettin' the cannon kill some Yankees before they hit our lines.'

'Is this an order or an enquiry?'

'It's a request, sir.'

'Goddammit.'

Tod tried to melt behind a tree.

'Captain Carter, I believe you were about to tell me how you've got everything squared away. Is that right?'

'Well, sir, I—'

'Pick twelve men from Company E who look fit enough to do some climbing.'

Tod turned and swore. Luther had won again.

*

General Newton led Opdycke away by his good arm; away from Barney and away from the sweat of the men. Opdycke sensed a hundred anxious eyes following them. Newton held on to him. 'It will be heavy work,' he said. 'Your three regiments of skirmishers need to clear the front for the attacking columns.'

Opdycke took in the order but his mind held a second thread: how much Newton looked born to be a general. His barrel chest and strong bearded jaw would sit easily on a bronze statue one day. Newton was fighting against his home state: Virginia. Opdycke admired that, it took a particular type of courage but, no matter how unfair, it was impossible to dismiss every last doubt.

'Go smack up to the Rebel works, pass over them if you can.'

That got Opdycke's full attention. 'You want me to attack without the column, sir? Not wait for them?' These were harsh orders. Where in this war had a line of skirmishers taken entrenched positions?

'Use your experience, Colonel. I have no idea what you'll hit. Judge the ground, judge the defenses. If you have to wait on the main effort, so be it, but if the columns are knocked to pieces and can't get up, you must protect the withdrawal.'

Opdycke's heart fluttered. This was ample latitude; Newton was showing real trust.

Harker ghosted out of the mist on his white horse and rode over to them, reigning in more harshly than was needed. Opdycke felt he'd been caught cheating; taking orders from Newton rather than Harker, but that was the way Newton had things organized.

'It would be good to attack soon, General,' said Harker, 'under the cover of the mist.' His horse sawed back and forth beneath him.

Newton got out his timepiece. Opdycke read it upside down despite the slight shake in the general's hand. 'It's seven thirty,' Newton said. 'We're to wait until eight and go in with the whole front.'

Harker looked uneasy, Opdycke thought. And why not, the day he'd wanted had arrived. His whole brigade would be thrown in. Compared to Newton, Harker was a work in progress – only twenty-six. In fifteen or twenty years, when the boyish look in his eyes died away, when his smooth brow took on some ruts and ridges and his sideburns a wisp or two of gray, then he might look the general. Today he looked more like a boy soldier trying on his father's uniform.

'Are your men in position?' asked Newton.

'There's little space to form.'

'But you are in column of division as ordered?'

'We are, but my front is narrow, only two companies wide.' Harker had complained to Opdycke concerning the formation, how the regiments would be closed up one behind the other. It was dated thinking, Harker had said; a battering ram that once moving forced on the front ranks. It would be hard to maintain control. Opdycke considered how his three regiments would be ahead of the three brigades; *three* battering rams.

Newton waved to a staff officer to bring his horse. 'Go to it, gentlemen. Talk with your officers, talk with your men.'

Harker and his brigade commanders had a hard place for sure, and the Rebels held the rock. Opdycke was in between.

*

Shire sat on the grass, tired from the early start and the marching, tired from the accumulation of such days as this. Nearby the captains clumped around Colonel Moore. The sun was up somewhere and, judging by the incandescence of the mist, soon to show itself.

Tuck lay beside him. 'You think our future wellbeing may be swaying this way and that in the little muddle over there?'

'Why couldn't they tell us last night what we're about?' said Mason. 'You can't help feeling they're only now making up their mind.'

'We're always the last to know,' said Shire.

'Maybe that's as it should be,' said Tuck. 'A man doesn't sleep any the better for knowing the shape of the next day, 'specially not given the shape they been takin' of late.'

Captain Elmer walked toward Company B like every step was a new effort for him. Shire and Tuck stood. Men fell into line. 'He has a face on him like Noah when it started to spit,' said Tuck.

Elmer took a breath, straightened his back. 'We're skirmishers today,' he said, 'clearing the front. We're to get right into the enemy works if we can, create confusion while the brigade comes up.'

'Dear Lord above.' The thought spilled from Shire.

Men crossed themselves, some took a knee. First Lieutenant Rice, his usual unkempt self, took off his hat and scratched the back of his head. 'Pretty severe orders, Captain.'

'The day has the regiment's name on it for sure,' said Elmer.

'You want to detail someone to guard the baggage?' asked Rice.

Elmer cast his eye over the men but settled on no one. 'You see to it.' He walked away.

Rice tried to fix his collar button but gave up and turned to the men. 'Any volunteers?'

Shire held his head up the same as everyone else, met Rice's gaze steadily when it passed to him. His deserter tag had never entirely faded; he was damned if he'd be left behind today. Cleves took a step forward just as a whip cracked out in the mist. Hubbard jumped like it was meant for him.

'Hubbard,' said Rice. 'You'll stay with the packs.'

'No.' It was Wick. 'Not today. He can't be spared.'

Hubbard and Wick glanced at each other. Shire wondered what passed between them.

Rice stepped close to Wick. 'It may prove to be our last day, Lieutenant, but you will call me *Sir* on God's earth. I may settle for Mr Rice in the hereafter.'

Wick smiled. 'His squad is so small… sir. Why not Denton? He's the oldest.'

'Alright, let's angle it that way.'

Denton made to protest but Rice forestalled him. 'Pile your packs by Denton, men. Denton.'

'Sir?'

'When we go to the front, you leave these packs a short while.' Rice spoke loudly. 'Follow us up. When we go in, it looks like we'll have some open ground to cover. If I come back, I'll want to know the name of the tailing man. You understand?'

'Yes, sir.'

Rice pointed a finger. 'It had better not be you, Wick.'

Shire put down his pack, suddenly caring all the more for it. He wondered if he would ever shoulder it again. He checked his cartridge and cap boxes were securely attached to his belt, tied and retied his boots. He felt a sudden warmth on his cheek as the sun won through the mist. A light breeze lifted the mantle away. The hills and trees were revealed before them across two hundred yards of open ground. Shots snapped from the shadow of the forest and a ball slapped into the pile of packs. Over by Colonel Moore, Ephraim Evans, a lieutenant in company D, fell like he'd been chin struck. Union rifle pits, fifty yards ahead, opened up on the trees.

'Form up! Form up!' shouted Moore and the captains. 'Advance to the pits.'

There were detonations high on the hill. Before Shire could look for the smoke, shells tore in above them and exploded. Men and horses scattered. Shire bent, held an arm across his head as clods of wet earth fell around him. He gripped his rifle tight and hurried into line, eager to move out of the clearing before the Rebel battery reloaded. Union cannon roared from behind; angry, indignant. Moore screamed and waved them on. Opdycke was there on Barney, sword held high, cantering along their front. Tuck and Mason were by Shire's side. He tilted his head as if heading into a winter storm and stepped forward.

*

Tod shifted the weight of his burden. The longer tipped shells were easier than the rounded ones he'd carried until now. It was the same weight, but he could hold it close to his chest like a day-old baby. This was his fourth climb. He wondered how many more he could make.

An hour back, at the foot of the hill they'd met another dozen men pulled from the 37th Georgia. They'd decided to make a game of it: which team could move the most shells up to the guns. The Georgian lieutenant clearly wasn't a quartermaster as he'd foolishly tried to organize his men to work together and carry whole boxes. Twelve shells a box; twelve pounds a shell. And it was a steep slope. Even with the rope handles, it was awkward to get the four men needed onto one box. While the Georgian's struggled and cursed, Tod had his men take one shell each. The Georgians eventually followed suit but were well behind on the count.

Despite his earlier misgivings, he was enjoying this. It wasn't the same as being at the front but, so far as he could tell, there'd been no ground attack yet and this task served a purpose.

There was no sense trying to run. He'd be down on the leaves and gasping out the warming forest air before he was half way up. Instead he leaned his weight into the slope and took short steps, moved back and forth across the hill between the trees. His men passed him on their way back down.

'Slow down, Captain Carter,' one said. 'You're making us look slovenly.'

'Just keep ahead of Georgia,' he called, 'and take some water before you start up again.'

Halfway to the guns his thighs began to burn. He set down the shell and took a moment. The Georgians hurried on down and Tod lifted his near empty canteen and his smile to salute them. When he started up again, it got more open. He had to thread his way between great smoothed gray outcrops. He was up out of the mist and it was all blue sky above.

A cannon fired close above him, so thunderous it made him slip against a rock. He steadied himself with one hand and held tight to the shell. More shots followed at quick even intervals: two, three, four. His route took him below the battery. He put the shell down again and laughed through the shock. Below him the mist lifted away in great tears and dissolved. The forest canopy emerged fresh and green, suspicious of nothing more than a hot summer's day. In places there was open ground where he could see ranks of blue. *Many* ranks of blue. The salvo had overshot, but men and horses scattered for cover. More and more cannon fired from further up the line, to the north where the high double peak of Kennesaw Mountain was dotted with puffs of white smoke. How in the hell had his army gotten cannon up there? He was glad his was a smaller hill. He hefted the shell again, assured it was going to be put to good use.

As the path took him around behind the battery, the cannon all fired again and he watched the shells arc away and fall. The artillery officer had them depositing the shells backward of another tall smooth rock where a Yankee reply couldn't reach them. There were two new piles: three dozen courtesy of Tennessee and almost as many from Georgia to add to those already up. A battery of four firing a round a minute would eat these up in no time. Aside from the trouble of getting shells up here, he'd heard talk of ordinance shortages. They couldn't fire all day. Likely they were taking the chance to catch the enemy in the open as the mist cleared. The guns fired again, the detonations rebounding off the stone outcrops. He decided to wait behind the rock for his team to get up. He could go back down with them. He took off his jacket and pulled out his shirt, sweat cold across his back.

He heard his men before he saw them, their panting chorus audible before the path rounded the corner and crested the rise. Kirkland was in front and smiled when he saw Tod. 'Look boys,' he said. 'Captain Carter's spent at last.' More faces bobbed up behind. Each man carried his load as if delivering tribute to the gods. 'The Georgia boys will catch him if we don't roll him back down.'

Kirkland vanished when the shell tore home; as if he'd been taken up. The fuse was late. There was a long, empty half-second of nothing before the explosion. Tod was thrown against the rock as if he were a straw-filled scarecrow. The back of his head struck hard. What time passed, he couldn't say. He discovered himself sat like a drunkard. The first thing he saw was a gunner collecting another round. The man didn't spare him a look. He felt the back of his head. There was blood, but not much. He looked toward where his men had been and there was no one standing, one was on all fours. Tod struggled to rise, his legs next to useless. The Georgians arrived. They put down their shells to help the wounded, brought them over to Tod behind the safety of the rock. Another Union shell flew above them to explode on the leeside of the hill. Campbell had a deep gash that cut clean through one eye. Lawrence was trailing a leg held in place by nothing more than a strip of Confederate cotton.

Unsteadily, Tod looked for his jacket. It was too much effort to bend and collect it from the ground. 'More shells,' he said.

'Sit back down, Captain.'

'We'll need more shells. Can't let Georgia get the better of us.'

The wounded outnumbered the helpers. As the Rebel cannon continued the argument, Tod escaped to stagger and stumble down the hill.

*

Shire stepped between the rifle pits. In the one to his right a dusty soldier rolled onto his back and put a hand across his eyes to shield the sun.

'Which regiment?' he asked.

'125th Ohio,' said Shire.

'The Tigers, huh. Can you run like a tiger?'

Shire didn't care for the smile below the hand that read, *It's your day to die, not mine.*

'Come on with us and find out,' said Tuck. 'You ain't no use layin' there.'

The soldier propped himself on an arm. 'I think I like it better here. You can visit me on the way back.'

'We don't plan to come back,' said Shire, then realized the double meaning.

'Very commendable,' said the smile. 'Be sure to give my regards to General Johnston.'

Colonel Moore had them step forward of the pits. 'Four-foot spacing,' he shouted.

Shire had helped with the ploughing at Ridgmont once. He'd tacked up the horses and the ploughman had invited him to try his hand. 'Four-foot apart,' he'd said. Shire made a pig's ear of it, unable to keep a straight and deep furrow. The ploughman's laughter had left a wound on Shire's boyish pride. Now here he was with a four-foot allocation in which to race over the open field in front. Halfway to the tree line there was a shallow ravine that likely held a ditch. He couldn't quite see.

'No firing,' shouted Moore. He had the left wing, Major Bruff the right. 'Race to the Rebel pits, fast as you can so they have no time to reload.'

That must be two hundred yards to where the timber line began and the slope started up. How fast did the Colonel think they could be? There would be men in the shadow of those trees. Shire screwed down his hat as if that might somehow save him. He looked over to Tuck, hoping for reassurance: a nod, a wink, but Tuck was head down, adjusting his belt. On Shire's other side Mason was similarly in his own world, looking out across the ground, blowing his cheeks, his head rhythmically twitching.

Opdycke was further to the left on Barney, over in front of Wagner's Brigade but coming this way. Shire was surprised no Rebel took a potshot. Their cannon were subdued too, only the Union guns firing at the hills. He looked behind and the brigade was forming behind the Union pits. Flags evenly spaced among line after line of men, so close behind each other that bullets couldn't miss if the Rebels got them to fly within six feet of the ground. So many men. And here he was ahead. It was like being roped to the front of a steam train.

Ocks spun him around. 'Face the front,' he barked. 'Be ready to run. No double quick, just into the Rebel pits as fast as you can and lay into them.'

Who did Ocks think he was talking to? Shire had fought at Chickamauga, climbed the ridge at Chattanooga.

Bugles sounded left and right and Moore pointed his sword. The men roared and Shire was running with them down his own line, his imaginary furrow. Muskets flashed from the Rebel pits but he heard no bullets, saw no one go down. When had he last run? Really run. He was in a heavy jacket, ill-fitting boots and held a rifle at port, weighed down like a workhorse in full tack. Tuck outpaced him, outpaced everyone.

His breath came hard from high in his chest. The percussion caps in his belt-box bounced with every stride like so much loose grain. He didn't check at the shallow ravine but let his running weight carry him in, through the dribble of water and up the other side. The trees were ever closer. He expected a full volley with each stride. The week-old blister next to his nub toe rubbed and burst but the pain was immaterial. His eyes watered as if riding a fast horse on a winter evening. The earth bounced ahead of him. Almost there. He could see movement in the tree shadow. There was a fence, nothing much. A few Rebels started back up the slope but Tuck was on them, Mason was on them. Rifles dropped; hands went up. He was there himself but there was no one left to collar or push to the ground. There was no death; no fighting. Why had they not run away sooner if they didn't want to fight? Fifty men taken as easily as that. The quick success brought confusion. Lieutenant Rice was speaking with Captain Elmer. 'Send them back to our lines. Disarm them and send them back. We can't spare men to husband them.'

Shire caught his breath. He looked into the wide gray eyes of the nearest Rebel then grabbed him by the arm, spun him to face the rear, pushed him away. Rifle fire pricked in among them. His prisoner clutched at his thigh, collapsed and cried out. Shire turned back to look up through the patchy forest to the real Rebel line and his heart stalled.

Up the slope, no more than seventy-five paces away, an earth rampart made it steeper still. It was topped with a head-log; a row of rifles protruded from the gap beneath. He could see at least one embrasure housing a black, frowning cannon. Before the rampart was a further obstacle: a great abatis of long logs with sharpened stakes driven through them to present down the hill. They were backed by felled trees, branches left attached, to make a second impassable obstacle beyond the spikes. A volley blasted from the top of the rampart, thwacked into the trees, rattled the brush like it was haunted, kicked up the pine straw. Rice was down, a hand to his bloodied head.

Moore had them fire and then start up the slope. To what end? How were they ever to get past that abatis? If they did, their only reward would be the rampart. Tuck was to the fore again. Shire followed him closer to the abatis.

He heard a shout. 'Down!' He looked back and there was Opdycke on Barney, bellowing up at Moore, waving the flat of his hand. 'Get them to lie down.'

Shire didn't wait on Moore. He threw himself behind the nearest tree, which wasn't nearly wide enough. He wished to God he was back on the farm; he'd be content for the ploughman to laugh at him forever and a day.

*

Opdycke pulled sharply on the rein to wheel Barney and hasten back down the line. He was just short of the trees.

A bullet zipped between his nose and Barney's ears. It felt wrong to move away from the 125th but he had wider duties this day: he must see what was happening in front of the 57th Indiana.

They weren't as far up. The trees were patchy to their front which meant the men were in full view of the main Rebel line, taking heavy fire as they struggled to get across the ravine. Opdycke saw Colonel Blanch leading them on. Looking back to the hill, he could make out that the abatis ran fully across the front here as well. When the 57th reached the slope, they'd face the same problem as the 125th.

He turned Barney once more and rode back, found a staff officer and sent messages to Newton and Harker describing the abatis. What else could he do?

Harker's and Wagner's brigades pushed across the field, trying to catch up to the skirmishers. The fire from the Rebels intensified. The 51st Illinois was in front, their formation disrupted by the ditch. He winced as a blast of canister scythed into them. The line faltered – stuttered – before the men behind forced it forward again.

He couldn't let sights such as this be the master of him. He needed to think, but today the terrible weight of the crisis bore down on him. He should have requested pioneers to go in with his skirmishers. He'd never encountered a defense like the abatis before. He was the crux, the senior officer, the furthest forward, but with no authority to call off the attack. Should he ride back to Newton, impress upon him how impossible this would be? Newton couldn't do anymore himself. Units were going in for miles either side of them, yet it was here that Sherman had put in his best division. It was his hope, his gamble that pushed the men forward.

Moore ran out from the trees and looked in dismay at the

murder of the brigade. Opdycke dismounted and had to snap him back. 'Moore. Look at me, man. What's happening on your front?' He waited the few long seconds it took Moore to rally.

'The men are laid down, like you ordered. Some have crept up to the abatis but there's no way through. I have them shooting at the works to depress the fire on the brigade. Emerson... sir, if we charge those works, it'll be the end of the regiment.'

'We have to endure, until the brigade gets up. If we get enough men to the abatis maybe we can pull it apart.'

'We need cannon-fire on their line but the forest covers them. Our cannon are too far back. Theirs can fire low into the brigade.' As Moore spoke, another volley of canister dashed across the 51st, eviscerated a clutch of men in the front line.

'I need to see it again.'

Moore nodded. Opdycke handed Barney to an aide and ran back in with Moore, bent over, hurrying between trees. There was a squad of men up the slope and close to the abatis. 'Is that Wick?'

'Yes, and Mason's squad. Ocks is with them.'

The abatis screened them; half protected them. The Rebels were concentrating their fire on the brigade as it crossed the open ground; for the moment the pressure on the 125th was less. The men were doing well, taking time to aim at anyone that showed above the head-log.

'Keep up the rate of fire. It's all we can do.' He'd never felt so helpless. Kimbell's Brigade wasn't in. Not enough width had been given to the division so Newton had held them back. They were obliquely behind Wagner. 'Weight of men,' he said to himself.

'Sir?' asked Moore.

'It's the only way.' He looked Moore square in the face and spoke as if he were pleading to the Lord. 'Weight of men,' he shouted over the muskets and cannon. 'If Kimble can push in next to Wagner.' There might be room. 'We all throw ourselves forward. It worked at Missionary. You saw how their skirmish line gave way. If they are weak, it'll work.'

'Sir. I don't think—'

'If we don't commit ourselves then the day is as good as lost. I'll send word to Newton and ride over to Kimball.' He took hold of Moore's shoulders. 'Keep up the fire. As soon as the brigade reaches the regiment, go in. It's all or nothing.'

'Yes, sir. All or nothing, sir.'

*

This way didn't look familiar. It wasn't as steep going down as Tod remembered. It was hard to tell; there was so much rifle smoke rising from the trees below, a more acrid taste to it than from the cannon. It climbed the slope, hugged the ground as if slinking away like a coward. He was walking down into Hades. Rifles rattled away below. If he kept on, he'd hit the line and could work out which way to go to find the 20th. He reached up once more to touch the sticky and tender raised bump on the back of his head. It sure was hot today. This smoke was blurring his vision and making him dizzy. He was glad to have taken off his jacket but then realized he'd left it up the hill. That was his rank he'd left up there. No one outside his regiment would know he was a captain. He had to find his own men.

His legs wobbled and slipped on the slope. Unsteady in body and mind he decided the right thing to do was to sit down. Maybe he should head back up, collect his men. He recalled the explosion: Kirkland blown away, all the others bloodied and broken. They couldn't fight. Only he could. Yes, that was it. That was the plan all along: to get into the fight.

A ragged cheer swept up to him, called him to his feet again. The smoke cleared and he took a lungful of clean air. It bolstered him and he carried on down, let each tree catch him in turn until he could see men below and a line of works. Rifles were being passed forward; the men on the firing step took them eagerly and fired down the hill.

Everyone was facing away from him when he stumbled into the lines from behind. A long-haired sergeant, bearded and fierce, turned on him, eyes searching for a name. 'Soldier!' he shouted. 'Where's your jacket? Where's your gun?'

'I was hot,' said Tod. 'Do you have any water, Sergeant?'

'Who am I, your mother?' He seized Tod at the join of his neck and pushed him forward. 'Get up on that step.'

Tell him who you are. Tell him you're a captain. He tried to climb up onto the firing-step. He would have fallen if the sergeant hadn't shoved him by his backside then handed up a loaded rifle. Tod looked out through the gap below the head-log into the shifting smoke, here impenetrable, there thinning for a moment. A bullet passed close above him and he looked up as if it might still be there. The man beside him nudged his shoulder with a canteen, pushed a wooden toothed smile in close. 'You want some? My mouth is dry as Lincoln's titties.'

The water went down like a cold anchor. He looked down the hill with a clearer head. There was a fence out there, more than a fence, a mess of fallen trees and spikes. The breeze shifted and the smoke cleared. Out well beyond the obstruction, where it was flatter, a sudden sea of blue washed toward them, coming on despite the price in blood, a man falling each and every second, trodden under by the men behind. Dizziness found him again.

'Whoa, keep your balance. Lean into the wood and mind where you point that musket. That's it, get it up there. You can't miss. It's a goddamned turkey-shoot.'

*

Shire lay flat against the slope behind his thin tree. He could feel every discarded twig, smell the pine straw, breathe in the warm, damp earth. Tuck shouldn't have drawn them up this far. Why had he pulled them so close to the abatis and out ahead of the rest of the company? Mason had come on, so had Hubbard and so had Wick. Ocks was behind Shire down the slope. Cleves was further back. Shire called up to Tuck who was three body lengths up the hill. 'They're firing at the brigade. Can you work back down?'

Tuck twisted his head and glared at Shire. 'Why in the hell didn't you stop me? A friendly ankle-tap was all I needed.' Tuck wriggled so his weight on the slope slowly edged him down the hill. 'I'd hate for someone to notice me. Any room behind that tree?'

'Barely enough for a skinny Englishman. Shuffle over to the next one.'

Tuck half rose and jumped to his right, hurried on by a couple of bullets from up the hill, and lay flat behind his own inadequate cover. 'They sure do take offence easily. I 'magine my crawling away was a provocation.'

'Put some fire on those works.' Ocks shouted from behind. He set an example by emptying his pistol. 'Into that embrasure if you have the angle. That cannon is murdering our brigade.'

Shire fired then hid again, like a schoolboy throwing pebbles at a window.

A shout, almost a wail, rose between the shots. '*I can do all things through Him who strengthens me.*'

'Sweet Jesus,' said Ocks.

Wick was on his knees, gazing up through the trees in rapture, his hands supplicant before him unhindered by any weapon. '*Though I walk in the midst of trouble, You will revive me. You will stretch forth Your hand against the wrath of my enemies, and Your right hand will save me.*'

'Someone knock him on the head,' said Mason. Hubbard was nearest.

'*Be broken, O peoples, and be shattered,*' called Wick. '*And give ear, all remote places of the earth. Gird yourselves, yet be shattered.*'

Shire watched Hubbard roll onto his side and regard Wick as if he was a prophet for a soul starved of hope. 'Watch your front, Hubbard.' Shire shouted. 'Don't listen to him. Come to me. He's going to draw their fire. Come to me.' He wriggled out from behind his tree and began to snake across to Hubbard.

'*Put on the full armor of God.*' Wick's voice sounded clear above the din of war. A bullet kicked up the leaves a hand's width from his knee. Another struck the tree behind him.

'Hubbard!' Shire shouted again. 'Look at me. Come this way.'

Hubbard gathered his rifle, brought his knees up, got ready to rise.

'Not yet Hubbard. We can't go in yet.' Shire was almost there. 'We're to wait on the brigade.'

'*The Lord will go forth like a warrior. He will raise a war cry. He will prevail against His enemies.*'

Hubbard was on his knees, planting his rifle to pull himself up.

'Hubbard. No!'

He took one step, just one step up the hill with his gun leveled, his weight forward and his jaw set, before a flock of bullets struck his chest, stood him up, drove right through him. The final bullet chased a heartbeat later, a full stop that took him square in the temple and threw him down the slope and away from Shire's outstretched hand. Beyond the empty space where Hubbard had stood, Wick lay back down, smiling like a saint at the gates of paradise.

'You are my hammer and my weapon of war.'

*

Opdycke rode back toward the 125th from Kimbell's Brigade. He'd urged Kimbell to come in on Wagner's flank as best he could and put some weight on the line. Barney raced across the open ground in front of Wagner's Brigade, which was almost over the field. There was nothing between Opdycke and the Rebel front but air thick with metal. He tucked his head in behind the horse's neck, trusted to God and let Barney have his head.

God obliged and they reached the cover of the trees. He could see Harker's Brigade was nearly at the fence that had earlier been the Rebel skirmish line. Opdycke willed them forward through the hail of bullets and the murder of the cannon. 'Come on, come on.' Barney, blowing from his run, shied at a bullet that pinged a stone next to a front hoof. Opdycke caught his balance. There was Harker in the thick of things, conspicuous on his white horse, urging on the men. The first ranks, ragged from their ordeal in the open ground, made the fence but in crossing were broken up still more. Most of them went straight to ground once they made the dubious safety of the slope and the thin collection of trees. Others broke to the right where the forest was denser. A few pushed on up nearer the abatis and lay down with the 125th, hopelessly intermingled.

Opdycke heard a cheer and steered Barney back in under the trees. Dear Lord! Some of the Illinoisans had waded straight into the abatis and were pulling it apart. They were fighting their way through, but only a handful made the other side and climbed the rampart. Their flag flew on the parapet for the briefest instant and then was gone. Whether it had fallen back or was taken over, Opdycke couldn't tell. More of the brigade pushed their way onto the slope. There was a second try at the abatis but it was blasted back. Harker was closer now, coming over with the last regiment, the 64th Ohio. Once they were across and lay down, all movement stopped. Opdycke watched Harker wheel amid them, a god among fallen men, call them back to their feet. No one took heed. Opdycke's heart was in his mouth. He must get to Harker, get him to understand. A bleeding Captain Elmer stumbled out of the woods and across Barney's path. Two men stood to take Elmer in hand. Opdycke pushed on but the ground was carpeted with soldiers. Barney had to pick his way. Rebel fire concentrated on the prone men. They squeezed themselves this way and that as if they could dodge the bullets. Opdycke couldn't get to Harker who was up in his stirrups, sword waving, desperately trying to inspire his stalled brigade. 'With me,' Harker shouted and jumped the fence, heedless of the men beyond.

Opdycke couldn't deny the valor of his young friend; pride and fear bloomed together. Captain Whitesides, Harker's adjutant, rode beside him. A few soldiers stood to follow, then more. 'Forward men!' shouted Harker. 'Forward with me and take these works.'

*

Shire kept his face pressed to the forest soil and his hands laced tight across his hat. He wanted to smother the shouted orders, the cries, the gunfire. He wanted to smother Wick. Why had he done that? What perverse purpose had it served? That was no hero's death; it was an execution, a goaded suicide. Hubbard's mind would have healed in time, after the war. Everyone could heal; you had to believe that, otherwise you might just as well stand up as Hubbard had.

'Shall your brothers go to the war while you sit here?'

Shire twisted his face in the dirt to stare at Wick. Wick smiled back.

'Death spread to all men because all sinned.'

Shire started to get up, ready to jump at Wick and throttle him, but soldiers ran in between them. The brigade had arrived at last. The new men threw themselves to the ground. Wick was suddenly three soldiers away.

Over to the right a clump of men charged on up to the abatis, began to tear at it. Shire wanted to spend his new fury. He looked back to Ocks. 'Now. We should go now.' He picked up his gun, took a breath.

Ocks clutched at Shire's ankle. 'Not yet. No orders yet. We go piecemeal and we'll be butchered.'

The men at the abatis were picked off. There was wire there, making it harder to pull apart, but yank by yank it was coming. One man was through, a flag followed, not Shire's flag but the 51st Illinois, the Chicago Legion. Through the mess of the abatis Shire watched a handful of men run up the rampart. Every man was either shot down or pulled into the works.

After the forlorn charge there was a lull in the firing.

Shire tried to ease his nerves by loading. The company had practiced it lying down but nobody had been intent on killing him at the time. The whole brigade was on the ground. There wasn't enough cover for everyone to hide. Some were scraping at the earth. He watched men killed just lying waiting, evil shots to the head or neck. The brigade couldn't stay here. They needed to go forward or go back.

Through the trees he saw a flash of white. Harker. His horse jumped the fence where they'd taken the Rebel pickets. That seemed an age ago. Whiteside, who'd left the 125th to be Harker's adjutant, rode with him. Harker pushed his horse up the slope. 'Forward men! Forward with me and take those works.' Around him men stood, started uphill into a splatter of new gunfire.

Surely it was now? Shire knelt, fired and then stood. Mason and Tuck were up too, bullets flew by them. Harker was ahead to the right. The Rebels were reloading; there was a chance to make some ground. Shire raced up the hill, feet wide and pumping. His rage at Hubbard's needless death ran with him. He reached the abatis and set his gun aside, gripped the shaft of a spike in both hands, pulled and twisted and grunted. Tuck was with him. Together they tugged and wrestled at the wood to make the slimmest of openings. *Forward or back*. Shire squeezed in between the spikes and felled trees, into the briar. Bullets cut at the wood like axe strokes. Tuck took a step back.

'Pass me my gun,' called Shire.

'It's hopeless.' The earth kicked up around them.

'Pass it!'

Tuck shoved the gun in butt first. Shire had to thread it between spikes and brush. Up the line more men were climbing in as he was, but he became caught: a spike split his jacket and held him. There was a thunderous volley. He looked behind to see Harker shot through arm and chest. His horse was struck, blood staining its pure white hair. Man and beast went down together hard onto the slope. The horse screamed and rolled once, legs flailing, then lay still. Whiteside was unhorsed too. Other officers were in the abatis and through – Lieutenants Dilley and Burnham. Both fell climbing the rampart. The attack was failing. Shire twisted and turned only to be snagged again. He couldn't get clear. Tuck had gone to ground, his arm up uselessly against the hail of bullets. Shire twisted out of his jacket, took a gash to his shoulder and slumped down in the tangled heart of the obstacle. Close by a breathless soldier was in the same state: scratched to hell and no way out. A bullet found his neck and he convulsed, a spike from the abatis driving into his side. Shire's own bullet would surely find him soon. How could it not? He hacked at a spike with his rifle butt and it snapped. He slid down further until he was lying on the ground, wholly trapped, utterly spent.

*

Tod swapped muskets with his wooden-toothed friend and loaded once more. 'I need cartridges,' Tod shouted over the gunfire.

'I'm about out,' said the soldier, pushing the musket under the head-log and taking careful aim. 'Get some from Wyndam.'

'Who's Wyndam?'

The soldier held fire rather than rush his shot. He nodded down to the body laying spread-eagled behind the works, a tidy ruby hole above its left eye. 'That's Wyndam. It's his rifle you was given.' The soldier took aim again and fired.

Tod stepped down and pillaged Wyndam's cartridge box, trying not to feel the warmth of the body. He needed percussion caps as well. In the end it was easier to roll the corpse over and remove the belt with the boxes attached. He buckled it on and climbed back up to the firing step, mindful not to stand up too straight. He resumed loading and swapping guns.

'Sure you won't try again?'

'I can't see a damn,' Tod lied. 'Must be the knock on my head.'

The truth was that when he had first come to fire, when the open ground was full of Union blue and he could have closed his eyes and still hit any one of a thousand men, his hands had begun to convulse and the muzzle shook like a sinner come to judgment. He fought it, but there was nothing he could do. His neighbor had laid a hand on the stock and said, 'Maybe let me do the shooting. You load.' They'd gotten into a rhythm: Tod's hands were steady as a rock for loading and his new friend did all the killing. That appeared to be the deal. Morally, Tod didn't see what odds it made; he was a party to the deed even if he couldn't pull the trigger. Chances were that this man was more practiced with a rifle and would do a better job. The last laugh was on Luther. He gave in to it, accepted he was destined to be a man one step back from the act itself: he would load guns, carry shells, hand out munitions. That would be his war.

'They's all across the open ground.'

'What's your name?'

'Winchester.'

'Truly?'

'Truly. You?'

'Carter.'

'Pleased to meet you, Carter.' Winchester squeezed off a careful shot then ducked as a ball took a chunk off the head-log. 'They's all laid down and wondering what the hell to do. It's a long day to sunset. Take a look.'

Tod handed Winchester a newly loaded gun and looked out below the head-log. There was a ragged cheer to his left. A few men were through the abatis and struggling up the rampart with their flag. It was hopeless. He watched Winchester swing his musket to the left along with all the men on the firing step. The brave little charge ended in a tumble of arched backs and wide arms.

Winchester laughed. 'They should dance together or not at all.'

Tod loaded then looked again. Whoever made that abatis had done a good morning's work. Without that and the felled trees there'd be a whole brigade charging their works rather than a squad.

'Looky here. They got a gen'ral down there in the trees. All white horse and shiny sword. Quick. Hand me that.'

There were cries from down the slope. A roar and twenty, thirty men stood and came on, some rose from close behind the abatis. Tod hadn't seen them there. They were right in front of his line, tugging at the spikes. Winchester was busy with the general, above the head-log this time, risking longer exposure to settle his shot. He fired but a drift of smoke obscured the outcome. When it cleared the horse was down, a second handful won through the abatis but were shot to death on the rampart. The charge withered, leaving a few desperate souls stuck and struggling on the spikes. A rifle fired from Tod's right and killed one of the trapped men. They were just twenty yards away. You couldn't miss. This wasn't battle, it was slaughter.

'Best tidy these fellas up,' said Winchester. 'This one can't go forward nor back. I'll settle it for him.' He reached for the gun.

Tod didn't let go. 'He ain't no threat. Let him be.'

Winchester pulled at the gun. 'If he ain't no threat then what the hell's he doin' in Georgia?'

'Let him be.'

Winchester thrust his powder smudged face in close under Tod. 'Who in the blazes are you? You even from this regiment? Give me that gun and git off this step, Carter.'

Tod put a firm hand against Winchester's chest. 'That's *Captain* Carter. And you'll do what the hell I say.'

*

The dead soldier hung on the spikes a few yards away, leaking his life-blood onto this Georgia hill. Shire lay panting in the tangle of branches and waited for the end. He carefully turned his head to look out between the branches and the spikes. Tuck was down the slope; not far away, tight to the ground, his body tensed as if he was about to make a last try to pull away the abatis. They locked eyes and Shire shook his head, raised a hand as far as he could. It was hopeless. He didn't want Tuck throwing his life away. That would make a poor last scene.

The firing went on but not at Shire. It all passed above. Where he was stuck the abatis crossed a shallow gully that ran down the hill. The Rebels must be able to see him because he could clearly see the top of the rampart and the rifles pushed out below the head-log.

'*My kingdom is not of this world.*'
Wick.

'*Do not think that I have come to bring peace to the earth. I have not come to bring peace, but a sword.*'

Shire looked past Tuck down the gully to where Wick was kneeling again. He held no weapon and seemed immune from Rebel gunfire. Beside him was Corry, a boy who'd joined in the spring as Hubbard had. Even from where he was Shire could see Corry shaking. It was close to a fit.

Wick stretched a slow open hand toward him. '*The Lord is a man of war.*'

Shire's rifle lay awkwardly, the barrel under his thigh. He twisted to lift his weight and pull the rifle up beside him. He needed to turn it around, thread it this way and that between the branches and the spikes until he had it pointed down the hill.

He caught Tuck's questioning eye but ignored him; there was no time for doubt. He arched his back so he could reach a percussion cap from his box. Next to Wick, Corry had his gun in both hands.

'*Give them according to their deeds, and according to the wickedness of their endeavors.*'

It was impossible for Shire to kneel or turn to lay facing down the slope where he might get a better shot. All he could do was rest the barrel across one bent leg and set the butt against his right shoulder. Sighting the shot was near to impossible.

'Shire. What the hell are you doing?'

'Lay flat.'

He watched his good friend twist to look down the gully at Wick. The shot would have to pass close beside Tuck, but he would understand, because of the gully, no one else would see. It would be as if the shot had come from the Rebels. Tuck looked back at Shire who made a last shuffle to get the final alignment. He was grateful for all the things Tuck didn't say: *This is murder*, or, *Don't put this on your soul when you're about to meet your maker.* He merely nodded and edged a little to the side.

Despite being trapped, despite being bent so awkwardly to try the shot, Shire felt strangely serene, detached. The noise of battle eased or at least moved away. He loved Tuck; it was a sad thought that he would see him no more. He half smiled at the irony that it was Tuck who had taught him to shoot straight and that his friend would have to trust to that teaching now. Looking down the length of the gun he saw Corry gather himself to rise. This was the only thing left to do. He was saving Corry as he should have saved Hubbard, protecting the regiment.

Wick was still kneeling, head back, both hands upturned to heaven.

Shire moved the gun a hair to the left and let his breath slide away as if it were his last.

'*For they loved not their lives even unto death.*'

Corry started to rise and Shire fired. The butt kicked painfully into his shoulder, but he held himself steady. Wick took the bullet high in the chest and jerked, his smile, at the last, deserting him. His hands collapsed to the wound before he fell forward. Corry lay back down. Shire couldn't tell if he had seen what Shire had done. It didn't matter. He let his rifle slide off his body.

He closed his eyes, felt no remorse. He wanted to rest now. He hoped, when it came, his own end would be as quick. Smoke drifted into the tangle and his eyes shot back open as he registered a change: mixed in among the sulfur of the muskets was the strong and homely smell of woodsmoke. He could hear the crackle and snap of flame between the gunfire. A warm breeze picked up. Above the cut branches that held him pinned, drifting flecks of ash mixed into thin white smoke.

A new depth of fear took hold and he began to struggle in earnest. 'Tuck!' There was a pitiful scream from somewhere along the abatis, somewhere close. The smoke thickened above. 'Tuck!' He managed to sit up, heedless of new scratches. His friend rose and hurried toward him, braving the bullets to get a hand on the abatis and tug away at it with two arms and all his wiry strength. It didn't budge. Shire followed Tuck's fearful glance. He could see the orange of the flames through and above the abatis. They ate greedily toward the dead soldier held erect by the spikes. The man's blue jacket began to burn, then his pale hair. The blood around his wound boiled and steamed.

Shire tried desperately to stand, managed to only at the expense of a gouge across his thigh. Tuck was getting nowhere. 'Go forward!' he screamed. 'Go forward, Shire. I can't move it.'

Forward was as thick as a hawthorn hedge. 'I can't.' He turned again and buckled at the look of terror on Tuck's face. Tuck went down, bullets striking all around him. By the time he was up again the fire was too close. The smoke and the flame interposed. Tuck was gone. Shire could feel the heat of it now, like no furnace on earth. Fire scorched the skin from the dead soldier's face and rose up, a column of flame, damnation come to take Shire in swift retribution. He turned to pull desperately at the branches, ignoring the rents and tears to his hands and face but with not an ounce of hope, only a final surge of unthinking animal fear.

*

Opdycke watched from below as a clump of men lifted Harker from beside his dead horse and carried him back into the trees. The abatis was alight, the crackle of burning wood competing with sporadic rifle shots fired randomly through the smoke. He received word from Wagner and Kimball's front, acknowledged it. It was the same appalling story: they too were being hammered before the abatis. No more than a handful of men had made it through.

Harker was being stretchered downhill. Opdycke weaved Barney between the trees and the prone men to see if there was any chance for him. He dismounted and waited, angled Barney's head up the hill so he was less likely to be hit. His throat was bone dry from the smoke and the shouting.

Harker was carried by. He was conscious. For a second Opdycke dared to hope until he looked more closely: one arm was shattered and there was a heavy glut of blood at Harker's waist beside a flowing wound.

'Is that you, Emerson?'

'Yes, Charles.'

Harker raised a hand. Opdycke reached out but the litter hurried on.

'Come and find me when the day's done.'

A spent bullet slapped the rear stretcher bearer's jacket but he didn't so much as flinch.

'I will.' Opdycke doubted that Harker would last that long. This was their unuttered goodbye then, after a year together there was simply no time. Whether Harker had been foolhardy or not no longer mattered. Opdycke should have told him how bravely he'd fought, but it was too late, the litter was gone. He turned his mind back up the hill, back to the tuneless cacophony of war. The Rebels were beyond reach, behind their works and the growing flames.

Who would take command of the brigade? Bradley, yes, it would be Colonel Bradley of the 51st Illinois. He mounted and turned Barney full circle but Bradley was nowhere to be seen. Opdycke sent an aide to find him, tell him that Harker had left the field and ask for orders, though they were inevitable: they would have to withdraw, the brigade would flee back across that murder field and suffer going back as it had coming across. What a waste. Walking wounded stumbled down the hill. The tide of men was on the ebb. He would need to follow Newton's prescient orders and cover the retreat with his skirmishers. He shouted to Moore who ran down to him.

'The order to pull back will come soon. When it does, the 125th is last off this hill and then holds the fence we took coming up.' Moore looked dazed, as if his pale eyes had drunk their fill. 'Colonel Moore, do you understand?'

'The fence, yes, sir. We never had a chance, sir. Poor Harker.'

A shout from up the slope drew Opdycke's attention. The fire in the abatis was sweeping from right to left.

'Sir,' said Moore. 'If the abatis burns away, we would be clear to attack.'

Opdycke considered it. 'We're too disorganized, too damaged. I don't think Newton will ask that of us.' He wished he'd thought to burn the abatis earlier, when the skirmishers first got up. Panicking men were trying to pull it apart. There were trapped soldiers in there. Screams rose above the gunfire and the popping of burning wood. The blaze generated its own rising, twisting wind, swept along at the pace of a walking man. One soldier was desperately fighting to get out, his comrade beaten back by the heat and the bullets. The would-be rescuer was tall and gangly, all arms and legs: it must be Private Tuck. Could that then be the Englishman, Shire, in the abatis? He prayed not. Tuck was defeated by the flames. Mercifully, the smoke hid the scene before the fire swept across. No one should have to suffer an end like that. Opdycke turned away.

'Go to it, Moore,' he said. 'Protect the brigade. That's all we can do. Protect the brigade.'

*

'Hogwash! If you're gonna be a captain, then I'm promotin' myself to colonel.'

Tod gripped the rifle as Winchester tried to pull it free. A bullet smacked into the head-log. Tod decided this argument would be better finished off the step. He pulled Winchester down with him. 'My jacket's up the hill, is all. Just shoot at someone else. Someone who's not trapped.'

'He'll be shootin' back soon enough if he gets free.'

The long-haired sergeant waded in, pushed them apart with bull arms. He glared at Tod but spoke to Winchester, 'What's going on, Chester? You run out of Yankees?'

'No danger of that, but this fella you stood up next to me says he's a captain and won't let me shoot.'

'That so?'

Tod saw the sergeant belatedly take in his side arm. 'That's *not* so, Sergeant,' he said. 'I merely ordered him not to kill the boy stuck in the tangle. And I expect you to do the same. Any man with a conscience would.'

Winchester gave up the fight for the rifle, recovered his own and drew the ramrod.

'What regiment are you from?' demanded the sergeant.

'Twentieth Tennessee.'

'Hell, you ain't even in our division. Captain or not, don't be givin' orders to my men. I'd get my own captain over only he's kinda busy. We all are, in case you ain't noticed.'

'What division is this?' asked Tod, wondering just how far off track he'd come.

'Cleburne's. This is Polk's Brigade. Why are you so far from home... Captain?'

'We were delivering shells. The squad was hit. I was dazed. I guess I came the wrong way off the hill.'

Winchester edged away to climb back up the step. Tod grabbed his arm. 'Not the boy! It's murder if you do, plain and simple.'

Winchester shook him off and looked under the head-log. 'Well, Captain Carter, I'd say about now I'd be doin' him a personal favor... Come see.'

Tod and the sergeant climbed up beside Winchester. To the left the abatis was alight. Flames were sweeping this way. The shooting had all but stopped while the fire and smoke intervened. The boy was still alive, no one else had seen fit to shoot him. He was fighting to stand up but was caught fast.

'You want I should shoot him now?'

'It's no good unless you kill him clean,' said the sergeant. 'Otherwise he just bleeds and burns at the same time.' He nodded at Tod's revolver. 'The smoke'll hide you. If you're so fond of the boy, why not step out there and see to him? You'd do it for a dog.'

Winchester wore a wooden smile. Tod felt the dare from the sergeant and from the other men who looked on, leaning on their rifles and taking water in the lull. This boy, this one life among so many newly spent, was balanced in the moment. The bigger challenge would come from Luther, but this would be a mercy killing, a kindness.

'Better be quick,' said Winchester. 'That's a fast fire. The shootin'll start up again when the fire's burned out.'

Winchester was right. This was a passing calm in the universe of the battle, a brief scene set to test him. There was no time to think. He climbed up and out and dropped onto the rampart, took out his revolver. He glanced back to see the head-log lined with powder-smoked faces. He arced to his left so the full height of fire was between him and the Yankees, kept his head low. A bullet fired hopefully through the flames struck the earth close to his hand as he balanced himself. The heat was intense, the smoke thickening and boiling away to the right. He overtook the flames and came up on the boy who was fighting like a jackrabbit trapped in a snare. The piled branches were so thick. Best if the boy didn't see him. As soon as he raised the gun the shaking started again. 'Damn it, Luther!'

The boy turned his head, eyes wide. He stopped struggling for the briefest moment and there was something, some slight connection, as if the boy understood. Tod tightened his finger on the trigger. The fire roared and towered above them. It burned Tod's cheek, stung his eyes. There was an anguished cry from the other side of the abatis. The boy was fighting again, heedless of the scratches to his hands and face.

To hell with it. Tod holstered his gun and grabbed at the nearest branch, began to pull frantically, but they were stuck tight. 'After this we're square, Luther,' he shouted. 'You hear me? I'm done with you, Luther.'

The boy fought toward him, coughing all the while. The flames burned ever closer, branch after branch bursting alight. It was hopeless, he wasn't strong enough. He thought about his gun again. There was a cheer from the men behind. Hands appeared beside his, filthy skinny hands.

'I don't want you takin' this as meanin' you was right.'

The branches inched out.

'Only he's on our front, so I don't see as someone from a lesser regiment should get to play hero.'

They got up a rhythm, yanking at the branches in tandem until they started to give.

'Alright, Chester,' Tod grunted between yanks. 'Glory's all yours.'

Stubbornly, the branches parted. The boy fought his way toward them but got snagged again. The fire was almost upon them. They were too late. A twist of wind held the flames away for a heartbeat. 'Hold still!' The Yankee didn't. Tod reached in and pulled a spike from the boy's jacket, the hot wood burning his palm. And then they were free, all stumbling away from the flames and climbing the rampart to more cheers. Eager hands helped them over. Tod collapsed to the ground next to the Yank. Water was handed down to them. Winchester was standing tall and having his back slapped. The boy tipped water over his head and hands then took a long draught before he turned breathless to Tod. They smiled at each other like drunkards.

'Who the hell is Luther?'

PART III

The Isabella Mine, Ducktown – June 1864

Clara lay wide awake on her chaise lounge, decoding the drip and slap of water. It was entirely dark. She had no idea how long it would be before Tonkin woke, before he made her get up and found something for them to do. It was important to keep to normal hours, he'd said. That frightened her: that they were consciously settling into a routine. Her stomached ached from want of food and added its complaint to the sound of the water.

If ever she got out of this mine, she'd be able to tell people a great deal concerning drips. To begin with, you might think the sequence entirely random, every drip with its own arbitrary genesis, but that wasn't true at all. She had come to know seven distinct notes, each with its own fixed rhythm.

She patted her hand on the stone floor to find her whiskey glass and drank the cool metallic water, trying to ease the hunger. There were other things she would like to un-know. She couldn't believe that Hany was dead. 'I had to shoot her,' Bowman had said. That seemed to allow for the possibility she was alive. It was a small hope to cling to, but down here, where nothing moved on in the world, it couldn't be proved or disproved. All she had to go by were the cruel words of a murderer. Yet if she was to trust to anything in respect of Bowman, it would be that he *was* a murderer. The boy Calvin lay dead somewhere above them, along with who else? Bowman had meant to kill her and Tonkin. She wanted to grieve for Hany, but without confirmation, without proof, she couldn't. The mine held her heart fixed as well as her body.

Tonkin's easy breathing told her he was asleep. He sounded close in the dark but she knew he was across the void, as far away as he could be without taking to another cavern and leaving her completely alone. Sleep came easier to him. Being underground, being trapped and lost to the world above, came easier to him. She tried constantly to calm her mind; worry didn't present ideas, no plan of action. There was nothing to do but endure and ration out the hope.

After the cage had come crashing down the shaft, Tonkin had led her away to one of the chambers and they'd waited for the dust to settle. They sat on the cold rock and he'd insisted they only whisper lest Bowman had set someone to listen from above. All Clara had wanted to do was run screaming back to the shattered cage and call for help. Tonkin kept the lamp so low she feared it would expire. After he'd checked his pocket-watch for the hundredth time, he led them back to where a weak infusion of evening light bled in down the shaft. Only two in the row of hanging lamps had survived the crash, but there was a supply of matches. Tonkin doused the light entirely in case it drew unwanted attention. They rarely spoke. What light there was, faded to utter darkness. Clara had never listened so acutely in her life but heard nothing above the local drips and a breeze occasionally lifting through the shaft, escaping to where she could not. Tonkin wouldn't let her call out. 'We need to be sure they're gone,' he said. 'Better to wait.' He hadn't said how long. That was two days ago.

They'd carried the small windfall of lamps back to their living chamber, but Tonkin hoarded the oil as if it were food. In the daytime, they would return to the free light near the shaft again to listen – whisper and listen. They placed two Comrie parlor chairs there, angled and close, like she and Tonkin planned to sew together in the company of the picks and crowbars. Her eyes grew so used to the quarter-light that she imagined if she dug in the Comrie boxes for a book she might be able to read. Perhaps that would allow her to set aside the weight of her new world, if only for a moment, but she couldn't bear to try: it would be like distracting herself from drowning.

Before the first night, back in their living chamber, they had dug into the Comrie goods and found Tonkin a mattress. The next day they had assembled the full bed. Clara insisted she would stay where she was rather than swap. The chaise lounge felt more temporary. Tonkin put out a table and chairs. It was a bizarre thing, setting up a subterranean home with a man she barely knew, all the while, Taylor's ruined face watching from his murdered portrait. There was little to put on the table except their crystal drinking glasses which sparkled the yellow lamplight around the chamber. Tonkin placed a decanter beneath one of the drips to collect the water. There was no want of that. Clara drank constantly. Trapped with Comrie's goods, she felt entirely differently about them. They were never truly hers. Why would she want to set Comrie as it was? It had only ever been a practical step, a statement of intent. Taylor and his family resided in every piece, be it furniture, porcelain or crystal. She was again living with Taylor as much as she was with Tonkin.

Tonkin asked about Matlock, curious of Bowman's parting words: '*Matlock sends his compliments.*' While Clara chose to hope that Hany might be alive, Matlock's part in this was clear: he'd sent Bowman after her to make sure she never came out of the hills. That was her new measure of Matlock;

he was as much a murderer as Bowman. When despair pressed down on her in the darkness, she concentrated on Matlock. Memories of Shire or Tod, thoughts of Comrie, even longing to see a warm and bright sun, didn't work as well as cold hatred. It steadied her, allowed her to face forward again. She would endure to spite him. She would ride back to Comrie and see him condemned and, when the time came, she would stand closest to the rope.

Away in the dark she heard Tonkin rouse. He exhaled a lazy yawning breath as if he were waking slowly on a Sunday. Tonkin struck a match, painfully bright, set it into a lamp to illuminate their prison. Somehow it shrunk in her mind's eye when it was dark. She would forget how high the chamber was, how rough-hewn the walls. She considered that today, for lack of anything else to do, she could hunt the drips and match them to their notes. How depressing a thought.

Tonkin smiled at her and in the weak lamplight his face creased in a thousand places. 'Good morning.'

His positive tone was at once reassuring and annoying.

'Did you sleep well?'

'I've rather given up on that.'

Tonkin opened the case on his pocket-watch and then wound the stem. 'I've a thought to keep us busy.'

'What time is it?'

'A little after six. We could take some of the boxes and line them up toward the mine shaft and your latrine. That way, you can feel your way more easily in the dark.'

She had woken him then, with her blind stumbling in the night, edging her way a step at a time along the wall and down the tunnel toward the copper hall. There was a small side chamber. Tonkin had designated it her latrine. He had found somewhere else for himself. Beside the chaise lounge there was a washbowl she'd recovered from the pile and she considered using it in the night, but instead she'd braved the dark. 'Can you not leave me a lamp and a match?'

'With the boxes we wouldn't need to waste those.'

Clara didn't consider it a waste. 'How long will the lamps last?'

'A week, if we're careful.'

'A week.' Her voice echoed away. 'If I don't eat for a week, I'll have no need of light.'

Tonkin put down his watch and picked up a hand-drill, began absently to turn the cog as he had done at times yesterday, adding a steady hum to the percussion of the drips. Clara gripped the edge of the chaise lounge.

'I've a further idea,' he said. 'It may work. Your mirror. It'll be heavy, but if we can get it to where the passage from the shaft joins the main run through the chambers, and angle it, it might push some light this way in the daytime. We can use a minecart to help move it.'

'Mr Tonkin, why don't we move ourselves closer to the shaft? To the copper hall at least. We sit by the shaft in the day anyway.'

Tonkin didn't answer and Clara didn't press the question; they'd had this debate once before. Tonkin seemed more of a mind to hide than to escape. 'Truth be told,' he'd said, 'I'm afraid of what we'll find. Someone should have come. George should have come. Maybe Bowman has taken them all.'

People could live for weeks without food he told her. She imagined this underground torture stretched out endlessly. He cited any number of Cornish rescues and one in the neighboring Hiwassee mine, where men were pulled out skinny but smiling a month or more after a collapse. Like Tonkin's mood, it was hopeful and depressing at the same time.

She wanted to ask again if the mine connected to other works, if there was another way out, but he'd told her already that this part of the Isabella was all dead ends. There was only the one way out.

She helped him move the boxes into a line. It was too awkward to lift the mirror into a minecart. In the end they carried it in short stages all the way to the corner for his little light experiment. The effort exhausted her. She took some water and went to sit at the mineshaft in the thin light of the upper world while Tonkin went back to the Comrie chamber to see if his idea had worked.

She stepped in among the shattered wood and tangled piano wires and looked up. At the top was a small square of light that she knew was only the inside of the hut, a further interdiction between herself and the sky. Without warning, the feeble dam she had constructed burst. She heard again Bowman's parting laugher which morphed into Taylor's and echoed through the mine. Desperation arrived in a rushing wave, overtook her completely. She collapsed to sit among the wreckage. 'Help,' she cried, quietly at first, but then louder, 'help us.' Tonkin wasn't here to stop her. 'Please,' she called, and then lost herself in the release, screamed up the shaft, angry at anybody and everybody who hadn't come to help. Tonkin arrived, fear in his face but then, the risk already taken, he joined her and they shouted together, shrill and strident, soprano and bass. Clara had no idea how long they tried, but she stopped first, hoarse and spent. When Tonkin stopped too, the silence was worse than ever, as if they had taken their entire yet meagre supply of hope and hurled it toward God.

Georgia – June 1864

Shire sat in the thin shadow of the wagon and sipped from the canteen. C.S.A was stenciled across the stained cloth cover. His jacket had been lost to the fire though, somehow, he still had his hat. He peeled off his sweat-soaked flannel shirt and twisted to look at the gouge in his right shoulder, poured some precious water over it to try and wash away the dirt that crusted the beginnings of a scab. He judged it was light enough to close itself in time. When he edged down his trousers, the wound on his thigh was longer. He feathered it with his fingers and gently prized it apart to check the depth. It stung and oozed fresh blood but he was reassured. He would just need to clean them. More scars for his collection.

His hands and wrists were scratched to hell and back. His face was too. What hurt more was the lasting heat which had taken hold across and within his right cheekbone. Perhaps it was only the fresh memory of the fire. It felt real enough. He wanted to pour water over his head too, ease the heat and give thanks for this rebirth, his baptism of fire, but he couldn't spare any more.

After they'd found the 20th Tennessee, Tod had left him here on his honor to sit quietly while he attended to the needs of his regiment. The long chance of them meeting for the second time on a battlefield, their roles reversed from Missionary Ridge, was not lost on Shire. The coincidence wore a strange symmetry that hinted at some unseen hand but, just now, other emotions overpowered mere surprise.

He'd been delivered from death but into captivity, a benign one at present, but couldn't gauge his fate beyond the next five minutes, no matter who might be tending to it.

Surreptitiously, he pressed trembling hands together and prayed that Tuck had made it away. Would God be listening? He remembered Harker going down, felt the overpowering sadness that the 125th and the brigade had been defeated. Under all, was the cold truth that he was become a murderer. The extremity of the moment that allowed him to pull the trigger, to be glad as the bullet took Wick in the chest, had passed. He didn't know what to make of himself any more than God might.

There was no fighting of note to their front; guns fired north and south, but it wasn't the roll after roll of musketry and repeating boom of cannon that accompanied a full attack. The Union Army must be falling back; it had all been such a mess. He doubted they would attack again today.

There was no panic in the Rebel ranks below. They manned the works, sent out the occasional shot, but were otherwise relaxed. He watched Tod move among them, checking on ammunition, directing men to bring up more water. He picked up a spade and used the handle to knock a head-log back into place. He was doing more than anyone else down there, perhaps making up for his time away from the regiment.

After he'd rescued Shire, Tod had tried to leave him with some big red-headed sergeant. 'He's no good to me,' the man had said. 'Ten prisoners you can organize for, one is plain awkward. You saved the man, you tend to him.'

To start with Tod had looked at Shire as if he was a stray dog he'd rather have nothing to do with, but there was something more: a thoughtful frown that Shire realized he was mirroring.

'Come on,' Tod had said. 'I need to get back to my regiment. I've stayed too long as it is.' There was a moment while their new prisoner–guard relationship hung in the air. 'I guess you'd better go in front. This way. Up the hill.'

Shire's legs would barely carry him. His wounds hurt but it was as much the aftershock of his salvation. It was as if he needed to learn to walk again. Flames still crackled and burned the other side of the works, muskets still fired. After no more than a minute, he turned and asked, 'Can I rest a moment?' He sat back on the slope before his legs gave way.

Tod's frown was back but softened to comprehension. 'You're English.' It wasn't a question.

Shire nodded all the same.

'I met an Englishman last year, on top of Missionary Ridge, after I was captured. It was you, wasn't it? You gave me back my pack.'

Shire blinked his smoke-sore eyes, looked up anew at his captor, felt a dawning familiarity. 'You're Tod Carter?' He tried to take in the sheer absurdity of it all. 'I might never have known.'

Tod smiled. 'I guess we've both worn since then.'

'It's only eight months ago.'

'You see a lot of faces in a war.'

'Were you exchanged? I thought they'd stopped all that.'

'I escaped. In Pennsylvania. Found my way back.' Tod said it like he'd taken an afternoon stroll rather than journeyed half a continent. He put out a hand. 'We can go slow.'

Shire pulled himself up. Tod held on to him while he steadied.

'I never felt I thanked you properly last year, up on the ridge,' Tod said. 'I was low, the defeat an' all.'

The same emotions were crowding Shire today. 'I wrote

to your brother, Moscow, told him you'd been taken, that you weren't injured. He was kind to me when I was stationed in Franklin.'

'That would have set his mind at ease. I've written to him since. I can do the same for you once this fight is over. You got someone I can let know?'

There was only Clara. Why would she need to know? 'Not really,' he said. 'only my regiment.'

'They'll pass over a list in time.'

They walked on slowly side by side, exchanged experiences from the day. When they reached the 20th Tennessee, Tod had found him some water and parked him under this wagon.

There was a walking stick propped against the wheel. Shire stretched for it with his good left arm. Only the top half was carved, the thinner end still twisted and covered with bark. He first took the bulbous-handle to be an inverted cauldron but came to see it was a mortar. Beneath it five cannon were carved to surround the shaft, all pointed down, each discharging a ball fashioned into a skull. Below those was a tangle of bones and ribs untidily piled as they might be in an ossuary. He traced his fingers across it and wondered at the craftsmanship.

'You lookin' to make use of that?'

The voice startled him and he looked up into gray eyes fixed in a weathered face.

'Cos I don't think I could bring myself to gift it to a Yankee.'

Shire used the stick to stand. 'I was admiring it.' He leaned it back against the wheel. 'I don't think I have need of it.'

'We all have need in time. You don't look so steady.'

'I'll mend. Besides, I don't have any money.' He fleetingly wondered what would become of his pack left back in the company pile the other side of the lines. There was nothing in it but a few dollars and his old map; perhaps Tuck would keep that or sell it for coffee. 'You have some imagination in your carving.'

'I just work the shape that comes to mind.' The man stepped up into the wagon and spoke from inside. 'Captain says I'm to find you something to eat.'

Shire wasn't sure he could manage anything but took the crackers and scrag-end of salt pork passed to him from the top step of the wagon. 'It's quiet to your front.'

'It is that. Your Union is spent for this day. Was a bad idea to come at us here. Lot of men dead or dying out there. The sun's hot. We'll smell them soon.'

Shire took a bite of a cracker for want of anything to say. There was a spatter of rifle fire a little closer. He saw Tod climbing the hill toward them. 'I see you've met Waddell,' he said as he arrived.

'We was gettin' acquainted,' said Waddell.

Tod caught his breath then said, 'Hop back in the wagon and look out a jacket. Shire will have need of one once this weather passes. No sense being a quartermaster and not using the benefits.'

'We givin' comfort to Yankees now?'

'He's a prisoner. I was treated well enough. Kindness breeds kindness, they say.'

'Who says?'

'Just get the damn jacket. Then you can climb up to the gun emplacement I carried shells to this morning and find mine.'

Waddell came out and down the steps of the wagon and handed Shire a jacket. 'My foot's hurtin' some,' Waddell said.

'Then don't feel obliged to rush.'

Waddell spat tobacco juice onto the pine straw before he started up the hill with a limp Shire hadn't noticed until now.

He tried on the jacket. 'It's a little big.'

'Hell,' said Tod, 'I'm not about to measure you up. It looks plain wrong with a Union cap above, but you might be a long time in prison. You'll be glad of the extra length when fall arrives.'

'Maybe I'll escape like you.'

'You've already missed your best chance.'

A cannon fired somewhere above them and Shire heard the shell scream away toward his old army. 'Perhaps my fighting days are behind me.'

'My colonel ain't expecting much more to happen here. He says I'm to get my head tended to. There's a field hospital back a way. They'll clean you up as well. Then I'll have to find someone to give you up to.'

Shire considered that he preferred living under fire to being anywhere near a field hospital after a battle. The place was busy without being overwhelmed. The surgeons treated at least as many Union soldiers as Confederates. Given the boys in blue must have been pulled into the lines as Shire was, it suggested Rebel casualties were light. Not all the wounds were. There were men stretchered up with leg and arm injuries, waiting their wide-eyed turn for the bone-saw. Cries and desperate entreaties came from inside the largest tent. There was a less conscious queue laid under the shade of the trees, waiting on a different trial. A black boy walked up and down the line with a leafy branch. He waved away excited flies from head-wounds and opened guts. It smelled like the backroom of a butcher shop.

'Do we need to be here?' asked Shire. 'I have nothing that needs stitching. We could clean ourselves just as well.'

'I hear you. Surgeons make me nervous too.'

Before they could turn themselves around, they were pulled into the triage line. Shire was dispatched to a soldier who himself had a bandage wrapped around his head. Once Shire told him where his wounds were, he got him to strip, tore off a piece of cloth and dipped it into a bucket; white cloth going in, damp pink coming out. He proceeded to rub away at Shire's wounds as if he was polishing tarnished silver. Both his shoulder and leg started bleeding freely again. He was bandaged up and at least that was done well. He said he'd wash his other cuts himself, dressed and went to find Tod, who had a head bandage akin to Shire's soldier-nurse.

Tod didn't look any happier than he was. 'Let's go,' he said.

They walked further away from the front. The guns still fired, seemingly from all directions, but it was like light rain after a deluge and Shire paid it no mind other than to consider he'd come out of the storm on the wrong side. Tod appeared to know where he was going. Ahead was a crossroads and in one corner two dozen or so Union soldiers, many bandaged also, some looking bereft, others looking angry. There was a guard of four Rebels.

Tod stopped back in the trees. 'I don't know where they will take you. Most of the camps are well south of Atlanta. One of those most likely.' He pressed a piece of paper into Shire's hand. 'Send a letter if you can and tell me where you are. I hear the camps aren't good, Shire. I'll try and get food to you and write to the authorities, get my colonel to do the same and press for an exchange. It still happens sometimes.'

'Thank you,' Shire said. Being exchanged back to the fighting wasn't something that appealed right at this moment, but he'd heard tales of the prison camps. His chances might be better back in the war. 'I mean…' He offered his scratched hand, as he'd done once on Missionary Ridge. 'I mean I truly want to thank you, for saving my life.'

Tod smiled and shook, his's hand as scratched as Shire's own.

'Like I said to Waddell, kindness breeds kindness.'

'You pulled me from a fire, risked being killed to do it. I only gave you back your pack.'

'You've no idea how much that mattered to me.'

'I'll write if I can,' said Shire.

'Good,' said Tod, and smiled, 'though I wonder if there's truly the need. We appear to be fated to meet on a regular basis at these shindigs.'

They stepped up to the crowd, their parting awkward with so many men looking on. Shire figured they'd said enough in the trees. When Tod walked away it felt as if he was losing his newest and oldest friend in the world.

He was held with the other prisoners until the heat started to wear thin and the gunfire died away to almost nothing. One guard took a liking to his new jacket and insisted on swapping it for his own tattered and stained butternut one. There was no sense in arguing. A handful more prisoners joined them and in the early dusk they were marched off the back of the hill and down into a town thick with wagons, mules and men. After dark they were quickstepped to a station. By torchlight, Shire could see the name *Marietta* carved in stone above *Western and Atlantic*. They took their sad turn at a trestle table giving name, rank and regiment to a clerk who stayed low to his paper. Inventory taken, they were pushed up into a hot boxcar and the door slid closed, locked in and left to wait out the warm night. No one spoke much. His spirits sank with the weight of what he'd left behind. Tuck, the squad, the 125th. Clara. Maybe as well some last shred of innocence killed by his murder of Wick. He felt guilt but no regret. Whatever it was, this new knowledge of himself sat prisoner alongside him.

Sometime before dawn came the bump and clank of the coupling and they were pulled away at the speed of a sleeping mule. Speed didn't matter, thought Shire, and put his nose to a gap around the door in search of clean air. There was no hurry to reach wherever it was he was going.

Comrie, Tennessee – June 1864

Matlock was reading. There was little else to do and it stopped him from thinking. Thinking how he'd invited Bowman to murder Clara, who he'd known for all her young life and was tied to by blood, loose tie as it was. Thinking how that invite held him here all the more, and that if Bowman did return for the money, what was to stop him burning Comrie to the ground anyway? Thinking that this wasn't his first murder, how last time he'd had a more direct hand, two in fact, that pressed the cushion tight over Shire's father's face.

He dropped his book when he heard horses in the yard, the sound he'd been constantly anticipating. There was an almost overpowering impulse to run. He'd told Bowman it would take ten days to get the money. Why was he back so soon? He edged to the window and saw it was only two troopers, already dismounted and leading their horses to the trough. Moses shuffled toward them. Matlock hurried outside and called on his way across the yard. The taller of the men turned and pulled off his gloves. Matlock offered a hand. 'What can I do for you…?' He could see no insignia.

'Corporal.' The man said, lifting his hat and running a hand through sweaty black hair before damply shaking Matlock's hand.

'Then what can I do for you, Corporal?' He was giddy with relief that it was Union men. 'Moses here can see to your horses.'

The shorter soldier stretched his back and cricked his neck. The two mares were drinking noisily from the trough.

Moses wasn't obliged to go anywhere.

'Will you come inside? It's a hot day.'

'The shade of your house will do,' said the corporal. 'We'd like to fill our canteens.'

'Moses, take these gentlemen's canteens to the spring house and find some cool water.' There was no baggage on the horses, only holstered rifles. 'Where are you headed?'

'Where we're at. We've come to find Clara Ridgmont.'

'She's not here. I'm… associated with her family.'

'And you are?'

'Isiah Matlock.'

'Are you expecting her any time soon?'

He hoped never to set eyes on her again. 'Why do you want to see her?'

Moses had collected the canteens but lingered. 'She's gone up to Ducktown,' he said.

The corporal spat into the dirt. 'She have a good reason for that?'

'Yes and no, sir.'

'Either of you gonna give me a straight answer?'

Other blacks, men and women both, stepped out from their huts.

'I'll deal with this, Moses. Go and fill the canteens.' Matlock drew the corporal toward the house. Mitilde was at the kitchen door, wiping her hands on her apron. Cele peeked out from behind her dress, wide-eyed and quiet.

They had all turned against him since the shooting. The boy with his eyes on Hany had shouldered a sack and marched away from Comrie the next day. Matlock had to claim his own food from the kitchen; no one collected his worn clothes from his room. He hated feeling unkempt, even in front of two scruffy soldiers, but he had larger cares than that. Only a few more days. Then he'd be free of the place. 'Are you sure you won't come inside?'

'Mr Matlock, our regiment is posted down in Cleveland and there's plenty for us to do there what with most of the army busy away in Georgia. A couple of days ago our colonel received a telegram from a Julius Raht. It suggested Mrs Ridgmont was in some danger.'

How could Raht have come to know about Clara?

'Now there are lots of people in danger, what with us being in the middle of a war, but he sent a rash of telegrams, some up the line to our brigade commander, and some to the citizenry. We had the mayor come and make representations. He told us Mr Raht was on his way from Cincinnati. The mayor wouldn't leave my captain alone until he promised to send us up here to have a look.' The corporal beat the dust from his jacket. 'It's a long, dry ride, Mr Matlock.'

Matlock knew as much, having made the same journey to the bank and back only days ago. It was no simple matter pulling together six-thousand dollars. The bank manager was malleable but Matlock worried over his discretion. He'd enquired as to the need for the money and Matlock had put him in his place: the funds belonged to the Duke, Matlock had the authority and it was none of his concern. He would need to go back and collect it all when the time came. That was a pretty thought: carrying six-thousand dollars to Comrie alone.

'Mr Matlock?'

'I'm sorry.'

'I need to go back and tell them she is safe. Do you think you can oblige me in that, sir?'

'Why would Mr Raht think she is otherwise?'

'There you go again,' the corporal waved his hat in the air, 'answering a question with a question.' The second soldier leaned against the wall and closed his eyes.

Matlock decided he could safely give some ground. 'She went to recover furniture that was hidden at Ducktown before the Union came. I advised her against going. The hills are full of trouble.'

Mitilde shooed Cele inside and came down off the kitchen step. 'Mr soldier, sir.'

'Not now,' said Matlock. 'Go back inside.'

Mitilde stayed where she was. The corporal looked to her then turned back to Matlock.

'There's more to this. The mayor told us that Raht had received a telegram his self, raising the scare. Only it was short on detail. We checked with the telegraph office and they told us an old black boy, a bit like the nigger you sent away to fill our canteens, came in a few days back and gave them Mr Raht's address in Cincinnati along with a scribbled note, but he didn't have more than a few cents to send it with. It had to be shortened to one line stating that Mrs Ridgmont – Clara as he called her, on account of that being fewer letters I imagine – was gone to Ducktown and was in danger. That's all it said. Perhaps when he comes back with our water, it's the nigger I should be talkin' to?'

'You're free to, of course,' said Matlock, 'if it helps. It really would be easier inside.' He led them into the cool of the hall and sat them on the stone benches while he gathered his wits. Mitilde must have found something out from Cele. But she was too young, surely, too distressed at the loss of her mother to make sense of what he had asked Bowman to do. She can't have understood. They could only have guessed at the truth. When had Moses gone into town? It must have been soon after the shooting.

The corporal gave him more time to think by adding to his side of the story. 'We also hear Rebel irregulars are in the hills. It's gone quiet. No news has come out these past days. That ain't a good sign. There's a Mrs Barnes down in Cleveland waiting on a husband who is a couple of days beyond her expectation.'

'If you have spoken to Mrs Barnes, then you must know of Lady Ridgmont's intentions in respect to her furniture.' He dug for authority, used a tone he might to the assembled staff at Ridgmont. 'Were you testing me, Corporal?'

The corporal sat back against the wall, struggled to hold Matlock's gaze. 'I'm after the truth, is all.'

There was no further value in embarrassing him. 'I know about the irregulars,' Matlock said. That seemed a starting point rooted in truth. 'They were here three days ago. Rough men. They shot one of the blacks, mother to that child outside. I thought they might kill us all.' He considered showing them the fresh blood stain on the hunting room floor, it was all that was left when he came back from the bank. 'The old boy was fond of the mother and he has a care for Mrs Ridgmont. We all have. He must have taken it on himself to raise the alarm.'

'Without askin' you?'

'They haven't taken to me. They have their own mind on things, but they have no more idea of which way the irregulars went than I do.'

The corporal put his boot across a knee and picked at some dirt. 'You don't seem overly concerned for Mrs Ridgmont, you being *associated* with her family.'

'She's a resourceful lady. And she's with George Barnes. He'll know where to hide.'

'You're not of a mind that I should suggest to my captain

he should send a squad up to Ducktown, escort her back along the road?'

'Forgive me, are you aware of Mr Raht's interests?'

'I'm told he used to run the mines. Captain said he wasn't convinced as to the man's loyalties.'

'Quite so. He has a handful of men up there. Of course, I'm sure he's partly thinking of Clara, but perhaps also of his mines. He knows the hills are lawless. It would be to his benefit if he could persuade a squad or two to visit Ducktown and show the Union flag. By all means ask your captain to send some men. We all need protection, but it's as well he knows whose interests he's serving.'

'How exactly are you *associated* with Mrs Ridgmont?'

'I'm in her father's employ.'

'He English too?'

'He is. He's a duke.'

'A duke now?' Both soldiers laughed. 'Well, no wonder her friends get all uppity. I didn't know we was lookin' for a princess or whatever she is.'

Matlock smiled and joined the lightened mood. 'I'm sorry for your trouble. Let me see if we have some food you can take for the road back.' The corporal stood and Matlock followed them outside. Mitilde was still on the kitchen step, Moses next to her with the canteens. Matlock told Mitilde to find the soldiers something and she reluctantly headed back into the kitchen. The soldiers took the canteens and walked across the yard to their mounts.

'Your horses need a feed?' asked Moses, walking along with them.

Matlock kept close behind.

'No.'

'Or I can wash them down. It's a hot day.'

'Not much sense in that, old boy. We're just on our way again.' The corporal pulled on his gloves.

Mitilde arrived with a knotted cloth. Matlock saw her glaring at Moses who squared his shoulders and cleared his throat. 'Mr Corporal, sir, I'd like to talk with you.'

The corporal glanced at Matlock who held his palms up in resignation.

''Bout Miss Clara, that's to say Mrs Ridgmont.'

'I think I understand well enough. I'll tell my captain that she's been fool enough to ride up into the hills and will have to take her chances. We'll see what he thinks about that. And I'll tell him I found two old blacks so flushed with freedom they thought they could take to sendin' telegrams and kickin' up a ruckus.'

Mitilde stepped in. 'But, sir—'

'But nothin'. I got a hot ride back to Cleveland to match the hot one out and what in the hell for? You take your lead from Mr Matlock, you hear?' He took the food parcel, tucked it into his saddlebag, then mounted.

Matlock exhaled. He'd turned them around, left Bowman to do what was necessary. The horses walked away. Mitilde had such a look on her it made Matlock think he should have left with the soldiers. A few more days. He need stay only a few more days. The other blacks had advanced half across the yard.

'This ain't done yet,' Mitilde said. 'Mr Raht will be here soon.' Moses took her arm and walked toward the kitchen where Cele was waiting. 'Then we'll see,' she said. 'Then we'll see.'

Georgia – July 1864

Sleep was a good friend to Shire: it sought out his company, blessed him with a deep and dreamless state. He hadn't known a man could be this tired. After the weeks of fighting, after Kennesaw and his salvation, it was as if fifty years had been added to his span. Sleep excused him from imagining what sort of prison awaited to the south, from thoughts of Tuck, Mason and Ocks. Sleep was an attendant nurse, constantly close to him, pulling over a blanket of pure weariness. He wound himself into it like a played out infant.

They spent two days on the train, most of it as stationary as a gatepost. Thin slants of light angled in through gaps in the planking. It was hot. There was no escape unless the train started to move and a trickle breeze found a way in. The prisoners sat with their backs against the warm wood. Shire mostly lay down and slept. There was room enough. He wished in his baking half-sleep for a storm to come and cool the air but none obliged.

They were let out only the once into nothing but low scrub forest beside the track, no hint of where they were or where they were going. They grouped into the shade of the boxcar and drank what little water was granted them.

On the second night, Shire was constantly bumped and buffeted, the train starting and stopping, backing up and lurching forward. He got himself sideways to the side-planking, looked out through a knothole and saw shadow-houses slip slowly by in the moonlight, an occasional thin glow behind a curtain. Atlanta, most likely.

One prisoner, a bullet graze at the join of his neck, had a fever. The next time they were watered they each gave up a tithe and asked for more to bathe the wound, but none came. He went into delirium and Shire chose sleep again over the man's lost thoughts and pleas for comfort. There was nothing to be done. It was the same as Shire's future. There was no steering toward any outcome. He'd lost all volition. He would go to prison to endure or die. That was all.

When the boxcar door slid open the next morning, they were invited out. 'Him too,' said the guard, pointing at the fevered man, who they half-slid to the opening and passed down. It became clear they wouldn't be getting back in. A hot hour passed before a stretcher was brought and the wounded man taken away. Shire didn't see him again.

They spent the morning in a shadeless stockade, part of a larger haul. Rebels with rifles perched on the corners of the rail fence. For lack of anything to do, Shire counted the crowd at a hundred and forty. By noon, the direct sun was so cruel that he had to lay his hot jacket over his face to stop himself from burning. He heard raised voices and looked out to see a Union officer arguing with a guard, demanding water and food, insisting he see their captain. The guard pressed him away with the butt of his rifle. Water arrived and the men queued to use the single tin cup.

'Owen Stanton!'

Shire was nearing the front of the line. His whole attention on the water, he barely heard the call.

'I'm looking for Owen Stanton, 125th Ohio.'

It was odd to hear his given name. 'Here,' he said dryly and raised his better arm.

'Come with me.'

'I need some water.'

'Right now. We'll get you water.'

The Rebel corporal wouldn't share what this was about. Shire was marched over the tracks and put on a train going back the way he'd come. Not in a boxcar but a passenger car in blissful shade. He had his own guard who, from his worn garb and gaunt underfed look, might have been a prisoner himself but for the gun. He sat across from Shire, as relaxed as if they were starting on a day out.

'Where are we going?' Shire asked.

'Atlanta.'

'Why?'

'I have no idea. I'm to take you to the Trout House Hotel.'

Shire could make no sense of it. Why should he be singled out? This could only be down to Tod. No one else knew where he was. After the water there was a cracker and a half-burned but cold cob of corn. Shire took his time with it. The train was no faster than the one down and the afternoon was over before, once again, he was between the houses of Atlanta, creaking past machine works and factories, other engines and sidings full of boxcars. They disembarked in a great high-roofed station. They walked down the busy platform and no one gave Shire a second look despite his Union hat. He took it off anyway. It would have been the easiest thing to race away and lose himself in the crowd but for the wound in his leg; that and his curiosity. They emerged onto a square as busy as the station. His guard gripped him by the arm and led him round to the right. Dodging carriages, they cut the corner and headed for a four-story box of a building with the name 'Trout House' spelled out one giant letter at a time between the windows on the highest floor. He was led in and parked against a paneled wall while the guard visited the desk. Then they sat together, the guard more nervous of the place than Shire was. 'You have some wealthy friends?'

'Not in Georgia.'

They waited long enough for Shire to consider this all might be a mistake and that he'd soon be back at the stockade, when a tall silver-haired gentleman in full dinner-dress approached them.

Shire stood. The man took time to survey him.

'Well, well,' the man smiled. 'I never truly thought we'd meet, Shire.' He offered his hand. Shire hesitated lest he dirty the starched white cuffs.

*

Trenholm noted how Shire made hard work of the stairs. He was used to entertaining soldiers in the reception room that was part of his suite, but exclusively officers, and usually those who'd the time and means to wash and dress. This boy was all in, but there was nothing for it; time wasn't on Atlanta's side. 'You can get cleaned up later. Best we talk first.'

Trenholm tried to reconcile the Shire that stood before him with the mental picture he'd created of the boy. It was over a year since he'd first heard his name. In truth, there wasn't much of a boy left. He looked older than Trenholm had expected. Perhaps that was the half-grown beard and the dirt. There were blood stains on his sleeve and pants. Beneath all that, Shire was tall and broad.

'How bad are your wounds?'

'I just need to keep them clean.'

He spoke well. The Queen's English. 'There'll be time for that. And we'll get you some fresh clothes.'

'I don't know why I'm here or who you are,' Shire said flatly.

He behaved like a man not unused to elevated company. 'Please, sit down. Don't mind the furnishings. I have brandy or coffee? Real coffee.'

Shire appeared genuinely torn.

'Brandy first,' said Trenholm. 'Coffee to follow.'

Shire lowered himself into the leather chair like it was an over-hot bath. 'Forgive me,' he said. 'I haven't sat in a chair like this for a good while.'

Trenholm passed a crystal glass into a steady but filthy hand. 'It's been a tough fight for you boys down from Chattanooga.'

'There were objections from your side.'

'Quite so. Quite so. General Johnston insists that you pay your way.' Trenholm raised his glass. 'But here's a belated toast to your efforts last year, for reaching Clara.'

Caution entered Shire's eyes.

'There's no need to close up on me. I know all about you. My name is George Trenholm. Did Clara ever speak of me?'

'She did… with affection.'

'Well, that's gratifying. I'd hate to think otherwise. You owe me none, though. For most of last year, I was trying to have you killed.'

'Lots of people seem to have a mind to that.'

'I prefer to think my reasons were patriotic. You see, and it shames me to say this, I came to know about Taylor's behavior toward Clara. I hoped, stupidly as it transpired, that he might mend his ways.'

'I'd be lying if I said I thought that was to your credit. Taylor was a long way beyond redemption.'

'Indeed. Clara wrote to me after you saved her.' He handed Shire another crystal glass, this one full of water. 'I want you to know that I care for Clara, I made a promise to her as I understand you did. It's why you're here.'

'I kept my promise to Clara. That's done.'

Trenholm heard the enmity and decided to dig a little. 'Did you not get the outcome you desired?'

'When last I saw her, she was safe. That was the desired outcome.'

'We're all allowed to dream, Shire. The world's built on dreams.'

Shire drank his water. Trenholm moved on. 'I had thought all that behind us too, but I have a wider world view than you have been afforded of late. Two days ago, I received a telegram from a friend of mine in Cincinnati. News comes through the lines if you have the right connections. My friend, Julius Raht, used to run the mines at Ducktown. He's a friend of Clara's too.'

'I have met Mr Raht.'

'Good. Then you'll know he can be trusted. His note told me he was concerned for Clara. He'd received a telegram himself from one of the Negroes at Comrie. It didn't say much except that she had gone to Ducktown and was thought to be in danger. Raht plans to get to Comrie himself as soon as he can.'

Shire sat forward in his seat. 'What sort of danger?'

'I truly don't know.'

'Her furniture was taken to the mines in the autumn. Hidden there. She must have gone to retrieve it. I was at Comrie in April.'

'Still seeing to her safety, no doubt.'

'I was wounded, there to convalesce.'

'Nothing quite so handsome as a wounded soldier. Was Matlock there?'

Shire looked pained. 'Isiah Matlock?'

'The same. Steward to the Duke of Ridgmont.'

'Why would he be there?'

'He was mentioned in a letter from Raht a few weeks back. I had dealings with Mr Matlock, last year in Nassau. He's a money man. I'm guessing, but perhaps, after Taylor's death, the Duke sent him to take stock.'

'Matlock will put money before people every day of the week.'

'I have the measure of the man. The danger to Clara might be connected.'

'I don't see how a Union prisoner can help.'

Trenholm noted the intent. 'We'll come to that. As I said, I received Raht's note only two days ago. Then your name popped up. I put you on a watch-list last year so I could hear if you had been taken prisoner or killed. It was never removed so, yesterday, I was notified of your capture. We're rarely this efficient in the South. Or maybe some higher order took a hand. The day after I hear Clara is in danger, her hero surfaces. At the very least it's serendipitous, wouldn't you say?'

'I'm not a hero, and certainly not hers.'

'Duty and reward aren't always bedfellows.'

'What are you asking? That I ride to Ducktown and find her again?'

'Actually, yes, but not alone. You'd never get there.' Trenholm walked to his desk and searched among his papers. 'First I need to know where your loyalties lie.'

'I'm a Union soldier.'

'A *captured* Union soldier, one destined to wait out the war in prison. The Confederacy has barely enough food for its own soldiers. The odds are that the war will last longer than you.' He found what he was looking for and held it up. 'Parole papers. Releasing you if you promise not to fight again.'

'And go where?'

'Anywhere you please. Ducktown to begin with, then perhaps Comrie, into the West? Home?'

*

Home was an idea Shire had learned to live without, it avoided facing up to the final loss that awaited him there but, when Trenholm said the word, he felt the simple power of it, the sudden idea that he might be done with the war and see Ridgmont again. His brandy smelled of freedom and he put it down lest it cloud his mind. 'My home isn't what it was, Mr Trenholm.'

'Very few are in these times. You could have gone back to England after you saved Clara, but you didn't.'

Clara had spoken fondly of Trenholm. He didn't look as far past his prime as Shire might have expected. 'It would have made me a deserter. There were people depending on me.'

'In the army?'

'Have you fought, Mr Trenholm? Do you know what it means to leave your friends to struggle on without you?'

'I know what it's like to have people rely on me. Lots of people. I'm recently become the Financial Secretary for the Confederacy. You might say the whole Confederacy depends on me, at least in regard to our economy.' He sat back on his desk and looked out the window. 'It's like tending to a dying child.'

Shire surveyed the room, began to understand that he was speaking to a man with power over many things, not least Shire's own future. He was many flights of steps up from the prisoner stockade where he'd spent the morning.

Trenholm turned back to Shire and waved the paper.

'This would free you from obligation. You have fought, you are captured. There is no dishonor in parole.'

'What do I have to do to earn this parole?'

'It's not a question of earning it. I just couldn't have a Union prisoner as part of a mission to Ducktown.'

'A mission to save Clara?'

'That's your part. There is another.'

'Perhaps you had better tell me what that is.'

Trenholm held the papers higher. 'I'll tell you when you're a civilian.'

Shire asked himself what there was to lose? Any soldier he knew would sign a parole rather than go to prison. Trenholm arranged the papers on the desk, inked a pen, held it out and smiled like a wise uncle. Shire pushed himself up from the chair and looked at the document. It was smartly drawn up with 'to whomever it may concern' in thick capitals at the top, then the promise not to take up arms unless fairly exchanged. There was space for his name and regiment. That's all that was required. Thoughts of home bunched up inside him: Father's house at Ridgmont, empty and waiting; his place in the regiment with Tuck, Mason and Ocks. That was the nearer home. How could he ever go back? He had murdered Wick. The reason didn't excuse the crime. He wrestled his mind to face the other way. This wasn't about going back. It was about moving forward, away from the war. He took the pen, steadied the paper with his left hand and signed, leaving three dirty smudges where his fingertips had been.

'You're going to need a new hat.'

Shire lifted off his Union kepi and tidied a loose thread, then set it down and attended to his brandy.

'Copper, *Mr* Stanton. My other care is copper. The Confederacy is running out and if we are to hold Atlanta until the other side of the Union presidential election, we're going to need a supply, if only to keep our rifles firing. Now, as an old shareholder, and as a friend of Mr Raht, I happen to know there's a ready supply of smelted copper stockpiled in the Ducktown mines. I've had my mind on it for some time.'

'There's no railroad to Ducktown, and no decent road except from the west. And if you could get there, how would you bring out enough copper to make a difference?'

'Mules. I've been collecting them, and not the run-down skeletons that the army employs. I've paid top dollar and have over two hundred collected a fast ride northeast of Atlanta, each with new leather saddlebags and strong enough to carry a man's weight in copper. It's a one trip deal. If we can get them back here before Sherman surrounds us, it might buy us a month.'

Shire envisioned a month of rifle fire in one apocalyptic volley.

'But the copper isn't your concern. The mule train will simply deliver you to Ducktown. I'm relying on your heretofore demonstrated persistence to find Clara.'

'How long will it take?'

'If you leave tomorrow, once you reach the mules, maybe a week.'

'She might already be safely back at Comrie.' He felt a sudden and deep stab of alarm as if, in trying not to think of Clara all these weeks, he'd simply hoarded up the worry. 'Or we might be too late.'

'As I said, I have a lot of people depending on me. Sending you as my proxy is the best I can do. If Clara is safe, then you can ride down to Comrie and pitch up as a free man. If you make it back to me, here or in Charleston, I'll do my best to get you through the blockade and back to England.'

There it was again, the heartfelt tug of England. 'That's my choice then. Walk out of here or go to Ducktown and get a free ride home?'

Trenholm walked around behind his desk and sat in his chair. 'To be honest, I don't believe you need any encouragement from me, but if you choose not to go to Ducktown, I'll get you home anyway, in recompense for my treatment of you last year. Clara would want as much.' He smiled. 'But we both know you have no real choice.'

'I suppose we do.'

'That's settled then. I'll arrange a room for you here tonight. We'll find you civilian clothes and a physician, though the latter's a tall order.'

'I'm grateful.'

'One thing might delay you starting. I have ten troopers lined up as an escort to the mule train but the lieutenant I'd earmarked to lead them got himself killed east of Marietta. I need to find someone new.'

'What sort of man?'

'An officer. Someone resourceful enough to operate in Union territory. Someone with an eye to logistics.'

'A quartermaster?'

'Possibly, but he has to be on my side of the argument.'

'Then I may have a name you can throw into my new hat.'

Northern Georgia – July 1864

Free from the press of the Union Army, Shire felt more inclined to lift his head and look around. What he noted, here northeast of Atlanta, was that the trees were taller, bare straight trunks right up to the canopy. You could have built a three-story house beneath them and the roof wouldn't have troubled the first bough. Tod rode beside him, quiet for the moment. Ahead was their guide, Clemens. If Shire cared to turn he would see, following on behind, two hundred mules roped into tens, each set led by a trooper or one of the hired teamsters.

'We're passing west of Garland,' called Clemens over his shoulder. He wore a long, dark coat in denial of the heat. His gray hair escaped his hat and spread every which way across his shoulders. Slouched on the lead mule, rein in hand, he was in the habit of telling Shire where they were, or at least where they were near to. Thus far, he'd avoided even the smallest of settlements, lest news of their long mule train moving toward the mountains got ahead of them. Shire had suggested earlier that surely the news couldn't travel much faster than they did themselves. Clemens said he'd been guiding in these hills long before there was a war to be concerned with and that he'd come to believe the hills could talk. He told Shire of a time when, 'As a younger man, I'd been carrying a letter to the sheriff in Ellijay, riding hard all the way. The matter was somewhat urgent as it concerned a hanging that needed to be forestalled. I shared the message with a cousin of mine when I stopped to eat not far out of Atlanta. When I got to Ellijay, they had a room made up for me and the Sheriff knew the contents of the letter.'

It was easy, and not unpleasant, to set Clemens off on these stories while the mules rocked them all onwards. It helped distract Shire from thoughts of Clara. He sniffed the musky air and considered the stink of two hundred mules on a hot day would certainly get ahead of them.

Clemens spat tobacco juice in an impressive arc to the side of the track. 'Before the war, if I hankered for whiskey, I could steer to most any farm hereabouts and be obliged with a nip or two, but the army took the stills for the copper early on. Those left are well hidden. No church bells neither. All melted down for cannon to call you Union boys to the congregation in the sky. All gone. We'll pass north of Dahlonega tomorrow. Not so flat there.'

Considering the ups and downs on his advance to Chattanooga last summer, Shire thought it not unreasonable to call where they were flat. The rises and falls were gentle enough. Flatness could be considered a relative term. The vistas were certainly even, except for Kennesaw Mountain which he'd glimpsed way back to the west after setting out yesterday. He thought of how what transpired at Kennesaw had translated him in so many ways: from Union to Confederacy, from a soldier to a free man, from an honest soul to a murderer. He was struggling with all three, but mostly with the latter.

The high trees were well spaced, shade only ever temporary. Shire strained to recall an English sky but was sure none were ever as painfully bright as they were here. There was a constant sheen, a hot veil that took the edge off the blue. Georgia might be pleasant enough any other time than summer. He tugged the brim of his new slouch hat over his eyes. His old Union kepi was in his saddlebag. He'd not had the heart to part with it.

A mule train wasn't something you could hurry along. Tod had made it clear he didn't want the mules blown on the journey up, not when they were each going to carry a personal load of copper all the way back. It was about making the quickest roundtrip, not just the leg up to Ducktown. But then Tod knew nothing of Clara – no one else did. Trenholm had been firm on that point. 'It wouldn't do,' he'd said to Shire before they'd parted, 'for people to get the idea I've taken men from the army for my own ends.' So Shire silently chafed at the pace Clemens and Tod set and tried to keep Clara from his mind.

He'd been happier on the dawn train that took them east out of Atlanta to Stone Mountain and then on the fast two-day ride up to Gainesville where the mule train was waiting. There had been some urgency then, but at Gainesville Tod had reverted to a quartermaster and spent a whole morning satisfying himself that Trenholm had supplied everything they would need. It would avoid delays later on, he said.

Waddell kept permanent close station behind Tod. Trenholm seemed to have no trouble springing Tod from the army and Tod had insisted that Waddell should come along, telling Shire he wanted at least one man on this trip that he knew.

'You know me,' Shire had said.

Tod had smiled. 'Two then.'

Middle afternoon was the hottest time of all. The insects provided an endless vibrating whistle. The ground beneath Shire's plodding horse was dry, the earth a rich red where it was exposed, but the air was heavy and moist, so that each breath had a tangible substance to it. 'Air you can chew on,'

Tod said. Despite the heat and the slow pace, Shire was content to be riding a horse again, a mare that, for a while at least, he could pretend was his own. He stroked her neck and wondered if he was expected to give her up at Ducktown.

He was surprised, given the slow pace, not to find himself more concerned for Clara. There was no denying his mood was light. Maybe it was that after months of fretting he was almost free of obligation to her or to anyone else, free to find his own future away from the cannon and the slaughter. Or maybe it was the simple fact that he'd turned two points of the compass and was heading straight toward Clara once more, and that his heart was at ease with that.

The track entered a long, grassy clearing where the insects were louder than ever. A trooper edged his mount alongside Shire so they were three abreast: Tod, himself and the trooper.

'Mr Shire, sir.' The man wore a wide smile. 'I was wonderin' if you might tell me again 'bout England.'

The novelty of being English, which had largely worn off in the 125th, was playing out all over again. Reb's would seek him out and walk their horses beside him or sit next to him on a halt. They'd engage in any dialogue at all just to laugh at his accent. Some wouldn't bother with a topic but simply ask him to say something and then do their best at an imitation.

'I think we've heard that story,' said Tod. 'Look to your mules, or they'll be away in the long grass.'

The soldier turned his horse and left, but Waddell spoke up. 'Why in the hell are you fighting for the Yankees, anyhow?'

Shire said he no longer was. He thought it best to leave aside any personal motivation and said it had been largely down to happenstance in the first place. That didn't satisfy.

'You should fight with us,' Waddell said. 'We're the injured party in this war. Nothin' but Dutch and Irish in the Yankee Army.'

Shire considered himself living disproof of the assertion. The conversation led to thoughts of sailing home. He simply had to accept Trenholm's offer. The mistake was to think about England with any precision. If he imagined himself at Ridgmont, then he had to face again the loss of his father as well as an empty and crumbling house. Matlock, who'd had such a hand in his misfortune, might by then have returned and once again be running the estate. If he thought only of the word, *England*, it was easier. Into those two syllables he could pile his happier memories; bundled together, they glowed with some unspecified agglomerated comfort. But Clara would, once again, be an ocean away.

He caught Tod looking at him sideways.

'What?'

'If you don't mind me saying, your story lacks something.'

Shire did mind him saying. 'What does it lack?'

'Motivation. *Man is his desire.*'

'Aristotle.'

'Very good. The way you talk about home you had it all buttoned up but for a girl. Teaching with your father, plans to study. No famine, no war to drive you across the Atlantic.'

'My desire was America. You don't feel the pull from the inside. There were plenty like me in New York.'

'Not a good time to pitch up though, in the middle of a war.'

'I hadn't intended to participate.'

'Have it your way.' Tod smiled. 'But I know a little concerning stories and yours has me thoughtful. Not many Union privates are known to the likes of Secretary Trenholm.'

'I told you. It's all family connections.'

'It's still an odd route back into the Union, via Ducktown, but I'll do as I'm told and give you *every assistance*. No matter that I saved your life.'

Shire could see Tod was only half serious. He liked the man. When they were camped and Waddell wasn't in such close attendance, he might tell him more. What harm could it do?

*

Tod would have been deceiving himself if he didn't admit he was happy. Of course he felt guilty being away from the 20th Tennessee, given he'd spent the best part of three months getting back to them, but here he was, with his own independent command, ten troopers, a dozen teamsters and, above all, a mission that truly mattered. The best way to help the 20th Tennessee, which even now he knew would be withdrawing toward Atlanta, was to make sure they had the means to fire back as the summer wore on. That meant reaching Ducktown, finding the copper, and making it back into Atlanta before the Yankees arrived. It would mean promotion for sure, especially with Trenholm in the mix.

They made good ground each day. By not pushing the pace he was able to keep the mules moving for longer. Before Dahlonega the land began to ruck up a little more and the climbs became steeper. They crested a ridge and the mountains proper came into view as a retreating line of gray-blue silhouettes. The next day was nothing but up. The red soil gave way to gray outcrops of rock on the high side of the path. On the low side the land fell away so steeply that they passed by half way up the tree trunks. And the trees were denser, smaller, hugging the mountains. Civilization was a rare thing. There were one-room farms with fields of maze so small you could have finished planting them before breakfast.

On the second night out of Gainesville, they camped in the dark of the forest. Shire was good company. He was a scholar as Tod had been. They had fought the same battles, albeit on opposite sides. Though they were much the same age, Tod somehow felt the more worldly-wise of the two. Despite his travels, his scars and his solid frame, Shire retained the air of an innocent, like he didn't belong in a war. It was hard to imagine him charging the line or making evil use of a bayonet. More than that, there was no good reason for Shire to be here. Soldiers were exchanged across army lines all the time; you didn't have to trek into the Appalachians to achieve the same end. It was hard not to be curious.

After they had eaten and Tod had checked on the men, he sat and took a tin mug of some truly excellent coffee that Trenholm had supplied. He tried to get Shire to open up while Waddell whittled away just beyond the light of the fire. Shire seemed at ease and gave him a tour of his wounds. The burn on his cheek was from a riot in New York; the round dent in his chest he'd gained cresting Missionary Ridge only minutes before they met last year. The new shoulder and leg gashes he'd taken in the abatis at Kennesaw were healing but would add to his collection. 'I'd given up on the world that day. I truly had.'

Interesting as it was to hear of battles seen from the other side, Tod suspected that wasn't where the secrets lay. 'When they tell the history of all this, it'll be about the battles. Tell me of the times between. How did you come to Franklin?'

'Down the Ohio. We were in Louisville a while and then

steamed up the Cumberland to Nashville and marched down the pike to Franklin. I liked Franklin. I liked your farm.'

Tod suffered a sudden bout of jealousy: though Shire had left Franklin more than a year ago, he'd been in Tod's home and spoken to his father and brother more recently than Tod had. This mission in the hills might be a welcome change, but it was a long way from Franklin. The Confederacy would have to win or lose the war for Tod to make it home. 'How did you go at Chickamauga?'

'I thought you didn't want to discuss the battles?'

'I'm happy to talk about the ones we won.'

'I was captured after the first day's fighting, but I escaped and found my way back to my regiment. A little like you, except I did it in one morning.'

Tod realized Shire was telling him everything and nothing at all. It was all where he'd been and what he'd done, but light as to why. He took a chance. 'Shire,' he said, 'tell me one thing, yes or no. Somewhere in all this, is there a woman?'

It was left hanging for a while.

'Yes.'

'I'm guessing it didn't end well?'

'I'm still trying to work out if it's ended.'

'Ha. Some of them stick with you, don't they? It's never finished if you keep thinking on them. I came down the Ohio too. There was this lady on my boat and, well, if this coffee was whiskey, I might tell you a thing or two that would make your toes blush. That might be a Yankee river, but I'll bless it as long as I live.'

'Trenholm gave me some whiskey. Scottish whiskey, would you believe?'

'I'm sorely tempted, but we'd have to share it with Waddell.' He spoke loudly into the dark. 'I can hear you whittling out there, Waddell. How the hell can a man whittle in the dark, anyway?' Tod moved away from the fire. It was cooler in these mountains and he reached for his blanket. 'We'll save your whiskey for another night.'

Isabella Mine, Ducktown – July 1864

Clara drifted in and out of shallow sleep to the accompaniment of cave music, the never-ending drips. She was spirited to her bed at Comrie. Through the window came the distant snap, snap of gunfire. She knew within the utter certainty of the dream that it came from the mountain church where she'd married. Moldered soldiers, carted back from Chickamauga and Chattanooga, clambered from their graves. Taylor was with them, restored in body, handsome as he ever was. To escape him she flew over the hills to Ducktown only to fall screaming down the mineshaft. Taylor ordered the soldiers into line. They would march the Copper Road and come for her.

She woke to burning cramps, tried to ride out the discomfort, thinking them nothing more than an extension of the hunger pains that had grown worse as the real days, days filled with people and light, passed by above her. This latest stab was so acute that she moaned and worried Tonkin might wake.

When they were down to their last hour of lamp oil, she had finally persuaded him they should move closer to the bottom of the shaft. Otherwise, she argued, they would have no light by which to move their beds. It meant they slept only a few feet apart, their new bedroom no more than the widest part of the passageway.

Tonkin's breathing was unchanged and Clara tightened her eyes until the pain began to ebb. She should go to the latrine. She sat up in the heavy darkness. It must still be night as there wasn't any hint of light from the shaft. She edged off the chaise lounge and felt for the wall. She began taking the smallest of steps, wary she might stub her toe on the hidden thrusts of rock that lined the passage.

Though she moved carefully, she was sure enough of her way. She'd done this so many times. The ridges in the wall were familiar, the drips guided her. She was become a creature adapted to the dark, a mole who, but for lack of food, might live out a life here in Taylor's domain. Not content with haunting her above ground, he had conspired to have her join him in the underworld. The sharp pain returned, insisted that she hurry. Twice before she reached the copper hall, she stopped and doubled over.

The stink of the latrine grew stronger until, surrendering to the impulse, she bent and dry-retched. Amid the unproductive heaving, she felt something give and a dampness between her legs. She couldn't bear going closer to the latrine. Instead, risking harm, she hurried on as best she could to the mound of copper and clambered behind, slipping on the loose, outlying ingots. She knew there was a low depression here in the cave wall and desperately felt for it. She found it and backed in, lifted her dress and hurried to draw down her undergarments, though they were already wet. She braced herself in her refuge, squatted with one hand on the wall and the other holding her bunched dress. All those times with Taylor and nothing took. She waited and wept through spasm after spasm, lost to the world, utterly alone, until there was a final and full rush that splashed onto the rock floor. She might endure for a while without food, as Tonkin said people did, but the life within her, could not.

Northern Georgia – July 1864

Shire swigged the last from his canteen then knelt on a smooth rock to reach into the stream and fill it, enjoying the cool water that ran over his skin. Higher in the mountains, they were never far from water; it tumbled and babbled between the trees, provided a constant and soothing accompaniment.

They needed more halts like this one to rest the mules. The paths were become narrow and awkward, winding around barn-sized boulders. Shire had been forced to dismount and lead his horse up this latest climb. The steepness tugged at his leg wound.

Clemens came to stand above him, the guide's gray hair hung forward like a greasy waterfall. 'Hold out your hands.'

Shire put down his canteen and stood. 'Why?'

'Hold them out.'

He did. Clemens, with childlike glee, poured a long yellow and black millipede into the cup Shire had made. Shire fought the first impulse to drop it. The creature hurried from hand to hand until he set it down out of the way.

'Sniff your fingers.'

There was a rich smell of cherries and almonds, so strong it made Shire dizzy. He smiled, transformed into a ten-year-old like Clemens.

'Shame you can't eat them, ain't it? These you can. Partridge berries.' Clemens picked a half-dozen red berries from a low creeping plant that lived among the dead mossy wood. He shared them with Shire. They tasted of nothing, the merest hint of sweetness.

When Tod started them upward again, Shire roped his horse to the lead mules so that he could walk beside Clemens. Where the path crossed a stream, Clemens lifted a salamander from under a rock. He pointed to ironwood trees, their trunks corded like muscle, to yellow poplars. 'We call them yellow poppers on account of the racket they make when you use them for firewood.' The forest was not much better than twilight where the canopy was unbroken, but here and there old hemlocks lay like slain goliaths, letting in the sky. The clouds were building out there.

Later, the path emerged into the open air high on the side of a deep ravine. The slope down to some hidden watercourse was so steep that the trees had given it over to bracken and bush. Shire and Clemens walked abreast, Shire nearest the drop as the path hugged the hill. At one spot the path was replaced by underpinned planking where, at some time or another, it had been swept away. The army of mules became noisy as they took to the wood. Shire stretched his neck to look down and could see where the lost soil had run out below, the ferns beginning to claim it.

'You not one for heights?' asked Clemens.

'I just trust whoever built this bridge of sorts considered that one day a weight of mules might test his engineering.'

'It's endured a few years. There ain't many paths good enough for us. It's a day's detour to avoid it.'

They reached solid ground again. Further along, above the path, was a single small tree and Clemens waved at it.

'See that red tree, its leaves on the turn though it's only mid-summer? Some call that an Ohio buckeye, though I've never discovered why. You were in an Ohio regiment they tell me.'

'I was,' said Shire, conscious of the past tense.

'Were your boys the first to turn?'

Shire felt an undeniable pang of loss. 'We never got into the habit.'

The open ground didn't last and before long they were back in the forest. The weather broke early afternoon and soon breached the canopy. Tod called another halt and the men left the mules on the path to find what cover they could. Shire fought through the downpour and retrieved his horse. He led it to the partial shelter of a tall mossy rock and took himself into a burned-out hemlock trunk with Tod. The tree stood tall and alive but with a charcoal cave big enough for them both. 'Let's hope the rumors concerning lightning have some substance,' Shire said.

Tod smiled. 'There's a simple pleasure in looking out on a storm and being powerless to do anything. Some sort of freedom.'

'We're imprisoned though. No freedom in that.'

'We know it will pass. I knew some men that found freedom in prison, freedom from fighting.'

'You never thought to wait it out? The war, I mean. You'd done your share.'

'My brother Moscow, he did his fighting early on and was captured. After that, he signed a parole thinking that his first duty was to his children, him being a widower. I don't have children, but I never could see it that way. You can't step out of a fight while the other fella is still swinging.'

'I never heard of anyone who traveled so far as you to get back into the war.'

'You came a long way to join one.'

'I was foolish. I had no idea what was ahead of me.' If anything, the rain was harder out there. Shire could barely see the nearest mule for the thickness of it.

329

Tod brushed out a space, sat down and took off his hat. Shire followed suit.

'That journey changed me some,' Tod said.

'Some journeys do.'

'This one more than most.'

Shire sensed that Tod would tell more if he just waited.

'After I escaped the train, I was a night in some wet woods. Miserable cold rain, not a washing rain like this. The next day I was all but finished but I found a farm. They took me in, hid me a while then sent me on my way with a set of clothes and a hopeful dollar.'

'Why didn't they turn you in?'

'It was against their way. They were Amish. They extracted their price though. I didn't promise exactly, but the farmer, Luther, he said that if the time came to kill again, I was to remember there was a choice. I didn't think much on it at the time, but since then, no matter what the circumstance, I can't bring myself to fight.' Tod threw a twig out into the rain. 'I've not told anyone this before.'

'Why tell me?'

'Well, to begin with, you can't deny that the war insists on re-introducing us from time to time. It only seems right that we get to know one another, but more than that, it appears to me that what Luther said was to your benefit. At Kennesaw I couldn't fire a shot. If I'd been busy killing, I doubt I'd have come and dragged you from the fire.'

Shire leaned back on the blackened wood and considered what he was hearing: that some man unknown to him in Pennsylvania had, by nothing more than peaceful intent, saved his life. The rain eased a little and the silence between them drew out. Shire felt called on to say something, to pass some sort of judgment. 'You're a quartermaster. It's not so hard to avoid the killing if you want to.'

'That's true enough, I just don't think I should. Besides, Luther had a view on that too. He said my being a quartermaster merely facilitated killing by others. And he's right. I've been thinking on what he would make of this venture. If I'm successful and get the copper back to Atlanta, there's no telling how many men will die as a result, on both sides if it extends the war. Sometimes I think it might have been better if I had missed that farm. I might have gotten my neck stretched but, up to that point, I'd been clearer in my thinking… Look, the rain has stopped. Let's get going, the mules will dry all the quicker.'

Soon after they started again, the path flattened and widened. Shire was able to ride for a while. He kept his own company, thinking about the flipside to Tod's confession, if that's what it was, and how it applied to him. He'd been so caught up in the notion of his own future, so secretly content to be tending toward Clara again, that he'd had little mind as to how what he was doing might eventually sit with him. Every tiny piece of copper retrieved for the Confederacy might ultimately spark the end of Tuck or Mason or Ocks. Parole papers didn't address the issue of friends. What if the copper was enough for the Rebels to slaughter a Union attack as they did at Kennesaw, enough to hold Atlanta until the presidential election? You could argue up any circumstance into a larger consequence, but what was clear was that if these mules returned to Atlanta in good time, then many more Union soldiers would die. That small matter aside, Shire considered he had his own ethical dilemma, though dilemma wasn't really the word for something in the past. He *had* done some killing recently.

After the rain, the sweet forest scent multiplied ten-fold

to rival that of damp mule. They crested a ridge without ever seeing beyond the trees and began to descend. Shire was riding again when Waddell, on foot, caught up to him and handed up a walking stick, saying nothing more than, 'Here.'

Shire dropped his reins and held the stick flat in both hands. It was a moment before he started to see it for what it was. By then, Waddell had dropped back down the train. The rounded handle was an eagle head, a *bald* eagle such that you could see on so many Union flags, including that of the 125th. The grain of its proud neck-feathers linked to the shaft above a lead band. For a palm's width below the band the wood was carved into a stormy sea. The waves merged to form a twisted rope that noosed a man, a black man by his features. Shire turned the stick over to see he had four faces, each bearing a different complexion of agony. His bare feet rested on the caps of four soldiers, each standing to attention and they, in turn, stood on a muddle of bones and skulls in the midst of which was a simple heart, such as a lover might carve. Below, the thinning wood was shaped into four flat sides with a word carved in harsh angled letters onto each. Shire read them one at a time: Chickamauga, Missionary Ridge, Kennesaw and Franklin. The tip was banded by the same gray lead as the handle.

It was Shire's story. Waddell had sat out in the dark, listened to him speaking with Tod and fashioned what he'd heard into the wood. It was wonderful and terrible. How had he done this in so short a time? Shire examined it endlessly as he rode, the forest forgotten. He discovered that of the four soldiers, one was smart as a new recruit. The next had a scar on his face, the third the same with his uniform torn. The last was the most ragged of all, unshaven, his eyes hollowed out and, unlike the others, he held no gun, but in among the bones at his feet there was a small, discarded book, a Bible perhaps. This was who he had become, this last ragged soldier without a guiding hand. All this time Shire had been soul-searching as to what sort of man he might now be and Waddell had done a better job just by listening in.

At their next stop he sought Waddell out and thanked him. 'I have nothing to pay you with.'

'I don't need no payment. We are not a people devoid of generosity. Thought it might keep the weight off that leg wound.'

'The battles,' Shire said, 'when we fought our way into Franklin, it was only a skirmish. It wouldn't rank alongside the other three.'

'It's what came to me, is all.'

Later in the afternoon, the way turned upward again, so steep that there was no way of forcing the pace. Shire led his horse, his eyes on the ground. He made use of his new walking stick and learned not to step off path where the age-old decay was more mulch than solid. He concentrated on each step. It became hypnotic: roots and rocks, roots and rocks, the occasional orchid his only distraction.

The air began to cool and the light to thin. Clemens led them out onto a great bald, a high meadow with hand-sized monarch butterflies dancing above knee-high grass. Tod concurred with Clemens that it was a good place to camp for the night and they let the mules free to graze under a pale blue sky. The troopers and the teamsters spread out to make their own fires and rest.

Shire helped Clemens collect wood and they bounded their intended fire with heavy logs. Clemens set to lighting it. 'One more full day,' he said, as Tod joined them, 'morning after we'll come to Ducktown.'

Shire swallowed hard, as if there was a battle beyond the next day. Would there be any news of Clara? 'Best we drink my whiskey tonight then. I'd hate to part from you with it unopened.'

Waddell was suddenly at his shoulder with a tin mug. Shire found the bottle in his saddlebag and poured the mug more than half full in partial thanks for his walking stick, though it had put Shire in a melancholic mood: the idea that his recent life could be summarized so darkly on a piece of wood.

The night and the stars swept slowly in above them and they ate and drank. Trenholm's Scottish whiskey all gone, Clemens produced something more local and altogether harsher. He retired first, his bed away somewhere near his horse and Shire realized that Waddell was no longer sitting close. He could hear him whittling again somewhere beyond the firelight. There was never a guard set. He figured he could wander off, get lost and die alone in the wilderness anytime he wanted to. Only what would he be escaping from? He was a paroled man after all.

'You got any idea where you're headed after Ducktown?' asked Tod. 'It's a far-flung place to start from alone.'

'It depends how I find things.'

'What might you expect to find?'

Having put himself in a fix, Shire struggled for an answer. 'There's a road down towards Chattanooga. I may take that.'

The fire snapped.

'Fine stick Waddell made you,' said Tod. 'Can I see?' And then, aimed into the darkness, 'He ain't never made one for me.'

Shire passed it over and Tod examined it by the firelight. 'About right for Waddell, I've never known him carve a summer dance.'

'It's something to show my grandchildren.'

'Only if you want to scare them half to death.'

Tod passed it back.

'I was thinking on what you said yesterday. About the killing, about what happened before you saved me.'

'What of it?'

'There's a story to tell from the other side of the abatis. Not one I'm proud of.'

'Only me and the stars listening.'

And Waddell, thought Shire.

Shire went back all the way to Wick's arrival in the spring, to Hubbard and the hung Confederate and how he was never right after that. He told of Wick's Bible classes and how in battle he would preach men to their deaths. Tod didn't interrupt except to share the last of the whiskey. Shire finally reached Kennesaw where Wick had sacrificed Hubbard for his own perverted glory. 'I don't think I would have done it if I'd known I was going to live. The way I was laying, no one else could see but my friend Tuck. I'd seen a hundred men killed that morning, and believed I was going to die any moment. It doesn't excuse what I did, but death was there among us and, well, it made it easier. It was just one more death.'

'Was it a clean kill?'

'Yes. In the chest.'

Tod put a drunk hand on Shire's shoulder. Shire turned to look at him.

'Then I think you did wrong,' Tod said. 'A man like that might have cured me of Luther. I'd have lowered my aim and shot him in the guts.'

Shire listened to the trill of the crickets for a while, found the true spot in his heart where he understood he'd killed

Wick for his friends, for the regiment. 'When I think over what he did, tell the story to myself as I've told it to you, I imagine I'd do it again, but I don't always have the time. It catches me unawares and I think myself a murderer.'

'Doesn't sound like murder. Sounds like justice. Tell me about the girl.'

'What girl?'

'While you're in a telling mood. You said there was one. Two days and we're parted again most likely. What's the harm?'

Shire smiled. 'She's why I'm here.' He lay back and the stars began to spin. He rode it out long enough to tell the tale once more of how he'd come to America, only this time with Clara front and center. He told of their childhood promise, of the false marriage, of how his coming had led to Taylor's death. How, when he'd left her at the end of winter, Clara was still tortured by his shadow, and how, beyond everything else in this world, he loved Clara Ridgmont and was come to try and rescue her a second time.

When he finished, all was quiet except the night insects. He stayed prone on his back. 'You still awake?'

Tod was silent. He must have gone to sleep. Shire followed suit.

Ducktown, Tennessee – July 1864

Consciousness insisted on a new relationship with Clara, one in which she no longer had a majority share. Her miscarriage had stolen a child, blood and any reserves of hope she had hitherto protected. For all of the previous day, she had lain on her chaise lounge, not rousing herself to call up the shaft as Tonkin had done, the little energy she could muster entirely spent on round trips to the latrine. But for Tonkin sitting her up and holding a glass to her lips, she wouldn't have troubled herself to drink. Why should she? The water moved through her as if she were a cleared gutter.

Taylor had become a constant; his spite and laughter ever-present in the darkness, as if there were three of them down here. He moved in and out of her dreams at will. Sometimes a child, other times a colonel. Just now he was a corpse, reaching to hold and pin her for a kiss. She fought, woke, her dream-fear still fully formed.

Tonkin was gently shaking her. 'Come and look.' In the dim light she could see the hollows in his face. There was a tremor in his voice. 'People have come.' He helped her to sit.

There was no visible change, only the two of them, no evidence that he was anything other than mad. Then a new voice echoed from above. 'We're dropping down the harness.'

Tonkin moved to the shaft. 'Alright,' he shouted, and came back to Clara. 'They've been here an hour but needed to fashion a way to pull us up. You'll go first.'

Emotions fought like tomcats inside her, not least anger. Why hadn't Tonkin woken her? Why let her suffer an extra hour, even in sleep? She stood too quickly and found herself lightheaded and unsteady. Tonkin sat her back down. 'Take some water,' he said. 'If you can't endure the harness, we can stay a day more while they get a whim and a cage set up. They can lower food down.'

He was mad then. 'I'll be fine,' she said. 'I just need a moment.'

Something dropped onto the rubble at the bottom of the shaft and Tonkin moved toward it. Clara's head cleared. It was a shock: something new had entered their closed world. She heard herself laughing.

'It's a canvas harness,' said Tonkin. 'It ain't very ladylike.'

'Should I wait for a horse and carriage then?' She tried to hurry over to him, a hand against the wall. He shaped the canvas onto her cotton dress. She was indifferent to the practicalities with her person.

'Take up the slack,' Tonkin called. The rope tightened. 'Sit into it. They have you.'

Her feet dragged clear of the debris and she turned on the rope, rose above Tonkin. He briefly held her feet to balance her and then she proceeded up in sharp repeated jerks. She became fearful again, that in the act of being rescued she might yet perish. She clutched the taut fiber of the rope, a pendulum weight; there was nothing she could do to be otherwise. She hit one rough side of the shaft with her hip, bounced and hit the other. Freeing one weak hand, she fended off the shaft wall and turned again, crying out. A voice called down. 'Push away gently.' Even in those three words she heard something familiar. It was someone from her real life, someone before the mine, someone without a Tennessee twang. She grabbed the rope with both hands again and looked up. The face, outlined in silhouette against the light of the world, was known to her, but the rope, twisted by her actions, began to unwind and spin her so that the face swirled around. She thought she would pass out. There was a strong smell of planed wood and earth, soil rather than rock. She was pulled into bright light and there were faces above her.

'Carry her outside,' said the voice, 'into the sunlight.'

She'd thought herself already outside, but then felt the life of the sun upon her face and closed her eyes against it. She wept. Soon there was shade again.

'Clara?'

She opened her eyes and tried to make out who it was.

'I came as fast as I could.'

The face retreated above her. Behind it was an unfeasibly blue sky, reinvented just for her.

'You should never have come here, but all will be fine.'

She lifted a heavy hand, shielded her eyes and looked into the jowly Germanic face of Julius Raht.

Clara sat in the rocker on Tonkin's porch and looked past Julius Raht's hitched horse and down the street. A half-dozen broken-down buildings, barely a glass pane in place, stood either side of the parched sandy ground. Doors hung crooked on their hinges. Bowman's men had left their mark on Ducktown, but to her the place was a miracle and each dilapidated element a wonder of its own, right down to the horse leavings. She would never see the world in the same way again. Eating had been a novelty, washing with soap had been a novelty, having her life ahead of her was a novelty.

'Would you like more coffee?' asked Julius.

She held out her mug and Julius reached over and tipped the pot.

'Thank you.'

'Are you sure you won't go inside?'

'I like it outside.'

After her rescue yesterday, she'd been lifted onto a horse and led to Tonkin's house. She'd found she could hardly eat. Julius had helped her up the stairs to bed. Once alone, she took off her mine-dress, intent on never wearing it again. She hadn't woken until past noon today. Tonkin was asleep still. She sat on the porch in a clean loose-fitting dress with a strange evenness of mind.

'I said I'd visit George today,' said Julius. 'Will you come? You can ride my horse.'

'I don't have the energy. I wouldn't want Tonkin to wake and find himself alone.'

Julius stood and put on his hat.

'Tell George I will come tomorrow. And thank him for me.'

Julius walked his horse to the porch step and climbed aboard heavily from there. Clara watched until the animal broke into a reluctant trot.

Based on their conversation this afternoon, she believed she had a grip on the events that had brought him to Ducktown. Julius had received a telegraph in Cincinnati from Moses saying she was in danger. The trains were all reserved for the army due to the battle outside Atlanta. Julius was delayed for many days in departing and again on route. When he had eventually reached Cleveland, he had raised hell with the Union regiment stationed there. The colonel said they had already visited Comrie once at his urging. Others were waiting on loved ones: George Barnes' wife, for one. It was only when Julius started putting together a posse of citizenry that the colonel had stepped in and dispatched a squad of his New Yorkers into the hills. Julius had insisted he ride with them. Rather than divert to Comrie they had sent a trooper who caught up to them on the Copper Road. He reported that Clara hadn't been seen at her home. There was just some superior Englishman living in the big house on his own, demanding the trooper stay with him and protect him from the blacks.

The sergeant wasted two days tracking rumors of irregulars up over Big Frog Mountain, Julius all the while saying it was Ducktown where they needed to go. At every farm people hid behind locked doors or showed a shotgun at the window. When, finally, they came into Ducktown yesterday morning, a handful of Bowman's men were astride the road but the Union squad saw them off. An old boy had come out of nowhere to tell them George Barnes was laid up at the Oliver house, shot in the head but newly conscious. George managed to tell them what had happened and sent them to the Isabella where they'd heard Tonkin calling. There were three poorly dug graves behind the mine-head: the two copper-haulers and Tonkin's man Steffan, George had told them. There was no sign of Tonkin's other men. Either Bowman had them or they had made it away. After helping lift her and Tonkin from the mine, the Union squad set off to track down Bowman, though George had told them that the numbers would be against them.

It was hard to reconcile her own redemption with the deaths of the people she'd ridden to Ducktown with. The plain truth couldn't be avoided that they had come at her urging and for furniture that she no longer truly wanted. She sipped cold coffee and watched the sun sink toward the hills and the shadows of the houses creep across the road.

When the horse came around the corner at the far end of the street, she thought it must be Julius back sooner than expected, but the rider was lighter in the saddle. For one terrible moment she thought of Bowman. She should hurry inside and wake Tonkin. The rider was in Confederate uniform, but even from this distance she could see he was better attired than Bowman or his men – an officer perhaps. Behind him a second man rode into view, older and a civilian, and then a trooper leading a mule, which in turn led another and another. She pushed herself up from the rocker and stood on the edge of the porch, shielding her eyes into the setting sun. Before long, the length and width of the street was full of mules, most of them with no burden other than hanging, empty saddlebags. The officer pushed his horse on ahead. As he came closer, she had to let the porch rail take her weight.

It wasn't possible. 'Luke…'

He dismounted quickly, the second rider almost with them, and stepped toward her. 'You have me mistaken, ma'am.' He gave her a look that plainly suggested otherwise. 'I am Tod Carter.'

'But how can you—'

'Please, ma'am,' he insisted quietly. 'Trust me. I am Captain Tod Carter and not known to you. I will not be your last surprise today.' More loudly, he said. 'This is our guide, Clemens.'

Tonkin appeared at the door, pulling braces over his shoulders, clearly anxious. He stepped up beside Clara. 'Who are these people? What do they want?'

'This officer tells me he is Tod Carter.'

'More irregulars?' asked Tonkin.

'I'm a captain in the 20th Tennessee.'

Clara looked away from Tod, as Luke had seemingly become, to the sea of dusty animals. 'Are you trading in mules, *Captain*?'

'We're here for copper.'

Across the street, over the heads of the mules, a man out of uniform drew Clara's eye. He climbed carefully down from his horse and hitched it before walking toward her, steering between mules, over and under ropes. The last animal negotiated, he walked to the porch with a barely perceptible limp. She searched for his eyes beneath the brim of his slouch hat, which, as he stopped beside Tod, he removed and held across his stomach, as if he'd come to visit royalty. Clara believed she must still be in the mine; this unlikely scene nothing more than a dying dream brought on by starvation and despair.

'Hello, Clara,' Shire said. 'Here I am again.'

She drew herself hand over hand along the porch rail. A step above him she came level with Shire's brown eyes and found in them echoes of another life, distant notes of childhood. She lifted one hand to push gently at his shoulder. He was real. She cupped his week-old beard, let her trembling fingers find the tear shaped scar high on his cheek and fell into his arms.

*

Shire held on to Clara, her light frame shuddering against him. There was no weight to her at all. The moment drew out. Over her shoulder he smiled at Tod, who turned away.

'Sir,' said Tod to a man on the porch. 'Who's in charge here? Of the mines, I mean.'

The man looked a little lost. 'My men are all dead or gone, but I'm a mine captain, or I was.'

'That makes you the man I need to talk to. Can we go inside?'

After they disappeared, Shire eased Clara away so he could look at her while holding her hands. Her face was so thin. She must have been ill. Clemens asked for the best place to water the mules and Clara directed him away to a water race that fed a disused steam furnace.

'I need to see to my horse too,' Shire said.

'There's a pail down the side of the house and a pump out the back.'

Together they collected water and crossed the street. When Shire's horse had drunk its fill, he dunked a cloth from his saddlebag and washed away the salt stains on its flanks while he and Clara dovetailed stories. He told her of his capture at Kennesaw, how Tod had saved him, how Trenholm had summoned him from the prisoner stockade. 'It seems I wasn't needed.'

'You were needed,' she said. 'You *are* needed. I was trapped, Shire, in the mines. Julius only found us yesterday.'

Shire stopped wiping his horse. Clara told him all she suspected of events at Comrie, how things had soured since Matlock arrived. Her fears for Hany. He learned about Bowman's arrival at the Isabella and the murders. His guilt mounted as he worked back the days. Clara, and this man, Tonkin, had been in the mine since before he fought at Kennesaw. When he met with Trenholm in Atlanta, she'd been trapped for the best part of a week. Every stop they'd made on the trail, every campfire meal with Tod, all the while Clara had been starving underground.

The shadow of the hills settled across the buildings. They left the horse and returned to sit on the porch. 'Small wonder you are so slight. I'm so sorry. I should have ridden ahead, come on alone.'

'Bowman left men close by I'm told. You wouldn't have been able to chase them away by yourself. And unless you found George, you wouldn't have known where we were.'

They sat a while in silence. Matlock so close, Shire thought, still the root of suffering and pain. He wished Clemens had brought them to Ducktown a day earlier, that *he* had been the one to pull Clara from the mine.

'That captain, Tod, was it?' asked Clara. 'He said he was here for copper.'

'The army, *my army*, is close to Atlanta. The Rebels need copper to make caps to fire their rifles, among other things.'

'Are you their prisoner then? Will you go back with them?'

'No. I'm not a soldier anymore.' He turned his head, held her almond eyes. 'I have parole papers in my saddlebag. I'm free.'

Clara looked away. 'What will you do?'

He'd sooner she hadn't voiced the question. Unasked, the quiet implication might have been that they would do something together. 'I'm not sure. To be honest, I didn't really expect you to be here. The news of you was old. I thought I'd probably find you at Comrie, but even that place doesn't seem to hold much safety for you anymore.'

'It never truly has.'

'Trenholm offered me a berth back to England if I return to Atlanta or make it down to Charleston.' He found it hard to read her face in the failing light.

'It's getting dark,' she said. 'We should go inside.'

The conversation felt unfinished, but he helped Clara up, opened the door and followed her in. A lamp was lit in the kitchen. Tod stood up as they entered the room.

'There's no need, sir,' Clara said.

Tonkin followed suit and offered his chair. Clara forestalled him. 'You must be as weary as I am. Let the

Captain display his manners if he feels he needs to.'

It was obvious to Shire she had taken a dislike to Tod, but then she didn't have a good history with Confederate officers.

'He has good reason to be courteous,' said Tonkin. 'He's come to rob you.'

'How d'you figure that?' said Tod.

'Clara, Mrs Ridgmont, is a shareholder in the mines. It's her copper as much as anyone else's that you're planning to steal.'

Tod drew himself up. 'Then I shall make my apologies, but we are in Tennessee, a Confederate state.'

Shire couldn't let that stand. 'Forgive me. I know Tennessee is your home, but I spent most of last year moving it back into the Union. The fight is for Georgia now.'

Tod's face set hard. 'Not your fight,' he said. 'Your fight's over. Mine goes on and we have need of the copper. There are shareholders in the Confederacy too, Mr Trenholm being one.'

'Well,' said Tonkin, 'I defer to Mr Raht. You can take it up with him.'

'He's not here to take it up with.'

'He'll be along,' said Tonkin. 'Did I not say? He came looking for Clara with a bunch of Union troopers.'

'How many troopers?'

'Six, by my count.'

'Where are they?'

'Tracking Confederate bushwhackers.'

'And Mr Raht?'

'Mr Tonkin told you he'll be here soon,' said Clara.

Tod looked agitated. 'This can't wait,' he said.

'Well, we won't be getting into the mines tonight,' said Tonkin.

'Can you take me to him?'

'Mr Tonkin doesn't have his strength back,' said Clara.

'I'm fine,' said Tonkin. 'Can you lend me a horse?'

'Take mine,' said Shire. 'Across the road.'

Tod and Tonkin left. Clara stared at the closed kitchen door. Shire waited.

'I don't know what there is for us to eat,' she said, and began opening up the cupboards.

'We brought plenty of supplies,' said Shire, but Clara carried on looking. Shire took her hand and turned her to him. 'Don't think badly of Tod,' he said. 'He's a good man. He's been a long time away from home.'

'Is that what you intend, to sail home?' It was delivered like an accusation.

'Would that be so wrong of me? What do I have here?'

Clara slipped her hand from his.

'Why not come with me?' he said.

'I couldn't.'

'We could make it down to Charleston. Trenholm wants to see you safe. We could sail home together. Why not, Clara?'

'What's there for me? A widowed Lady, damaged goods fit only to be gifted to the first landed nobility my father takes a liking to. And you? Will you be the little teacher again or work on the farm? I like you better here. I like *me* better here, despite everything. What about Moses, Mitilde, all of them? I can't abandon them. You go if that's what you want. I'll be damned if I ever will.'

'I don't have anywhere else to go.'

The fight appeared to go out of Clara. 'You *know* you can come to Comrie.'

'We didn't part well the last time I was there.'

'I know, but you're free of the army now.'

'Yes. I suppose I am.'

'You want to fight again?'

'My friends are still fighting.'

'I'm your friend. Come back to Comrie. So much has happened. We both need some peace.'

'I'll come,' he said. Clara had won out over home long before now and there was a reckoning overdue with Matlock.

She came to him again. He closed his eyes and put his cheek to her hair, felt again how slight she was. 'Stay here,' he said. 'I'll go and fetch us some food.'

Ducktown, Tennessee – July 1864

Having slept so late yesterday, Clara lay awake long into the hot night. The window was open and the curtains back, begging for a breeze. She needed no blanket and there was no sheet. Her nightdress she'd found torn to shreds by Bowman's men. Even naked she was too hot, the mattress warm and damp beneath her as she turned over and over. She almost missed the cool and constant climate of the mine. She caught herself trying to replace the monotonous crickets with the drip, drip. She sat up and swung her legs off the bed, the planking warm and dry beneath her feet.

Shire and Tod vied for her attention. Shire won for the most part. For some reason she was angry at him again. He instantly made her feel she was his keeper, waiting as he had on her say so to come to Comrie. For once, why didn't he just tell her what he was going to do? There was something deeper though. She thought again of his rejection when she had crept into his bed at Comrie. He'd had his own mind then. And now, at Tod's behest, she was deceiving him. Shire was the only person who knew her absolutely, and here she was, forced to lie.

Tod remained a mystery. She had learned precious little from him when they were on the Ohio, preoccupied as they had been with physical matters. She'd carried his child before the mine claimed it. The one sure thing she had known about him, his name, turned out to be a lie. Strange, how you were pulled toward the man you knew nothing of rather than the one you had known all your life, who you could depend on, who you knew beyond any doubt loved you. She stood and looked down at her body, pale and skeletal in the weak moonlight. She smoothed her hands around skinny thighs. Her hip-bones were sharp, her breasts smaller. She lay back down and, preferring their company to her other thoughts, let the imagined drips of the cave begin to play. An infant breeze flicked the curtain and at last she slept.

In her dream Comrie was made whole again, furnished and adorned as it had been, but Taylor set about it with a hand axe, laughing all the time. He climbed the stairs slashing at portraits, jumped up to cut down the heavy curtains, swung full arcing blows into the polished wood of the walnut dining table, again and again, no matter how she screamed.

She woke bathed in bright sunlight to the distant banging of a hammer and the brutal knowledge that she'd carried Taylor with her from the mine, the certainty that he would, henceforth, contend with Tod and Shire for her attention.

She dressed and, after finding some food, followed the noise back to the Isabella. The hut above the mineshaft was being torn down. She stood well away and looked on. Julius and Tonkin were there with teamsters that had come with the mule train. Tod was stripped to his waist, working as hard as anyone to pull apart the hut. He caught her eye but turned back to his labors. For a flushed moment Clara recalled the warmth of his body, remembered her hands gripping the round of those shoulders. An older soldier sat on a box to one side, taking no interest and instead whittling a length of wood. There was no sign of Shire.

Julius detached himself from the work, walked across to her and took off his hat. His face was boiled red. He mopped at the beaded sweat on his face and neck with a balled handkerchief and invited her to climb a short way up a spoil-heap. He struggled up behind her. They sat and looked down on the work. It was a while before Julius caught his breath. 'It's my own fault as much as anyone's that we're left with this wasteland,' he said. 'The sulfur from the smelting kills all the trees.'

Clara remembered her visit before the war came to Tennessee, when the mines were in full swing.

'Does that make it unfair of me to wish for a little shade?' said Raht.

Clara thought that for two long weeks she had endured nothing *but* shade. A beating sun in a blue sky was a miracle to her. All that time in the mine, that spiteful hut, sited as it was over the mineshaft, had denied her any sight of the sky. 'Perhaps,' she said. 'Why are they destroying the hut?'

'Because they are vandals,' said Julius, sullenly. 'Vandals and thieves as all soldiers believe they have a right to be.'

Clara waited.

'I am sorry,' he said. 'We need a new cage for the shaft and it is simplest to remove one from the Hiwassee mine and bring it here in one piece. It would take time to disassemble it and then build it again inside the hut so they decided to knock the hut down. The new cage is smaller and it'll rattle in the shaft, but it will serve their purpose to rob me of my copper. Trenholm shouldn't ask this of me. I'm not part of his Confederacy.'

Julius was so glum, but Clara voiced her thought anyway. 'Surely it's the shareholder's copper. It's mine more than yours.'

Julius looked hurt. 'It'll be me who has to account for the loss. I have shares too, not so many as you, but yes, *our* copper.'

'Why help them then?'

'They are soldiers with guns.'

'Tod wouldn't threaten us.'

'Not you. Me, I'm not so sure. They'll go all the sooner if I help. The Union troopers will either find Bowman or they won't, but sooner or later they planned to come back this way. And if they find Rebels here then there'll be more bloodshed. Luke has his soldiers guarding the mules and the approach from the north.'

'You mean Tod.'

'Yes, Tod, as he wants us to call him. What do you make of that? A Rebel all along. Last night he practically dragged me from George Barnes' bedside, took me out and asked me to pretend I'd never met him.'

'He must have his reasons.' Clara had begun to guess at what they might be.

'Whoever he is, he is stealing my copper – *our* copper.'

There was a crash from below as one side of the hut fell flat to the ground and blew out a burst of dust. Clara could see the maw of the mine. 'Will you come and see George again?' she said. 'I promised I would go today.'

Julius said he'd be happier away from here. Clara borrowed a horse and together they rode out of town to the east, far enough to reach the first stunted trees and find Julius his shade.

Ducktown, Tennessee – July 1864

Shire had ridden further than intended, much further than he'd come yesterday. He had started down the Copper Road until he reached the Ocoee River. In high summer it was doing little more than trickling its way between sun the bleached rocks. There was a pebble beach and he steered his horse across and into the water. He dropped the reins so she could drink then flipped a leg over the saddle and, sitting sideways, undid his shoes – another gift from Trenholm. He tied them to the pommel and then slipped down into the water to enjoy the cool. Leaving his horse, he paddled to a rock to sit and wash his feet.

It was good to be among the trees and away from the wasteland of the mines, but as the afternoon wore on the air became hot and heavy. The road wasn't a sensible place to be. He had no gun. Anyone could come this way, but he couldn't bring himself to help at the mines, to fetch up the copper when he could draw a clear, straight line between doing so and the bullets slapping into his friends in the 125th. Since they had reached Ducktown two days ago, and after it became evident that Tod really would take back the copper, Shire had felt more and more like a turncoat.

Clara was avoiding him again, just as at Comrie. How quickly they had come back to that. Most of yesterday, she'd spent away with Raht visiting some copper-hauler almost killed by this Bowman renegade. Shire had asked Tonkin the way but thought better of it. He wasn't about to start chasing her again although, in truth, he'd gone to her house in the evening, armed with more supplies and a rabbit that Waddell had snared. They talked while he skinned and boiled it, but the conversation was stilted, as if she already regretted inviting him to Comrie. Tod arrived later, looking for Shire he'd said, and it had been worse still. Clara invited Tod to stay and eat but he said duty called, insisted that Shire stayed on. After the meal, Clara said she needed to sleep. He had no idea where she was today.

There were fish in the water: trout. You could see them clearly if you got the sunlight behind you. He wondered if he might tickle one and throw it onto the pebbles. Another offering: rabbit one day and fish the next. He tried for a few minutes but never got close. It would only make for another awkward supper anyway. He should get back.

The road climbed steeply away from the river toward the mines. Tod had a couple of men posted where the last sickly trees surrendered to the cracked and barren soil. He called ahead and they joked with him; their tame Yankee.

He'd rather have gone to Tonkin's house than the mines, but he wanted to know how the work was progressing; it would determine when Tod would leave, so he walked his horse toward the Isabella, already missing the shade.

Things had moved on since he was here yesterday. The ground around the mineshaft was cleared. The raised soil of the three unmarked graves was trampled where the men had worked to build a pyramid frame which held a winding-drum below its apex. A thick rope departed the pyramid in two directions: across to a whim device which allowed two mules to walk in a circle to work the drum, and arrow straight down the shaft. A number of men were crowded there, all looking down, like they were waiting on news of the underworld. News must have come because the mules were led forward and the taut rope began to wind. A cage – a frame really, since its sides were nothing but air – was pulled clear of the shaft and steadied by many hands. Tod jumped the gap, put down a lamp and held a pocked brown ingot aloft like it was solid gold. There was a brief cheer and a few waved hats. Tod walked to Shire and half-tossed, half-passed him the ingot. Surprised by its weight, he nearly dropped it. He turned it over. In his mind's eye, he saw a thousand shiny percussion caps.

'Quite something down there,' said Tod, 'and I had a way out. Your Clara is a tough one alright. You ever been in a mine?'

'Not so many mines in Bedfordshire. Just clay pits.'

'You should try it. I won't ask you to carry up any copper.' Tod was smiling.

Shire couldn't find an answer but handed back the copper. He turned and walked to his horse. As he looked over the saddle, he saw movement up on the barren hill capped by the wooden church, as desolate a spot for worship as you could imagine. There was a woman up there and that could only be Clara. She wasn't one for prayer. Tod followed his eyeline. 'There she is. I imagine she doesn't want to be near the mine. Can't say I blame her. All her things are down there though, laid out like she and Tonkin were setting up home.'

Shire couldn't see the humor in it. He looked at the copper in Tod's hands. 'What if you didn't go back?'

'What?'

'Or if you went slowly, got there too late.'

'Now hold on.'

'It'll just mean more men die… on both sides. You'll stretch out a war that's already lost.'

'It wasn't lost last time I checked.'

'It will be when Atlanta falls, and it'll fall sooner or later, with or without that copper. You said Luther told you a time would come when you had a choice, to kill or not. Maybe this is that time. Maybe you saved me just so I could tell you that.'

'Take your way, you mean?'

'What else could I do?'

'You've had a choice ever since we left Atlanta. If you'd hightailed it, I couldn't have spared the time to come after you.'

'I signed parole papers.'

'Hell, half the Confederate Army has signed parole at one time or another.'

'It's not the same. If I went back, it would be one man. This copper...' He struggled. 'You might as well take back a thousand headstones.'

'You know, I didn't tell you about Luther so you could start speaking up for him.' Tod tossed the copper to one side.

'You've had the same thought. You told me as much.'

'When you were in uniform, could you have abandoned your friends? No, I didn't think so. You've gone back to them before, when you could have just left them and America to it. If I betray my own people now, then what was I fighting for these last three years? No. I'm getting this copper up, out, and back to Atlanta as fast as I can. I don't need your help and I wouldn't expect it, but don't ask me to go against my loyalties.'

Shire thought how many lives might hang on this argument, on his rhetoric, but he could find nothing more to say. 'I needed to ask.'

'I know... Let's talk no more on it.' Tod retrieved the ingot. 'Look,' he said, 'you don't have to haul any copper up. You can go down the mine all the same, see where Clara has been all this time, find something she'll be glad of.'

Shire hesitated. Perhaps it would help him understand how Clara was feeling, what it must have been like. 'With you?'

'Clemens wants a look. Said he's ridden these hills for a lifetime so he might as well see what they're made of. Raht's down there. I need to check on my men in case Bowman or your Union friends show up. Can I borrow your horse? Mine's over with the mules.'

'Why not. It's a Rebel horse.'

Having made the decision to go down, Shire wanted to unmake it, but couldn't turn tail in front of the southerners. He was representing the Union Army and England at the same time. He stepped onto the open platform after Clemens; the helpers had to lessen the sway. They were lowered faster than seemed necessary. The cage, undersized for the shaft, rattled and swung all the way down.

He followed Clemens along the tunnel, each of them with a lamp. They passed a chaise lounge and a mattress, turned right at an angled mirror, these day-to-day things utterly at odds with their surroundings. He fought his own fear and imagined what it must have been like for Clara, down here so long with scant hope of rescue. He hadn't understood at all.

They emerged into a cavern and found Raht next to a huge mound of copper ingots that shone dull green and gold in the lamplight. Morosely, he watched as his hoarded treasure was plundered. Next to him a man finished filling a minecart with ingots. Clemens, ever one for getting on with things, helped to push away the cart. Long after it left the chamber, Shire could hear it squeak and scrape the metal rail on its journey to the mineshaft. He was left alone with Raht.

'You as well, Shire? You've come to steal from me too?'

'No, Mr Raht. If it was down to me you would keep your copper. I just wanted to see the mine and take up something of Clara's.'

Raht didn't seem to have heard him.

'Will it all go?' Shire asked.

'Two hundred mules. Tod says he plans to put a hundred and eighty pounds on each animal. I think they might take a third. The problem they will have is unloading the mules every night and loading them in the morning. Heavy work. There is a trade-off between how much copper Tod takes and how fast they can get to Atlanta.'

'You will be able to keep most of it then.'

Raht turned to him. 'You think I should be grateful? Clara's things are in the next chamber. It's not far. You can't get lost.'

Shire would have preferred Raht to come with him but didn't feel he could ask. He took each step as if approaching a cliff edge. In the next chamber he found Comrie's things: tables, chairs and cupboards; boxes, some open, others nailed closed; a painting of what looked like Taylor shot through. Clara could never quite get away from that man. He spent some time foraging, wondered what single thing would make her happy. In the end he settled on an old riding hat of hers he recognized from England.

He moved back through to the copper cavern, happy to be on the return leg. Raht hadn't moved, but there were two or three others as well as Clemens, it was hard to see exactly how many in the lamplight. They were loading the minecart once more.

'Do you understand all the sweat and toil it took to build this pile?' Raht said.

Shire supposed that Raht was talking to him. 'I imagine it's an effort to dig it out.'

'The digging is only part of it. First, someone has to ride the mountains and understand the geology, drill boreholes or sink shafts for samples, send them away for grading. Then you have to bring in the men. People think anyone can dig, but it's in the blood. We recruited men from Cornwall and Wales. You need the right skills: engineers, men who can work with explosives. Only once they're here can you begin to dig and blast. When you get the ore out it has to be roasted for weeks and then smelted in a furnace you've somehow built in the mountains. Only then do we get to this, to copper.' Raht picked up an ingot but then dropped it back on the pile. 'I thought it would be safe if I put it back down here, but Trenholm has sent Captain Tod to steal it for his precious war.'

Shire couldn't rouse more than a nugget of sympathy. For Raht, it seemed, the copper was an end in itself, before the final alchemy when it would be transformed into dollars. The fact it was destined for Trenholm's *precious war*, that it would come to kill and maim people in due course, didn't appear to weigh much. 'It's not like you've lost a limb, Mr Raht. I've seen stinking piles of arms and legs beside a surgeon's tent. Do you know what effort it took to produce those? There'll be another pile like that soon on account of this copper.'

Raht pulled Shire away and lowered his voice. 'Do you like Captain Carter?'

'He saved my life.'

'But do you *trust* him?'

'Sir, I appreciate he's taking your copper, but I think he's an honest man.'

'Truly?' Raht held the lamp up beside them, brought his

round face in close. 'Why then,' he whispered, 'has he asked Clara and I to lie to you?'

'What do you mean?'

'I've met Tod Carter before. Clara has too. We shared a steamboat with him from Cincinnati to Memphis in the spring. Only then he wasn't a Confederate captain and went by the name of Luke Edwards.'

I came down the Ohio as well, Tod had said. *There was a girl on my boat. I might tell you a thing or two that would make your toes blush.*

Shire was no longer anxious about the mine for the confined walk back to the shaft; he could have been in an open field. He climbed into the cage and shouted to be lifted up. Near the surface he realized he still held Clara's hat and threw it back down the shaft. He stepped off the cage and tried to decide if he would look for Tod or Clara first. At least he knew where Clara was. He looked up to the wooden church, squinting into the sunlight. There was someone up there. He put his hand above his eyes and the shape resolved into a horse, his horse.

*

Tod leaned forward on the horse as they climbed the steep path to the church. He stroked her neck, like damp silk, a light sweat drawn out by the heavy air. Above the church, clouds boiled high into the sky, white turning to gray.

Was this such a good idea? Based on what Shire had drunkenly told him around the campfire about Taylor, about the lasting hurt he'd done to Clara, he'd had time to think again about what had happened on the Ohio: where her driving need might have come from, her urgency. He wasn't sure if that put him in the wrong, he didn't know after all, but

360

he wondered what he'd have done if he had. People needed comfort. Maybe he'd have behaved no differently.

Beside the church was a great brush arbor, long since dead but sturdy enough to tie the horse to. He opened the church door and removed his hat. Clara was sitting with her back to him in the front row, left of the aisle. Her head lifted as he stepped inside. She stood and turned, the concern in her face replaced by something else, something tighter. He looked at the dust and the broken glass. 'It's seen better days, I imagine.'

'We all have,' Clara said. 'It's still a church.' She turned away and sat down again.

Tod walked slowly down between the pews. 'I'm sorry if I interrupted your prayers. May I sit?'

'Which side of the aisle?' she said. 'Luke on one side and Tod on the other?'

He stepped past her, put his hat on the pew and sat down. 'There's been no chance to explain.'

'What makes you think I need you to?'

Something in her tone, something English and better than he was, irked him. 'There's no need to get all artful about it.'

'You could have told me who you were.'

'Neither of us were trading secrets as I recall. I gave you the letter. I thought you might read it or, if you took it to Franklin, you might find out the truth.'

'It wasn't addressed to me. Some children answered the door and took the letter.'

'You went to my house?'

'Yes.'

Tod wondered which children they had been and was surprised how much that hurt. 'Seems everyone gets to go

361

to my home but me.' The wind whipped up outside and blew more dust in through the glassless windows. 'I couldn't tell you on the boat. They would have hanged me.'

'I wouldn't have betrayed you.'

'Not purposefully… I never expected to see you again.'

'And now? Why are you making Raht and I lie for you?'

'Isn't it obvious?'

Clara stood and walked toward the pulpit. He followed her.

'Shire loves you, Clara. You can't doubt that. He crossed an ocean to reach you, joined in a war that wasn't his. He was on the way to save you again. He and I are connected somehow, by the war. Brothers in arms, though on opposite sides. What would it do to him if he found out?'

Clara turned. 'How would he? Raht never did.'

Tod wasn't able to meet her eyes. 'There was a certain amount of soldier talk around the campfire. Before Shire told me about you, I had no way of knowing you might be here.'

'How much talk?'

'Enough. If he comes to know we met on the boat, he'll work out we did more than sit and watch the sunset over the river. I'm sorry. There's no need to tell him. I'll be gone tomorrow.'

'So soon?'

'We're going to work through the night.'

'And what about us? What about our connection?'

Tod rose and walked to her, put his hands on her shoulders and slid them down to her waist. She was so slight; the remembered swell of her hips barely there at all. 'I can't tell you how much I think back to that river, how I'd like things to be different than they are.'

She put her head on his shoulder and he wrapped his arms

around her. 'There's something I have to tell you,' she said.

Over her head Tod saw the church door swing open. He thought it must be the wind until he saw Shire framed by the door arch against a gray sky. He gently separated himself from Clara.

Shire took a step inside. 'I thought you said it was the men you were going to check on.'

'Shire,' Tod said. 'There's a lot to explain. I—'

'There's been ample time for that. It must have been entertaining for you, hearing my story and keeping yours in your pocket.'

'It's just the war toying with us. I didn't think you would ever need to know.'

'Who decided *you* get to play God? Are you so sure you know everything?'

A sudden onset of rain drummed the wooden roof. Tod looked to Clara for help. She stood tall but appeared close to tears. 'Perhaps you two need to go somewhere to finish your stories,' she said.

'I'm always too late, aren't I Clara?' said Shire. 'Too late to stop you last time, too late to save you this time. Maybe I should switch sides, see if I can work my way up to being a Confederate officer. That appears the most direct route to your affections.'

'Maybe I'm not some journey's end?'

Tod saw Shire turn his head and step outside. He'd heard it too, above the heavy rain the crack of a rifle. Another shot followed. Still more. Sweet Jesus. He should have checked on his men. He hurried toward the door, but when he emerged into the pelting rain, Shire was riding the horse wildly away down the steep path.

*

Shire knew he'd likely fall, racing down the wet slope with the rain needling his eyes, but there was a strange comfort in being reckless. It didn't do to stop and think. When had thinking about Clara *ever* turned a profit?

He reached the bottom of the slope and fought the horse to a stop. Rain sheeted across the barren land, pressing dust into a first thin layer of mud, but there was no lightning, no thunder to match his mood. He thought he saw a muzzle flash away to his right. Yes, there was another. Whoever it was, they were attacking from the north, probably on the track that came in from the other mines. It could be Bowman or it could be Raht's Union squad. He urged his horse that way. There was also comfort in thinking like a soldier. It's what he was become, after all.

He got closer and the firefight in the rain became better defined. A few of Tod's men were shooting around the crumbling corner of an old kiln. Up the track were troopers, he counted six, wheeling and firing, falling back, wheeling and firing again. Through sheets of rain, he could see they were in blue: solid, dark Union blue, the color he had lived in for the last year and a half.

He leaned back on his horse and reached deep into his saddlebag, pushed aside a tin cup and the empty whiskey bottle until he felt the firm rim of his Union kepi hat. He sat up and twisted it on, good and tight. He flanked the fight, staying behind slagheaps and mine-workings where he could.

The Union troopers retreated out of range and he moved parallel to them. They would take him for a Rebel; his hat wasn't going to be enough to save him. In his saddlebag was a second shirt, more gray than white, but it would have to do. He pulled his walking stick from the rifle holster and tied on the shirt.

The first rush of rain began to ease. He rounded an old furnace with an outsized waterwheel to its side and found himself almost upon the Union men. One was slumped on his horse, rain diluting the blood flowing from his thigh. Two rifles rose, so close that Shire could look down the barrel of each.

He put up the walking stick. 'I'm Union! I'm Union!'

One of the troopers hurried to him while the other gun stayed level. The man with a bead on Shire's chest said, 'The only part of you that's Union is your hat. Sergeant, we ain't got time to figure this fella out if those Reb's come after us.' His barrel rose a final inch.

'Private Owen Stanton,' Shire said. '125th Ohio Infantry under Colonel Emerson Opdycke.'

'Have to do better.'

'Parole papers. I have them in my saddlebag. I'm unarmed.'

'Last 'pears to be true,' said the soldier closest to him.

'Can you ride, Wilson?' said the sergeant.

The wounded man said he could.

'Jenkins, Morland, cover us then follow on. You, Ohio, ride out in front where we can see you. Back down the track.'

Shire led them on. There were no shots from behind. 'They don't have enough men to come after us.'

'Quiet.'

Half a mile out they reached the trees and stopped. The clouds were spent. The squad was from a New York regiment. The wounded man was helped down and the dismounted sergeant waved Shire off his horse with a pistol. 'I'll take a look at that parole.'

Shire slid to the ground and searched again in his bag. For one heart-stopping moment he thought it was gone. 'Here,' he said, unfolding it and passing it over.

'Appears in order.' A fat drop smacked the paper. 'Shame it bars you from the fight. I'm a man down.'

'It doesn't say I can't help.' He thought again of Clara in Tod's arms. How at ease she'd looked. 'There's something you need to know.'

Comrie, Tennessee – July 1864

'Of course, there are the slave huts,' said Matlock, waving his arm to take them all in then pulling the satchel strap back over his shoulder. He had no wish to extend the tour in that direction. At their doors or from their thin porches the blacks looked on. 'It depends how you want to run the place. No need for Negroes at all if you don't want to work the land. You could find white help for the house.'

Dark clouds were building above the hills to the east. Comrie had been spared the rain but the wind was fresh and tore dust-devils from the yard.

'This place is further from town than you intimated. I'd have to work at least some of the land.'

Matlock saw this buyer as a trial run rather than a genuine prospect. The man complained that the fields were too steep and the stables oversized unless he wanted to open a stud – which he didn't.

'The journey back is much easier,' said Matlock, 'given it's downhill. And the road will improve once the war's over. Let me show you the house.'

When he'd gone back into Cleveland yesterday, to collect the six thousand dollars for Bowman, Matlock had sought out an agent, someone to find a buyer for Comrie. It might have been as easy to find a buyer himself. Despite the war still raging down in Georgia, there was an influx of northerners arriving with a view to cheap land in this dispossessed corner of Tennessee. There was no shortage of sellers either: war-widows, one-armed veterans, mostly offering up small-scale farms scratched from the hills. Comrie was in a different league with its acreage, all the tenant farms and the grand house itself.

There had been a long minute when he'd stood frozen in the town square, letting the world turn around him, a rare moment of clarity. Why not simply leave his horse at the hitching post and board a train, disappear into the churn of America? If he could find some strength and courage, he could make a solid start with six thousand dollars. He could go north, to New England perhaps or Canada. He wasn't so old that he couldn't yet marry, maybe under a new name, build a reputation and respect away from Ridgmont.

The answer from his core didn't even entertain the argument for the same reason that he'd embezzled from the Duke in the first place. It had never been about the money. It had been about blood, disenfranchised bastard blood, generations old, that should by rights have granted him a part share of Ridgmont. Instead he'd had to claim it for himself. What would he be away from Ridgmont? Just another immigrant, just another man. No. He was head steward to Ridgmont or he was nothing at all. Comrie had to survive and be sold. It was the only way.

He hated agents; they could smell easy money. Within the hour, he'd been introduced to a buyer from Indiana fresh off the train. Comrie wasn't an easy sell: who wanted a mansion in the middle of nowhere? But with the money secreted in his satchel, Matlock didn't want to journey back alone and the buyer had a sidearm. He'd painted Comrie and its tenancies as the best land in the state, the bargain of a lifetime.

Now he'd brought him to Comrie, he wanted rid of the man. He hurried through the house, his hand ever at the man's back.

'Why would anyone need so many rooms?'

Moses surprised them in the hall, pretending to do precisely nothing. 'Mr Matlock, it ain't right you showing folks 'round when Mrs Ridgmont ain't given her permission.'

'What's he sayin'?'

'You know,' said Matlock, 'if you want to get back to town before dark, it would be best you were on your way.'

'You said I could ride back in the morning.'

'So I did. We're short on furniture as I explained, but some of the slave huts have a bed.'

The man rode away two minutes later. Matlock hurried back inside, intending to berate Moses for trying to scupper the sale. There was no sign of him. Matlock wanted to find him, tell him, *'Clara's not coming back. It's been twenty days or more and she's been dead for most of them.'* Moses and Mitilde must suspect as much. Why else had they summoned this mine captain?

Speculation about the squad that had gone to Ducktown with Raht had been all over town but, after this amount of time, Matlock was confident Bowman had kept his end of the deal. If the Union managed to chase the irregulars from the hills, so much the better; he'd be six thousand dollars to the good. Nevertheless, it was as well to have the money on hand. Bowman wasn't a man it would be easy for anyone to corner. He'd considered holding three thousand back at the bank, as security on Comrie's wellbeing, but he couldn't see that playing out well for him. What to do with it all though? He couldn't carry this satchel around forever and a day. Moses might start to wonder.

Unspent anger still bubbled inside him having failed to find Moses. He climbed the stairs, intending to go to his room, but instead kept on up to the top of the spiral. He paused, leaned over the bannister to listen and be sure the house was empty then turned to the attic door. He slid back the bolt, pulled open the door and stepped inside. Nobody ventured up here anymore. It would be a better place to hide the money than his room. It was a big, high-vaulted space, a few boxes pushed under the eaves.

His eye was drawn to the fine rocking horse. There were lines in the dust ahead of and behind the rockers. He walked over and tapped its head and body with his knuckles. Hollow. He put the satchel down and laid the rocking horse on its side. There was a round hole between the front legs. He opened the satchel and placed the wound rolls of bills carefully inside. As he righted the horse, he felt a click under his fingers and a small drawer sprang free of the painted wood. Inside was a double-folded piece of paper. He opened it.

Here it was: the marriage license of Taylor Spencer-Ridgmont and Grace Harland, the prize they'd all fought over so hard last year; the evidence Shire had brought with him to America proving Taylor was a bigamist. Why had Clara kept it? The name of the other witness, Abel Stanton, Shire's father, was torn, but Matlock's was intact, a full flowing signature that, if ever it came to light, would cost him his position with the Duke, his home and his reputation.

He sensed a wide circle closing. He was cast back to a cold and barely lit church at Ridgmont, just the four of them and Grace's father, the vicar. A hollow service, no marriage kiss, just pen and paper.

Clara must have been keeping it as a last resort to use against him. She would never have the chance. He should destroy it, take it and burn it, but he found himself folding it up and tucking it back into the secret drawer. He might have cause to use it himself one day. He must think on it. He would come back tomorrow.

He clicked the drawer closed and then heard the attic door complain as it was pushed shut. He stood and turned. The bolt slid home.

'No!' He rushed over. There was no handle, nothing more than a knotted rope to close it from the inside. He beat on the wood. 'Open this door. Open this door!'

'You be quiet, Mr Matlock.' It was Moses. 'We don't want no more buyers to come visit. Ain't right. Best make yourself comfortable and pray Miss Clara is home soon.'

Ducktown, Tennessee – July 1864

Clara stood and watched the exodus. The slow and weighty mule train, with Tod and Clemens out front, toiled up the first bare hill to the south. It was raining again; vertical, heavy, warm rain. Shire and Tod had arrived three days ago. Shire had disappeared with the Union soldiers yesterday, and now Tod was leaving as well. Her heart would have to split in two if it wanted to follow them both. She lost sight of Tod: too many mules, too much rain.

Tod had spared no time for her since coming to the church, preferring, it appeared, to stand guard with his men or hurry things along at the mine. She had decided to find him this morning while the mules were being loaded with copper, a drawn-out process as the ingots were slipped into the saddlebags one at a time before each weighted mule was led away. Tod had looked anxious, he hadn't given her a welcome. 'It will take forever to load and unload at the end of each march. During the day the mules will have to rest fully loaded, which is to say they will barely be resting at all.'

'Why not lift off the saddlebags with the copper inside?'

'Too heavy.'

'Take less then,' she said, not wanting to talk about copper.

'I'm already taking less than I want.'

'Take none at all.'

Tod turned to her. 'Shire said the same thing. Are you going to try and pacify me as well?'

She hadn't come to talk about Shire, either.

'You know,' said Tod, 'coming back with me might be the safest thing for you.'

'Atlanta doesn't sound so safe.'

'Will you look for Shire, then? Try to explain?'

Clara couldn't imagine how she might begin to do that. 'Look for him where? Trenholm offered him a berth back to England.'

'I know.'

'Maybe it would be better for him,' she said. 'He can start again over there.'

'A lot of people are going to need to start again after this war. Many will never get the chance. He'll calm down, come find you at Comrie.'

It was hard to reach back to the state of mind that had determined her to come to Ducktown, but they'd be no peace once back at Comrie. Matlock would be there. Taylor too. He had no plans to leave her. The next mule was led forward.

'Should I come and find you?' Tod whispered. 'After the war.'

The need to tell him of the child that never was surged through her: the sadness that if she had stayed safe at Comrie she might yet be carrying it; the crumb of hope it had given her for the future. But it would only make it harder for him to leave. She spoke only in tears. Tod took her in his arms, heedless of the men looking on. 'Is that so bad a prospect?'

'No,' she'd said. 'It isn't.'

Now she stood alone in the rain. The last pair of long ears, the last bent back and the last drooping tail disappeared over the crest. All that was left to show the mules and Tod had ever been here was the wide churn of mud at her feet. Tearful once more, she picked her way back toward Tonkin's house. As she entered the street she saw four mules tied to his porch.

She smiled despite herself, knowing how hard it must have been for Tod to give up four loads of copper. Tonkin and Julius were in the kitchen. Tonkin pointed to a note on the table. 'You need to get dry.'

'Have you seen the mules?' She opened the note.

'We have.'

The note said that the mules were to help her get out of the hills. Bowman wasn't accounted for, he'd written. She should either hide out with George Barnes at the Oliver house or head back quickly all the way to Cleveland.

'Help me get the mules under cover. I'll get dry after that.'

Julius stood up. 'Tonkin and I will see to it,' he said.

After they left, Clara climbed to her room and was forced to put back on her mine-dress for want of anything else. She heard the front door sooner than expected and walked to the balcony. Wet Union soldiers were crowded into the narrow hall below, supporting an injured man. Shire stood at the bottom of the stairs, water dripping from the peak of his soldier's hat.

*

Shire looked up the stairs to Clara. Back in England, when her noble parents still deemed him harmless enough to visit their ducal home, he'd seen a younger Clara in a dress fit for royalty descend a sweeping marble staircase, her hair high and pinned with a jeweled comb. Here, she came out of the shadows to the top, narrow step in a dirty, creased dress, her hair half-dried and wild. For all that, she was every bit as beautiful, the upward tilt of her chin remained proud, her dark eyes enough to stop his breath.

'We need to see Raht,' he said, 'or Tonkin. 'Are they here?'

'Who are these men?'

Sergeant Dryden answered. 'Pardon the intrusion, Ma'am. We were with Mr Raht a few days back and helped to pull you from the mine. It wasn't a time for introductions.'

'It wasn't. And thank you. I'm in your debt.' Clara came down the stairs and stopped on the last step.

Shire fought a foolish urge to kiss her.

'Wilson has a leg wound,' said Dryden. 'We need to clean him up.'

'Of course. Shire, bring down the mattress from my room and put it in the parlor. You know where the pump is.'

He held Clara's gaze. 'Raht and Tonkin. I asked if they are here.'

'They'll be back presently. I'll get the mattress.'

He pushed past her and climbed the stairs, thinking it was as well he wouldn't be staying long.

It had been one thing yesterday to get Dryden to accept that he was a Union soldier, albeit a paroled one, quite another to persuade him to support his plan, such as it was. They had been making camp back in the forest north of Ducktown. 'That copper is headed for Atlanta,' Shire had told him. 'It's going to kill men from every state in the Union, including New York.'

'I don't doubt it,' Dryden had said, pulling his short rifle from its saddle holster and leaning it against a tree. 'But my orders were to see what had become of Mrs Ridgmont, and I have a man in need of a surgeon.' He slid the saddle from the horse and put it down.

Shire was a head taller than the heavyset sergeant. 'He can't ride all the way to Cleveland,' said Shire. 'The copper will leave tomorrow, I'm certain of it. Then we can find your man a bed and someone to look after him while we go after Carter.' It was easier to call him Carter.

Dryden placed his saddle on the ground then sat leaning against it. 'We're five men, six if you break your parole.' He yawned, rubbed through the bristles on his cheeks. 'You tell me they are more than twenty if we include the teamsters. What is it you expect us to do?'

'Catch up to them. Slow them down. That mule train is half a mile long. It's not easy to defend.' He nodded toward the gun. 'Do you all have repeating rifles?'

'We do.'

'They are worth a few extra men.'

'I'm not leaving Wilson alone. Bowman is out there somewhere. What do you think he'll do if he comes back and finds a wounded Union soldier?'

'Leave some men with him then. They can hide out. You have to protect Clara anyway. You can't leave that to Raht and Tonkin.'

In the end, it was the necessity of getting Wilson somewhere dry that settled it. The wound in his leg looked a good one to a soldier's eye, clean in and clean out, no broken bone and hopefully no lead lingering in his thigh. Shire had crept back with Dryden toward Ducktown. He had watched the mule train load up through the sergeant's field glasses but passed them back when he saw Tod take Clara in his arms.

Now he was back at Tonkin's house with Clara and Tod was gone. She brought hot water from the kitchen into the parlor. Wilson's comrades cleaned his wound. Raht and Tonkin arrived, wary, having seen horses outside. Sergeant Dryden went with them into the kitchen. Shire followed along and they all crowded in, everyone wet but Clara.

Dryden came straight to it. 'I need to leave Wilson here, for a few days at least. After that, maybe we can find a wagon and get him back to Cleveland.'

'Leave him alone?' asked Tonkin. 'Bowman could be half a state away by now.'

'We're not going after Bowman. I'll leave three men with Wilson in case he comes back. This house might not be the best place.'

'We can take him to the Oliver house,' said Raht. 'Mrs Oliver already has one patient. I think she'll be glad of the guns, even Union guns. Where *are* you going?'

Dryden scratched his head and held out his wet hat toward Shire. 'It's your big idea.'

Shire looked at the expectant faces, Clara's last of all. 'After the mule train,' he said.

'After Tod?' asked Clara.

'After the copper,' Shire said. 'We have to slow them down or stop them getting to Atlanta.'

The accusation was clear in Clara's eyes. 'You weren't so concerned about the copper before yesterday.'

'Before yesterday, there was nothing I could do. The sergeant's here now... It matters, Clara. It matters for the war.' *It matters for people I care about.*

'By my count that leaves three of you to go after them,' said Tonkin. 'What will you do, take pot-shots at the mules? His troopers will come at you.'

Shire didn't want to shoot at men or mules. 'We'll be able to get around ahead of them,' said Shire. 'We're on horseback. The mules are loaded and will be slow in the rain. If we only delay them a day it might matter to the army in front of Atlanta. We're going to need a guide.'

Tonkin laughed. 'Good luck finding one. Things have

changed here, but not so much that anyone will want to be seen helping the Union. More so with Bowman on the loose.'

Shire turned away from Tonkin and addressed Raht. 'When we were in the mine, you said something about explosives.'

Northern Georgia – July 1864

There was a mule-squeal back down the trail; a sound of pure agony. It was the middle of the second day out from Ducktown. Tod dismounted. He needed to wait, having gotten ahead of the mules again. He also needed to rethink his plan. Water streamed down his oilskin poncho. This rain was changing everything.

They'd made no more than five miles yesterday and that was when the mules were fresh. He spotted Clemens back in the trees, the lead mules behind. Poor beasts: this war was harder on mules than it was on men. They came on slowly, heads down, the whips of the teamsters slapped into their flanks but made little difference. Somewhere behind them the lone mule continued to scream. It shouldn't bother him, he'd seen them suffer in battle often enough, but then it had been part of the tumult of war. This single tortured cry in the wet forest reached right into his gut. Clemens arrived and dismounted. They pulled their mounts back from the path to let the mules trudge by.

'This isn't going to work,' said Clemens.

'I know it,' said Tod, curtly.

'The mules will give out long before Atlanta.'

'I said I know it.' There was a single shot and the braying cut out. Tod turned and collected his canteen. After he'd drunk, he offered it to Clemens instead of an apology. It was accepted in silence.

Last night it had taken a full hour to unburden the mules and another full hour this morning to load them again.

He didn't dare use his troopers to help, not this close to Ducktown when there were Union soldiers about, few though they were. He had two of his own casting ahead, four as a rearguard and the other four detailed to flank the march out in the woods, at least where the terrain allowed.

The muddy mules passed by like an endless funeral procession. The path churned up before his eyes. 'They need to rest,' he said to Clemens. 'Is there a place to stop soon?'

'There's a small clearing, but it's a mile or more.'

'Not much of a rest is it? Standing in the rain and mud loaded with a hundred and eighty pounds of copper.'

One of the teamsters led his horse over and spoke from below his dripping hat-brim. 'A mule slipped and broke a leg coming down that last section. We'll lose more with the weight and the rain.'

'Did you have to use a bullet?'

'You ever tried getting near a mule that's in pain?'

'It signals where we are.'

'With respect, sir,' the man unstuck a boot from the mud, 'we ain't exactly hard to follow. Our line is stretched out. The mules at the back are walking in ground mushed all to hell. What should I do with the copper from the dead mule?'

Tod didn't regret leaving the four mules with Clara, just the necessity of it. He regretted leaving her though. He recalled her standing by the path in Ducktown watching them leave, beautiful in the rain. His mind clicked back to her cabin on the Ohio.

'Sir?'

'Leave the copper.'

The man turned away.

'Wait. Clemens tells me that there's a clearing a mile on.

We'll break there. I want you to remove twenty pounds of copper from each mule.'

'Yes, sir.'

'Then I want half the teamsters to walk and spell each other to free up some horses. Clemens and I will do the same. Alright, Clemens?'

'I guess. I'll ride up ahead, let your scouts know where we're stopping.'

Tod turned back to the teamster. 'Load the freed horses with copper.'

'They won't take as much as the mules.'

'They can take some. And empty four mules altogether. Use them to spell others that get worn out. We'll stop an hour earlier tonight, start later in the morning. Hopefully the rain will let up. We can go back to a full day's march once the path's dry.'

Clemens and the teamster left him to his thoughts and the mud while the train struggled on by. It had all been so much easier on the way up: sunshine and stories, campfires and whiskey. His best intentions to protect Shire had misfired. Perhaps he'd become too accustomed to keeping secrets. Now Clara didn't even have Shire's protection, though he'd likely have gone back into Ducktown after the mule train left; he'd find it impossible to ride away from her. Tod felt a stab of jealousy; the most worthless of emotions, his father used to say. Shire might have found Clara in Tod's arms, but there was something deeper between those two, more than a shared past. He thought of the way Clara collapsed into Shire when they arrived in Ducktown, disarmed by the surprise. There was a reliance there, a need she didn't care to admit.

Beneath his oilskin in his jacket pocket was a note with her address at Comrie. He didn't doubt that the teasing wheels of fate would circle them back together again. You had to believe in fate or destiny or something, otherwise everything was just a godawful mess.

He waited a good half-hour for the last of the mules to pass and then rode with the rearguard as far as the clearing. The mules were gathered at all angles in a great steaming circle. The teamsters were busy removing portions of the copper from the saddlebags as ordered – a small mercy at least. Clemens suggested they load his horse and share Tod's; Tod agreed, said he was happy to walk for the next couple of hours. The rain stopped.

When they started out again, Tod hung back. He'd see how the mules fared by following on; once he had his horse again, he'd work his way back to the front. As he left the clearing, he looked back at the cairn of copper that the teamsters had built; a monument to his over-optimism. High above the cairn and the nearest ridge was a small but hopeful pool of blue sky.

Georgia – July 1864

Shire looked up from the deep grave to the faces above. Tuck, Mason, Ocks and Cleves were all there, over him, caps in hands, heads bowed in prayer. He wanted to scream. He wanted to climb out but dumbly fought in vain to move dead limbs. He could only watch as they put on their caps and raised their rifles to fire a salute but then, on command, aimed and fired into the grave, shocking him awake.

He lay under a soaked blanket. The first light was leaking into the forest. Broken patches of the troubled dream sank beyond rescue. He struggled up, his clothes almost as wet as the blanket, bent and shook Dryden by the shoulder.

'I'm awake,' said Dryden. 'Hard to sleep with you calling out. I hope it was Mrs Ridgmont you were dreaming of.'

Shire didn't disillusion him. Instead he moved onto their guide. They had found one readily enough, Tonkin had been wrong about that. When they took the injured Wilson up to the Oliver House, before they left, standing in the hall, Shire had asked Mrs Oliver if she knew of anyone. It had sparked a series of urgent knocks from beneath the floorboards. Mrs Oliver moved aside a hall rug and lifted away some floorboards. A boy climbed up and out. He was tall enough, but with a thin frame that suggested most of his height was a recent addition. 'I'll guide you,' he said.

Dryden stuck to his plan to leave three healthy troopers with Wilson. One trooper, the burly Jenkins, had come along with Shire, Dryden and their new guide, who said his name was Elrod and claimed to be sixteen. Sixteen or not, he was given Wilson's horse and Shire told him where they needed to get to, how they couldn't use the direct path or they'd only come up behind the mule train.

Elrod said he wanted to help the Union. 'I was all for walking down to Cleveland to sign up. Ma hides me away when anyone comes to the farm.'

Dryden took him at his word. They'd been no more than two bends away from the Oliver House when Dryden had stopped, had the boy hold up his right hand, and swore him into the army.

The boy looked younger still asleep in the forest; he had the milky skin of a five-year-old. Shire shook him awake. There was no telling what ground they had made up on Tod so far, but it wouldn't be helped by laying here.

They'd left Ducktown the same day Tod did, albeit only an hour before dark. Elrod, keen as a cooped-up bloodhound, got them moving west after they bridged the Ocoee. Yesterday, he switched them south on narrow, steep trails. The day was nothing but rain. Shire had spent most of it fending off wet branches that crowded above the path. Shire lost all idea of where they were. He hoped Elrod knew better.

Shire and the boy mounted then waited for the two men in uniform. The forest gently steamed around them and there was a clear blue sky showing up between the tree tops. They would make better time, but then so would Tod. 'Will we get there today?' asked Shire.

'Yes,' said Elrod.

He looked confident enough.

'By midday, I think.'

Once Raht had let slip about the four mules left by Tod, Dryden had commandeered two of them: one to carry a twenty-pound barrel of gunpowder, and the other two sledgehammers. Raht had been tight-lipped concerning the powder until Dryden's hand had slipped to his pistol. He'd said Raht could show them where the powder was or ride back to Cleveland with his hands tied behind his back and explain his reluctance to their colonel. Laying a powder trail as a fuse was an art though, Tonkin had told them. 'The trail will burn faster than you can run.'

Dryden fed bullets into his repeating rifle. Shire had handled one before, a trooper friend of Tuck's back in camp at Cleveland had shown them the miracle of how to lever the next bullet through in seconds. He had the same weapon in his saddle holster.

Dryden and Jenkins were ready at last. Once underway, Shire tried to recall the layout where the path had been repaired. 'The hill's called the Hogsback,' Elrod told him. 'The Toccoa River runs through the bottom of the gorge. The path slid away before the war. Some of the miners helped bridge the gap. My pa was one of them.'

Shire's main recollection was that it was dizzyingly steep below the planking. As he'd done most of yesterday, he tried to calculate how long it would take Tod to reach there, but it was all guesswork. Either they would arrive before him or they would find a long line of hoofprints heading south and Shire would have wasted Dryden's time. His heart whispered perhaps that would be for the best. Best for Tod maybe, not for Tuck and the 125th.

He'd had time to reconsider his motivation in coming after Tod and could see that it was well seasoned with his own personal hurt. Clara tried to persuade him not to go, becoming exasperated and claiming he was doing it to punish her. He'd rounded on her then, surprised himself with how direct he'd been. 'The world isn't preoccupied with you just now.

Neither am I. You haven't seen what I have. At Chickamauga, on Missionary Ridge, at Kennesaw. Rows of men cut low by lead, scythed down like they were no more than summer wheat, the lucky left dead, the unlucky taken to have their arms and legs sawn away because in the mess of bone and muscle is buried that same metal. Without Tod's copper they can't shoot. Every ingot is enough to fire a thousand bullets at my army, my regiment, my friends.'

She'd just walked away.

He'd called after. 'I won't set eyes on Tod. We'll blow the path ahead of him.'

It was true, he thought, riding through the woods behind Elrod, that delaying Tod a day or two might help, but it was a half-measure. If he was truly loyal to his friends and the army, that mule train should never make it back to Atlanta.

Elrod, smiling as if he'd won a foot race, brought them to the overlook around midday: a shelf barely wide enough to accommodate their horses. There was a single, man-high boulder to the right side. The shelf was open to the sky and ended at a sudden edge above a deep gorge. As he dismounted, Shire registered the busy sound of fast running water somewhere below. They stood together and looked across the chasm to the other side where the mule-path hugged a steep, scrub hill, disappearing beyond its sloped horizons in either direction. The mend, the plank road and the trestle-work that supported it, lay exactly opposite.

Dryden took off his hat and proceeded to beat Elrod about his shoulders. 'Damn lunkhead. You expectin' us to fly over? Here.' He grabbed Elrod by his coat and walked him to the edge. 'You first.'

Elrod twisted out of his grip. 'There's a way down,' he said. 'A bridge over the river. Look.'

Shire braved the edge to see where Elrod was pointing. Way below he could make out a thin plank and rope bridge. 'That won't take a horse.'

'Is there a path up the other side?' asked Dryden.

'Pretty dumb place for a bridge if there weren't,' said Elrod.

'Watch your mouth, kid.'

'There's a way,' said Elrod, 'but it cuts up to the right and joins the main path to the south. You would have to come back along the road to get to the trestle. Or you could work your way up the scrub slope from the river.'

'It's too steep, 'specially carrying a twenty-pound barrel,' said Dryden.

Shire gazed across to the mule-path. 'We can't tell if they've gone by.'

'Take the horses back into the woods. I need to think,' said Dryden. He hadn't moved when they returned. 'Is there another crossing? Somewhere we can get the horses and the mules over so we can take the hammers?'

'Yes.'

'How far?'

'Couple of hours, but this way was the quickest. You said you wanted the quickest.'

'We don't have the time,' said Shire.

Jenkins shot out a meaty arm, pulled Shire behind the rock and called in the others. 'Look,' he said, nodding north. Two horses had come into view on the mule-path, their riders relaxed. Shire watched around the rock as they walked closer. 'There's no one following them,' he said. 'They must be scouting ahead.'

'How far ahead is the question,' said Dryden.

It took what felt like a full quarter hour for the riders to amble to the trestle opposite the overlook and then on and out of sight around the southern slope of the hill.

'If we are going to do this, it has to be now,' said Shire, stepping out from cover. 'I'll go. This was my idea.'

'Not you,' Dryden said. 'New York will do this.' He nodded at Jenkins. 'It's a heavy barrel to get up that hill. Jenkins is the man for that. Alright, Jenkins?'

'Alright, Sergeant.'

'Elrod will take you down to the bridge and point the way from there. You judge if you want to take the path up and risk the road or cut straight up to the trestle. Send the boy back up to us. Our English friend and I can cover you from here. We can hit anything that comes along that road if you need to get away.'

They all went back into the woods and helped rope the small barrel across Jenkin's broad back. 'It ain't so heavy.'

Elrod led off and Jenkins followed.

'Oh, Jenkins,' Dryden hurried after them. He handed Jenkins a tin of matches. 'Make sure it's a long fuse.'

Shire took his rifle from the saddle-holster and went to sit with Dryden on the overlook, alternately watching the road opposite and the rope-bridge below. It felt an age before they saw Jenkins and Elrod gingerly make their way across, the bridge swaying beneath them over a river running fast and furious. Elrod started to climb across the scrub, leaning into the slope and taking the direct route rather than the path. Jenkins climbed behind him.

'What the hell?' said Dryden. 'I told him to send Elrod back.'

'The boy's finding the way,' said Shire. 'I should have gone.'

Their progress was painfully slow but step by step Elrod

and Jenkins climbed until they came up almost to the level of the overlook. Dryden shouted encouragement but cut it short when it echoed down the gorge. Shire watched both ends of the road. Tod must come soon.

When they reached the trestle work beneath the planking, Elrod helped Jenkins take the barrel from his back. Boy and man looked spent.

'No time to rest,' Dryden called across in a whispered-shout.

Shire watched Jenkins send the boy back down then cast about in the shadow beneath the planks. The ground fell away so steeply.

'I'll need to put the barrel above,' Jenkins said loudly, 'run the fuse along the road.'

'No,' Shire called back. 'That won't do it. The barrel needs to be underneath.'

Jenkins struggled on under the wood. Soon, Shire saw him tip the barrel and edge carefully backward, managing his balance as he spilt a line of powder down the slope. He ran it for maybe twenty feet, no more, then climbed back up to set the barrel behind a stanchion.

Elrod was halfway down and across the slope, making his way back to the rope-bridge. A breeze swept up the gorge from the north, carrying with it a scent Shire had come to know well – wet mule. Even from this distance he knew it was Tod as he rode into view. Shire eased Dryden back behind the rock. 'Here they come.'

There was nothing they could do: if they called out to Jenkins, they would alert Tod. It would be some time before he reached the planking, but there was no way he could yet see Jenkins at work or Elrod down the slope. Jenkins came out of the shadows and climbed down to light the fuse.

'How in the hell is he going to get away before it blows?' said Dryden.

'He's not,' said Shire. 'All he can do is step to the side and hug the slope.'

'Goddammit!'

They watched him strike the match; once, twice, then touch it to the fuse, which fizzled and wiggled its way upward between scrub bushes as Jenkins hurried as best he could across the slope. There was a rising wraith of smoke carried away to the south, melting to nothing. The burning fuse disappeared under the bridge. Jenkins laid flat against the slope. Shire put everything but one eye behind the rock. He could hear nothing but the breeze. The moment stretched out. Jenkins lifted his head. He glanced back to where Shire and Dryden were hiding. Tod was halfway to the trestle ahead of a long line of sullen, muddied mules. Clemens was not far behind, leading a heavy-laden horse. Waddell was further back. Shire risked being spotted and tried to wave Jenkins down the slope.

Jenkins didn't see him. Oblivious of the danger, he started to climb back toward the barrel. Dryden readied his rifle.

'Wait,' said Shire. 'He can hide under the bridge.'

'Only if he sees them first.'

Whether it was the scent of the mules or the rising noise of leather harness and heavy hooves, Jenkins stopped in his tracks and stood up straight to look. He might have remained unseen, but as he turned and began to hurry down the slope he slipped, a loose, flat rock shooting out from under his foot and then end over end. Tod led his horse to the edge and leaned out. 'Union!' he shouted, pulling out his pistol. Troopers fought their way forward through the mules to the edge of the path. Jenkins picked himself up and struggled on.

Tod rode onto the trestle. 'He's not armed!'

The troopers fired anyway, hit Jenkins in the back. He was thrown forward off the slope, tumbling and cartwheeling until he disappeared into a patch of fern and bramble.

Dryden stood out from behind the rock. 'Bastard Rebels.'

Tod was almost opposite them, he'd ridden forward over the trestle.

'No!' said Shire. 'He tried to stop them.'

Dryden lifted his rifle. 'He didn't try hard enough.'

Shire threw himself at Dryden, caught him around the waist as he fired. They both went down.

'You crazy sonofabitch.'

'We didn't come to kill them. We came to stop the copper.'

Bullets cracked off the rock and kicked up the dirt.

Dryden, wild-eyed, rolled on top of Shire. 'Tell that to Jenkins.'

Shire fought to subdue Dryden. Dryden fought without limits. He brought his rifle butt up to the side of Shire's face. It was only a glancing blow, but Shire lost a second to the jolt and the pain. Dryden rose over him and lifted his rifle for a final downward blow but was swept away by a bullet to the side of the head. More bullets split the air above Shire. He scrambled and clawed back to the rock, breathing hard. The firing stopped and he crept to the other side where there was tree cover. The troopers were north of the trestle with the mules, three of them dismounted and ready to fire again. Tod was still on his horse, the only man over the trestle. 'Shire! Is that you, Shire? There's no sense in this.'

Shire didn't answer. He was the only one left apart from Elrod. He should get the boy out.

'Bring the mules on,' Tod shouted. The line, stretching a quarter mile back down the track and out of sight around the corner, began to move once more; a line of death snaking its way toward Atlanta and his friends. He sat behind the rock. He thought of Tuck and he thought of Mason. Another bullet slapped wetly into Dryden's body. Dryden was only here because of him. *Jenkins* had only come because of him. He couldn't slink away now. He gulped at the air, then forced his breathing to slow. He was in battle. Nothing new there. His rifle lay out in the open. He jumped out to grab it, span back to the rock through a brace of shots. He levered through a bullet, edged out the far side of the rock under cover of the trees. Tod had moved a short way down the track. Clemens was crossing and leading on the first of the mules. Under the planking, in the shadows, Shire could just make out a quarter outline of the powder-barrel where it protruded from behind a stanchion. Waddell dismounted short of the trestle and fired his rifle across the gorge. The bullet glanced off the smooth rock above Shire's head. He ducked away and then back, sighted the barrel and fired, saw splinters fly from the stanchion. He levered through another bullet. More shots struck the tree beside the rock. He would have to hold himself out there a moment longer, risk it all, allow himself time to aim. He took a final long, slow breath then pushed out further from the rock. In his side vision the troopers fired, Waddell fired, Tod twisted on his horse with his pistol pointed at the sky. Bullets struck rock and tree and Shire waited, waited until the bead drew onto the powder-barrel. He squeezed the trigger.

Clemens simply disappeared, swallowed up by a hot yellow burst of flame. The planking exploded upward pursued by a billowing, self-eating ball of black smoke. The shockwave of heat forced Shire to turn away. Wood, planking and thick stanchions rained down around him, into the trees, on top of

Dryden's body. Shire dropped his rifle, folded down in the join of the rock and the dirt, his hands over his head until the wooden deluge slowed and passed. He dared to look again.

Tod was unhorsed but getting to his feet, his mount galloping away to the south. There was a fifty-foot gap where the trestle-work had been, leaving Tod alone and stranded. The other side, a half-dozen mules were on the ground, dead or writhing. Copper ingots lay scattered on the track.

Shire thought the explosion, or Dryden's blow, had unhinged him, since the world began to move in an unnatural way. The track to the north of the new gap took a great jolt and reset itself a foot lower, then it began to slide. Everything slid along with it, accelerating: mules, scrub trees, boulders, men. A sound like distant thunder rose and rose. The slide worked back from the gap, a straight tear in a piece cloth. Helpless men and mules could see it coming. It could only have been a matter of seconds, but Shire seemed to be gifted the time to witness it all. He saw Waddell fall outward; for a moment he was clear of the sliding mass until he was gathered into it and lost. He saw a line of tied mules go over one at a time, somehow braying over the roar of the earth, hooves flailing, necks and legs breaking. He saw copper ingots fly from saddle-packs and spin out all the way down to the water. He saw a trooper scramble to the slope above the path, almost save himself until the tear reached up and claimed him too. He saw the fanning tide of earth sweep Jenkins from his newly found resting place and on down toward the river. The slide ate away at the path, working back and back and back, until finally it slowed and stopped. The first lucky mule did no more than look over this new and adjacent cliff and press forward her ears. The rumbling subsided. Deep below the mud reached the end of its slide and settled fully astride the river. Shire stared after it and stepped out into the clear; the only thought he could shape was that Raht's copper was buried once more.

All was silent. When he eventually looked up and across the gorge it was into the maddened eyes of Tod Carter, a pistol held at his side. Shire wanted to say *I only came to destroy the bridge*, but he knew it wouldn't wash, not with Tod and not with himself. He'd broken his parole, he'd killed Waddell, Clemens, other men who'd shared the road with him this last week, and so many mules. It was all down to him and he was too weary to ever face up to it. He didn't deserve any more than Tod's men who were dead and buried at the bottom of the gorge. This extended life had been Tod's gift anyway. He threw aside his hat, tried to silently convey across the chasm how sorry he was, how in the end he'd had no choice. He held his arms wide, inviting a bullet. Tod raised his pistol and held it there. The whole length of his arm began to shake. He threw a wild scream across the gorge and fired. The bullet grazed so close to Shire that he felt it whip the air, but he stood steady. Tod fired again and again and Shire was hit sudden and hard from the side, knocked to the ground and then bundled back behind the rock. The shots echoed and died down the gorge.

'Mr Shire, sir.'

Dazed, Shire sat himself up.

It was Elrod, young Elrod, kneeling beside him and breathing hard, dirt across his face. 'You can't leave me to go back alone.'

Shire lay his head back against the rock, the weight of a longer life settling back into him.

'Did we help the Union, sir?'

Shire struggled to get the words out. 'Perhaps, Elrod.

We'll have to hope so. Come on. Let's get you home.'

'Home? I'm in the army now.'

Shire looked into the boy's proud eyes. 'There's no one who knows that but you and me, and I wouldn't wish it on you, Elrod.'

Nancy Creek, Georgia – July 1864

Opdycke had duties elsewhere but stood silently under the old oak tree beside the road. He could have come on Tempest, but that didn't seem right. Somehow it would have been unfaithful.

The days and the names all blurred together of late: the Chattahoochee, Roswell. Today, they were somewhere called Nancy Creek. He supposed he would remember this place. It was busy; a cannon was dragged along a sticky road by a long team of horses, heads down, legs straining, the artillerymen dismounted and pulling as well. Infantry followed on, a few men glancing at the scene beside the oak, no doubt wondering what pour soul was being laid to rest. Opdycke avoided the eyes of their officers.

Beyond the circumference of the tree and its roots the three men were all but finished. They tidied and patted around the edges of the grave as if reluctant to put down their spades. 'That'll do,' said Opdycke.

Without orders the three men retrieved their rifles and brought their muddied selves back to the graveside. Opdycke's heart cracked a little more. They had been the three men to hand when it happened.

Yesterday, he'd ridden Barney up an isolated hill, intent on reconnoitering a signal station. Moore was with him. It was no great peak but rose above the trees and the flatter land that they'd fought their way onto since Kennesaw. From the top they could just make out Atlanta's spires, seven miles away by Moore's estimation. They might have shaken hands in celebration but for the Rebel army that lay between, an army that could give no more ground unless Johnston wanted to hand over the keys to the city. It had proved harder to drive the Rebels back these last few days. Opdycke and his regiments had slewed to the north along with the rest of Sherman's Army, like a stream rounding a river boulder. It would be harder still from here on.

On their way down the hill they'd dismounted to pick early blackberries. He'd shared them with Barney. Orders had come from division HQ for the next move along with rumors that Joe Johnston had been replaced by General Hood. Opdycke thought it unlikely. Johnston had made it so hard for them all the way from Rocky Face Ridge.

They'd attacked this morning at five o'clock. Opdycke's command had the advance and once more he had the 125th out in front as skirmishers. They were expert at that business nowadays. The enemy contested Nancy Creek and he'd been obliged to draw forward another regiment and bring a battery of cannon to bear. The Rebels were on the run when the bullet struck under Barney's right shoulder and into his heart. He stood shivering long enough for Opdycke to dismount. Then the old boy lay down. There was nothing more.

He ordered Tempest brought up. After the battle, he walked back to find Barney. The soldiers were there, guarding his corpse like he was some dearly loved uncle. Ocks was nearby and Opdycke asked him if he could borrow the men. Ocks looked surprised at such courtesy.

Their job done, at a whispered order from Mason, the three men snapped to attention and smartly shouldered arms, as if it was a famed general that they had just buried. He knew them of course, he knew all the veterans of the 125th and Tuck was hard to miss, stretched up as he was a head above Corporal Mason and a neck more above Private Cleves. They were waiting on him. Other men moved closer, silently approached the graveside, one by one coming to attention until the grave was surrounded in muddy blue.

A prayer was called for. What if Sherman should chance by? He was in the habit of riding out into the lines unattended. What would he think to see Company B gathered in prayer over a dead horse? To say nothing would be to let the men down. He understood. There had been so much death since Rocky Face Ridge, so little time to mourn. Barney had led them as much as he had. 'Let us pray,' he said, and the men took off their caps. He lifted his head, found the right words, at the same time watching tears wash clean white lines down Tuck's face.

They all had someone to cry for. Opdycke thought of Harker and then of Tuck's friend, Shire, killed at Kennesaw. That Englishman had a soft spot for horses. He recalled how he'd loaned Barney to Shire when he was straggling on the road to Chattanooga last summer. In the fall, Shire had looked after Barney under siege in that same town, then soothed him when he took a bullet in the mouth below Missionary Ridge. Tuck might shed tears for Barney, but he was surely crying for Shire as well. Poor boy. No prisoner lists had come down to Opdycke of late, but he'd seen Shire trapped when the fire swept through the abatis; he didn't care to dwell on it.

He finished up the prayer and nodded to Sergeant Ocks.

'Right, you lot,' said the sergeant, not unkindly, 'you've said your goodbyes. Face front. March.'

Opdycke's baggage caught up with him that evening. Before he did anything else, he found pen and paper and wrote to Lucy.

I am sad and lonely tonight – for my good horse Barney is dead.

The Copper Road, Tennessee – July 1864

The Ocoee River ran fast and free beside the Copper Road. Shire turned his horse and waited once more for the short but curious wagon train. The first wagon, canvas down, belonged to Mrs Oliver. Her husband, Shire now understood, had fled the hills at the beginning of the war and was, as far as Mrs Oliver knew, fighting for the Union in the east. Elrod rode beside her and held the reins. Piled behind them was all they could bring from their home that two mules might reasonably be expected to haul. 'Elrod's a good boy,' Mrs Oliver had said. 'I'm proud that he struck a blow, but word will get out. I wish we'd left with his father.'

The second wagon, a flatbed hauled by the remaining two mules, belonged to Clara who rode alongside on the late Sergeant Dryden's horse, another prod to Shire's conscience. There were so many. As Clara came nearer, Shire could see she wore a smile, but it was solely for George Barnes' benefit. He had a way of working a little happiness into anyone. George was perched on a chaise lounge that Clara had insisted Shire help bring up from the mines. It was the only thing she said she wanted.

Since there was precious little room in the wagon, what with the injured Wilson lying next to Barnes on a thin mattress, Clara had argued that the chaise lounge could pay its way as a bed. She appeared to have some attachment to it. Barnes had asked Shire to turn it so he could face forward. After hauling copper out of these hills a hundred times, today he was carried like a king and would roll a royal hand whenever Shire passed by.

Raht and Tonkin brought up the rear but for the trailing soldier a quarter mile back. Another of Dryden's diminished squad was a similar distance ahead. The third drove Clara's wagon.

Shire had no idea if she had forgiven him for going after Tod or, indeed, if he should be soliciting forgiveness. He hadn't gone looking to kill anyone, death made its own appointments in this war. Wriggle as he might with the rights and wrongs of the matter, try to claim a degree of innocence under the cover of an unfeeling fate, he couldn't deny that he had been, at the very least, fate's provocateur. If he'd not persuaded Dryden of the necessity to stop the copper, Dryden would still be alive. Jenkins would be alive, Clemens and Waddell, a hatful of teamsters and Rebel troopers and the greater share of the mules. All but Dryden now resided in a shared and untidy grave of men, mules and copper. He fought to stop himself imagining the innards beneath the settled soil. He couldn't have borne it at all if it wasn't for the fact that somewhere at his core, part of him remembered the greater crop of death that the copper would have germinated. The horror he had instigated and witnessed remained the lesser evil. That thought gave him no peace: the explosion and the sliding, churning mess played out again and again.

He'd taken the spare rifle holster from Dryden's horse so he had one on either side. One carried a rifle and the other the walking stick, his gift from the late Waddell. There was the urge to pull it out, throw it end over end into the fast-flowing river. No. The stick was his to keep and to bear, a reminder of Waddell and that lesser evil.

None of this, not the smallest part, meant he needed to seek forgiveness from Clara.

He steered his horse off the road, let the Olivers pass,

then waited, a silent invitation. George came along and gave his familiar lofty wave. 'You stealing her away from me, Mr Shire?'

'I'm not sure if she's of a mind to be stolen.'

In answer, Clara peeled away and stood her horse beside his. Raht and Tonkin did no more than touch their hats as they followed on. Shire and Clara fell in behind. Shire let the gap play out.

'I'm not anyone's to steal,' she said, as soon as they were out of earshot.

'George put it that way. I wouldn't have dared.'

'You are more daring in some things.'

Despite her smiles for George, her mood appeared no lighter than it had been for the couple of days they'd spent in Ducktown since Shire and Elrod had returned, trailing two empty saddles plus the mules. Elrod had told the tale and Shire had been glad to be spared that duty. Still more so that Elrod was alive to tell it: the troopers might have taken a dim view if Shire had returned alone to tell them their sergeant and Jenkins were dead. He'd watched Clara close her eyes at the moment she'd learned that Tod was alive and safe. He'd put in details where they were called for. No one needed to know of his struggle with Dryden. Shire and Elrod had loaded his body on a mule but buried him the same evening. The heat wouldn't allow them to bring him further. Elrod could find the wooden marker again at need, he said, though it wasn't clear who that need might belong to. Jenkins was beyond recovery. When they'd left the gorge, Tod and his surviving men were starting down the slope to see if anyone had survived, unlikely as that seemed.

'Will we make Comrie, today?' he asked Clara over the noise of the river.

'George thinks so, even with only two mules per wagon. We started early.'

'It must feel a long time since you were there.'

'I'm frightened of what's waiting for me. I hadn't expected to leave Matlock alone for so long.'

'I have business with him too,' said Shire.

'You have no proof that Matlock killed your father.'

'You have no proof that he asked Bowman to kill you. It all mounts up though, doesn't it? Perhaps we're beyond the need for proof. But for Matlock, you might never have come away to America and there'd have been no need for me to follow. We might both have been at home yet, our old selves, ignorant of copper mines and war.'

They reached a bend where the road banked the river. The water rushed on by. They stopped their horses to watch. 'We've made our decisions,' said Clara, 'back then and every day since. We are not the product of Matlock's deceptions. I refuse to see myself as such. When you decided to go after the mule train, you made your own choice.'

She would have them talk on this then, finally, after days of avoiding the nub of it. 'I don't deny it,' said Shire. 'To do otherwise would have been the greater betrayal.'

'Even there you make a choice in allegiance. You can only betray those you have given your loyalty to.'

If it was an accusation it was a subtle one. 'And sometimes…' Shire twitched his rein to start his horse forward again. Clara could follow is she wanted to. 'Sometimes it's impossible to be loyal to everyone.'

The sound of a cantering horse rose above the water. Shire turned back. The rearguard trooper raced toward them and slewed to a halt. 'Did you hear the shot?' he asked, breathless.

They caught up to Raht, Tonkin and the trailing wagon. A shot could be something and nothing but the trooper swore it was a pistol, not a rifle. Hunters didn't use pistols. George Barnes said they weren't far from the Halfway. They could hide in the barn. There was no other place to get the wagons off the road. Before Shire could stop her, Clara rode to collect the man out front. George Barnes declared that if he could sit up in a fancy bed then he could drive a wagon. He took over from the trooper who went to help guard the road behind.

Half an hour later, every last one of them was hidden in the barns and the stables behind the Halfway. Shire, rifle in hand, squinted between slats in the barn door and out across the yard to the road. The sound of horses wasn't long in coming. Tonkin gave feed bags to the mules to keep them quiet. Abandoned though it was, the Halfway made a natural stopping point.

Two men rode into view and half-turned into the yard. Their uniforms were partial. One had on a Rebel kepi, the other butternut pants. They looked back the way they had come. More men, many more than Shire had expected, rode up and stopped, bunching in the yard, so close that the nearest horse put Shire's eye into shadow. If the shooting started, the hideaways would come off second best. The barn wood was old and thin. It wouldn't stop anything. He thought to get Clara and Mrs Oliver away before it came to that, but it was all open field across to the river. There was nothing to be done. Raht cracked open a pistol barrel and Shire winced. Mercifully, the horses' stamping in the yard covered the sound.

Through the melee of men and horses Shire watched a bigger man ride up. He barely stopped. Instead he angrily shouted and waved the crowd on down the valley, taking his feathered hat from his red hair and slapping at a man who came within range. The milling horses found their direction and set off at pace. The sound of them receded until Shire could hear nothing but the run of the river beyond the field and the happy mastication of the mules.

*

Matlock totaled the column again, desperate to find an error. So far, he'd discovered only two in the twelve years of Comrie ledgers he'd worked through. The nub pencil he'd found was ever poised to make a correction. The numbers were a comfort, better than fretting in this hot attic hour after hour.

The column totaled correctly. Disappointed, he looked up into the wide and brightly painted eyes of the rocking horse. He hated that horse. Its bright colors and varnished coat spoke of things that had long been absent from his world: of taking pleasure in a child's simple joy, of well-meant indulgence, of kinship. It was impossible to look at it without thinking of Cele and thereby Hany. Not that those events were down to him. The rocking horse was a mute cellmate, dumbly reminding him that he was locked in the attic, while Moses and Mitilde waited on the impossible return of their long-dead mistress.

He had found no way to tell them. When Moses came to leave his food and replace his chamber pot, backed each time by a towering field-hand, he could hardly say, *'Clara isn't ever going to return. I know it for a fact. You see, I arranged to have her killed.'* He had tried everything else: an appeal to basic humanity, threats to see them hang, a straight bribe. Nothing dented that old black face. Moses never uttered a word.

He considered keeping a diary but had nothing to say. He'd found a blank ledger and started to go over the Ridgmont finances in summary; most of the figures were lodged in his head, but the Comrie records were more detailed, more absorbing. If ever he escaped this attic he would move into town and sell Comrie from there. The agent could take care of the showings. In fact, why not start for England and take the sad news of Clara's loss back to the Duke?

He tried to conjure scenarios that would lead to his release, but who would miss him? His greatest fear and his only hope was Bowman: that the renegade hadn't changed plans or been chased from the county.

He moved to the low window seat and looked out; nothing but the hills to the south. There was little he could see of Comrie's business. If he opened the window and put out his head, only then could he manage to see the scrag-end of the yard and some of the old slave huts. That was all.

His belongings were slowly migrating to the attic. He'd asked for his razor and a shaving bowl, a change of clothes, a mattress and linen. All were mutely brought up.

He collected a ledger and took it to the seat where at least there was a breeze. How quiet it was. Where was the usual babble from outside? Then he heard the low rumble of horses, lots of horses. Whoever it was, Bowman or Union, he judged from the sound that they were riding up the switchback drive. He hurried back to the rocking horse, pulled the dollar-rolls from inside. The clatter of hooves and tack dulled as the host rode around the far end of the mansion. He left the money-rolls piled beside the horse and returned to the window, ready to call. The clatter had moved down to the left. They must have come around the corner into the yard.

'Search the house.'

Matlock recognized the deep, lazy authority of Bowman's voice. He backed away from the window when he saw two of the irregulars hurry to the slave huts and kick their way inside. He should wait. Experience had taught him not to play his hand too early.

'There's no one here.' Grady's voice perhaps, Bowman's lieutenant.

'You in a hurry to be right?' asked Bowman.

'The blacks are gone into the hills again. There's no surprising this place.'

'We got no business with them, only Matlock.'

He heard footsteps echoing in the hall below. If he banged on the door, they would find him.

'You think that old butler has waited all this time? He only wanted rid of us. No one can get six thousand dollars together just like that.'

'You don't move in the right circles, Grady. Matlock does. Look around. The size of the house, of the stables. How many slave huts do you count? To people like Matlock, or at least the people he deals with, that money don't amount to much. He's slippery alright, but I don't think he'd welch on the deal, not if he got what he wanted, he needed this place still standing.'

There were steps on the stairs. Matlock took a breath, formed the first word.

'Only he didn't get what he wanted,' said Grady. 'Not if the rumors around Ducktown are true.'

'I'm bettin' we're out ahead of those rumors. As far as Matlock knows, she's dead.'

Matlock breathed out. *Clara not dead.* He couldn't hand over the money if she wasn't dead. He stood stock still, not risking a creak of the floor. The attic door rattled once then twice. There was a shout from below and steps back down the stairs. He could make out reports fed back to Bowman. 'Nothing, Captain.' 'Slave huts are all empty.' 'No one in the house.'

Bowman swore. 'I'm findin' it hard to contemplate riding away from six thousand dollars.'

'It was never here to start with.'

'Torch it. The stables, the huts and the house. Everything.'

Matlock ran to the window. His first cry of 'no' was drowned out by whoops and hollers. Then all was commotion and excitement. The dog barked and barked, pistols fired, glass shattered. Matlock shouted until his voice was hoarse. He had the money. They would spare him if he handed over the money.

He heard wood break and splinter. More cries. He leaned from his window and saw a trooper carry a lighted torch into a slave hut then emerge, the first thin trails of smoke following him out the door. Matlock waved and called but the man was into the next hut. He ran to the attic door, battered at it with his hand, kicked at it.

When the first scent of smoke reached him, he discovered a deeper well of fear. He ran back to the window. Dirty smoke killed the view; inside, white wraiths insisted themselves in around the edges of the door. He saw the air shimmer outside the window. The snap and crackle of flames sounded from below. He felt the heat rise around him. The smoke thickened and he sank to the floor to breathe. He mustn't stay here. He should find his way to the window, squeeze out. He got to his knees, only to find himself face to face with the rocking horse. The horse stared back. The varnished palomino coat began to blister and drip flaming gobs to the wooden floor where they lit the dollar rolls. The yellow tail and mane burst into flame, the red saddle melted and the painted face distorted and slid down the long nose. The floor gave way all at once. Screaming, Matlock fell with the horse and the burning money down into the black smoke and the reaching flames.

*

Clara saw the smoke first. She had been casting her mind toward Comrie and had looked that way though they were deep in the cut of the Ocoee. There was a dirty smudge high in the late afternoon sky above where she imagined Comrie to be. A cry escaped her: some inarticulate mixture of shock and fear.

Shire was beside her. 'What is it?'

She tightened her rein and kicked, her horse reared before starting at a canter down the Copper Road. She raced past Julius and Tonkin who had seen the smoke too.

'Stay together!' Tonkin shouted.

She paid him no heed and sped past the wagons and away down the road. It was wider here alongside the river, two sets of hoofbeats echoing off the steep valley sides. There was no need to look back to see who was with her.

She overtook their scout and heard Shire shout at him that they were going on to Comrie. The road followed a bend in the river and she urged her horse on down the long straight beyond, overtaking the speeding water, until she reached the tight path on the right and cut up into the hills. Once in the trees, she steered the horse on a hurried walk between oak and hickory, up beyond the church and onto the wider path to Comrie.

She wasn't aware she had stopped until Shire drew

up alongside her. She stared up the steep meadow that accommodated the switchback drive as it climbed to the mansion. The classical columns remained standing on the porch, but to no purpose; the red-tiled roof they used to support was gone. The columns stretched up only into a forest of smoke trails.

'We should stay in the trees,' said Shire, 'come around the side. Bowman might still be here.'

Where were all the people? She started her horse up the drive.

'Clara! Just for once, would you listen?'

With each sharp turn she could see more. The walls had survived, but above each and every window Comrie's whitewash had been turned black. As she neared the level of the house, she could see the stables were gone, only the great square arch of the carriage house was left burnt but standing, an entrance to nowhere. Shire, rifle drawn, darted past her to check the yard. She came on slowly into the acrid stench of smoke.

The redbrick kitchen, built separately to protect the house from fire, had itself survived, so had the smokehouse and the springhouse. Three huts were standing, the rest were rectangles of ash. In the slave graveyard, fully visible with the huts gone, stood the people of Comrie, the living as silent and bereft as the poorly marked dead.

Clara climbed from her horse and walked toward them. Moses was there, standing close to old George. There was a tired rope between them; Moses looking more in need of it than the horse. Mitilde had Cele balanced on her hip. The child leaned out and Mitilde had to let her down but held on to her hand. She had grown. Behind Mitilde and Moses others pressed forward. A keening wail rose from amongst them and a sea of grief and loss and love welled up in Clara. Cele broke away from Mitilde and back through the crowd. Clara wanted to collapse into Mitilde's embrace but instead took the wet black face to her shoulder. The crowd parted and she looked beyond to where Cele sat on the mound of a fresh grave, brushing at her dark hair with Clara's ivory comb.

*

When he learned from Moses that Matlock had burned with the house, Shire didn't know how to feel. He'd prepared himself for a reckoning, revenge even, and it had been served, meted out, before he'd arrived. He'd had no part in it. He tried to tell himself it was divine justice but, if so, it was delivered at the hand of another evil man. Perhaps the Divine didn't care overmuch how it went about its business.

More unsettling still was the undeniable feeling that he had lost another link to England, to home. In truth, Matlock had been a block to him ever returning to Ridgmont, but the man was *of that place* and, irrationally, distant as it was, Ridgmont seemed diminished by his violent passing. There were more pressing matters to think about. He kept a wary eye on Clara who was busy helping Mitilde.

By the time the tired mules had dragged the wagons around and up to Comrie via the long road, the thin black trails of smoke were fronting a red Tennessee sunset. No one was of a mind to press on to Cleveland in the dark. In the fading light, Shire helped the soldiers rope and pull down the entrance to the carriage house then searched through the warm ashes with Moses for tack or tools that could be recovered.

They set up camp to the north side of the burned-out house – out of reach of the walls should they fall – where

410

the ground was open and mostly flat. The night sky was no stranger to Shire.

Mitilde's hut was one of those spared and she said she would clear out in favor of Clara, having by now learned of Clara's ordeal and poked and prodded at her diminished frame. Clara said there were others who needed shelter; she would not take a roof from someone who had lost their own. Mitilde asked if she had taken a look at Comrie's roof lately. Shire thought maybe he should lead Mitilde away after Clara said that Moses had lost *his* hut and that, 'For once perhaps it would be useful if he shared Mitilde's bed for the whole night.' To everyone's surprise, not least Moses, she said perhaps he would. She had Cele sleeping there and later took in Mrs Oliver as well to give it an air of decency.

The sleeping arrangements wouldn't matter after tomorrow or beyond a few days at most, thought Shire. Comrie was a ruin. Young and old, the blacks would all have to head away and take their chance with freedom someplace else. Bowman had settled that much.

Others lodged in the outbuildings left standing. Tonkin and Raht took the smokehouse with George Barnes, Wilson and Elrod. Shire picked a spot close to one of the wagons. The night was hot and he lay above his blanket, wondering what came next. Unsure as the future was, it was better than thinking of the recent past. He didn't notice Clara arrive above him until he lost a clump of stars.

'There's a dearth of blankets,' she said.

He was slow on the uptake. 'I'm fine,' he said. 'It's not going to be a cold night.'

'George offered me the chaise lounge but he has more need of it, besides, I might dream I was back in the mine. Mitilde gave me this quilt… I'd feel safer here.'

'Oh. Of course.' He hurriedly got up.

Clara spread the quilt out beside him. 'It's easily big enough for two, and we can share your blanket.'

'It's been traveling a while.'

'None of us are freshly scrubbed,' she said, sitting herself down. 'We slept out when we were very little. Do you remember?'

'I do. Down by the lake. How old were we?'

'Seven or eight.'

'Your sister watched over us.'

They lay back and looked at the stars. 'You seem alright,' said Shire.

Clara said nothing.

'I mean, all things considered…'

'I'm trying not to consider all things. Not yet. I've been helping, being useful for once.'

It wasn't only the blacks that would need to leave Comrie, thought Shire. What was left for Clara to stay for? 'You underestimate yourself.'

'I think perhaps I have the opposite problem. If I hadn't insisted on recovering the furniture,' her voice ebbed back toward sadness, 'Hany, any number of people, might be alive. Comrie might still be whole.'

'You don't know that. Bowman might have burned it a month back with you inside instead of Matlock.'

'There remains a debt to Hany. Out of friendship as much as anything.'

Shire wondered if he could ever make good on his own debts. If Clara's guilt was tenuous, his was less so. He needed to pay. Atonement, that was the word. The 125th called to him, at once the safest and most dangerous place. 'What will you do?' he asked Clara.

The conversation stalled under the enormity of the question.

'More helping,' Clara said, finally. 'I'm homeless, but not penniless. I have a property leased out in Western Tennessee, further from the war. There are shares in the mines when they open again. For now, it just feels like something is over.'

'Clara.'

'Yes.'

'I don't think you could ever have recovered here.'

She turned her head and he held her gaze. 'You think Taylor's ghost burned with Matlock?'

'I have to believe, sometimes at least, we can leave our ghosts behind. Where will you go?'

'Julius still has his old house down in Cleveland. He says I can live there for as long as I like. They'll be room, if you want to stay?'

'I'm not sure,' he said, and sensed a further question in the silence that followed. 'I made noises to the New Yorkers that I might. It's not how they see things.' The corporal's exact words had been, '*The hell you will. You turned our sergeant to your plan and now he's dead and so is Jenkins.*'

'They want me to explain to their colonel what happened.'

'And after that?'

'I broke my parole, killed any number of men and mules. If Tod makes it back, he's sure to tell Trenholm. If I'm lucky, the army will be able to exchange my parole with a Rebel, so we can both fight again legally, but I'd better not get recaptured.'

'It sounds like you want to fight.'

'I don't think I have a choice. Whichever way I look at it, I'm back in the army.'

'We can talk about Tod if you like?' Clara said.

'Not now.'

'He wasn't trying to deceive you, only protect you.'

'And did *you* think I needed protecting?'

'I've always looked after you.'

'In a roundabout sort of way.'

'What does that mean?'

He wasn't really sure. Instead he said, 'I think it means we're forever doomed to look after each other.'

They slept then. Shire woke once in the night, a fox barking somewhere away in the trees. Clara's head was on his chest, her arm over him. He lay there and watched the stars wheel, fought off more sleep to enjoy the sweet, smoky scent of her hair.

Epilogue – De Greffin – September 1864

Trenholm stood at his desk, his red, studded work-chair having gone ahead. He emptied his papers from the drawers to make two piles: one to take, one to burn. The irony that he was abandoning his safe haven wasn't lost on him but, with Atlanta gone, De Greffin was no longer a refuge; few places were. He'd go east, back to his true home in Charleston. The Army of Northern Virginia fought on. He would retreat toward that last stubborn strength.

The chandelier was fully lit; why leave oil for Sherman? But the long, bulky curtains that shut out the September night would have to stay. There was constant noise beyond his study door: hurried directions, strained effort.

Sorting his papers was a chore but some tasks couldn't be left to others. There were letters from the President, fair copies of his replies and advice. Another drawer held acceptances and apologies for Emily's wedding, held here back in June. So much hope had been conquered since then. He put them onto the burn pile.

There were more raised voices out in the hall; everyone was anxious to get away. No one knew where Sherman's armies were. Rumor and alarm colored the truth, but De Greffin might be ashes within days.

The walls were bare. Pictures that had come from Ashley Hall would have to return, that was if room could be found for them on the journey. There were artworks here worth more than their weight in gold alongside keepsakes valued only by a treasured memory. He had a whole boxcar waiting; it was moving the valuables to the station that was the problem. What good was all his money and influence when there were no horses or mules to buy?

The handle on the study door squeaked. He looked up, curious that there was no knock. A ragged soldier let himself in. Trenholm's hand moved toward his pistol in the drawer, but the man wore no obvious malice. He carried a saddlebag and looked played out.

'You don't recognize me,' the soldier said, stepping closer.

'I don't think so.'

'Captain Carter, 20th Tennessee.'

It took a moment for the name to shuffle up through Trenholm's long list of cares.

'Carter. Of course. My apologies, Captain.'

'Your people are preoccupied. I let myself in.'

Trenholm's valet hurried into the room, stepped around Carter. 'I'm sorry, sir. Everyone is in and out.' He tried to herd Carter away.

'It's alright, Hampton. I know this man. Bring some whiskey.'

'The whiskey is packed, sir.'

'Then unpack it. Go on!'

Trenholm had met this captain just the once, before sending him to Ducktown. And he'd become accustomed to disheveled soldiers, but the change in Tod Carter was severe. The muddied boots, the stained jacket and the weather-beaten hat were all to be expected, but Carter looked as if he'd aged twenty years. He struggled to bring himself erect, his eyes weary and deep-set.

'The chairs are all gone. Here, there is a window seat behind the curtain.'

Carter looked as if his legs might fail him. He half-dropped a saddlebag down on the polished wooden floor. 'I will stand, sir.'

Trenholm walked to him and offered his hand.

Carter chose to give him a tired salute instead. 'You're leaving? Clearing out?'

'By necessity. There are rumors that the Union is headed this way. Plantations are burning west of here.'

'It's no more than a raid. Sherman's army is away around Atlanta.'

'A raid might still burn us out. You are not with your unit?'

'I am not. I was seconded to you. Do you not recall?'

'Of course, of course, but it's two weeks since Atlanta fell.'

'You had given us up for lost then.'

Hampton returned with a whiskey decanter and two crystal glasses held by the fingers of one hand. He cleared a space on the desk among the papers and poured out a frugal measure.

'Leave that,' said Trenholm. As Hampton left, he half-filled the glasses and held one out to Carter.

'Shire told me you were ever generous with your whiskey. Is this Scottish too? He and I shared a bottle from you on the way to Ducktown. It freed up some secrets.'

He must know about Clara then. Trenholm kept the glass raised, considered the peculiar similarity between this scene and when he met Shire in Atlanta: another bedraggled soldier reluctant to drink free whiskey. 'A failing of mine perhaps. Please. You look like you need it.'

The resentment gave way a fraction. Tod's dirty hand took the glass, but he didn't drink.

'I'd not given you up. The army command was told to look out for you, that you would come in from the north, that you should be given safe passage and news sent to me.

Other matters became more pressing. We had to move what we could from the rolling-mills and the machine works.'

'I was there.'

'Where?'

'At your rolling-mill.'

'Why?'

There was an angry press above Carter's eyes. 'To find you. To report.'

'Drink some whiskey, Captain.'

'But you were gone. Most of the city was gone.'

Trenholm leaned back on his desk. 'Do you want to report now? Did you find Clara?'

'Was that the real mission?'

'If she were, then you wouldn't have needed the mules. I've tried to get news from across the lines, but those channels are closed now. Please, tell me.'

Carter looked into his whiskey as if he might divine something. 'Let's start with the girl, shall we? My unknown objective. Judged by that measure, it was a success. She was trapped in Ducktown – in a mine would you believe – but freed before we got there by your friend Raht.'

Trenholm had to walk to the other side of his desk to hide the moment.

'We left her with him when we started back with the copper. Lots of copper. Too much copper.'

'And Shire. You left him with Clara?'

Carter smiled. 'Shire. Now he's the real story. I imagine you have to gauge people a great deal to get as wealthy as you have, Mr Secretary. Take their measure and then gamble on your judgment. Am I right?'

'People are everything, in business, in politics. I live and die by my judgment.'

'We both misjudged Shire.'

'How so?'

'Without him, I might have gotten you your copper. Raht had a few Union troopers along. Shire couldn't resist the old blue. He switched sides and came after us.'

'Truly? I honestly thought he'd settle out of the war if he found Clara.'

'It might have gone better if you'd told me about her. Shire blew up our path in the hills. The explosion knocked the whole hillside loose. They all slid away behind me, sir, down and down, like I was owed some sort of redemption, but they were taken for the devil. Quite a sight. The few of us left climbed down after them, but they were all buried. Our guide, Clemens. My friend, Waddell. Troopers, teamsters and mules.'

Trenholm saw the scene in his minds-eye. 'Dear Lord.'

'We backtracked, but it was useless without Clemens. We wasted a week finding a new path. The mules we had left became exhausted, no matter how much copper we dumped. Some collapsed, others just gave up and lay down like they wanted a bullet. We were still fifty miles from Atlanta when we worked out the Union Army was across our line of march. The hills were thick with cavalry. A blind man could have tracked us. We had to leave the mules and run. We could hear them being shot, a mule every few seconds. After that, it was just me and two troopers.'

Trenholm kept silent. Carter needed to tell his story, and he had a duty to listen.

'The three of us came all the way to Stone Mountain. I let the troopers go search for their unit but found my way through the lines and into the city. Everything was gone to hell, but I wanted to find you. They were clearing everyone away from the rolling-mill. Boxcars had been brought up alongside on the tracks, close to the works and packed with munitions. All the rail routes out were blocked and they couldn't leave them for the Yankees. One of your men was still there. He told me of this place, said I might find you here.

'I stayed on until after dark. I wanted to see the cars go up, see the end, but I should have moved further away. I had no idea. My horse and I went down together when the first car blew. I lost count of how many explosions there were. There can't be a glass pane left in Atlanta. A great fire took hold, swept through the city. I couldn't tell which way to go. I found the remains of a house with wide steps down to a cellar. I lead my horse in there.

'At first light we came out and it was all smoke and ashes. We were back close to your rolling-mill. Nothing but your chimneystacks standing, sir. Everything else gone.'

Trenholm lifted his glass to his lips but saw it was empty. 'I'm sorry I sent Shire with you.'

Carter swilled his untouched whiskey. 'As I recall, it was Shire that volunteered me. Seemed like an act of friendship at the time.'

'I'm sure it was.'

'Well… That's buried with the copper.'

'But you needed to find me?'

'I did.'

Carter put his glass down on the table and picked up his saddlebag. He unbuckled the strap and, reaching inside, drew out an irregular, brown, pocked ingot that grudgingly reflected the light from the chandelier. He held it out.

Trenholm took it in both hands. 'Thank you,' he said, and smiled. 'My judgment in Shire may have been lacking, but I was right about you. If you want the God's honest truth, I don't think you could ever have made it to Atlanta in time, not the way things moved on.'

'I'm sorry. That's all there is.'

'It's like everything else in this war. Men, money, resources. We don't have enough.'

'We still have some fight. We've never been short of that.'

'Maybe that's not the blessing it seems.'

'I know a good man in Pennsylvania who would agree with you.'

'It occurs to me, Captain, that you remain under my direction. I've not released you.'

'I'm done. I'd like to get back to my regiment.'

'I have two final orders. Firstly, drink your damn whiskey. Secondly, you're to rest here the night. We're not giving up De Greffin until the morning. I'll find out where your regiment is and send you back with my commendation, for what it's worth.'

It was the small hours of the night before Trenholm finished with his papers. His legs ached from standing for so long so he sat on his desk, drained the last of the whiskey and let the smoky peat linger on his tongue. The house was still at last, Carter hopefully sleeping soundly somewhere above. Despite everything, the lives spent, the copper lost, he couldn't quite bring himself to regret sending Shire back to Clara. You had to cherish the little victories in this long war, even if they weren't, strictly speaking, your own.

He picked up the heavy ingot and searched for a small box, found one that contained some ancient vase he'd bid for in Venice years before the war. He set the vase on the desk. Sherman could have that. He wrapped the copper and placed it inside, closed the box and marked it, *Most Precious – Priority*.

Historical Note

Whenever I'm invited to talk on historical fiction, I often hover at length on the constant dilemma writers face between truth and fiction. Of course, when considering history, truth is largely taken on faith. '*History is not the past,*' Hilary Mantel tells us, '*it's the method we've evolved for organising our ignorance of the past.*' (2017 Reith Lectures). We may have a mountain of facts: names, dates, places, casualty lists; we may have an idea of the weather and personal accounts abound from the Civil War. But all this is just a fraction; the vast majority of the past is lost to us, just empty pages waiting for a passing fiction writer.

Yet that doesn't make it open season on history. Every writer needs to decide on their own red lines, how far they are prepared to bend history to support the story. Perhaps historical fiction writers are best considered as sketchers, illustrators, not quite precise enough to be called draughtsman. We're softer around the edges.

For me, the joy in this form of writing is finding a fictional narrative that can live comfortably within the history as I understand it. The backbone of *The Copper Road*, as it was in *Whirligig*, is the wonderful 125th Ohio Infantry. The opening chapter is set at the winter battle of Dandridge. Later we follow them faithfully through the Atlanta campaign, touching on just a few of the battles that piled one on top of the other all the way to Kennesaw Mountain and beyond. Following that path myself, visiting ridge after ridge down through Georgia, was one way of getting closer to the past. If you half-close your eyes to filter out the houses and the highways, you can at least be confident you are sharing the view with Sherman's soldiers. Less so their hardships, but there are several books written by men of the 125th to help with that. Opdycke's own letters were a constant guide. As a rule of thumb, the officers in *The Copper Road* are real historical characters and the rank and file men are fictional. The exception is Wick, who although fictional, does represent a real thread of abolitionist sentiment at the time that it might be God's will that the sin of slavery had to be paid for in death. '*Until every* drop of blood drawn with the *lash* shall be paid by another drawn with the sword,' as Lincoln said in his second inaugural address.

Moore and Opdycke did share a tent and Opdycke was a close friend to the ill-fated Harker. Opdycke did receive his wound at Resaca and Harker's death at Kennesaw was as recorded. Apologies are due to Captain Moses of the 125th who I renamed Captain Elmer (his given name) to avoid contention with Moses at Comrie.

Barney's death is based on Opdycke's letters and was a tough chapter to write. I wish I could have kept him for the third book. Opdycke himself has become a strange sort of friend to me, despite the intervening centuries. It's all a little one-way but was strong enough for me to drive many hundreds of miles on one of my transatlantic trips to visit his grave in Warren, Ohio. I hope I have represented him well, though I doubt very much Shire and Tuck would have survived their desertion if it had been the real Emerson Opdycke who held their fate in his hands.

On the same drive north to Ohio I visited the Confederate prison cemetery on Johnson's Island in Lake Erie. Tod Carter was held prisoner there in the winter of 1864 and did escape by jumping from a train in Pennsylvania while en route to a new prison in Baltimore. How he got back from there to his regiment in Georgia is a mystery and something of a miracle. I have guessed at his route and invented his stopovers with the Amish and in Pittsburgh, but I can well imagine that the industrial might of the north would have appalled him as I portrayed when he sat on Mount Washington overlooking the birth of the Ohio River. It's a view I recommend to anyone who pays Pittsburgh a visit.

The Copper Road was, and is, very real. It was the Appalachian folk stories surrounding the road that drew me to the bottom right-hand corner of Tennessee in the first place and why I placed Comrie close by. You can still walk a section of the road if you drop into the Ocoee Whitewater Centre on route 74. The 'Beware of the bears' sign stopped this Englishman following it very far.

Just up the road is Ducktown with its own unique history rooted in copper. George Barnes did haul supplies up from Cleveland, Tennessee and copper back down. He was also shot by the Confederate bushwhacker gang led by John P. Gatewood who inspired the character of Bowman. George Barnes survived into old age. He was actually born in 1840 but I have tended him to middle age to represent the wisdom of the hills. Sorry, George.

My other George, Trenholm, was very much historically real. His idea of a mission to recover copper from the mines is not. It's entirely mine. Though I think there's a reasonable chance that someone might have considered it. The Confederacy was desperate for copper and had emptied the church bell towers from the towns and confiscated the copper stills from the hills. I suspect the latter was the sadder experience for many.

For the military purists the 125th only came down to

Cleveland, Tennessee by April 21st 1864. They wintered in Loudon, but I needed them to be closer to Comrie so Clara could come to collect Shire and so that Opdycke could pay his visit. Also, I concatenated the action from two days on Rocky Face Ridge (8th and 9th of May) into one.

Shire and Clara are, of course, fictional. My English compatriots somehow allow me to be as wide-eyed about Civil War America as I was when I ventured to Upstate New York as a student in the 1980s. Shire and Clara are slowly becoming Americans, I think. Both have their roots in Bedfordshire as did my parents who are no longer with us. In some strange way Shire and Clara grant me a tenuous connection to them.

Shire's squad are perhaps my favorite invention and if I return too often to the firelight, the coffee and the whiskey bottle, it's because I crave their company, especially Tuck. Latterly I donned Ohio blue myself and fought a friendly skirmish in West Virginia to get closer still to the soldiers of the Civil War, but I didn't put in the marching yards or the heartache. I hope, while writing *The Copper Road*, I've never made light of their sacrifice. That part of history isn't in doubt.

Richard Buxton

Acknowledgements

Many of the books read to underpin the historical context in *The Copper Road* were also those used to support the first Shire's Union novel, *Whirligig*. I simply read a little further on. I therefore continue to be in debt to all the soldiers of the 125th Ohio who wrote letters from the front and to those survivors who documented their memories in the years that followed the war. Most useful of all were the letters of Emerson Opdycke collected together by Glenn V. Longacre and John E. Haas in *The Battle for God and the Right*. Also the wartime memoirs of Company B's Ralsa C. Rice in *Yankee Tigers*, the collected letters in *Opdycke's Tigers* by Charles T. Clark and *Yankee Tigers II* edited by Richard A. Baumgartner. I would also like to thank Ethel T. S. Nepveux for writing *George A. Trenholm – Financial Genius of the Confederacy*. And it's always a pleasure to return to the renowned *Company Aytch* by Sam Watkins.

Among the books used which are more specific to just *The Copper Road* are *Kennesaw Mountain* by Earl J. Hess and, for the wartime history of Atlanta, *What the Yankees Did to Us* by Stephen Davis. Charles Frazier remains an inspiration and his latest novel, *Varina*, if I can paraphrase a Jack Nicholson line from the movie *As Good as it Gets*, simply makes me want to be a better writer.

I'd also like to thank the Civil War Trust for their detailed battle maps and for all they do in helping to preserve civil war sites so we can get closer to the history. Thanks to Ken Rush, Director of the Ducktown Basin Museum, who continues to answer my obscure questions about nineteenth century copper mining in the bottom right hand corner of Tennessee.

Thank you to everyone who has helped or encouraged me. Firstly, my wonderful editor Patrick LoBrutto who taught me so much about my own characters. Also friends, writing colleagues, relatives and everyone who has asked after the sequel to *Whirligig*. Huge thanks to my M.A. colleagues Glen Brown, Tracy Fells and Jacqui Pack for their above and beyond help in reviewing and advising on full drafts, also to Zoe Mitchell and Bea Mitchell-Turner for their expert feedback. My gratitude to Juliet Croydon for beautifully sketching the walking stick carved by my father. Many thanks to my neighbor Julia Brown for her precision in producing the battle maps. Huge thanks to my friend Major Jeff Houston for his unwavering enthusiasm, for hosting me in Ohio, teaching me the drill and going into battle with me at Droop Mountain, West Virginia. Last of all my biggest thanks and love to Sally for, well, pretty much everything.

A note from the author

Thank you for reading *The Copper Road*. I hope you enjoyed it. If you have time, please consider taking a moment to post a brief review on the site where you purchased the novel. Your feedback is important to me and will help other readers decide whether it's a book for them.

If you would like to get notifications of new releases, please visit www.richardbuxton.net where you can join my email list or contact me.

Richard Buxton